DEMONS IN THE GOLDEN EMPIRE

GONZALO PIZARRO DURING THE SPANISH CONQUEST OF THE INCA EMPIRE

MARCOS ANTONIO HERNANDEZ

THE EMPEROR MEETS THE ORACLE

THE ORACLE REQUIRED death before anyone received her wisdom. Nobody knew if it was the price of her far-sight, or if it was the source of the ageless woman's power, but generations of powerful Inca from all four parts of the realm came to see her despite the high toll.

Including Atahualpa.

His father, Huayna Capac, was the former Incan Emperor and a direct descendant of the sun. Huayna's body no longer worked because of the strange illness spreading throughout the empire from the north. The fever had kept him in his bed before the rashes began on his face and hands. His remains were still at his palace in Cuzco, however, attended by the same servants who had waited on him while he could move under his own volition. His connection to the Earth taken care of, it was up to the citizens to keep Huayna in their hearts and minds, the same way they remembered and sustained Pachacuti, the sun's progeny who had expanded the Incan Empire far beyond the Cuzco valley in the first place.

Atahualpa commanded the troops following him to stay on the banks of the river while he dismounted from his litter in front of the oracle's cave. The same dozen warriors had stayed close to his person for five full years, ever since the body of his brother, Huayna's oldest son and heir, also stopped working soon after their father's, victim of the same strange malady. Without clear instructions as to who would lead the empire, both Atahualpa and Huascar—half brothers with different mothers—claimed the role for themselves, dividing the empire in two. Atahualpa had the north, Huascar the south and Cuzco.

"Huascar doesn't believe in the old ways either," Atahualpa said when his captain stared at his chest with doubt not quite hidden behind his eyes. None dared look at the sun's descendant in the face for fear they would lose their eyesight, the same way they would if they stared at the sun in the sky; the captain had taken a risk raising his eyes from the ground in the first place. "He probably doesn't even know where this place is," Atahualpa added, turning around and inspecting the cave's entrance.

It reminded him of the caves in the mountains around Cuzco he used to play in as a child. Back before rumors of bearded men appearing on the coast, before the plague began eviscerating the population of the empire. *His* empire. The opening was a thin slit in the rock, barely enough room for a full-grown man to squeeze through. The rock was damp and covered in moss, and he stepped on bits of crushed bone and fur as he turned sideways and slid into the darkness.

The passage turned right, somehow narrowing, and Atahualpa continued on with his left shoulder leading. He felt the slick rock against his back and chest with every deep breath he took. There was a moment of anxiety when he thought he could go no farther, that somehow he had gotten the location of the oracle's cave incorrect, until a breeze struck the back of his left arm. He turned his head to the left, looked behind him, and caught the stuttering light of a fire against the cave wall.

There was no continuing forward no matter how he contorted his body. Annoyed, he backed out and turned around in view of his confused guards, facing the other direction before plunging back into the rock. This time, when he got to the choke point, he managed to squeeze through—but received a long gash on his chest for the effort.

The cave opened up and Atahualpa strode into the firelight. The room was no bigger than two royal litters sitting side by side, the fire burning low in the center of the room. In front of him stood a wooden woman with a belt made of gold, golden breasts, and golden eyes, dressed in tattered queen's clothes splattered with blood from previous sacrifices. Bones and rotted flesh from both humans and animals lined the spaces where the floor met the wall.

A living woman sat cross-legged next to the idol; she stood when Atahualpa approached.

"The oracle said we'd be receiving a celestial visitor. Tell me, has one truly entered the chamber?" the woman said without bowing her head, her face cloaked in shadow.

Her brazenness when meeting the Emperor of the Four Realms shocked the man who fancied himself a god. "I am Atahualpa, the true heir to the throne," he said with authority.

The woman smiled. "I am Sarpay, the humble interpreter of the oracle's message." When Sarpay turned to the side and bowed as if allowing an audience with the wooden idol, Atahualpa saw that scars covered the sunken holes where her eyes had been.

"The idol . . . is the oracle?" Atahualpa said.

"It certainly isn't me!" Sarpay said, cackling.

Atahualpa wondered why his father—or any of the other Incan nobility who had visited her—never mentioned the oracle's true nature. Realizing it must have been because he wasn't the named heir to the throne, he set his jaw in anger at his father's oversight.

Remembering the few lessons about the oracle he'd pieced together from whispers during his campaign against Huascar, Atahualpa went to one knee between the wooden idol and the flames.

Sarpay sniffed. "You came alone."

"Yes. I've come to make the true sacrifice."

Sarpay flashed a smile filled with rotten teeth. "You know what it requires?"

"Of course," Atahualpa snapped.

"Well, you didn't know the oracle's true nature," Sarpay replied without pause.

Anyone else in the Four Realms would have been thrown off a cliff for such a retort.

"Lie down," Sarpay commanded as she walked behind the oracle.

Atahualpa set his jaw, swallowed his displeasure at the command, and did as he was told. From his position on the floor, he saw the flames dancing in the idol's golden eyes—it looked like she was watching him with glee.

Sarpay returned carrying a golden bowl in two hands, walking so as to not spill a drop. "Most people bring animals as tribute; some sacrifice slaves. Only the most desperate for the truth lay down their own lives."

Atahualpa shuddered as he took a deep breath. His army, superior to that of Huascar, had enjoyed a recent string of victories. In what he had hoped was the decisive blow, Atahualpa had sent the majority of his army—including the powerful general Quizquiz—ahead to Cuzco in hopes of capturing Huascar and ending the war once and for all. But like his father had said many times before, "Hope for abundance, prepare for famine."

Now, lying on a dirty cave floor, Atahualpa hoped the oracle could shed light on the unseen path ahead.

Sarpay got down on her knees next to Atahualpa's head and began lowering the bowl to his face without any indication that she couldn't see. Something about the way the firelight reflected off the bottom of the golden bowl caught his eye . . .

The Incan Emperor grabbed Sarpay's wrist. He sat up with care so that not a drop of the sacred liquid spilled. Inspecting the bowl, he realized it was the gilded skull of Atoq, Huascar's former top general. It was one of his prized possessions; along with his queen, Azarpay, it traveled with him everywhere. It should have been outside the cave, waiting for his return.

"How did you get this?" he said, his eyes wide in awed horror. All twelve men of his guard would soon find themselves joining the condors in their flight among the cliffs.

"Shh," Sarpay said, laying a hand on Atahualpa's chest, pushing on his fresh wound to force him back down. "Your men are still outside—" She lifted her head as if she could see them through the cave's wall. "Guarding your queen."

Thrown off by the entire affair, Atahualpa didn't realize she was the first person to touch his body outside of the bedroom since before he'd proclaimed himself divine ruler of the Four Realms. "Then how—"

"The same way the oracle will tell you what it is you wish to know," Sarpay said, her voice turning the words into a song. Atahualpa decided there was no other vessel he'd rather drink from, that the golden skull of his former enemy was another good omen for his continued ascension.

Sarpay poured a thick liquid into Atahualpa's open mouth; he swore she'd pulled a coal from the fire and placed it on his tongue. Strong hands pressed his shoulders to the earth when he swallowed, pushing him deeper into the packed dirt. Thick gray smoke emerged from his lips as the ground overtook him . . .

Atahualpa woke up with a start. He sat up near the cavern's entrance, the fire's brightness burning his eyes. Sarpay sat cross-legged between the fire and the oracle, leaning back and forth to an unheard rhythm.

"Tell them to wait outside," Sarpay hissed, her voice deeper than he remembered.

Before Atahualpa could question the woman, he heard one of his guards calling his name.

"Stay outside," Atahualpa shouted. His voice sounded strange to his ears, raspy.

"There's water in the skull," Sarpay said, still rocking.

Atahualpa grabbed his favorite goblet and took long sips of fresh water. It wasn't until the vessel was almost drained that he wondered what had happened to the oracle's potion.

"It was water the whole time," Sarpay muttered, reading his thoughts.

"Did you move me when I was asleep?" Atahualpa said when he realized she sat where the ground had swallowed him.

"When you were dead, yes."

"So I did die . . ." Atahualpa said in awe.

"And your body was then healed by the oracle. The wound in your chest?"

Atahualpa put a hand to where the cave's wall had scratched him. "It's gone."

"We know."

Sarpay's hands shot straight down, her fingers breaking with a loud crunch against the packed-dirt floor. Her head snapped back, and her entire torso bent backwards at an unnatural angle so that she faced Atahualpa. "Now, are you sure you want to know what lies ahead?"

Atahualpa scrambled onto all fours and sat on his knees. "Yes, yes, tell me."

"Invaders threaten the Realm of Four Parts."

Huascar?

"Death heralds their arrival, but what we have seen is only a taste of what's to come. They will ride in on the water before ripping the bones from the living Earth and blocking the sun like a flock of condors flying in the sky."

"Nothing can stand against the power of the sun," Atahualpa said, rage building as Sarpay slandered his celestial ancestor.

"Two brothers united can defend our land against death. Divided? The underworld has space for us all."

Atahualpa closed his eyes and allowed the escape of a slow exhale. Part of being a divine ruler was mastering a human's fleeting emotions. His anger subsided, and he opened his eyes and looked at the upside-down face of the oracle's interpreter. "Who are the invaders, and when do they arrive?"

Sarpay frowned, but upside down, it seemed like a smile. "Two brothers united." With that, her body snapped forward as if pulled by an unseen rope connected to the idol's head before collapsing in a heap. Atahualpa stood up and stared at the idol's golden eyes, each daring the other to blink. He grabbed Atoq's golden skull without taking his eyes from the idol, turned, and made his way out of the cave.

The guards snapped to attention once Atahualpa reappeared. Azarpay, standing near the river accompanied by her litter-carriers, meandered back to the group in case Atahualpa decided they were leaving.

"I need to send a message to Quizquiz," Atahualpa declared while gazing at the river in the distance.

The royal recorder approached the emperor, long strings of different-colored ropes hanging from a special yoke resting on his shoulders. He withdrew a singular golden thread from a leather pouch hanging at his side, the color only the emperor could use, and readied himself to make a new quipu—knotted strings that recorded information for transport. Quizquiz's recorder would decipher the message and carry out the emperor's instructions.

Atahualpa began when he was certain his recorder was ready. "Tell him not to capture Huascar . . ."

The recorder's hands flew as he began tying the knots on different-colored threads.

"I want him executed." Then, to himself, he muttered, "It's time to end this war."

1

THE MASSACRE OF CAJAMARCA

THE INCAN EMPEROR was waiting outside, and Gonzalo Pizarro was adjusting a friar's habit.

"Hurry up, will you?" Friar Vincente de Valverde told the twenty-two-year-old Spaniard. The priest turned his head and cast his perpetual frown on the young man.

"I'm trying; your cincture's all twisted," Gonzalo replied as he fumbled with the braided rope around Friar Valverde's waist while standing behind the holy man. His shaking hands didn't make the task any easier—all he could think about were the hordes of native men alongside the emperor streaming into the town square of Cajamarca.

The one hundred and sixty-eight Spaniards, led by Gonzalo's brother Francisco Pizarro, had chosen Cajamarca as their destination after landing on the coast for one specific reason: the leader of the Incan Empire, Atahualpa, was encamped nearby. The ruler had just won the civil war against his half brother, Huascar, and Francisco was eager to establish contact with yet another indigenous civilization in the New World, hoping for the same success Hernán Cortés had experienced against the Aztec Empire. Hernando de Soto's envoy, with support from another Pizarro brother, a second Hernando, had strode through the vast Incan camp days before and invited the emperor to that day's meeting in the town square. In preparation, Francisco had hidden his men and horses in three of the square's adjacent buildings where they could rush through one of numerous doors if needed; their artillery was in the fourth building, across from the entrance closest to the Incan camp, one of two into the square.

In truth, Francisco Pizarro had no firm idea on the best course of action. The Hernandos' envoy had reported close to eighty thousand native warriors, so the Spaniards were outnumbered at least four hundred to one. There were two main options: either offer themselves as allies in the fight against Atahualpa's remaining enemies or capture the emperor just like Cortés had done in Mexico. But there was no way of knowing how the Incan army would respond to either course of action. In the end, Francisco let all of his men know that he would rely on divine inspiration for his decision. In essence, the Spaniards would have to wait until the precise moment when the correct path presented itself to their leader.

Gonzalo, the youngest Pizarro brother, was chosen to accompany Friar Valverde and their Quechua interpreter Felipillo when the priest read Atahualpa the *Requerimiento*, the declaration by the Spanish monarchy that they had the divine right to take possession of the New World and the peoples within. He had watched the first Incan warriors arrive in the square, singing and dancing, and retreated back into the building when he caught sight of Atahualpa being carried on a litter surrounded by many men wearing golden armor and crowns.

"Finally," the exasperated priest said when Gonzalo reported that the cincture was in place. They stood side by side for a moment, with Felipillo behind them, until Friar Valverde broke the silence by asking if Gonzalo had seen all of the gold adorning the warriors.

Gonzalo reported that he had.

Friar Valverde slapped Gonzalo's back. "Then smile, boy! We're about to become very rich men."

Gonzalo wondered why a man of God cared about riches. Weren't the men of the cloth supposed to live to serve God and obtain new converts? He knew why he wanted the status money could bring: to show the noblewoman who had rejected him because of his low birth what a mistake she had made. Even his father, so quick to praise Francisco for his eldest son's exploits in the New World despite Francisco being a bastard like Gonzalo, had laughed when Gonzalo told him that he had requested Don Antonio's daughter's hand in marriage. Francisco's offer of an expedition in the New World soon after the failed proposal had been a blessing—Gonzalo couldn't go into town without his face flushing red with shame from the stares of those who knew about his attempt at reaching beyond his station.

The silence in the square pulled Gonzalo from his reverie. Juan Pizarro, the fourth and final Pizarro in the New World and Gonzalo's full brother, was stationed alongside the artillery with the priest and his entourage. He stood at such an angle that he could see Francisco at one of the doors on the adjacent wall.

"Those bastards are laughing at us—they think we're hiding scared in the buildings!" Juan whispered through clenched teeth. Then, a moment later, he turned to Gonzalo and Friar Valverde. "You're up," he said.

Friar Valverde stood tall, clutched the Bible at his side, and held his wooden cross at arm's length as he emerged from the shadows into the town square with Gonzalo at his side. Felipillo followed behind.

Five thousand Incan warriors filled the Cajamarca town square. The horde parted when they saw the Spanish contingent approaching the emperor, who was seated on a litter lined with colorful feathers tickling plates of gold and silver. The men beneath him could have been statues. He sat on a thick cushion atop a golden throne, with an ornate golden crown on his head and large emeralds around his neck. Other nobles carried atop litters behind the emperor looked plain compared to the splendor of their leader.

It was obvious that the warriors had different factions within their ranks. The main differentiator was the variation in shields—there were large rectangular shields worn on the back by archers, small round shields at the sides of men carrying slings, and square shields with sides the length of a torso carried by the men with a mace in their hands. One of the Incan men slammed his mace against his shield, startling Felipillo. Gonzalo stared at the warrior's wide eyes and locked his jaw; Friar Valverde ignored the man altogether.

"Felipillo, come here," Friar Valverde snarled. The young interpreter hurried forward and stood between the priest and the Incan Emperor.

"Tell him that Governor Pizarro is in that building over there," Friar Valverde said, pointing to the building where Gonzalo's older brother waited. "And that he'd very much like to share a meal."

Felipillo nodded and started speaking to Atahualpa in Quechua. Gonzalo wondered how effectively Felipillo could translate even this simple request—the young man had learned the language of Cuzco on the coast, far from where it was the common tongue, and his grasp on Spanish was tenuous at best, having learned on his own by spending time around ordinary soldiers.

Despite the challenges, Atahualpa understood the gist of the request. He rattled off a series of words while Felipillo interpreted them into broken Spanish. "I'm not leaving this spot until you return everything you've taken! I know what you've been doing."

Friar Valverde's face clouded over at the mention of the failed conversion. He had tried teaching the natives about the Christian God at a village south of Tumbez; instead of converts, he'd brought back rumors of an impending attack, courtesy of Felipillo. Francisco struck fear into the surrounding countryside by collecting the village elders and burning them at the stake. Then, the soldiers had looted the village. And every village from there to Cajamarca, following in the footsteps of the traveling news of their brutality.

Gonzalo placed a hand on Friar Valverde's back and leaned in close to the priest's ear. "Read him the *Requerimiento*."

The friar took a deep breath, reached into his pocket, and withdrew a scroll. He unfurled it and began reading, not pausing or even slowing down for Felipillo:

"On the part of the King and Queen of Spain, subduers of the barbarous nations, we their servants notify and make known to you, as best we can, that the Lord our God, Living and Eternal, created the Heaven and the Earth . . .

"We require that you acknowledge the Church as the Ruler and Superior of the whole world, the high priest called the Pope, and in his name the King and Queen, as superiors and lords of these lands . . .

"If you do that which you are obliged to do for their Highnesses, we in their name shall receive you in Christian love and charity, and shall leave you, your wives, and your children, and your lands, free without servitude, that you may do with them and with yourselves freely that which you like and think best . . .

"But, if you do not do this, I certify to you that, with the help of God, we shall powerfully enter into your country, and shall make war against you in all ways and manners that we can, and shall subject you to the yoke and obedience of the Church and of their Highnesses; we shall take you and your wives and your children, and shall make slaves of them, and as such shall sell and dispose of them as their Highnesses may command; and we shall take away your goods, and shall do you all the mischief and damage that we can, as to subjects who do not obey and refuse to receive their lord, and resist and contradict him; and we protest that the deaths and losses which shall accrue from this are your fault, and not that of their Highnesses, or ours, nor of these cavaliers who come with us."

Spittle escaped Valverde's lips when he said "are your fault."

Atahualpa stared at the enraged priest while Felipillo kept talking. His face didn't change when the interpreter finished, nor did he say anything acknowledging the information. Silence descended on the town square, without so much as a rustle of armor, and Gonzalo was struck by the question of whether a single king or queen in the Old World could ever exert so much effortless control.

Friar Valverde held up his Bible. "Tell the barbarian that everything about the Lord our God is contained within, his own words preserved in the pages," the priest said, tapping the text.

Atahualpa interrupted Felipillo mid-translation, pointing at the book and saying something to the young man.

"He wants to see your quipu," Felipillo said to the priest.

Friar Valverde gave a solemn nod and approached the emperor's litter. The warriors lining the path didn't move a muscle but stared in contempt as the priest handed over the book.

"Quipu?" Gonzalo whispered to Felipillo.

"Messages sent with rope," Felipillo responded in Spanish.

Gonzalo assumed that the young interpreter had used the wrong word and brushed the matter aside, not realizing that the entire empire ran on a complex system of record keeping using the knotted strings—everything from census data to tax obligations.

Atahualpa turned the Bible over in his hands, examining it from every angle. Realizing that the emperor didn't know how to open the book, Friar Valverde reached up . . .

Atahualpa slapped his hand away, annoyed.

A surprised Friar Valverde gestured opening the book with his hands. "Like this," he said.

Atahualpa pried open the pages with great care, as if he was opening a birdcage and was fearful the creature trapped within might escape. When nothing happened right away, he opened the text all the way and stared at the markings on the pages.

Gonzalo held his breath, wondering if he was witnessing the greatest mass conversion in history. His daydream evaporated when Atahualpa tossed the Bible to the ground.

"How dare you!" Friar Valverde roared, his anger returning in full force as he picked up the discarded book.

In response, Atahualpa stood on his litter—without the platform moving in any discernible fashion—and yelled towards the buildings where the rest of the Spaniards lay in wait.

"He's demanding that you return everything you took, again," Felipillo said.

Friar Valverde rushed away from the Incan Emperor with Gonzalo close behind. "Attack!" he yelled. "Come out, Christians, for I absolve you! These dogs reject the word of God!"

If Gonzalo could count on anything from his brother Francisco, it was his staunch faith in the power of the Catholic Church. Gonzalo, still fleeing with the priest and the interpreter from the center of the town square, looked at the building where he knew his brother waited and saw the red flag: the signal to attack.

Thunder from the artillery rattled the bones of every human in the square, indigenous and Spanish alike. Scores of native men fell. Then, before the sound had stopped echoing off the square's walls, dozens of Spaniards poured into the square from every direction at once—sixty-two of them on horseback—with cries of "Santiago!" They swung their swords, hacking the stunned warriors around them to pieces while the horses stomped anyone in their path. Wind carried the artillery smoke into the square, covering the bloodbath in a sulfurous haze.

The Incan men weren't fighting back. Gonzalo looked around, unsure of his role in the slaughter. Keeping the priest safe seemed like the obvious priority, but did that include attacking the closest warrior despite the native man's obvious confusion? In the end, Gonzalo escorted Friar Valverde and Felipillo back to the building that housed the artillery and made sure they were safe inside without raising his sword. He retrieved his horse, a beautiful dark brown beast he had named Castaño, and returned to the massacre.

Back outside, Gonzalo saw that both entrances to the square were held by Spanish forces, blocking all means of escape. Attempting to put distance between themselves and the cavaliers, the natives surged towards one side of the square, crushing their brethren against the plaza's wall. As Gonzalo watched, the wall crumbled and a stampede of men fled from the unprompted attack.

In the center of the square, the men beneath Atahualpa's litter were being hacked down in prodigious numbers. Others hurried to take the place of the fallen carriers so that their leader never got closer to the Earth. Nobles and warriors stood between the Spanish fighters and their leader without attacking, sacrificing themselves for his sake. Some of the warriors tried pulling the cavalrymen from their horses with little success; this was the extent of their resistance.

The supply of men responsible for carrying the litter soon ran out, and the emperor teetered on his platform as the remaining men struggled to keep it aloft. Atahualpa would have fallen to the ground if Gonzalo's brother Francisco hadn't caught the emperor, protecting the prize with his own body. He laid the ruler atop his horse, holding the man down with one arm while hacking whatever natives stood in his path on his way to the closest building. It was as if Atahualpa was frozen, so confused about the turn of events that he couldn't fathom taking any action to save himself.

A faint gurgling on the ground caught Gonzalo's attention. He turned from his broad view of the carnage and came to focus on a singular example of the day's gore: an Incan man with a hole clear through his neck. The bubbling was his dying breaths escaping before they reached his lips. Gonzalo dismounted from his horse, knelt down, and plunged his sword into the native's breast. He wasn't sure they deserved the mercy after rejecting the Christian God, but he decided he had the rest of his life to come up with a satisfactory rationale when asked for an explanation by Saint Peter.

He continued expediting fallen natives' path to the afterlife, one at a time, cursing them for not accepting the Christian God when given the chance. He continued until the two Hernandos, Pizarro and de Soto, returned on their horses through the broken wall with the Incan queen Azarpay slung over his brother's shoulder. Every Spaniard cheered their good fortune, thanking God for smiling down on them and convincing themselves that divine providence was responsible for the outcome of the day's events.

In all, more than five thousand natives lost their lives at the massacre of Cajamarca. The Spaniards? Not a single man was lost, and the only injury was a cut on Francisco's hand from an errant Spanish sword.

2

THE RANSOM ROOM

As NIGHT FELL, the leaders of the invading force sat down to a meal with Atahualpa. The Spanish contingent consisted of the four Pizarro brothers—Francisco, Hernando, Juan, and Gonzalo —and Hernando de Soto. The rest of the men were busy completing the work that Gonzalo had started, skewering the fallen men with injuries beyond treatment using the end of their lances.

"Now, first things first," Francisco said through a mouthful of food, gesticulating with a piece of bread in his hand. "Don't feel bad about what happened here today."

Felipillo translated for Atahualpa.

"This is just what happens when heathens encounter Christians; you're not the first sovereign to fall, nor will you be the last."

Juan nudged Gonzalo and snickered. They both knew their brother said "Christian" but meant "white men."

Francisco ignored his brothers. "Our sole aim is to spread the religion of Jesus Christ. He smiled on us today, making sure every one of his believers made it out of the encounter alive."

Atahualpa picked a grilled piece of meat off the bone and

placed it in his mouth, chewing with his eyes closed as he listened to the young translator.

"I've got to know though," Francisco continued. Bits of food fell from his mouth into his beard, and he wiped them away with the back of his hand. "What were you thinking when you walked into the town square with your army instead of coming peacefully?"

The Incan Emperor's relaxed face and purposeful movements reminded Gonzalo of a cat.

"Yours was a good plan," he began. "My men led me to believe that you were no threat; what could such a small force accomplish? Instead, you captured me from the middle of my own troops."

Atahualpa paused while the Spaniards laughed.

"I wanted to see for myself the men who dared pass through my lands and never doubted that my larger force would make quick work of you." Atahualpa looked at Castaño, tied up behind Gonzalo. "My plan was to capture your best men for my own service, take your animals for breeding, and kill the rest."

Not even Francisco, a lifelong military man, could take a bite after hearing the Incan's scheme laid out plain.

"Well, you're lucky you weren't captured by people as cruel as yourself!" Gonzalo said, his first words spoken to the emperor.

"We treat our conquered enemies with mercy—even those who defile our sacred text," Francisco added with a solemn nod.

Through Felipillo, Francisco made it clear that submission on the part of the Incan Emperor would guarantee his continued existence and offer the chance for his freedom. Atahualpa understood the offer because of how his great-grandfather had unified the empire in the first place: subjugating the various peoples for effective taxation instead of wiping them from the Earth.

After a moment's consideration, Atahualpa asked for counsel with one of the captured men. When he arrived, they spoke in front of the Spaniards while Felipillo translated the discussion from Quechua.

"He's asking if there are many men dead . . . He's saying that he wants this man to tell the rest of the troops not to attack any of you, on his royal order . . . asking for his servants . . ."

Gonzalo sidled up to Francisco. "You're going to let his people surround him?" he asked.

"Sure, if it guarantees his cooperation."

"Oh, and tell him that we want a few dozen of their sheep slaughtered and brought for our men," Hernando added.

Felipillo looked confused for a moment before realization dawned on him. "They're called llamas," the young man said with a lopsided smile.

"Well, tell him we want some!" Hernando snapped. He was the sole legitimate son of their father, raised and educated as one of noble birth. Because of this, he lacked his other brothers' easy way with those lower on the social hierarchy.

Felipillo conveyed the message to the emperor, who passed word along to his man.

The next morning, while the captured natives cleared the dead from the town square, a sizable group of native men and women appeared and were taken to Atahualpa straightaway. Francisco, curious about the extent of the natives' discipline, arranged for the investigation of Atahualpa's camp by thirty men on horses, led by Hernando de Soto.

Gonzalo, Hernando, and Juan were all eating breakfast together, still marveling at their good fortune. "Did you see the city's storehouse? There were enough clothes and blankets for everyone, and it looked like we hadn't even made a dent on the supply!" Juan said.

"And we're going to need it," Gonzalo said, rubbing his

hands together. "Any wounded men in the square that escaped our lances surely died from the cold last night."

"No wonder they take the production so seriously," Hernando observed.

All three brothers looked up when Francisco approached.

"Gonzo, a word," the eldest brother and leader of the expedition said.

Gonzalo didn't hesitate. After setting his meal on the table, he stood and followed his brother.

Francisco started on a path towards the outskirts of Cajamarca, in the opposite direction of the native camp. "How did you sleep?"

Gonzalo thought the question strange but replied, "Like the dead," the same joke he'd heard his brother Juan make earlier that morning. Gonzalo hadn't met Francisco until his older brother had turned up in Spain to request the formal rights to conquest from the King and Queen of Spain. They were thirty-two years apart in age, Gonzalo twenty-two and Francisco fifty-four; Francisco had left for the New World for the first time a year before Gonzalo was born. After hearing about Francisco's exploits from their shared father, achievements that included a stint as mayor of Panama City, Gonzalo had expected a refined nobleman when he heard that Francisco had returned. Instead, he had met an illiterate military man, disciplined but unrefined.

"Why do you ask?" said Gonzalo.

"I remember I had trouble sleeping when I first got to the New World," Francisco began, walking with his hands behind his back. "I showed up to this strange land with big dreams filling my small head."

This wasn't the first time that Gonzalo had heard his brother make an oblique reference to his lack of education.

"You know what struck me the most?" Francisco said, turning a wise eye toward his brother.

Gonzalo shrugged.

"How the natives don't appreciate learning about God. I was crossing the Isthmus of Panama with Balboa—this was before he was beheaded—and I convinced him to let the native tribe we found on the coast continue living there, thinking that they could be a part of our first settlement. I spent weeks telling them about the Ten Commandments and Christ's forgiveness. Things seemed to be going well until one day I found them dipping a small cross into the cavity of a slaughtered pig in a bastardized mix of their ways and ours. It was then that I realized their true nature."

Francisco let silence descend, the scuff of their boots on the ground the sole sound.

"What did you do?"

"Exactly what we did outside of Tumbez. We burned the chief and sent the families away. Some came back for worship on their own, but most stayed clear of the new town. That's the key, you see: they have to come on their own. We can't force them to believe in God, Jesus Christ, or the Pope, but we can cast them from the land and hope they come back. The Bible tells us about the prodigal son—these are the prodigal people."

"Why are you telling me this?" Gonzalo said, making an effort not to sound rude. The two men hadn't ever been alone together during the long voyage to the New World.

"Because I remember what it was like to be young," Francisco said in a faraway voice. "I meant to talk with you after we handled the chiefs outside of Tumbez but I never got the chance. Then, after yesterday's battle . . . Well, I've heard some men talking this morning about how you didn't participate." The elder brother stopped walking, put a hand on Gonzalo's shoulder, and faced his younger brother. "You're a Pizarro. We have a name to uphold, one that our father did us no favors by leaving our births illegitimate. It's up to us to make our own way in this world."

Gonzalo shook his head, anger clouding his thoughts. "I killed dozens of native warriors!" he said in defense of the prior day's actions, his pride wounded.

"After they had already fallen, so I hear. Is that not true?"

"It is," Gonzalo replied, hanging his head in shame.

Francisco continued walking. "I need your help in bringing this land to its knees; I can't do it alone. Can I count on you from here on out?"

Gonzalo set his jaw and nodded. He would bring the natives to heel—for Francisco, for the Pizarros, to show the woman who rejected his affection the kind of man she'd missed out on.

Hernando de Soto and his men returned early in the afternoon. Nobody in camp was quite prepared for what they brought.

"The dogs didn't do anything but stare at us!" de Soto said, laughing, as he dismounted his horse and threw a heavy sack onto the ground. "We strode right through the camp, straight to the biggest tent in the center, and they just watched us pass." Turning serious, he added, "Though there are so many of them still out there that it looks like we hardly made a dent in their numbers."

Gonzalo gulped at the thought of the natives deciding to overwhelm the Spanish forces. While his brother could count on him during their next encounter, the sheer numbers involved made him realize the unlikelihood of what they had pulled off the day before.

His awe at their luck intensified when he witnessed what Hernando de Soto pulled from the sack—more gold and silver than he'd ever seen in one place. And not even in bars!

"The emperor had all this just in his tent!" Hernando said,

excited. There were golden dishes of all sizes, jugs and pitchers, silver basins and bowls.

Francisco brought Atahualpa from the Temple of the Sun, where he had been kept prisoner. Pointing at the loot, he asked, "Is there more?"

Atahualpa looked confused after hearing Felipillo's translation. "Of course. I'm the son of the sun," Atahualpa replied. Despite being held prisoner, he still projected an air of refined nobility that could rival any in the Old World.

Some of the Spaniards in attendance giggled, some gasped, and still others clapped the backs of their closest comrades. They were going to be very rich men!

After translating Atahualpa's words, Felipillo added in a conspiratorial whisper to a stunned Gonzalo that the Inca believed that gold was the sun made real on Earth.

Atahualpa spoke a few words in his native tongue as if he was toying around with a thought in his mind. Amidst the tumult, Felipillo hadn't heard. Francisco told the men to be quiet, and the young interpreter said something to the Incan lord that received a momentary stern gaze before Atahualpa spoke, with everyone present enraptured.

"There is more, a lot more, in the capital of Cuzco. In exchange for his freedom," Felipillo translated, "he can cover the floor of that building over there with gold."

Everyone turned in the direction of the building Felipillo indicated, a large room used for storing weapons: spears, maces, shields, and a large quantity of high-quality rope. It was nine paces long and seven paces wide.

The Spanish men turned their eyes on Francisco, who was deep in thought.

Atahualpa sweetened the deal before he received a reply. Raising his hand, he said that he would fill that room up to the top of his hand with gold, and two more of silver. All he needed was time.

"He'll send out word across the Four Realms for collection to begin immediately," Felipillo said. "If that's what you wish, of course."

Gonzalo almost accepted on behalf of the Pizarro expedition. Hernando de Soto looked down at the precious metal taken from the Incan camp, then at the room, no doubt calculating the volume required. He met eyes with Francisco and raised his eyebrows.

Atahualpa added, "What you have at your feet is just from my table service."

Francisco chuckled, shaking his head. "Disband your army and tell them to begin collection."

Atahualpa nodded while staring at the ground.

The gold trickled in over the following weeks, convincing even the most doubtful Spaniards of the emperor's fidelity. But a new fear began creeping in, one that couldn't be dismissed by the amassed riches: that the natives were gathering for a renewed effort against the invaders.

Part of the belief came from the pace of the treasure collection. Traveling vast distances over rugged terrain took time, even more when carrying loads of metal, and the more suspicious Spaniards thought that the emperor was stalling while his troops were rallying in a new location.

Atahualpa became indignant when told of the sentiment by Gonzalo—who had become close with the captive after teaching him chess. "Not one of my subjects would dare raise a finger against you without my orders. Send some of your men alongside my own to Cuzco. I'll ensure them safe passage so that they can oversee the gold collection themselves and realize that I have no plans against you. General Quizquiz can assist you in the capital."

Gonzalo was struck by how the Incan said "I," as if nobody else in the empire would assume the mantle of responsibility in his absence. Nobody wanted to claim themselves descended from the sun? After telling Francisco about the offer, his older brother suggested Gonzalo go down himself.

"I need accurate information about the state of the country, from somebody I trust," Francisco explained, taking a break from drafting overseas correspondences with his scribe.

Gonzalo sighed before accepting the task.

"Do you doubt the Inca's words?" Francisco asked.

"No," Gonzalo said without hesitation.

"Good, then it's settled. You're getting too close to him anyway; it'll be good for you to spend some time apart." With that, Francisco went back to pacing while dictating his letters.

Gonzalo's trip to Cuzco took the better part of a month. As a show of his support to the Spanish cause, Atahualpa ordered litters for him and the two Spaniards accompanying him on the journey. They traveled along the great road to Cuzco, an engineering marvel paved with stones, complete with steps through the mountains and bridges across streams and mighty rivers. There were vast flocks of llamas and sprawling fields of crops between towns and hamlets, each of which received the travelers with the graciousness owed the emperor's royal guests.

Their first glimpse of Cuzco, in the early morning, included the three towers of the fortress Saqsaywaman, just outside the city and as well-constructed as any castle in Spain. One of Gonzalo's companions, a veteran soldier, remarked that it could hold thousands of Spaniards. "I bet it could withstand cannon fire, and nobody could tunnel on that rocky hill," he said in awe.

Besides the practical aspects of the fort, the three Spaniards wondered aloud, while their litter-carriers took them into the city proper, how the natives had moved so many large stones. The stone houses stood along right-angled stone streets, a gutter running down the middle for water drainage. Walls along their path were made of irregular stones, fit together as if they were made for the task—no space discovered at any seam. Similar to the town square at Cajamarca, there were four large buildings surrounding the plaza at the center of Cuzco, except these were larger and more magnificent, made of colored marble and painted. Through their translator, they learned that these belonged to past emperors who, according to the native, were still inside, along with their servants. Gonzalo thought something was lost in translation, not realizing the Incan custom of preserving the dead.

And everywhere they looked, industrious natives were going about the day's tasks.

Quizquiz met the trio in the town square wearing a black-and-white-checkered tunic and a wool mantle hanging from his shoulders. Around his neck hung a golden disk, and he had gold bracelets on each arm. He escorted them to Coricancha, Cuzco's Temple of the Sun and the preeminent one in the empire, a gleaming building on the east side of the city. Morning sunlight reflected off the eastern surface and illuminated the opposite side of the street.

"It's . . . it's gold," one of the soldiers stammered.

"The entire building is plated," the third Spaniard said in awe.

"There's more inside," their translator added with a smile. Over the course of the trip, Gonzalo had learned that the young man's family had supported Huascar during the Incan civil war. Atahualpa's victory had made them outcasts, and he welcomed anything that reduced the sun descendant's power on Earth.

The litter-carriers kneeled so that Gonzalo could step down, the first European in the Incan capital. His travel companions followed suit.

"Take all of these gold panels down and make a pile over

there," Gonzalo said to the surrounding natives, including General Quizquiz.

None of them moved after the translator relayed the command.

"They'll die if they enter the Temple of the Sun," the translator explained to a stunned Gonzalo.

Undeterred, Gonzalo and his two companions snatched whatever tools they could from the nearby natives and got to work themselves. After scaring away the priests and temple virgins, they pulled hundreds of golden panels from the temple walls, any one of which was worth more than they made in a year combined.

General Quizquiz stayed until the end, long after the sun went down. "If you don't release Atahualpa, I'll go rescue him myself," the proud man said.

Gonzalo stood right in front of the general, staring him up and down. He reached out and lifted the golden disk hanging from the man's neck. "You're lucky I don't take this too," he said.

3

THE ONE-EYED BASTARD

THERE WAS a surprise awaiting Gonzalo when he returned to Cajamarca three months later with a sampling of the golden panels in tow.

Diego de Almagro had arrived.

Thickset and shorter than the rest of the Spaniards, he was known as the rowdy man with one eye. When Francisco had received the right to conquer the land that would one day be known as Peru and become its governor, he brought back a title for Almagro as well, one that didn't quite match the grandeur of his own: mayor of Tumbez, the small town near the coast. Placated by promises of a future governorship, Almagro had agreed to continue helping Francisco with organizing the expedition in the New World, a skill set that was Francisco's main incentive in including the brutish Spaniard in the first place.

His arrival doubled the Spanish presence in Cajamarca and added fifteen African slaves to their number. Every Spaniard gathered around as Gonzalo told them about the trip through the countryside, the city of Cuzco, and the vast quantities of gold now on the way to their location with the other two men overseeing the thousands of required porters and llamas.

"And Cuzco is halfway through the empire, correct?" Francisco asked loud enough for all present to hear.

"According to Atahualpa," Gonzalo replied. He looked at the two guards standing outside of the temple where the emperor was held prisoner.

"See, there's a lot more treasure here for the taking!" Francisco said, spreading his arms.

Every man cheered to their good fortune.

Francisco later explained that the men accompanying Almagro were worried that they wouldn't receive any treasure for their efforts. "I told them quite simply that they have no claim to the room of gold and two rooms of silver." He was seated on the golden throne Atahualpa had ridden on into the Cajamarca town square. After handling the gold panels in Cuzco, Gonzalo guessed the royal chair weighed as much as twenty panels, maybe more.

"I'm sure they didn't like that one bit," Gonzalo replied. The four Pizarro brothers were in Francisco's living quarters, the guards outside under strict orders not to let anyone inside.

"And even if they didn't, there isn't much they can do about it," Juan said, cracking his knuckles, always ready for a fight.

"We took the risk; we get the reward. It's really quite simple," Hernando added. His noble education, which left him with more tact than the other three brothers, meant that he was a natural second-in-command among the brothers, behind Francisco. The status the brothers had grown up with in Spain stretched across the Atlantic Ocean and continued in the New World.

Gonzalo asked the question that had weighed on his mind since his return. "How's the prisoner doing?" He understood that overt signs of caring about a heathen's well-being were frowned upon by most and had waited until none of Almagro's men were around before making his inquiry. To them, the emperor was still an ignorant native, less than human until he accepted the Christian God. Even if Atahualpa ever accepted a Christian baptism, he would still face discrimination courtesy of the prevailing attitudes about blood purity and innate hierarchy.

"He's had de Soto keeping him company. Might even be better than you at chess now," Francisco said with a wink. To a lowborn military man like Francisco, Atahualpa was an asset, a casualty of their current expedition—under different circumstances, the native could have been another associate like Almagro. Plus, there was always hope that the emperor would embrace Christianity and transform the entire empire into a vast Christian realm.

Juan picked under his nails with a knife, uninterested; Hernando scowled. "Did you worry about the dog during your whole trip?" Hernando asked.

Gonzalo didn't dare utter a retort.

"Ignore him," Francisco said. "Go talk to him and give me your impressions—he's seemed distant ever since Almagro arrived."

Gonzalo got up from his seat, glared at Hernando, and left.

Atahualpa was sitting on a low stool in the shadows of a well-swept room when Gonzalo arrived. All of his attendants except Felipillo filed out with their heads bowed.

"I heard you've been playing chess with de Soto," Gonzalo said.

Felipillo didn't say a word.

"Aren't you going to tell him what I said?"

A mischievous smile spread across Felipillo's face. For a split second, Gonzalo got the feeling he had walked into an ambush. Upon realizing he possessed a sword at his side and numerous reinforcements outside, he demanded Felipillo tell him what was funny.

Felipillo closed his eyes, lowered his chin in deference, and pointed at Atahualpa.

"He's taught me a lot," Atahualpa said in rough Spanish. His eyes never left the ground.

Gonzalo laughed at his worries. He grabbed a stool from near the entrance and sat down across from the emperor.

"Should I set up the board?" Gonzalo said, looking around for the chess set.

"No, not today," Atahualpa said.

Gonzalo got the feeling that the man would have commanded his exit if he'd had the power.

"The trip to Cuzco was a success. Nobody stood in our way —General Quizquiz even showed us the gold and silver in your palace. Your men listened without question."

"Of course they did. I'm their ruler."

Did Atahualpa know about the past tense? And if he did, would he have still uttered those words?

"More men came," Atahualpa said, sadness heavy in his voice.

"They did. Our friends from across the ocean."

Atahualpa looked at Gonzalo as if seeing him for the first time. "You mean to stay," said the emperor.

A wave of confusion passed through Gonzalo. Felipillo's laughing broke his reverie.

"He thought he was buying his freedom, that your brother would take all of you back where you came from once he filled the room with gold and silver," the interpreter said, shaking his head. "I might have let him think it."

"A comet passed through the sky in the days before the one-eyed man arrived," Atahualpa said without any sign he had heard or understood Felipillo. "There was a similar omen before my father got sick."

Gonzalo scoffed. "Superstition," he said.

Atahualpa looked at Felipillo for a translation. After hearing it, he shrugged. "With so many of your men here to rule over the Four Realms, there's nothing left for me to do but die, just like my father."

None of the numerous reassurances could coax another word from the emperor. When consulting with Hernando de Soto about the state of their prisoner, Gonzalo learned that the emperor had compared Almagro's arrival to an unaccounted-for knight putting his king into check. "He said there was nothing he could do but accept defeat," de Soto explained.

FRANCISCO ORDERED the distribution of the treasure once the other two men returned from Cuzco in June 1533, even though the quantity in the room hadn't quite reached the agreed-upon height. Eight hundred native porters had brought two hundred loads of gold, each quantity doubled for the collected silver.

The presence of Almagro's men in the camp necessitated the quick dispensation of the plunder before the complete collection to the men who had taken the Incan Emperor prisoner. None of the new arrivals had claim to the treasure, yet they were working alongside those who did. To a man, they desired the further exploration of the empire so that they could earn their own fortunes, a task not possible with a condensed collection of treasure. The grumbles about not receiving a share of the haul, a daily source of frustration, wouldn't hold as much weight if the men who earned it already took their own share. Taking from the group was a faceless transaction; from a man made it personal.

Gonzalo himself broke up many of the fights between the two factions; as a Pizarro, the men held him in high regard. Francisco had larger problems requiring his attention,

Hernando felt the task beneath him, and Juan preferred fighting both men for disturbing the peace in the first place.

There was one task in particular that rankled Almagro's men more than any others: guarding the native metalworkers while they melted the gold artwork their predecessors had crafted with care and turned them into uniform bars. Goblets, vases, ornaments, and utensils all went into the furnaces. Of note, a sculpted golden ear of corn with silver leaves, complete with a tassel of delicate silver strings.

Gonzalo got word of yet another fistfight during the second week of the gold bar creation. It seemed the entire camp surrounded the two men rolling around in the dust. Gonzalo forced his way in and separated the two men, receiving a blow to the face for his efforts.

"What the hell is the matter with you two?" Gonzalo roared, giving oxygen to his anger.

The two men glared at each other, their chests rising and falling with their heavy breaths. One had a cut above his eye and the other's face was flushed red from exertion.

"We're a few hundred men in an empire of thousands upon thousands of natives! We die if we don't stick together," Gonzalo reminded them.

Almagro's man, a slender Spaniard with a prominent widow's peak who was a carpenter in Spain, pointed at the red-faced man. "He asked me to empty my pockets before my shift ended. We're eyed with suspicion just like you watch the native dogs!" he said.

"I saw him put something into his pocket!" his accuser responded.

Gonzalo looked at both men, thinking. "Do you have anything?" he asked the accused.

Almagro's man stared at Gonzalo in anger. "So you don't believe me either?" he snapped.

"I didn't say that," Gonzalo replied. Despite the ache in his jaw, he kept his hands away from his face.

Juan appeared from among the crowd. He walked right up to the slender Spaniard and put a hand around his throat. "Answer the question," he said, his other hand working through the man's pockets.

He didn't find anything.

Almagro's man spat on the ground when Juan released him. "You talk about sticking together but you don't even trust your fellow Spaniards," he said to Gonzalo before storming away.

For the rest of the month during the creation of the gold bars, Gonzalo made sure that none of the new arrivals oversaw the native metalworkers. In response, Almagro's men then complained that the original conquerers didn't trust them.

"Carry on with whatever you think best," Francisco said with a dismissive wave when Gonzalo approached him about the matter. "They'll be upset no matter what the arrangement."

Spaniards took over the tedious task of weighing and stamping the gold bars. In the end, the lowest ranking of the original captors received ninety pounds of silver and forty-five pounds of gold. The horsemen, by virtue of contributing their beasts to the effort and thereby earning a greater stake of the loot, received double the amount; three of the Pizarro brothers fell into this category. Francisco, for his efforts, received seven times as much as each of his brothers, plus the golden throne, melted down and turned into gold bars.

If any of Almagro's men wanted treasure, they would have to take it from an individual instead of the collective. And if they did, the laws of Spain regarding theft still applied.

None dared eye the portion of the loot set aside for the first Christian church in the land, now called New Castile, nor the fifth of the treasure set aside for the Spanish Crown. Hernando, by virtue of his noble birth, was chosen for the transport of the king's share back to Spain, and he began the long journey days after the distribution.

With that, the men were ready for a trip to Cuzco and the continued capture of the Incan Empire. But there was one glaring problem: What should they do with the captured emperor? Traveling with him presented a handful of challenges.

First, he required a constant guard, taking away men that could be better used in defense of the procession. Second, transporting a captive Atahualpa and his retinue opened the Spaniards up to attacks—what if the natives attempted a rescue mission? They already knew, courtesy of Gonzalo, that the great road to Cuzco offered many opportunities for an enemy ambush.

And there was no way they could let him go free. For one, he could turn the entire empire against the Spaniards. Then there was the fact that the gold hadn't reached the agreed-upon height . . .

Atahualpa argued that the panels from Coricancha should count for more and demanded his freedom. Francisco had laid them flat on the ground, however, and maintained that the emperor's debt wasn't paid.

After Felipillo relayed a rumor about native forces amassing in a town called Guamachucho—Atahualpa's birthplace—Almagro made no secret about his belief that killing the emperor was the best course of action. Part of his motivation included finding opportunities for him and his men, who had been promised vast riches on the expedition but had yet received none. Moving on to Cuzco offered them the chance for riches they had missed out on by not capturing the native lord.

Francisco asked Atahualpa outright about the allegations. Alongside him were Gonzalo and Hernando de Soto, Francisco believing that the two men could discern the truthfulness behind the emperor's claims.

"What treason is this against me, who has treated you like a brother? I let you have your servants and wives and you plot behind my back?"

Atahualpa looked at his two friends then laughed. "Another of your jokes! How could I ever turn against the Spaniards? I saw what you did to the men in the square."

Gonzalo felt his heartstrings pulling on his gut at the emperor's words. Francisco flexed his jaw.

Realization dawned on Atahualpa's face and he began his defense. "I'm your captive—how could I gather troops without you knowing? I'd be the first one killed if they attacked!" He continued when none of the Spaniards responded. "It seems you don't understand something. Nobody makes a move without my orders. Nobody and nothing. The birds won't even fly without my permission!"

Gonzalo hadn't seen the emperor's belief in his overwhelming power in weeks. He feared Francisco would take the emperor's words as blasphemous. "I'll go to Guamachucho and investigate myself," Gonzalo said, stepping forward.

Francisco didn't even look at him. "I can't risk the men."

"I'll go by myself," Gonzalo replied. He looked at Atahualpa. "I believe him."

"I'm going with him," de Soto added. "The two of us will go and report back."

Francisco turned his gaze on the two men. "You're asking me to risk my brother and one of my best men, along with their horses, because you believe a heathen?" Francisco said, more pensive than angry.

"No engagements. Just investigation," de Soto said. He had a knack for inspiring trust.

"You have three days," Francisco replied.

The two men set off right away. They crossed the countryside, found a peaceful Guamachucho without any gathering of natives larger than a family, and turned around so that they could relay the information to Francisco, proving Atahualpa's innocence.

They found the leader of the expedition in his quarters, lying down with a hat covering his face. "We didn't find anything!" Gonzalo reported. "Must have been a trick. Do you think Felipillo was in on it?" he said.

Francisco took his time in sitting up. There were tears in his eyes when he removed the hat from his face.

"I've been tricked. Atahualpa is already dead, executed alongside his queen."

Gonzalo sat down on a nearby chair; Hernando paced the room with his hands on his head.

"There was no enemy!" de Soto said, throwing his hands in the air. "Everywhere we went we were received with goodwill." He turned his eyes on his leader. "You acted rashly."

For a second, Gonzalo thought his comrade had gone too far. But once he saw Francisco bury his face in his hands, he realized Hernando said nothing that his brother didn't already realize.

"He accepted baptism from Valverde so that his body wouldn't be burned—according to their beliefs, one can't get into the afterlife without a body still present on Earth. They named him 'Francisco Atahualpa' in my honor, and he made one request before facing the garrote." Francisco lifted his tear-filled eyes and looked at the two men. "He asked me to look after his children in Quito."

"You killed him for no reason at all," Hernando said while shaking his head before storming out of the room.

4

"SEND ME TO HELL"

THE TRIP to Cuzco began in September 1533. Almost five hundred men—one hundred and fifty on horseback—left Cajamarca accompanied by Atahualpa's retinue, now in Francisco's personal service. The procession traveled along the great road to Cuzco, each night stopping at one of the houses built for royal couriers who carried quipus throughout the empire. Each location came furnished with storehouses of grain provided by the closest town, a system set up by the Incan government that contributed to the effective ruling of their vast empire.

Gonzalo regaled the men with stories about the riches in Cuzco each night. Despite taking all the gold from the sun temple and Atahualpa's royal palace, he assured the men that "we only took what we thought would fill up the ransom room."

"I wouldn't be surprised if there was twice as much still in the city," another of the men who had gone to Cuzco would chime in. "The other nobles, the palaces that Quizquiz assured us were empty—it was obvious the natives were hiding a lot more than we took."

Almagro's men salivated at the thought of seizing vast riches for themselves; the Pizarro faction daydreamed about adding to their bounty, like gluttons imagining fruit pies after a banquet.

"Did I tell you about the other temples too?" Gonzalo would add, despite knowing full well that he had told the story the previous night. "There were so many that we didn't enter; the heathens certainly have active imaginations!" he said. Of course, every man who heard about the temples knew about the panels taken from Coricancha and assumed the other locations would offer a similar haul.

Despite the road's quality, the Spaniards ran into two unexpected challenges along the way, both due to the unforgiving countryside. The mountains near the beginning of their journey had stone steps cut into them; the humans and llamas had no trouble traversing the mountain passes, but the horses proved a different matter. The rocks cut the hooves of the beasts even when they were led by the bridle, slowing the entire procession's travel. Diego de Almagro, notorious for his short temper, cursed both the natives and the horses. Francisco, on the other hand, had Friar Valverde lead the men in prayer each night, asking God for the safe passage of the horses through the mountains. The leader of the expedition understood the immense value of the animals, having seen how effective they had been in fighting against the natives. Before his death, Atahualpa had even remarked how the Inca had no counter for the horses, a comment that would presage the further clashes between native and Spanish forces.

The second issue the Spaniards faced concerned the bridges crossing the various streams and rivers on the way to Cuzco. While the bridges were durable enough for humans and llamas, it didn't take long for the column to realize that the much-heavier horses broke up the footpath across the water, the holes in the bridge making the route more dangerous for all. Because of this, the Spanish cavalry had to cross the water on rafts while leading their swimming horses.

Pockets of organized Incan resistance to Spanish occupation materialized halfway to Cuzco. The Spaniards' suspicion of the natives had never wavered, even after learning that Atahualpa had been murdered for nothing. In fact, since the execution, the invaders had been even more cautious, perking up at the mere mention of native gatherings like hunted deer.

The vanguard arrived in a lush valley with a broad but shallow river running through the middle. While their horses drank and soldiers rested, a contingent of warriors appeared on the far banks, materializing from the trees without a sound. By the time the first Spaniards spotted the group, one of the Inca had taken an axe to the woven bridge spanning the river—it fell into the water with a groan and a splash, the current pulling it at an angle from the shore.

"Gather your arms, men!" Gonzalo roared. His full brother Juan urged the men to the shore on their side of the river, where they stood facing the natives. The Inca let out a war cry, their painted faces contorting into furious masks and their weapons held aloft.

Juan looked at Gonzalo and smiled. Gonzalo didn't have the chance to ask for more time, to suggest they wait for Francisco and Almagro's arrival before making a move.

"Santiago!" Juan called out, urging his horse into the water.

The rest of the Spaniards followed suit.

After seeing the mad dash of their enemy, the Incan warriors unleashed a single volley of projectiles—small stones, arrows, and spears—that bounced off of the Spanish metal armor. Then, they took to their heels and disappeared back into the trees.

"After them!" Juan roared as he emerged from the water. He disappeared into the trees, tearing after the warriors at a frenetic pace with the fastest Spaniards close behind. Gonzalo made sure every Spaniard crossed the river without incident before following.

They cut down every Incan warrior they could find, riding behind them and slashing down at them from atop their horses. Gonzalo took great care with his strikes, ensuring a quick death, but Juan employed a different strategy, later bragging about his favorite maneuver around the fire:

"I'd overtake them and hit them on the head with the broad side of my sword," he said to the laughing men. "Then, once past them, I stabbed their belly or chest so that they'd bleed out."

The crueler men grew jealous that they hadn't thought of the scheme while kinder members of the company stared at the fire.

"Teach them to stand up to us!" Juan said.

A cheer went up from the Spaniards; the fire threw sparks in the air as the logs rearranged themselves.

Francisco decided that the skirmish's location was a perfect spot for another Spanish settlement: Jauja. They stayed at the location for a number of days while Francisco established a church, a school, and a hospital. He sent letters with offers of land in exchange for populating the new town and decided which of the men from his own forces would become the seed inhabitants.

A portion of the vanguard also left for further exploration, Francisco replacing Juan with Hernando de Soto in hopes of preventing another slaughter.

"We'll end up creating the resistance ourselves if we let Juan off leash," Francisco told Gonzalo in private. "Keep an eye out and report back. In particular, restore the bridges where they've been destroyed."

A number of natives accompanied Gonzalo and de Soto's

sixty-cavalry detachment, experts in bridge construction and enough workers for the task's completion. Gonzalo and de Soto rode out along the great road and soon encountered burned villages and paths blocked with heavy stones and trees, in addition to the expected bridge remnants. They soon lost the first Spaniards in their conquest of the Incan Empire—three men in a quick skirmish as they navigated a mountain pass.

The surviving Spaniards took the loss hard; it was the first time they'd faced their own mortality. Yet they continued marching towards Cuzco.

A native brought word of another ambush in an upcoming mountain pass. It was the end of the day, and both horses and men were exhausted. They had planned on making camp on the other side, and word of the native warriors didn't alter their objective. Instead, every Spaniard drew their weapons and readied for the attack.

The sun hung low in the sky, casting long shadows across the path. Silence descended on the invaders, the wildlife and wind waiting with bated breath. Halfway through the pass and in sight of a plateau up ahead, a horde of native warriors appeared from every nook and cranny as if the shadows themselves had turned into the darker-skinned attackers. The air filled with their war cries, the surrounding birds and animals contributing to the noise.

Horses were overturned on the rocky terrain and men scrambled back to their feet swinging their swords. Hernando de Soto and Gonzalo did all they could to restore order and press the attack, but the natives were hell-bent on driving the invaders back.

With a shout and a plea to almighty God, Hernando drove his horse forward, hacking at the natives that tried holding on to his horse's legs. He broke through the masses and made it to level ground, riding back and forth as he created distance between himself and the pressing native troops.

As the last remnants of daylight disappeared, the rest of the surviving Spaniards made it to his side. The Incan warriors didn't press the attack, instead gathering on one side of the clearing while the Spaniards withdrew to the opposite. The camps were close enough that they could hear each other throughout the night.

Gonzalo didn't need an interpreter to know that the Incan men were in high spirits. His own encampment recorded the day's losses, making special note of the natives' weapons that had cost them several men and horses and discussing counter-strategies.

"There's no way this wasn't commanded by a military man," de Soto proclaimed around the glowing embers of the night's fire. "They all surged forward at once and fought like well-disciplined troops."

"Quizquiz said that he'd rescue Atahualpa himself if we didn't release him. I don't doubt he's behind this, now that Atahualpa's gone."

De Soto shook his head. "They never should have executed him," he growled.

Gonzalo and de Soto both knew that his brother had made the final decision, but Hernando was tactful enough not to name the eldest Pizarro in front of the man's younger brother.

De Soto took a deep breath and exhaled before placing his hands on his knees and standing up. "Listen up, everyone!" he yelled. Since the natives couldn't understand what he said, he didn't bother lowering his voice.

The Spaniards gathered around.

"Tonight was rough, we can't deny that," he began. The assembled men murmured in agreement. "But we had traveled all day; both ourselves and our horses were exhausted! Imagine what we can do after a full night's rest on level ground!"

Gonzalo watched as hope returned to the faces of their men and felt a twinge of jealousy pierce his heart. He was the Pizarro in the company; he should have thought about what words could inspire his men.

"God has led us this far, and he'll deliver us to the promised land—there's nothing that can stand up to his almighty power!" Hernando said.

A cheer went up from the men. Hernando waited until the noise died down before handing the floor to Gonzalo, who relayed the battle plans they had made for the following morning.

Bugles woke the Spaniards in the middle of the night. They recognized the sound but had no idea why their countrymen would signal their position. Unworried about betraying their location—since the natives were right across the clearing—they responded with their own bugle call and guided the other group to their location.

It was Diego de Almagro with almost every other horse possessed by the Spanish in the Incan Empire. Almagro explained that Francisco, after hearing the reports from Gonzalo about the state of the countryside, worried about an imminent attack and had sent out reinforcements. Almagro had heard the battle the night before and urged his men and horses past the point of exhaustion so that they could provide support.

"And that's why he's the one leading the expedition!" Hernando said, clapping Gonzalo on the back. "Your brother is the best there is."

Yet another fortuitous decision by Francisco had preserved the Spanish cause within foreign territory. To every Spaniard awoken in the dead of night, it seemed that God did indeed smile upon their cause.

At daybreak, seeing how the Spanish ranks had swollen overnight, the natives retreated into the morning fog.

After discovering definitive proof of native resistance, the men decided they should go back to Francisco at Jauja. Almagro would go back straightaway, while Hernando and Gonzalo would travel farther west and strike north from another direction. "Stay away from mountain passes," Almagro joked before they went their separate ways.

In yet another serendipitous turn of events for the Spanish, Gonzalo and Hernando de Soto stumbled upon a native army a few days' march southwest of of Jauja. Because the opposing force numbered more than five thousand native soldiers, the Spanish cavalry decided against attack, instead opting for a diplomatic approach. After prolonged urging for a discussion, Gonzalo himself led the talks.

"Come meet our leader, my brother, and we can discuss how we can work together for the betterment of everyone in the Four Realms," Gonzalo said.

Through the interpreter, General Chalcuchímac made it clear that he knew about Atahualpa's execution. "You're lucky we don't exact our revenge right here and now!" the man said. His black hair had streaks of gray, and he had deep lines on his forehead and around his eyes from a lifetime of staring into the distance in the countryside.

Upon hearing his threat, the general's vast retinue put their hands on their weapons. The Spaniards all responded in kind, staring at their enemy until Gonzalo waved a hand and urged calm.

"I'm here to offer a trade. Come with us as our guest and meet with my brother. In exchange, we will give you Atahualpa's remains so you can give him the ceremony he deserves." Based on his discussions with the former emperor, and the way the natives he encountered spoke of the dead, he had a feeling his brother held on to a powerful bargaining chip.

Hernando turned his eyes to Gonzalo, giving him a look that said he had no right to make such an offer. Gonzalo, despite supporting his brother, still felt guilty at their treatment of the Incan royal and believed God had given him the chance to make things right.

Chalcuchímac, tears in his eyes at the mention of his fallen emperor, asked for a day to think. The Spaniards retreated to their nearby camp, ready for a hasty retreat if the Incan army readied for conflict.

The next morning, General Chalcuchímac appeared in front of the Spanish camp riding in a litter supported by a number of slaves. His advisers, assistants, and wives followed, along with a handful of warriors carrying an empty litter. "They'll take Atahualpa's remains away when we arrive," the general said, his gaze boring into Gonzalo.

Gonzalo agreed, and they set off. Along the way, natives from the towns and settlements came from their houses and greeted the general as if he was a royal—this was how Gonzalo realized the value of the prize he now brought to his brother.

The Spaniards at Jauja all stared at Gonzalo, Hernando, and Chalcuchímac as they strode into town and went straight to Francisco's quarters. Honoring Gonzalo's deal, Francisco handed over Atahualpa's remains after the Incan general said a few words to the corpse in his native tongue. Every Inca stared at the warriors carrying Atahualpa on a litter as they receded into the distance.

"To be honest with you," Francisco whispered to Gonzalo. "I fear they were gathering to take back his remains in the first place. Now, we have another prisoner, and we were never at risk." He clapped Gonzalo on the back twice, and Gonzalo felt a surge of pride swell in his chest.

A dark cloud blocked the sun when the Incan general turned to Francisco. "Now, I have some questions for you," he said via Felipillo.

Francisco's gaze darkened. "I was going to say the same to you."

The interrogation of Chalcuchímac took three days. On the first, both men feigned diplomacy. During the second, Francisco made it clear that the general was his prisoner, putting him in irons and taking away his attendants. By the third, Francisco spoke plain.

"You scouted out our movements and attacked our men," Francisco charged.

Yet again, Chalcuchímac reiterated his claim that his army was waiting while he decided the best course of action after hearing about the emperor's death.

"Then you told Quizquiz about our forward troops and he attacked us!" Gonzalo added. He had spoken his suspicion to Francisco before, but his brother hadn't brought it up to the general.

Francisco nodded in agreement. "You've been sending information about us to Quizquiz in Cuzco, is that it?"

Chalcuchímac insisted he never spoke to the other general. "We each have our own armies and took commands from Atahualpa," he said. "Now we don't have anyone telling us what to do, so we each operate independently."

Francisco wasn't listening. He sent for Friar Valverde and told him that the man would be burned at the stake. "See if you can get one more for the Lord our God," he said. To Gonzalo, he added, "Tell the men to get a stake ready."

Gonzalo was torn. While guilt racked his intestines because of the Incan belief about preserving the physical body for the afterlife, he also understood that every Spaniard would have an opinion about one of the Pizarros not following orders; they had to display a unified front.

Friar Valverde led Chalcuchímac to the stake at the appointed time. "Do you accept Jesus so you can go to heaven?" the priest asked.

After a moment's consideration, the general replied, "Is that where the Spaniards go?"

Valverde said yes with a solemn nod, his hand on the same Bible Atahualpa had tossed in Cajamarca.

"Then send me to hell so I don't have to see such cruel people."

The general didn't scream as the flames licked his feet, the fire fed by his fellow countrymen under the watchful eye of the Spanish.

5

THE PUPPET EMPEROR

"I CAN SMELL the gold from here!" Diego de Almagro said as the Spanish conquerors readied for their final march towards Cuzco. The rising sun warmed the faces of the men as it cut through the morning fog. According to their native guides, they would be getting to the Incan capital later that day. "I'll have to use the rest of my soap to wash the native stench off whatever we collect," he added.

"Use it for yourself first; you smell like you slept with the horses last night!" Juan replied.

Almagro lifted his arm and took a deep whiff of his armpit. "Not bad. One of the women in Cuzco will get their fill of this later on tonight," he said with a wink.

Gonzalo laughed from atop his horse. Francisco shook his head at his business partner's crude joke but had no room for judgement—he had taken one of Atahualpa's sisters for himself way back in Cajamarca. She rode atop a litter carried by native shoulders near the center of the caravan.

"Go gather the other two men who were with you in Cuzco," Francisco told Gonzalo. "The three of you will ride with me and Almagro so you can tell us everything you know of the city and, in particular, about General Quizquiz."

A murmur among the horde made Gonzalo pause soon after he had left his brother's side. A native litter had emerged through the trees at the front of their caravan, where the other Pizarros and leaders of the expedition waited. Gonzalo hurried back just after the initial introduction.

"Another one of Huayna Capac's sons?" Francisco said, his eyes alight with inspiration.

Felipillo continued his interpretation. "He's Huascar's full brother. Been on the run from Atahualpa and he's here to claim the throne."

A loud laugh escaped from Almagro before a look from Francisco silenced him. "We're here to uphold Huascar's claim to the throne, sent by the King of Spain," Francisco said.

Almagro's one eye narrowed on his partner before opening wide in understanding.

"The people of Cuzco are overjoyed that you have delivered them from the northman," the new arrival said through the interpreter.

"And we'll help you get rid of the last of them!" Francisco replied.

Almagro and the other Pizarro brothers raised their hands and cheered. Then, together with the Incan noble and his retinue, they all continued on towards Cuzco.

"What's his name?" Gonzalo asked Juan as they set off, eyeing the young native on his litter. Although still a teenager, the weariness in his face betrayed the time he had spent living on the run.

"Manco. Much easier to say than the last one," Juan replied. "And that's his adviser Villac Umu riding in the litter right behind him, the one decorated with black condor feathers." As it turned out, Villac Umu was more than just Manco's lead adviser; he was also the former head priest of Coricancha. As one of Huascar's staunchest supporters, he had abandoned the gold-plated temple and gone into hiding with Manco when Atahualpa won control of the empire.

Cuzco appeared late in the afternoon. From their position, Gonzalo could see the Incan fortress overlooking the city and the right-angled streets within. And in those streets, standing in ordered rows, were thousands of native troops under the command of General Quizquiz.

Francisco decided that they would enter Cuzco the following morning and sent Felipillo ahead with news that they were releasing the city from the general's grasp; it was the last time they saw the young man. He placed Juan, Gonzalo, and Hernando de Soto between their camp and Cuzco, along with four dozen cavalry and twice as many infantry. The rest of the soldiers protected the other sides of the camp. Finding sleep proved difficult, since every man lay down for the night wearing their armor with their weapons at their side.

Gonzalo awoke the next morning to Francisco standing between him and Cuzco while looking down at the city. He hadn't yet made a noise or moved anything but his eyelids, but Francisco started talking as if they were looking at the view together. "Tell me, what looks different this morning?" his older brother said.

After getting up and standing next to his brother, Gonzalo stared at the city. "The warriors in the streets—they're no longer organized."

"That's because they're not warriors. Those are the citizens awaiting Manco's arrival."

Gonzalo's mouth hung open in disbelief. "What happened to the army?"

"We'll find out soon enough. But I have a feeling the young Inca was right that the people of Cuzco are happy we're here."

Francisco turned a greedy eye towards Gonzalo. "Should make it easy to pull our new friend's strings."

According to Manco, it was more than just the citizens of Cuzco who lined the streets as they entered the city. People from the surrounding countryside had also heard about the men who got rid of Atahualpa and flocked to see them. The natives stood still and stared, wearing sandals and alpaca tunics without a single weapon drawn in opposition.

"I'm surprised they're not scared of us," Almagro observed.

Something about the way he said it made Gonzalo think that maybe the one-eyed man preferred fear over adulation. "And what about the soldiers we saw last night?" Gonzalo asked.

A new interpreter explained that General Quizquiz had abandoned the city in the dead of night. Then, he spoke with Manco in their native tongue.

Seeing the Incan capital didn't have the same draw for Gonzalo—since he'd already been there—so he spent the march watching the reactions of his fellow travelers to their arrival in the city. He thought Manco looked nervous but put on a brave face, while the rest of the natives accompanying him radiated relief. They had taken a chance in supporting a rival brother's claim to the throne and could have gotten killed for it. Instead, they had been catapulted into a position of power and now returned alongside the last living member of the royal family and a banished priest.

He chuckled at the slack-jawed disbelief common among the Spaniards. The stone city would have been marvelous even in Spain, and an argument broke out among his comrades about whether Cuzco was the finest city in the New World. "Let Cortés keep his Mexico City in the north, there's no way it's as well-constructed as this!" one of the men said. Every Spaniard knew about the conquistador's exploits in the Aztec Empire, but none had been there in person.

What Gonzalo thought most interesting was the interaction between Manco's natives and the Spaniards. Both groups displayed a certain haughtiness towards the other—who was really in charge? The Inca had the divine right, but there was no denying the Spanish strength.

Their procession ended at the town square. Francisco commanded his men set up camp there together in case the inhabitants attempted revolt. The Spanish leaders met with their Incan counterparts in the city while the men got to work securing the plaza.

"First order of business: the people need a leader. Manco, you'll become the new emperor."

While the interpreter gave Manco the news, Francisco muttered, "Can't have any of the natives defecting to Quizquiz."

Manco took a deep breath, steadied his nerves, and nodded at the news. He then said something in his language to the interpreter. "The Lord asks for help in taking care of General Quizquiz," the interpreter said. "He wants the last remnants of Atahualpa's reign wiped from the Four Realms before his coronation."

Francisco smiled while looking around at his brothers, de Soto, and Almagro. "Seems like this kid might know a thing or two!" He then turned his attention to the native lord. "I was going to suggest you raise an army as your first order of business, then take care of the general."

"The kid asked for help!" Almagro exclaimed. "Me and my men didn't get the chance for a fight yet, let us go help him out."

Francisco nodded. "Very well. Gather fifty cavalry and accompany him. Hernando, will you go too?" Francisco asked.

De Soto nodded. Francisco wouldn't let Almagro and his men go without one of his own there for information.

After the council, Francisco addressed the entire group of Spanish invaders in the town square. "The natives think we're liberators now, but that can change in an instant!" he said to his collected men. "And don't you dare do anything to instigate their wrath. No violence or taking of women whatsoever— remember, we're Christians."

The men groaned, Almagro the loudest of all.

"But that doesn't mean you can't start collecting your fair share of their treasure!" Francisco added after a long pause. Every pair of eyes lit up. "Bring everything here, and we'll take care of the distribution."

Like the sickness that had spread among the indigenous population and taken the life of Huayna Capac, the Spaniards rushed out from the town square and began taking everything valuable in sight. They took everything but the mummified remains from the palaces of past emperors, stripped the lesser temples of their silver and jewels, and opened every tomb once an enterprising Spaniard wondered if there could be treasure within and discovered a trove. Maggots on a carcass would have had trouble discerning one of their own from the ravenous Spaniards.

The men strained against Francisco's orders when more loot was discovered in a cave outside of Cuzco in the days following their arrival. "They're hiding more, we all know it!" Juan said, speaking on behalf of the men.

"And what do you propose we do?" Francisco asked.

"I say we torture them and make them tell us where it is!"

"They won't think of us as their allies if we do that," Gonzalo observed.

"They're bound to find out eventually," Juan said, pouting.

Francisco received a curious bit of news in the days before Almagro and Manco were set to leave. Don Pedro de Alvarado, one of Cortés' generals in Mexico, had landed on the coast and was making his way to Quito. Despite Francisco's royal grant of the land, another Spaniard had their eyes on the territory.

"Take care of the native threat then continue north when Manco returns for his coronation," Francisco told Almagro concerning the new Spanish forces. "Avoid conflict at all costs— if anything, offer to buy whatever men he can spare as reinforcements to our cause."

Almagro nodded with an avaricious glint in his eye. "Once I tell them about all the gold and silver we've gathered here, I'm sure the men will fight themselves for the chance to join us."

Francisco turned to Gonzalo as soon as the one-eyed man left the room. "I swear that man knows how to play men like a musical instrument."

"And you play them like a game of chance," Gonzalo observed. "And you always make the correct bets."

Francisco smiled. "Do this as long as I have and you learn from a lifetime of mistakes."

Almagro and Manco left Cuzco the next morning. In addition to Almagro's cavalry, Manco had amassed ten thousand native troops.

Since the pile of gold taken from Cuzco wasn't as large as the one amassed in Cajamarca, it didn't take long before rumors of native torture reached Francisco's ears, courtesy of Villac Umu. As the high priest, he was the most powerful native in Cuzco while Manco was gone.

Francisco took the priest's complaints in stride. "I promise you, if I ever catch one of the men doing it, they'll be burned alive."

The threat of this severe punishment was enough for Umu, who believed the consumption of a physical body offered no chance at an afterlife.

Francisco turned to Juan as soon as Villac Umu left. "Make sure I never catch them." It was common knowledge that the late arrivals, those who came with Almagro, were the ones most desperate for riches and therefore the ones who pushed the limits the furthest. Francisco had made their well-being and obedience Juan's personal mission.

Organizing where everyone lived, that was Gonzalo's mission.

After the first few days in Cuzco passed without incident, Francisco decreed that the men could take up residence in the buildings near the central plaza. Gonzalo became the last word of every housing dispute, and the one who managed the resources needed for daily life. Lucky for him, the Incan storehouses had plenty of food, blankets, and wood for the masses that had descended on the capital city. Although he made sure the men used their assets with discretion, there was never a plan for replenishing the stores.

There were four main palaces off the square. Gonzalo decided that one of them, Huascar and Huayna's former residence, would go to Manco. "We have to make sure it looks like Manco's in charge," he told Francisco while the pair were walking together and reviewing Gonzalo's proposed arrangement.

"Of course, of course," Francisco said, nodding.

"And you'll get whichever of these three you want," Gonzalo said, gesturing to the remaining three stone palaces around the square. He had his eye on the one they stood closest to, made of black marble.

Francisco stared at Gonzalo's preferred palace for a long time. "Where are the horses going to be?" he asked.

"Our personal stable will be in the town square, over there," Gonzalo said, pointing to the side opposite the black palace.

"Ah, that's a good place for it."

Gonzalo felt a flush of pride. His own father's praise had

been nonexistent until he told the old man that he was going to the New World with Francisco.

"And you know I love being around my horse, so I'll take that one." Francisco's chosen palace, like the others, was long and low, built of well-fitting stones painted a dark red. It had belonged to Pachacuti, Atahualpa's great-grandfather who started the Incan Empire's expansion. "Reminds me of the roofs in Spain," he said in a faraway voice.

"And I'm assuming you'll take this one?" Francisco said, pointing to the black marble building. It was the former home of Topa, the sun's descendant who'd captured Quito.

"Well, I was going to see which one Juan wants first. And I was going to ask you about Hernando . . ."

"Juan will take whatever we decide—he worries about the women in his bed more than the roof over his head. And Hernando has had a lifetime of living in palaces in Spain; he'll survive without one of the main ones over his head. There are plenty of other nice ones around the city."

"And Almagro?"

"Almagro might prefer living in the stables himself!" Francisco said, laughing. "In all seriousness, we'll give him a sumptuous residence just outside the plaza. He won't know the difference."

His brother's laid-back demeanor surprised Gonzalo. There had been so much work setting up the city—starting schools, churches, and a convent, making Valverde the first Bishop of Cuzco, and creating a monastery at the Temple of the Sun—that he expected Francisco would rush through his proposal on his way to the next issue.

"And what about the soldiers who have taken the large houses for their own?" Gonzalo said. "Every large dwelling in the city has a new owner. Some of the men didn't have a house in Spain and now they're living like princes!"

"Take the ones we need and make the ownership official. Maybe that way they'll stay instead of taking their wealth back to Spain." Francisco put an arm around his younger brother. "But enough about everyone else—let's take a look inside your new home!"

Gonzalo felt his face flush. Together with his brother, they walked across the threshold and into the palace. He imagined leading his love into the building in the future, if she could ever be convinced to leave Spain and her family behind. When she saw how wealthy he was after his time in the New World . . .

"And there was gold in this room too?" Francisco asked. He had been taking care of creating the city while Gonzalo was removing treasure from the palaces.

"This is where we found two of the golden llamas," Gonzalo said, pointing to a corner of the room. Light from the courtyard streamed in through a cut portion of the wall; almost every room had a source of natural daylight.

Continuing on, Gonzalo said, "And here is where—" He paused while peering into one of the few dark rooms.

"What? What is it?" Francisco said, peering into the darkness. His older eyes didn't adjust to the changing light as fast as his younger brother's could.

"I told them to get this thing out of here. It's unnatural."

Gonzalo yelled, and one of his men appeared out of the stonework. "Get this thing out of here," Gonzalo commanded.

Francisco, squinting into the darkness, stopped the soldier with an arm. "No. Get one of the natives to do it." He then turned to Gonzalo. "It costs us little to give them back their ancestor but could go a long way in maintaining order."

Gonzalo stared at his brother. "As a Christian, how can you let them worship a corpse? That's idolatry."

Francisco led his brother out of the building. They looked across the plaza at the building Francisco had taken for himself.

"I'm going to knock it down," Francisco said. "And build the first cathedral in this city. It will stand next to Manco's palace, a symbol of their combined rule over this land."

Anger coursed through Gonzalo's body. They were standing in front of his greatest accomplishment to date, the pride of his life, the home where he imagined his future. Francisco, upon receiving the same prize, decided to throw it away.

"And once they learn the truth about their revolting beliefs, they'll abandon these trifles and hate themselves for ever being so foolish."

6

THE DISPUTE OVER CUZCO

As the Spanish had expected, there was more wealth in Cuzco than in Cajamarca; less gold, but a good deal more silver. Within a month, the initial haul of treasure had been divided and the entire city had celebrated Manco's coronation with a three-day festival that included the mummified remains of the former emperors. The Spaniards took part, drinking and eating while scheming how they'd scour the rest of the country for more loot.

A dazzling jewel of a different sort caught Gonzalo's eye during the coronation. The unexpected desire rising in his breast could have occurred at any point since they'd first met Manco, but it took seeing her in queen's regalia for him to realize her true beauty. She rode on a litter, seated on a silver throne the same size as Manco's. Sunlight glinted off of the jewels and precious metals adorning her body, and the bright feathers of her headdress rippled in the breeze. All Gonzalo could see was her proud face, and he imagined what her lips looked like from up close.

Manco and Almagro had caught up to General Quizquiz outside of Jauja. The combined Spanish and native forces drove the famed Incan general north to Quito before he could damage Francisco's new Spanish town. His exhausted troops, kept on the warpath by the stubborn Incan general, revolted and killed Quizquiz themselves before returning to their families and farmland, ending the last remnants of Atahualpa's rule.

While Manco came back to Cuzco for his coronation, Almagro had continued towards the competing Spaniards from Cortes' expedition; he returned with more than three hundred new recruits hungry for gold. Upon his return, Almagro then had the loyalty of two-thirds of the men in Cuzco. The Pizarros counted the other third entrenched on their side, having made them wealthy beyond belief after capturing Atahualpa in Cajamarca.

Francisco left soon after Manco's official ascension to a son of the sun. Creating a Spanish settlement in Jauja and Cuzco had whetted his appetite for attending to civil matters, and he became convinced of the country's need for a port city. Lima was just a thought in his mind when he left, but it became a reality soon enough through sheer willpower alone.

Juan and Gonzalo were left in charge. It was Gonzalo's first taste of power, and he wished his beloved back in Spain could see how far he'd risen since her devastating rejection. While Juan slept late and kept a generous supply of native women and servants nearby, Gonzalo adopted his eldest brother's austere work habits. He lived alone and rose early so that he could supervise the native workers building the cathedral across the plaza. Breakfast with his men was followed by a visit to the stables, where he helped care for Castaño before touring the city on the back of his prized horse. Without iron for reshoeing, Gonzalo had the Spanish blacksmith use one of the metals they had in abundance: silver. Many of the other men in the Pizarro faction followed suit; they had plenty of gold and silver and could afford using some of the metal on their horses.

The Almagro faction, dubbed "The Almagristas," stared at the gaudy show of wealth. Half of them had received their share of the treasure from the distribution of the Cuzco loot, but the newest men were still as poor as they had been when they had first entered the country.

The two groups of Spaniards, each faction loyal to a different man, started appearing at each week's mass. When Friar Valverde had first started preaching in Cuzco, the split was between the Spaniards and the natives. The most prominent Spanish citizens sat at the front, the average Spaniard behind them, and the natives were lucky enough to find a seat filling in the back. Manco and his queen came to the last of the Sunday services—nobody knew if it was on his own volition or as part of the arrangement that kept him in power—and Gonzalo made sure he went to whichever mass they attended each week so that he could see her. He even started staying for two church services: the first so he could worship God and the second so he could worship the queen.

The division between the Spaniards grew clearer as the weeks went by. The Spanish leaders still sat at the front, closest to Friar Valverde and the cross, and the natives filled the back. But Gonzalo noticed that most of the Spaniards, all of them Almagristas, sat on the left side of the temporary church; the smaller group on the right was the men who had been with him in Cajamarca.

"What's going on?" Gonzalo asked Hernando de Soto on a Sunday afternoon after mass. De Soto had always been more in touch with the average man than he had, and Gonzalo's new position had made free association with the rank and file all but impossible. De Soto, despite having become a rich man twice in the New World, still maintained a presence among the humblest Spanish workers. Gonzalo thought he was like Francisco in that way.

De Soto inspected Gonzalo then looked down at his horse's feet. "Almagro's men feel shortchanged," he said.

Gonzalo couldn't contain the flash of anger that arose in his chest; it was unleashed through his tongue. "Oh, did they have better prospects of riches in Spain? Perhaps they should thank us for offering them the chance instead of throwing tantrums like so many babies."

"'Us' as in the men who were at Cajamarca?" Hernando ventured.

"No, us as in the Pizarros!" Gonzalo snapped. "My brother's the entire reason this expedition even exists. No Pizarro, no gold."

De Soto squeezed his lips together and looked down at his horse's mane.

Gonzalo knew that he had overstepped. "I didn't mean it like that," he said.

"You're not the only one who thinks like that," Hernando observed. "The rest of the men at Cajamarca also act like they deserve thanks for their efforts instead of appreciating the reinforcements."

"*The rest of the men,*" Gonzalo scoffed. "Like you're any different."

"If I'm not any different, why do they still talk to me?" de Soto said, looking at Gonzalo with patient eyes.

Gonzalo shook his head and looked away.

"I play dice with them and lose on purpose," de Soto explained. "I have more money than I know what to do with, and these men can't afford anything anymore. Do you have any idea how expensive everything is now that everyone has such vast amounts of gold and silver? Twenty-five sheets of paper costs ten gold pesos. Think about that: ten *gold* pesos, not even silver. A cloak? *One hundred.* And god forbid any of the men want a horse; you can't find one for less than twenty-five hundred. And we both know what a powerful advantage a horse is when fighting the natives . . ."

"I could swear I've seen some of the new men riding horses," a chastened Gonzalo muttered.

"On loan. The new men face a peculiar situation: either they continue their quest for treasure without a horse, indebted to none but with their lives at greater risk, or they take out a loan without any guarantee they see enough treasure to ever pay it back. Wouldn't you be upset?"

Gonzalo exhaled and shook his head. "So you say you've been finding ways to give them some of your money?"

"A little money in their pockets goes a long way. Even enough for the smaller pleasures, like a bottle of wine. Which costs sixty gold pesos, by the way."

As a leader in Cuzco, Gonzalo thought de Soto's methods worthy of emulating. He made plans to talk to Juan about a coordinated effort for getting more money into the average Spaniards' hands in the coming days and tipped the stable hand for "taking such good care of Castaño." Francisco had put him and his brother in charge of Cuzco, and there was no way he'd let the Spaniards become divided under his watch.

As it turned out, there was nothing he could do. News from overseas soon cleaved the two factions beyond repair.

Before leaving, Francisco had distributed a large number of *encomiendas* to the men who took Cuzco, which included some of Almagro's men. Each *encomendero* was responsible for the land and natives within his territory, gathering taxes from the holdings in exchange for protecting and Christianizing the natives. Any natives who objected to becoming a peasant for the new Spanish aristocracy faced death.

Manco played a pivotal role in the transition to an *encomienda* system. The Incan Empire had run on a similar concept before the arrival of the Spanish, with a hierarchical system where the labor and goods from the populace were funneled through the Incan elite for the good of the state. What Francisco had instituted was a change in who collected the products and the elimination of the state's ultimate involvement. Manco, in exchange for the elimination of Atahualpa and his ascension to the throne, made sure that his subjects followed the new system by giving it his blessing.

Back in Spain, King Charles had decided that Francisco would receive the northern portion of the empire and Almagro the south. According to Hernando Pizarro, who spoke with the king in person, their company had secured a vast land filled with rich agricultural resources and immense mineral stores, evidenced by the large quantity of gold for the crown that was just one-fifth of what they had collected. And who were the two people in charge of the company? Francisco Pizarro and Diego de Almagro. Therefore, the empire was split between them.

The location of Cuzco presented a problem; it was in the center of the territory. Hernando was on his way back with the formal documentation about the line of separation, but until then both the Pizarro and Almagro factions believed they had the right to rule the Incan capital city given to them by the king. Rumors flew about Almagro's advisers telling him to take the city that belonged to him from the clutches of the Pizarro brothers.

The murky state of affairs even affected those with an *encomienda*. Up until the king's decision, they had been ready for lives of luxury, having received their wealth in Cajamarca, Cuzco, or both, and with a source of steady income for the rest of their lives. But those *encomiendas* were given out by Francisco, not by Almagro. If the one-eyed man had in fact received Cuzco from the king as he believed, some of the city's associated *encomenderos* could find themselves losing their granted land— the ones who were aligned with the Pizarros.

All of a sudden, it wasn't just Almagro's new arrivals who looked at the men from the other faction with contempt; the wealthy men who aligned with the Pizarros also distanced themselves from their counterparts, furious at their leader's brother for pulling unseen strings at Spain's court that put their holdings at risk.

Nobody was madder about the king's decree than Juan. Gonzalo had made him promise not to leave his house unless they were together, thinking that he could at least calm his irascible older brother before the situation got out of control if anyone from Almagro's camp triggered him.

Despite staying home, Juan still provided the spark that ignited the combustible situation in Cuzco.

Gonzalo awoke before sunrise to the sound of shouting men and scraping on the cobblestone plaza. The sounds themselves weren't strange, just the time of day. Curious, he got up and got dressed before searching for the reason the men were working on Cuzco's cathedral so early in the morning.

A handful of men were holding torches, commanding a native workforce dragging three large covered sleds. Gonzalo couldn't tell what they contained. A horse snorted in the distance.

"Hurry up!" Juan shouted from the entrance to his residence. Gonzalo hurried across the town square and found his brother wearing his battle armor, his helmet under one arm.

"What's going on?" Gonzalo said.

"Almagro's going to take the city, it's just a matter of time," Juan replied, as straightforward as if he had been asked the color of the sky.

"He's what?" Gonzalo said, looking around. The rest of the city was still fast asleep.

"Hurry up, get those cannons over here." Juan pointed at three spaces in the wall of his palace facing the plaza.

"Cannons!" Gonzalo exclaimed. "What the hell is the matter with you?"

"I'm getting us ready to defend our homes against Almagro and his good-for-nothing men," Juan replied. He turned to Gonzalo and put an arm around his younger brother. "Didn't you get the three women I sent over last night? If I find out they didn't go . . ."

"No, no, they were there. I sent them to stay with the rest of the servants."

"After you were done with them?" Juan asked, a sly look in his eye.

"Done? Oh no, I didn't do anything with them."

A look of feigned hurt passed over Juan's face. "What! Those were my best. I thought for sure those would suit your tastes . . ." Juan said, trailing off.

"I told you to stop with that," Gonzalo said, his pulse rising. "What goes on in my bed is none of your business."

"Look, these aren't Christian women! Take what you want —we're in charge here, remember?" Realization struck and he roared, "We're in charge, not that one-eyed bastard Diego! And I'll be damned if I let him take the city we worked so hard to get."

A sharp sadness appeared under Gonzalo's ribs at hearing Juan's opinion of native women; the Incan queen wasn't Christian. Would she go to hell, or would God be merciful because of her native ignorance? He leaned back and tilted to one side, looking for relief from the pain.

"Juan, you can't just barricade yourself in the palace," he began.

Juan turned on him. "And why not? I knew you'd disagree, that's why I tried to make sure you didn't wake up so early this morning."

"Because Diego hasn't done anything!"

"Not *yet*! But he will. He's trickier than I gave him credit for, but anyone who can receive a royal grant of land from such a low position has schemes up his sleeve that we need to be prepared for." Juan helped guide the first of the cannons into position. "Now, are you going to help me or not?" he said to Gonzalo.

Gonzalo sighed. "If it'll keep you at home and away from the Almagristas, sure."

"Good, then go get the horses," Juan said.

By early afternoon, the Pizarro brothers had barricaded Juan's palace and secured it against potential attacks. To nobody's surprise, the Almagristas found out about the raised defenses and a number of them gathered on the plaza. The natives stood around waiting for a fight between the Spanish forces.

"Those dogs out there think they can wait for the right time to strike," Juan said through clenched teeth while inspecting the plaza from inside his palace. "Tell you what we need to do . . ."

Before Gonzalo could stop him, Juan had mounted his horse and was navigating out into the square. Gonzalo jumped on Castaño in pursuit.

"Any of you dogs want this city, you'll have to come through me!" he roared while pacing side to side on his horse.

Gonzalo stopped his horse behind his brother, aware they were outnumbered in the city. "Juan, come back inside and calm down," he hissed.

Juan ignored him.

"Ungrateful bastards." Juan spat on the ground. "The Pizarros lead you to riches in the New World and you plot our downfall!"

Hernando de Soto separated himself from the crowd and approached on horseback. He caught Gonzalo's eye and mimicked drinking with his hand, inquiring eyebrows raised. Gonzalo shook his head no to the nonverbal question.

"No, I'm not drunk, you duplicitous beast," Juan said.

"I'm not your enemy," a calm de Soto replied.

"I see you with them! Scheming, plotting, playing both sides like some kind of game. Waiting for our downfall so you can rise up yourself!"

"The only scheming in all of Cuzco is taking place right behind you," de Soto replied, gesturing towards Juan's palace.

Juan turned around, looking for what de Soto had mentioned. He realized too late that the joke was about him—snickers erupted from the crowd when he looked at de Soto again. Enraged, he grabbed a lance and thrust it at de Soto.

Years of experience between horse and rider saved de Soto from injury. With one of the fastest horses in the New World and extensive training in Spanish weaponry, de Soto stayed out of the range of Juan's lance on his way out of the plaza. Juan ran off in pursuit, with Gonzalo trailing behind them both and the rest of the men from the square bringing up the rear.

They ended up outside of Almagro's residence, where many of the newest Spaniards spent their time because of the goodwill Diego had earned with the average Spaniard in Cuzco. Upon seeing the Pizarros chasing Hernando de Soto into their domain, the men all grabbed their arms and raised them at Juan.

Gonzalo withdrew his own sword and held it aloft. The look of disappointment on de Soto's face almost made him put it away, but a pressing Almagrista forced a swing.

For a tense moment on a random spring day in the Andes, the majority of the Spaniards in the Incan Empire stood staring each other down. The natives, eager for revenge on their new elite overseers, watched in anticipation.

All of a sudden, Friar Valverde emerged from the gathering crowd. He walked right into the center of the standoff. "You all realize that whoever wins will be attacked by the natives, right?" he said. "No matter which side wins, everyone dies." Then, the priest erupted in a rare moment of anger. "And I, for one, won't get killed because you can't realize the enemy isn't us—it's the devil inside all of them!" he roared, pointing to the assembled indigenous men.

A slap in the face wouldn't have been as effective as the priest's words. Juan turned his horse around and urged the animal home. Gonzalo lingered, waiting for the chance to talk to de Soto and explain what had happened.

As he watched, de Soto followed Almagro into the one-eyed man's house without so much as a look back at his former friend.

7

THE EMPEROR'S ALLY

"THE FLOW of gold and silver is slowing down," Gonzalo told Manco weeks after Juan's confrontation with Hernando de Soto. "None has arrived from the countryside in weeks now."

"The Four Realms are vast, and men are slow," Manco said. "I sent the quipu out, so it's on the way."

Their afternoon meeting took place on the roof of the temporary church, as suggested by Friar Valverde, after days of logistical wrangling. Both men refused attending the other's palace on the grounds that they should receive visitors and not visit themselves. Manco was the sun's son, after all, and what divine ruler heeded a mere mortal's bidding? Even if those mortals had placed him on the throne in the first place, as Gonzalo believed.

"Just because you sent word doesn't mean they'll listen," Gonzalo replied. Manco's devout belief in his absolute authority rankled the youngest Pizarro. Since it outright infuriated Juan, Gonzalo took care of any communication they had with the young emperor.

"Why would they dare go against what I say?" Manco said

while staring at the sunset with pride, as if he himself had anything to do with the turning of the days.

"Because they know!"

Manco turned on the young Spaniard. "What do they know? That you'll take it all for yourselves?"

Gonzalo couldn't come up with a reply that didn't confirm Spanish greed.

Manco strode across the roof and put a foot on the stone parapet. "My great-great-grandfather's palace was one of my favorite places to go when I was a kid," he said, staring across the city towards the plaza. "I would go and look at him, dreaming of a day when I could lead the Four Realms, just like him." Manco turned around. "Although at that point there was little chance it would ever happen."

"And who do you have to thank for your ascension to the throne?" Gonzalo asked, his urging eyes wide.

"It's no secret that your brother's plans worked, and for that I'm forever grateful. But your men have picked Cuzco to her bones and still you want more." Manco continued before Gonzalo could get a word in. "And it's on the way. Even I can't make men move faster than their nature. Now, if you let us breed horses . . ."

Gonzalo put a hand up. "Out of the question." The horses were the Spanish equivalent of a superweapon, and there was no way he'd let the natives get their hands on one, let alone many.

"Then it appears you'll just have to wait." Manco walked over to the external staircase. "Was there anything else?"

"Send word to them again."

Manco nodded then disappeared.

Gonzalo stared at where Pachacuti's palace once stood and imagined the cathedral's spires enhancing the Cuzco skyline. He thought of the entire Incan Empire as his own *encomienda*, entrusted to him and his brother by Francisco while the older brother created more cities. Since Juan cared more about his women than his responsibilities, the brunt of the work fell to Gonzalo.

Part of being an *encomendero* included ensuring that the natives in his care continued production. He wondered how the Spaniards in charge of native labor in the rural parts of the empire encouraged consistent output. At least they had access to both carrot and stick—Gonzalo couldn't strike Manco without fear of retaliation from both the Inca population and the Almagristas, since Almagro and Manco had gotten close during their trip to battle General Quizquiz.

If only that one-eyed bastard hadn't tried to take the city from them! They could work together to wring every last drop of precious metal from the country for Mother Spain. Truth be told, the king had made a mistake in giving Almagro so much land and creating tension between him and the Pizarros. With Almagro working with Gonzalo instead of taking Cuzco for himself, they could send more taxes back and make more money themselves; everyone would win.

Gonzalo playing nice with Manco also benefitted the crown. Taxes can't be collected from a scattered, regional population, so having the Incan Emperor continue ruling guaranteed consistent profits for their country.

Another part of being an *encomendero* included Christianizing the population. Friar Valverde had approached Gonzalo about the possibility of a Christian wedding for the royal couple after both finalized their conversion. Gonzalo forbade it, even though he knew it could convince more native couples of God's legitimacy, for a simple reason: he didn't want Cura Ocllo, the Incan queen, beyond his reach. As long as her union with Manco wasn't formalized by a Christian marriage, there was still a chance that he could make her his. Once the priest bestowed

God's blessing on them, coveting her was a sin and put his own soul at risk.

All these thoughts swirled through Gonzalo's head, twisting and turning, disappearing and replacing one another while he walked back to the stables without paying attention.

"Looks like you've got something on your mind," Diego de Almagro said. He had his horse's reins in his hand and was leading the animal away from the plaza. Several sycophants followed in his wake.

Gonzalo blinked three times like a man just waking up. "Tell Manco to hurry up with the gold collection," Gonzalo said.

"I can't make men move faster than God intended," Almagro replied, brushing his horse's mane. He flashed a thin-lipped smile that rankled Gonzalo to the core. "Besides, he's got his hands full with his brother."

"Paullu?" Gonzalo asked. Gonzalo had first met Manco's brother and confidant in the days following their capture of Cuzco. He was one of the many nobles who had flooded back into Cuzco when General Quizquiz quit the capital. A number of them had found Spaniards living in their mansions—Almagro's budding relationship with Manco helped maintain the peace.

"No, he and Paullu are still close. Another one: Atoc. As I hear it, a bunch of the noble savages want that one in charge, something about Manco being too young and too close to us."

"Too close to *us*? To you, maybe."

Almagro grinned, displaying decayed teeth. "They want something done about Friar Valverde. According to them, he's not teaching the natives under his charge about Catholicism. Instead, he's using them as slaves and taking their land for himself."

"How did you find this out? I haven't heard anything

about it."

"Of course you haven't. Manco told me. He tells his people that Friar Valverde is our version of Villac Umu, that they need to follow his teachings. But no representative of the sun god took the liberties our good man Valverde now takes, according to them."

Gonzalo thought for a moment. "Why didn't he tell me about the treatment of the natives himself?" he asked.

"Gonzalo! What are you doing?" Juan yelled in the distance before Almagro could answer.

Both Almagro and Gonzalo turned and watched the other Pizarro in Cuzco march towards them.

"Juan," Almagro said when his main rival got close.

"Diego," Juan replied. He eyed the men with Almagro; each one had a hand on their sword.

"I was just leaving," Almagro said. With a nod to his men, he walked past Gonzalo towards his own residence.

Gonzalo couldn't tell if the stench that reached his nostrils came from the horse or the men.

"Don't waste your time with him; he's only looking out for himself," Juan said to Gonzalo as they watched Almagro walk away. "Why is he even talking to you?" he added, spitting on the ground.

"He really believes the king included Cuzco on his side of the map," Gonzalo said. "And as the leader in the city, it makes sense for him to play nice."

"He better not try that with me. I'm not so easily swayed."

Gonzalo sighed. "We know."

"What did you discuss?" Juan said as Gonzalo began walking away.

"He's going to talk to Manco about collecting more gold," Gonzalo replied without turning around, leaving Juan alone in the town square.

A few days later, one of Gonzalo's personal entourage came into his study with a surprise. "Almagro's asking for you outside."

Gonzalo organized his papers, stood up, smoothed his frayed white shirt, and walked out. "What's all this?" he asked Almagro.

The one-eyed Spaniard stood next to a large covered object. "I wanted to show you myself; look what Manco's found for us!" He pulled at the sheet and showed off a full-sized golden llama. "Look at the size of this thing!"

Gonzalo ran a hand over the precious metal. "How much do you think is here?"

"How should I know? I leave that to the numbers men."

Gonzalo chuckled. "And I don't blame you. Get it over to the smelters, let them melt it down into bars."

Almagro looked at his men. "You heard him!" he said. The men all scrambled forward and began dragging the heavy sculpture away.

"He 'found' the sculpture at a noble's house. Said there might be more in some of the nearby temples." Almagro leaned forward and beckoned Gonzalo closer.

Gonzalo approached and took care to keep his face relaxed when he smelled the man.

"He's asking for protection, thinks Atoc can pounce any day now."

Gonzalo stepped back. "The situation is that bad? Why haven't we heard about this?" he exclaimed, looking up towards the sky.

Almagro shrugged. "Maybe it's because every time you talk to him all you do is ask for more gold."

. . .

THE POWER STRUGGLE among the Incan elite came to a head that night. Juan himself stormed into Gonzalo's bedroom, yelling that they had to go to Manco's palace.

"The men are looting!"

"Which men?" Gonzalo said, still groggy. In the stuttering firelight, he could see his disheveled brother standing over him, the smell of wine diffusing throughout the room.

"Our men!"

Gonzalo didn't understand what was happening. He got dressed and followed his brother.

There was a crowd of men outside of the Incan Emperor's palace. Manco's native attendants stood a fair distance apart, watching the Spaniards streaming into and out of the building.

"What the hell is going on?" Gonzalo asked Juan.

"They say that Manco's hiding at Almagro's house because some of the other Incan nobles opposed to his rule are on the warpath."

"On the warpath? He's the emperor . . ."

"He ordered Atoc killed—that's who the opposition wanted on the throne in place of Manco."

Gonzalo thought back to that afternoon's discussion with Almagro and something clicked. "Do you know who did it? One of his men?"

"No! Get this: they say it was a couple of Spaniards. Killed him in his bed."

The golden llama was payment. Instead of taking it for himself, or distributing it to only his men, Almagro had taken advantage of the Spanish treasure collection infrastructure to hide his tracks and divert suspicion.

"Stop!" Gonzalo screamed, surging forward. A few of the closest men looked at him before stepping away. He got to the palace's entrance and almost ran into a man carrying a native woman on his shoulder. Gonzalo tore her from his arms and directed her to the other natives while pushing the man to the floor.

"Stay down," Juan said, pointing his sword at the man's chest when he tried to get up in anger.

The man crawled away.

"We have to stop this," Gonzalo told Juan.

"Do we though?" Juan said, his delight in the chaos obvious in the firelight.

Gonzalo stared at his brother, amazed at his ignorance. "He's already aligned with Almagro. Now our men are looting his palace? Almagro might as well take over tomorrow!"

"We could always adopt those opposed to Manco," Juan observed.

"And have another coronation? Francisco will have our heads if we don't figure this out!"

Securing Manco's palace took the brothers a full hour. Once the last of the intruders left, Gonzalo and Juan agreed that Juan would stay to protect the residence while Gonzalo would investigate the situation at Almagro's house.

Everything was calm in Almagro's corner of the city. Numerous guards outside stared down even more natives, though there were no signs of physical conflict. The front line let Gonzalo pass; Hernando de Soto met him at the door.

"Can't go past here," de Soto said. "Almagro's orders."

Gonzalo didn't bother with niceties. "What the hell was Diego thinking, killing an Incan noble?"

"He didn't kill anyone. We're protecting the emperor while figuring out who did it." De Soto leveled suspicious eyes at Gonzalo. "How do we know it wasn't any of you?"

"Oh, come off it. I know that the golden llama was payment. Almagro himself told me."

"Not sure what you're talking about. The emperor is terrified and we're keeping him safe for all of Spain. What kind of leaders are the two of you? Your men just looted the sovereign's palace—that puts this entire operation at risk!"

Gonzalo put a hand on his sword. The men surrounding de Soto all unsheathed their weapons before standing down on de Soto's orders.

"We have to work with the empire so we can collect taxes. There's more gold, sure, but this can only last for so long. We'll eventually have to use the people and labor; there's no better person to guarantee their continued cooperation than Manco. It's a simple fact you don't seem to understand."

Gonzalo wondered how he'd let the situation deteriorate so far beyond his control. There was an entire side of Incan politics he wasn't aware of because of Almagro and Manco's relationship. What de Soto had said wasn't wrong, and in fact it made sense: helping Manco maintain power was the best way to keep the empire in line. If that meant they had to murder a rival, so be it— they'd slaughtered thousands of natives before for lesser reasons.

But the proud Pizarro couldn't admit the one-eyed man's sound logic. Instead, he took his hand off of his own sword and backed away, walking to his own palace while reasoning what his eldest brother would do in the same situation.

His wondering didn't last long. Francisco, upon hearing about the Incan political situation and already knowing about the confrontation between his brother and his business partner, traveled from Lima to Cuzco as fast as he could.

"What's going on here?" he asked his two brothers in the shadow of Saqsaywaman, the stone fortress outside of Cuzco. Gonzalo and Juan had ridden out so that they could meet their brother on the road and prepare him for the state of affairs within the city.

"In short, everything split," Gonzalo said. "Clean down the middle."

"Manco and the Almagristas stay away from us and the Inca elites that are against his rule."

"And the people?" Francisco asked.

"The people?" Juan said, asking for clarification.

"The people. The common man. Are they fighting in the market, avoiding each other on the street as well? Or is it just the people in charge who act like children?"

"The average native doesn't pay much attention, I'd say," Gonzalo said, looking at Juan for his opinion.

"More or less. I don't see them that often."

"So the first order of business is making sure these squabbles don't trickle down to the rest of the city." He urged his horse forward.

"Hardly feels like squabbles," Juan said under his breath. Clear enough, but with no fortitude.

"What was that?" Francisco said.

"Nothing," Juan replied.

Francisco's first order of business was a meeting with Diego de Almagro at the temporary church. Gonzalo and Juan stayed outside on one side of the building with more of their allies, while Almagro's men, including Hernando de Soto, stayed on the opposite side. Each group played dice in the shade while the afternoon passed.

"Well, it's settled," Francisco said when he emerged an hour later.

"What's going on?"

"Well, for one, I told Diego how unbecoming his behavior has been. He should have waited for the official documentation from Spain before assuming his post or taking any action from a position of power. Until then, the two of you were and are in charge."

A cheer came up from Almagro's camp. Juan put an index

finger on a nostril, turned towards the sound, and blew snot from his nose. He wiped his fingers on his pants leg.

"What's all that about?" Gonzalo asked.

"He's going south to explore the rest of the empire. I'm financing it."

Gonzalo and Juan stared at their brother. "You're giving away any treasure that might be there?"

"Small price to pay to restore order. It's clear we can't have him around." Francisco continued before his brothers could utter a reply. "You'll have to handle Manco and the other Incan elites. No more political scheming; they need to understand that Manco is the emperor. Think you can control them?"

Juan scoffed. Gonzalo said, "Yes, they do what we say." It wasn't the exact truth, but he needed some vestige of power in light of the deteriorated situation.

"Then make them back Manco. We need them all on our side." Francisco mounted his horse. "Not just us; all of Spain."

The weeks leading up to the expedition's beginning carried on as if the strife over the previous months never occurred. Nobody doubted Francisco's authority, and this absolute hierarchy carried over to the Incan nobles as well in their backing of Manco. The emperor sent his brother Paullu and Villac Umu on the trip as Almagro's guides so that they could exert control over the subjects in the southern part of the empire in his name.

One man wasn't satisfied with how the entire ordeal unfolded: Hernando de Soto. Eager for a governorship, he had offered a considerable amount of money to Almagro in exchange for becoming second-in-command. Almagro, knowing the man's previous ties to the Pizarros, declined, deciding on the ever-loyal Rodrigo Orgóñez instead.

The Pizarros, Manco, the Incan elites, and the *encomenderos* all watched Almagro's expedition depart Cuzco.

With him went every Spaniard still searching for wealth in the New World.

Francisco and Hernando de Soto left for the coast soon after. Francisco back to his young city, and Hernando back to Spain.

Juan and Gonzalo found themselves alone in the plaza outside of their palaces; the sun had long since gone down.

"Guess we're really in charge now," Gonzalo said.

"Guess we are," Juan replied.

A tranquil moment passed between the brothers.

"How long do you think until Manco realizes he backed the wrong man?" Gonzalo asked.

Juan laughed and clapped his brother on the back. "He'll find out soon enough."

8

THE INCAN QUEEN

"Go in peace and serve the Lord," Friar Valverde said from the pulpit.

"Thanks be to God," the congregation responded. Gonzalo and Juan Pizarro were sitting in the front row.

The priest, in the white robe he'd begun wearing after becoming Bishop of Cuzco, started walking down the aisle while holding the Bible high overhead. Two other Spanish priests, local men who hadn't yet made their fortune but couldn't go with Almagro because of injuries, followed behind Valverde, both wearing brown robes.

A native boy walked in front of the priest swinging a thurible, the burning incense carving a path for the holy man. More native youths followed behind the trio of Spaniards, their stained, ragged garments hanging off of their too-thin frames. The priest swore he needed the children for help around the church, claiming he was saving their souls.

The boy leading the procession stumbled, and the metal incense burner struck the ground, startling the nearest worshippers. The clasp came undone, and the coal fell to the floor. Terrified eyes turned toward the priest.

"Pick it up, my child," the priest said in a soft voice. He smiled at the closest Spaniards.

The boy stared at the coal on the ground.

"Pick it up!" Friar Valverde repeated through clenched teeth.

Small fingers pecked at the coal like a bird lifting a large seed. Gonzalo chanced a sideways glance at Juan and noticed his brother smiling.

The boy took a deep, calming breath, then pinched the coal while suppressing a cry and put it back into the swinging container. He redid the clasp using his knuckles and stood up.

"Wait," Friar Valverde said before the group started moving again.

Everyone in the room held their breath.

"Turn around," the Lord's agent on Earth said to the hunched youth in front of him.

The native servant turned around, his eyes filled with tears.

"Give me your hand."

Gonzalo imagined an upcoming blessing for the pain, kind words like the ones Jesus said to the lepers. He was wrong.

Friar Valverde squeezed the boy's burned fingers and leaned in close. "God read the thoughts in your impure heart; that's why you fell."

The native child nodded. Despite the tears now flowing down his cheeks, he didn't scream. "Yes, Father," he choked out in accented Spanish.

"Let's go," Friar Valverde said as he released the boy's hand.

Gonzalo watched as the priest went to the back of the room then beckoned those seated in the front row forward. With Juan walking behind him, he stopped at the priest and kissed the rings on man's outstretched hand before leaving.

The sun outside the church's walls shone bright. Gonzalo, squinting, looked around at the natives and the Spaniards leaving mass. Hungry eyes settled on Cura Ocllo, Manco's primary wife.

After seeing how Friar Valverde handled his flock, Gonzalo realized he had been too lenient with those entrusted to his care. The royal couple, unwed in the eyes of God, lived in sin; how long would it be until they stumbled and fell because of the impurity in their veins?

"Don't worry about that," Juan said when Gonzalo brought his concerns to his brother. They had just eaten dinner and were walking around the courtyard in Juan's palace for help with digestion. It was no secret that the abundant vegetables gave Juan gas, and he walked instead of snoozed so the smell wouldn't accumulate in his home.

"We only need him until enough Spaniards arrive that we can take over tax collection throughout the entire kingdom ourselves. After that, no amount of his bad luck can affect what we've put in place here," Juan said, holding his arms wide and looking around.

"The queen's Christian marriage might bring more natives to Jesus," Gonzalo pressed. "The church needs all the help it can get—back in Spain, the Muslims are coming from the south and east, the Protestants from the north. We can fight back by saving souls here."

"That's the priests' problem. But you aren't wrong," Juan said. He inspected a hanging pink flower and laughed. "Do we really care about growing weeds?" He grew serious when Gonzalo didn't laugh along with him. "I'm sure we could make Valverde marry Manco and Cura Ocllo within the week."

A flush of red rose up Gonzalo's neck. "What if I told you that I wanted the queen?"

Juan turned to his brother with wide eyes. "For marriage? I'd say you're crazy. No Spaniard marries a native, especially one in our position. Just take her if you want her so bad; Manco can marry another one." A malicious twinkle appeared in Juan's eye. "Some of these native women aren't so bad in bed," he said with a wink.

Gonzalo stared straight ahead as they turned left at a corner. Taking her for himself would still leave her living in sin but prevented Manco's continued defiance of God's laws—for the good of Spain and the empire. Maybe one day, when Spanish attitudes shifted, he could explore a more permanent arrangement with the queen.

"Why don't we go tell him right now?" Juan said with a grin.

"Right now? It's almost sunset." Gonzalo's heart raced and his hands grew moist.

"So? We're in charge of the city and we can do whatever we want." It was his catchphrase ever since Almagro had left.

Manco showed up to Juan's palace right as the sun touched the horizon. Without Almagro in the city anymore, he didn't dare ignore a summons. He stared at the ground as Juan nudged Gonzalo.

Gonzalo felt an intense shame rising in his stomach at the prospect of demanding the Incan queen. It seized his tongue and arrested his breathing before rupturing a blood vessel in his eye. A whiff of his own sweat reached his nostrils, a sharpness that spoke of the fear coursing through his veins. The smell revolted him; he was disgusted with himself. In response, a cold anger began at the crown of his head and spread downward— since when did a Pizarro care about what a native thought? His hands formed into fists once his anger spread to his fingers, wiping out any remnants of shame left in his soul.

"I want Cura Ocllo," Gonzalo said. "The two of you have lived in sin long enough."

Manco lifted his eyes and looked at Gonzalo. There was no doubt that the young emperor had heard and understood Gonzalo's words.

Juan laughed. "You heard him! Bring her here before we go and take her."

The sound of Manco's shallow breathing overtook the space. His statuesque bodyguard made no sign that he had understood the command given in Spanish.

"When did you take your eyes from gold and silver?" a chastened Manco asked.

Gonzalo's rage boiled into a crescendo. Who was this native man asking questions of a Christian Spaniard? Didn't he understand the hierarchy? Gonzalo had languished for years without respect, without power, back in Spain, and had even lost the woman he loved because of it. Yet he still faced questions—from a native, no less—even when his right to rule was given to him by Francisco, who had the right given to *him* by the King of Spain, who received the right from the Pope, whose right had been bestowed by God.

Questioning God was Manco's stumble; what pitfalls did the empire now face? Would the spilled incense burn down the entire enterprise?

Remembering Valverde's methods, Gonzalo decided Manco must face the pain of making it right, just like the boy who picked up the coal with his bare hand. Gonzalo would be there to squeeze the wound afterward.

"We still want gold and silver; now we want Cura Ocllo too. Valverde will oversee your marriage to another so that you can rule this empire as a Christian."

Gonzalo yelled, "Go," before Manco could say another word.

A large trove of gold and silver appeared on Gonzalo's doorstep the next morning, delivered by Manco himself. "This is the last of the treasure in my palace." He lifted a gold basin. "I was bathed in this when I first came out of my mother." Setting it down, he showed Gonzalo a golden disk attached to a golden chain. "My father gave me this after I returned from settling a dispute in the south; it's the last thing I own that he gave to me." He laid it down on a silver platter, next to a miniature silver statue of a man's head, complete with ceremonial headdress.

Gonzalo inspected the treasure, nodding his head as he held each piece up to the sun's morning light. "It's not much, but it's all very high quality," he said.

"For you, as a token of our friendship. All I ask is that you reconsider your request."

"Come now, Manco, I have all the gold and silver I could want. Now I've got my eyes set on another prize. Bring her here by Saturday night or we'll be forced to march on your palace. The horses can't tell who's fighting back and who's fleeing."

Manco had one more trick up his sleeve. On Thursday, two nights before the deadline, twenty of the most beautiful women in Cuzco appeared at Gonzalo's door. Some of them were married, some were temple virgins, and some of them were from Manco's own harem, all taken by royal decree for the good of the empire—according to Manco. In fact, in trying to save his queen by taking the wives of other men, he took the same steps Gonzalo did on those below him in the hierarchy; though as a divine emperor it fell within his rights.

"I don't see Cura Ocllo here," Gonzalo said after inspecting the women. Juan, after receiving word from one of Gonzalo's messengers, had come to watch.

"No, no, she's right here!" Manco said, pulling one of the women forward.

Gonzalo strode forward and lifted her chin with a rough hand. His narrowed eyes inspected her face, and he turned her around and squeezed her hips.

Manco stared at Gonzalo while holding his breath.

"I didn't recognize her without the queen's headdress!" Gonzalo said. He laughed then held out a hand as if to give

Manco a comrade's slap on the back. Remembering the Incan emperor's strict decorum and in a fine mood, he changed his mind, made a fist, and let his arm fall to his side.

"I thought maybe you'd take another instead of my queen," Manco said before turning to the second Pizarro. "And Juan, please feel free to take one as a personal gift from me," he added.

The women all stood still as Juan selected two, pulling them from the lineup and sending them towards his palace with a smack on the rear end. "We won't be getting much work done tomorrow morning," Juan said to Gonzalo, laughing.

Gonzalo waited until Juan and Manco walked away with the rest of the women before leading the queen into his palace. He exhaled as soon as he walked inside, transforming into a breathless young lover.

The queen stayed as still as if she was carved from the mountains; only her wide eyes moved. As she watched, Gonzalo approached with food and the presents he had accumulated in hopes of one day giving to the woman he loved back in Spain. A pitiful creature in the presence of a deity. It had taken a trip across the ocean and months of hard work in a foreign land, but he now possessed the type of woman he deserved.

Despite the pounding in his chest, he couldn't shake the fear of Juan's potential discovery of his fawning. He led the stunned queen to the back of the house and into the bedroom, where he laid her down on the bed without taking off her clothes. While she stared at the ceiling in the semi-dark, Gonzalo curled up beside her, his head at her ribs, and laid a hand across her stomach. He woke up a short while later and found the sheets soaked with tears.

Gonzalo became curious after the third time the queen didn't respond to her name, outright suspicious when an Incan servant didn't drop his gaze enough in her presence. In the end, he asked her outright, sweetening the deal with an offer of freedom.

"I have no use for you if you're not the queen," Gonzalo said. A great man deserved a crown jewel of a woman at his side, and Gonzalo Pizarro knew in his heart that he was a great man. Everyone on both sides of the ocean would find out after he saved the church with the influx of new souls saved by the one true religion.

The woman broke down sobbing. With the help of a translator, Gonzalo learned that she was the queen's sister, that she had been married to another nobleman when Manco made her come to Gonzalo's home.

"Go then, and tell your husband the truth—that I never touched you as a husband touches a wife," Gonzalo said.

The woman fled from the house, her dress tickling the tops of her feet as it blew in the wind.

"Get out," he told the translator and his primary attendant before sitting down and burying his face in his hands.

The translator left, but the attendant assumed the order wasn't meant for him.

"I said get out!" Gonzalo roared.

The attendant left too.

Gonzalo sat still for hours. Rapid breathing followed spikes in his rage at being tricked, tears when the frustration of his loneliness emerged from his heart. In time, rage won, and he vowed revenge on Manco and the natives for making him look like a fool. He stood up, gathered his sword and lance, then walked into the plaza.

Juan wasn't surprised when he saw Gonzalo pacing from left to right outside his palace; the look in his brother's eye said enough. "Where are we going?" the older Pizarro brother asked.

"Manco's." Gonzalo replied, gesturing with his head to the emperor's side of the plaza.

The Pizarro brothers and a handful of comrades who happened to be in the stables marched into Manco's palace without notice. They walked past surprised guards who didn't raise a hand in objection, startled a group of women working on exquisite fabrics, and disrupted old men studying ornate quipus. Gonzalo told the stable hands to spread out, find the queen, and bring her to him.

The brothers weren't prepared for who was waiting for them in the courtyard.

Gonzalo walked into the sun first, followed by Juan. On the far side of the space, Manco and another man turned around at the sound of the intrusion. Manco's guards stood by in silence.

"That's the priest," Juan whispered, confused.

"Villac Umu," Gonzalo replied. "What's he doing here?"

Manco held up a hand, and the priest stayed where he was while Manco approached the Spaniards.

"He's returned from Diego's trip south, reporting on what he's seen."

Gonzalo, surprised out of his vengeful spirit for the moment, waited.

"The porters are working all day long without food or rest, then imprisoned at night," Manco began. "He's told me about how our people are kept in chains around their neck, twelve at a time—if one dies, they cut off his head and keep moving."

Juan shrugged. "Sounds like they're keeping them in line," he said before nudging Gonzalo.

Gonzalo thought for a moment then laughed.

"They kidnap women and children and hold them while demanding gold and silver. No matter how much of the metal the chiefs give them, it's never enough—the captured natives always accompany the convoy as servants. The servants are dying off faster than they can be replaced."

Gonzalo looked past Manco at Villac Umu. The man was

holding a leaf in his hand, brushing it with his thumb while he stared at the Spaniards with contempt.

"What Diego does isn't our problem," Gonzalo said.

"The men are poor! Maybe if you'd have given more gold and silver when they were here they wouldn't resort to such measures," Juan added.

"I've given everything I have!" Manco replied, one of the few times Gonzalo had ever seen him frustrated.

"Not everything," Gonzalo said, cold regard heavy in his voice. "Not Cura Ocllo."

Manco blanched and lowered his eyes.

"Yes, I know about your little deception. Did you think you could keep it going forever, that I wouldn't know?" Gonzalo said while placing a hand on the emperor's shoulder. Villac Umu's eyes grew wide at the gesture. "Where is she?"

"We found her, sir," a Spaniard called out. He dragged Manco's queen into the courtyard by the arm. "She was getting into her litter and had a whole caravan of llamas packed and ready to go."

"There was another litter too," another Spaniard reported.

Gonzalo looked at Manco and his eyes rested on Villac Umu. "You were going to send her away with him so I never found out about the switch," Gonzalo growled. "What kind of fool do you take me for!"

Manco looked at the Incan priest; the pair exchanged a wordless gaze.

Gonzalo fumed, lost for words, until Juan put an arm around his shoulders. "Let's go, brother," he said. "You're in for a long night!"

The pair cackled as they left the courtyard.

All of Gonzalo's tenderness had escaped his body upon the discovery of Manco's deception. Brutality reigned supreme that night, the queen silent throughout.

The Saturday morning sun rose on Gonzalo's silent palace, sending long shadows reaching into the building. They striped Gonzalo's back while he spent the day as a jailer, his lone prisoner powerless against his torment.

It wasn't until well after the light had retreated and plunged Gonzalo back into darkness that the world outside his palace came calling. It was a messenger from his brother, the urgency evident in his shouts.

"Manco has escaped."

9

"EXTERMINATE THE INVADERS"

GONZALO DRESSED while telling Cura Ocllo about the guards he kept outside the palace. "You might not see them, but they're everywhere. Go wherever you want inside, but don't leave these walls."

The Incan queen made no sign that she had heard or understood his words. She didn't move a muscle when Gonzalo approached her, brushed stray hairs away from her face, and kissed her forehead.

"One of the natives can fetch anything you need."

Gonzalo met Juan's messenger outside his palace. "Your brother went to Manco's house and found it empty. He said to meet him at the stables."

Juan stood between his own horse and a saddled Castaño behind the stables. "What took you so long?" he said.

"I came right away. Don't forget, it's the middle of the night."

"I'm sure he thought we wouldn't discover his absence until the morning," Juan said, handing the reins to his brother.

They both climbed onto their horses.

"How did you find out?" Gonzalo asked. Confident in their

God-granted authority, neither brother paid much attention to the emperor's day-to-day activities.

"Native spy. A bunch of the Incan elite met just after sundown, where Manco called them all to resistance. He wants an attack in four months' time, 'to exterminate the invaders,' the spy told me. No doubt the other nobles already sent word to the four corners of the empire," Juan said before spitting on the ground.

"After we put him on the throne? The ungrateful dog," Gonzalo said, shaking his head.

The Pizarro brothers gathered half a dozen of their best horsemen on the city's outskirts. "Manco's escaped to the south, thinking he's going to lead a rebellion. Let's teach him a lesson he won't forget!" Juan shouted.

The men all raised their weapons—harquebuses, lances, and swords—and cheered.

With the moon high overhead in a cloudless sky and broad, clear roads unobscured by trees, the Spaniards pushed their horses in pursuit of the escaped emperor. The sound of silver horseshoes on stone streets pierced the night air while Gonzalo strained his eyes looking for hints of the emperor's entourage. The road split off into smaller streets, some paved and some dirt, but the group stayed on the main road south.

The Spaniards caught up with two Incan nobles walking along the right side of the road just past the intersection of a substantial adjoining highway. The men stopped and stepped to the side as if letting the Spaniards pass. There was no reason for their travel at that hour unless they were a part of the flee from Cuzco.

Juan pulled his horse to a stop. "Where is he?" he snarled.

The nobles stared without saying a word.

Juan cursed the men, calling them dogs who were spreading rebellion through Spain's rightful land. He dismounted and took the shirt of one of the men in two hands. "Manco!"

A scared noble's shaky finger pointed in the direction the pursuers had passed in their haste. Juan turned rabid eyes on the second man, who also pointed in that direction.

Juan pushed the noble into the dirt. He turned around, paused, then approached the second noble and pushed him down too.

"Let's go," Juan said, climbing back onto his horse.

Gonzalo, his horse faster than the rest, led the way. He pushed Castaño until the heat from the horse's body singed the hair on his legs and foamed horse spittle fell to the road. He spotted another traveling noble up ahead. While the rest of the men caught up with him, he leapt from his horse and marched up to the Incan man.

"Manco," Gonzalo said.

The Incan man didn't say a word.

Gonzalo struck him in the face with the back of his hand before repeating the one-word question.

The noble stayed silent.

"Still no sign of him?" one of the Spaniards called out as he pulled his horse to a stop. "No way he got this far, we've been pushing our horses for a long time now."

"It doesn't make sense," Juan added, looking around.

"Let's teach this man some manners," Gonzalo said. He went back to Castaño and rooted around in a small saddlebag, emerging with a piece of rope. "Get down and help me hold him still," he said to the other Spaniards.

The native man twisted and turned on the ground against the men holding him down as Gonzalo exposed his genitals to the night air, then kicked and shouted as Gonzalo tied the rope tight around his scrotum. With cold determination, Gonzalo walked the other end of the rope to Castaño, looping it around the horse's neck. Because of the slack in the rope, the part closest to the man rested on the ground.

"Now, I'll ask again. Where's Manco?" Gonzalo said in the native lord's face, accentuating the emperor's name.

Juan's grin shone white in the moonlight. Gonzalo wondered if his own teeth gleamed—they were both Pizarros, after all.

The terrified Incan man said something in his native tongue with tears streaming down his face.

Gonzalo, tired of the games the ungrateful natives played, walked over to Castaño. He raised a hand high, staring at the native with a malicious smile. He brought the hand down fast and hard . . .

And stopped it right before the horse's hindquarter. Instead of a slap, he opted for a tap.

The horse took the tiniest step forward, but it was enough to take the slack from the rope.

Screams erupted from the native man as the rope strained against his testicles.

Every Spaniard but Gonzalo laughed. Gonzalo scurried forward and stood over the man's face.

"Manco," he repeated.

The Incan man, sweating and taking short, quick breaths, pointed back in the direction they'd come. He pointed to himself and said "Nazca," the name of a city farther on the road ahead of them. Then he said "Manco," followed by "Titicaca," the name of the large lake that was the center of the cosmos, according to Incan lore.

"He's heading to the lake?" one of the men said.

"Nice big landmark where everyone can gather," Juan said. None of the men had been that far south and therefore had no idea about the gargantuan size of the body of water.

"Road there is the opposite of the way we turned," Gonzalo

grumbled. He stood up. "I'm so tired of these damned tricks! No matter how nice you treat them, trying to save them by teaching them about God, they all continue disrespecting us. I bet the first two we met are laughing now!"

Gonzalo stepped on the taut rope, pulling the man's testicles even further. The detainee screamed, then whimpered.

"Let him wriggle on the ground like a worm," Gonzalo said to his men.

The Spaniards let the native man relieve some of the pressure in the rope but pushed him back to the earth when he tried rolling onto one elbow.

"Hold him still," Gonzalo said. He took a knife from his pocket.

The man's eyes grew wide, and he struggled against his captors.

Gonzalo made a show of leaning close to the man's genitals, tapping the tight scrotum skin with the edge of the knife. A thin line of red appeared. He held the knife so that the sharp side of the blade pointed to the sky, then slashed.

The rope fell limp on the ground, severed right below where it had been attached to the man.

After doubling back, the Spaniards made it back to the main road running south from Cuzco. They looked for the duplicitous nobles who had sent them in the wrong direction but couldn't find any sign of them. Gonzalo looked to the sky. The night wore on him, the burst of energy from the initial hunt wearing off, and he wondered how long it was until dawn.

They took the road to Titicaca when it became clear the nobles were gone. Confident they were on the right path, they urged their horses on despite the animals' fading energy.

The first wisps of sunlight were sneaking into the night sky when Gonzalo, leading the pursuit, caught sight of the discarded royal litter up ahead. He slowed his horse, both waiting for his comrades and wary of a surprise attack. Despite the overwhelming Spanish success in the conquest—they had lost a handful of men while thousands of natives were dead—he still held respect for what could lurk in the shadows.

Juan drew his sword when he arrived; the rest of the men withdrew their weapons, Gonzalo and one other man preferring the lance. They crept forward in pairs, looking into the dense brush on each side of the road, until they got to the litter.

"They've got to be around here somewhere," Gonzalo said. "Probably heard my horse and fled into the trees."

Juan looked farther down the road. "You didn't see anyone up ahead, did you?"

Gonzalo shook his head.

"If we don't catch him now, he'll organize the entire country against us," Juan hissed. "Let's split up."

"Sir, do you think that's wise? It could be a trap," one of the riders said. He had been a cobbler back in Spain before coming to the New World in search of riches.

"Either we face a few here and now, or we face thousands back in Cuzco. Which would you prefer?" Gonzalo asked.

The man gulped then nodded.

"Besides, it's probably all servants anyway," Juan added.

Juan led a group left, Gonzalo a group right. Their horses needed urging into the undergrowth, but every Spaniard knew the beasts were the best defense and weapon against the natives and wouldn't dare going in on foot. They had seen time and time again how the natives had no response to the hacking from above, the heavy hooves tearing through anyone who dared get close.

Castaño hadn't gone more than three steps into the trees when Manco appeared from behind a nearby bush.

"It's me!" Manco said, his hands in the air. More servants coalesced from the shadows, surrounding the emperor.

"Get out here onto the road where we can see you," Gonzalo commanded. He maneuvered his horse so that Manco could pass.

"Juan, we got him!" Gonzalo shouted.

"Coming!" his brother replied from the other side of the road.

The mounted Spaniards surrounded the Incan group as the sun appeared over the horizon, their weapons all pointed at the natives.

"There's no need for this," Manco said. He reached out and pushed Gonzalo's outstretched lance down.

Gonzalo didn't fight the weapon's lowering.

"Diego sent me a message asking me to join him in Chile," Manco said with a smile. "We were headed there when we heard your animals on the road and thought you needed us out of your way."

"So that's why you hid in the trees," Gonzalo said as if the truth had just dawned on him.

"Exactly!"

"And what about your meeting with the nobles today in Cuzco? The one where you called for your country's resistance 'until every last one of us are dead'?"

"I guess that was Diego too," Juan said with a laugh.

Manco's face lost all expression. "How do you know about that?" he whispered.

"We know everything," Gonzalo replied. He pointed to the servants, then the litter. "Pick it up; we're going back to Cuzco."

Juan and Gonzalo rode side by side at the back of the caravan. Two of their group rode in front, followed by Manco's litter and the natives, then the remaining Spaniards.

"We should be bringing him back in chains for attempting a coup," Gonzalo mused, fighting his deep exhaustion.

Juan shrugged. "He'll have plenty of time in chains once we get back."

Upon their return to Cuzco, Gonzalo directed the litter-carriers towards Coricancha, the Incan Temple of the Sun that now served as a Spanish monastery. Francisco's imprisonment of Atahualpa in the Cajamarca Temple of the Sun was the Pizarro brother's inspiration.

Although there were precious few Spanish men of the faith in Cuzco, natives from the noble families bolstered their number, most from the lineages that had backed Atoc instead of Manco. Despite their grievances emanating from the closeness of Manco and the Spaniards, they now harbored deep resentment at the assassination of one of their own.

They were the perfect jailers for Cuzco's newest prisoner.

The Pizarro brothers let the Incan Emperor walk into the temple under his own volition then put him in chains as soon as he got inside. With an iron ring around his neck and two around his feet connected by a chain—the two shackles connected by a second chain running down the front of his body—they led him to one of the rooms once reserved for the priests or temple virgins, they didn't know or care which.

"Now that we don't have to pretend anymore—" Juan said, cracking his knuckles.

Gonzalo put a hand on his brother's shoulder. "Wait. We've been up all night; why don't we get some rest and come back later?"

Juan grinned. "Great idea. It's not like he can go anywhere!"

Gonzalo sent for two Spaniards who could serve as additional guards right outside Manco's door, ordering fresh horses from the stables stationed outside the temple as well, before going back to his palace.

He found Cura Ocllo still in the exact same spot as he had left her. After sending her away, telling her it didn't matter to him where she spent her day as long as she stayed within the palace, he collapsed into bed and slept. She crept away in a daze.

A refreshed Gonzalo found Juan already at the Temple of the Sun that afternoon.

"Oh good, you're here. I was waiting for you," Juan said with glee. He waved Gonzalo over to the former altar, where Gonzalo himself had taken down a dozen golden panels.

"I went to the blacksmith before I laid down," Juan said, walking towards a bundle wrapped in rough cloth.

Gonzalo wondered what sadistic device his brother had commissioned.

Juan unwrapped a silver bowl. He rotated it in his hands, then showed Gonzalo an inscription. "See?" he said. "M-A-N-C-O." Juan couldn't read well, but he knew his letters.

"Man-co," Gonzalo said, sounding it out. He said "man" on the first try, then he realized the truth. "Manco!" he said, pronouncing the emperor's name.

"It's a bowl like Hernando gave his dogs back in Spain!" Juan said, roaring with laughter. Their highborn brother always kept dogs for hunting and treated them better than he treated the peasants who worked for him.

"Let's go give the emperor his present," Juan said before sending a nearby servant for water.

Juan walked into the makeshift prison with the bowl held behind his back; Gonzalo followed.

"Have you had time to think about how you betrayed us?" Gonzalo said.

Manco didn't move. He sat still on the bed while staring out the window and made no sign that he recognized that his captors had entered.

"Hey, we're talking to you!" Juan said, smacking the emperor on the back of the head.

Manco's head snapped forward. He sighed and turned towards the Spaniards.

"Now I know that I'm your prisoner," he muttered.

Juan presented the engraved silver bowl. "You're nothing but a dog we have to keep on a leash," he said. "And here's your bowl!" he added, tossing the dish to the ground at the emperor's feet.

The servant appeared with a pitcher of water. Juan made a show of pouring it into the bowl before reaching out for Manco's head, grabbing the man's hair from the back in an attempt to force his face to the ground.

Gonzalo reached out and stopped him. "Listen, dog," he said, addressing Manco. "Give us gold. We don't care where you get it, who you have to command, or what they have to do, just get it brought to us right away. If not . . ."

"You'll be burned, just like Chalcuchímac!" Juan added. Both Pizarros knew what burning meant to the natives, how the destruction of their physical body prevented a prosperous afterlife.

Gonzalo leaned in close. "We're taking the rest of your wives too, as punishment for running away."

"You were given gold and silver in Cajamarca and I've given you everything in Cuzco—it's never enough. What more can I give; what more can you take?"

"Manco, you were planning a rebellion," Gonzalo said as if explaining a child's punishment to them.

"And now there's a death sentence hanging over us thanks to you!" Juan exclaimed.

Manco sighed and hung his head.

Gonzalo knelt and put a hand on Manco's shoulder. "Look. Just give us what we want—gold and silver—and we'll set you free. Until then, you have to face the consequences for your actions." He stood up and told Juan, "I'll be back, I need to take a piss."

Juan pointed to the corner of the room next to Manco. "Just go there, that's where he'll have to do it."

Manco hung his head, then started standing up.

"No, stay where you are," Juan said. When Manco sat back down, he told Gonzalo, "Go on."

Gonzalo shrugged, pulled down his pants, and relieved himself in the corner. Droplets splashed on the Incan Emperor, who sat with his arms hugging his knees.

"You're lucky I don't have to go too," Juan told Manco. "I won't bother pointing away from you."

10

A LESSON THEY WON'T FORGET

FEAR SPREAD among the Spaniards in Cuzco in the following weeks.

As the year 1535 came to a close, news about the effects of Manco's revolt began trickling in from the countryside. It began with rumors that Manco's uncle, General Tiso, had collected an army in the north.

"Should we tell Francisco about it?" Gonzalo asked Juan on a cloudy morning. The two had started meeting every day since taking Manco captive, often visiting the emperor together for continued demands of more gold and silver.

"We told him about Manco's deception—telling him every little development will just put more on his plate."

"What about Jauja? They could be at risk."

Francisco had stationed a formidable garrison at the fledgling town. "Well, then we send word for them to prepare. We'll keep the men ready to march at a moment's notice."

"And leave Cuzco with less defenders? We should prioritize this city."

Juan looked at the sky and thought for a moment. "Guess we'll just have to see what happens."

Gonzalo looked skyward too. "Even from this far away you can tell how massive those birds are," he said. The black dot floated on the mountain air currents. Its path looked straight at first glance, but over time it became clear that the bird was circling the entire city. "Have you ever seen one up close?" he asked Juan.

Juan pulled his eyes from the sky and stared at his brother with condescension—a favorite tactic of their shared mother. "We've been together the entire time I've been in the New World. When would I have seen a condor up close?"

"I don't know. Cura told me that they're the messengers of the skies," Gonzalo said, still staring.

"Maybe it's finding out what we're doing here so it can tell Tiso about our movements," Juan said, deadpan, looking at a group of passing natives on the city streets.

Gonzalo looked at Juan in disbelief at his brother's imagination; the possibility of such a union with nature had never occurred to him.

Juan laughed and slapped his brother's thigh. "Nobody can talk to birds; it was just a joke."

Gonzalo decided he would ask the stolen queen if the priests ever communicated with the condors but forgot by the time he got home.

The news of a gathering army worried the Spaniards in Cuzco, but the first *encomendero* killings turned the blood in their veins to ice.

Two *encomendero*s had gone out to inspect their land and collect the associated tribute in the countryside. Neither traveled with any more security than their own weapons and horses despite the recent political unrest. At some point in the journey, the natives attacked the pair and killed them, sending their stinking, rotted heads back to Cuzco, leaving them at the base of the walls of Saqsaywaman, the Incan fortress with three towers.

"Think the natives have two horses now?" Juan said when Gonzalo told him the news in the morning; he never asked the names of the Spaniards they lost. The older Pizarro still wore his nightclothes while he sat with his brother within the walls of his palace.

"If they're smart they do," Gonzalo replied. "There's a service today, make sure you're there," he said to his brother before standing up. "And you reek of wine—do something about the smell."

One of the few Spanish women in the New World stopped the brothers outside of the temporary church. Her tear-soaked dress was in tatters, her hair disheveled, and her red eyes rubbed raw.

"It's all your fault!" she screamed, pointing an accusatory finger at the two brothers.

"What's our fault?" Juan said with disdain.

"Pedro's dead because of you!"

"Which Pedro?" Juan said, his patience wearing thin. "I know a lot of Pedros."

"De Moguer," Gonzalo whispered.

"He's the one who was killed! He's been with us since the beginning. Didn't he come with you to Cuzco the first time?"

A solemn Gonzalo nodded. "We're very sorry for your loss, señora. But how is this our fault?"

The murdered *encomendero* had chosen a country life but stayed near the city—his house was a single day's ride away while his lands were a full five. "You didn't tell us how bad it had gotten! He went out there alone with no idea about the revolt. I only found out when I came to Cuzco; I'm too afraid to live in the country now—even a day's ride away is too far."

"We'll make sure you're taken care of," Gonzalo said, taking one of the woman's hands in both of his own.

She pulled away, revolted. "I don't want anything from you. I'm leaving on the next ship to Spain."

Juan pulled Gonzalo away from the distraught woman. "Look, there aren't many Spanish women in the city. We can't let her leave."

Gonzalo chuckled. "So we'll convince her to stay." He turned around and insisted the woman sit next to them during mass, an offer she couldn't refuse without facing ostracism from the Spanish community for a breach of etiquette. "And afterwards, we'll get you set up so that your time in Cuzco is as pleasant as possible."

The woman went through the service as if sleepwalking, then followed Gonzalo as he took her to the house of a local Spaniard whose wife had a reputation for being charitable and caring. Gonzalo himself dispensed a handful of natives for the woman's care and gave her a loan until her husband's monetary affairs were settled.

"No woman should have to go through this; you have to tell the people living outside the city about what's happening with the natives," she said in a moment of serenity before Gonzalo could walk out of the door.

Gonzalo paused, turned around, then looked her square in the eye. "You have my word."

At dinner later that night, Juan couldn't contain his laughter. "What did you go and say that for? All that would do is stir up fear in the countryside, giving the natives the upper hand."

Gonzalo stared into his cup of wine and took a swig. "She was hurting."

"And we'll be hurting if Francisco finds out we can't even keep control of one city. What do you think will happen if we fail?" He continued when Gonzalo didn't answer. "No, we keep this local."

"And what, sit in our palaces waiting for it to stop? We'll run out of countrymen before long."

Juan took a big bite of llama meat and thought. "A lot of the people I've talked to want us to go teach the natives a lesson," he said with his mouth full, bits of meat flying onto the table. "Let word of the punishment spread among the natives."

"And what about leaving the city at risk?"

"We'll go ourselves, with three other handpicked men. We're the best fighters here; it shouldn't take long." Although Juan had a reputation for being boastful, it was common knowledge that the two Pizarros were among the best fighters on horseback in the entire Incan Empire—Juan with the sword and Gonzalo with the lance.

Preparations took three days. In that time, the city got word of a third *encomendero* killing, this time in the southwest of Cuzco. "We're marching out right away," the Pizarro brothers told the city's worried Spanish citizens. "We'll send them a message they won't forget!"

Five Spaniards set out at the beginning of the new year, following the same road the Pizarro brothers had when chasing the escaping Manco. They rode at a relaxed pace in hopes that word of their departure from the city would spread and bring their enemies to them.

The hills and valleys blended together, the land becoming more regular as the group got closer to Lake Titicaca. Along the way, stares from the natives graduated from curious glances to scheming hostility; recent harvests became purposeful resource deprivation. The haughty Spaniards kept their heads high as their horses meandered through the countryside. They commandeered food at native towns while asking after gold and silver despite their lack of transportation for any volume of stolen valuables, always hopeful but never finding any.

Their first encounter with resistance of any sort took place on their third night away from Cuzco. They had spent a relaxed day following a stream through a valley, the hills nearby covered in green from the recent rains while the mountains beyond were peaked with snow. One of their number, a thin man with sharp cheekbones and a pockmarked face known for having the eyesight of an eagle, spotted a native herder disappearing over a ridge on their right.

"He's been tracking us," he said. "That's the second time I've seen him. Those colorful cloaks they wear make it too easy."

"Let's make camp early tonight," Gonzalo replied. "Maybe even have two people on watch."

Juan groaned. It was common knowledge he snoozed whenever he was on lookout duty.

"Better than waking up to an attack," Gonzalo added.

They stayed at one of the one-room Incan dwellings built for the quipu carriers. During a light dinner of roasted meat, the thin man reported three natives were watching them from the closest hill. Before Manco's escape, the local chiefs often met any travelers at the inn—Incan or Spanish—and offered food, drink, and blankets. Now, because of their emperor's resistance, they observed the Spaniards' every move, no doubt preparing for potential hostilities.

"Think they'd attack if we had fewer numbers?" another of the handpicked Spaniards said, a thick brawler who had earned a reputation for savagery at Cajamarca.

"No doubt about it," Juan said, lying down before the group figured out who would take first watch.

"If we didn't have the eagle here we'd have no idea they were there," the fifth member of their party said. Built like Gonzalo and Juan but bald, he specialized in trampling natives with his horse, the best trained in the empire. "Those poor *encomenderos* probably went to sleep without a worry in their head."

All five men crossed themselves.

Gonzalo took first watch with the eagle-eyed man. There was nothing to do but wait once the daylight ended, but the pair took solace in the strength of the stone walls surrounding their party.

"How many natives you think it would take to get through that door?" the thin man whispered, gesturing towards the single entrance to the room.

"More than they have, I'm sure," Gonzalo replied. "Unless there's another army gathered nearby we don't know about."

Both men grew quiet at the thought.

The night grew heavy, pulling at both men's eyelids. Snorting from the horses made both men bolt upright.

"Wake up," Gonzalo said, shoving Juan's shoulder.

His older brother didn't show any signs of his usual sluggishness. Instead, he shook his head and sat up. "Now they've gone too far," he said without bothering with the volume of his voice. After lighting a torch, he stormed outside with his sword in hand.

"Come into the light and I'll introduce you to steel!" he said as he walked into the night.

His four countrymen came out and stood by his side. A single rock whizzed past over the conquistadors' heads, striking the stone wall behind them. Hushed Quechua words followed, then silence.

"Someone talked some sense into whoever threw that," Gonzalo said after the Spaniards strained their ears listening to the night. "Doubt they'll be coming back."

"Should we bring the horses inside?" the brawler asked.

"And get rid of our alarm? No, they'll be fine. We'd have to worry about the archers, but they're far to the east, over in the jungle."

"Put out that flame," the thin man said to Juan.

Juan turned on the man in anger. "Are you giving me an order?" he snarled.

Gonzalo stepped in, knowing how his brother acted when woken up.

"They can see their targets," Gonzalo said. He reached out and grabbed the torch before taking it inside, throwing the entire thing into the main fire.

The men waited outside until the adrenaline wore off. Moonlight came and went depending on the heavy cloud cover, the landscape plunging in and out of total darkness.

"Let's go to bed," Gonzalo told the thin man. "Two of you take the second shift."

"You two do it; I'm going back to sleep," Juan said. He led the way back into the dwelling, and his breaths were the first to steady in slumber.

The vigilant Spaniards didn't enjoy a restful night's sleep for the remainder of their time away from Cuzco. They arrived at the murdered *encomendero*'s land cranky, tired, and soaked to the bone, after a continuous rain since the previous day.

"Supposed to be right here," Gonzalo said, surveying the land from atop his horse. Short grasses covered the desolate ground, green because of the recent rain. The land would be light brown in other times of the year.

"What tribute was he going to collect? Dirt?" Juan said.

"Guess we'll have to find some of the natives and ask them ourselves," the bald one said.

Together, they climbed to the highest peak nearby and surveyed the land, not finding any settlements or natives. The Spaniards had grown used to receiving a traveler's welcome on behalf of Manco whenever they entered an *encomienda*; its absence made them again realize the deep sentiment shift taking hold of the land.

A well-worn trail crested the top of the next hill. "Could be llamas or people," the thin man said.

"Find llamas and you'll find people soon enough," Juan growled, spurring his horse forward. His choleric mood infected the others, reminding them of their reason for the unplanned excursion into the countryside: the killing of the two *encomenderos*, one of whom helped captured Atahualpa at Cajamarca.

The group crossed the next ridge and discovered a settlement. On the far side of the handful of stone houses, a pair of horses grazed while tied to a post in the ground.

"Those filthy dogs," Juan roared, pulling the sword from his scabbard and sending his horse charging through the small town.

Upon hearing the Spanish words, a native man ran from one of the stone buildings closest to the horses. He pulled the post from the ground and slapped one of the horses on the rear. As he turned around looking for the Spaniards, a single stroke separated his head from his body.

Juan didn't stop until there wasn't a single native male alive in the settlement.

Gonzalo made him stop before he turned on the women too. He sent the brawler and the bald man after the escaped horses, then gathered the rest of the townspeople.

"*Curaca*," he said to the quavering women and children. The Quechua word meant an official in the Incan system of government in charge of tax collection from families assigned to him, similar to a chief.

The oldest woman present, her hair more gray than black, stepped forward and pointed away from the direction from which the Spaniards had arrived.

Juan walked his horse forward, grabbed the woman, and laid her across his horse. "You're going to take us there."

The Pizarro brothers left the eagle-eyed man at the town to wait for their two comrades chasing the fleeing horses then set off. They found the *curaca*'s settlement; it was three times larger than the one they had just raided.

Juan tossed the elder woman onto the ground like a discarded fruit rind and pointed into the town.

"We should've waited for the others," Gonzalo said.

"To hell with them. I'll take care of these dogs myself," Juan replied.

"Just wait; we'll see what happens."

The *curaca* appeared at the edge of the town with fifteen native warriors behind him. They each held a mace in one hand and a square shield in the other, their bodies protected by thick woven armor.

Juan smiled. "I'm not sure we can wait much longer."

As if on cue, the elder woman cried out to the men in her native tongue, tears streaming from her eyes. At her insistence, the men all rushed forward, the *curaca* alone standing back.

Gonzalo and Juan pressed the attack instead of holding back. They charged forward on their horses, trusting the animals would stomp and kick anyone in their path. From their elevated position, Juan hacked and slashed his sword while Gonzalo thrust and swung his lance.

The native warriors stood no chance.

Adrift in his bloodlust, Juan dismounted and began dismembering the fallen men. Ignoring his brother, Gonzalo approached the stunned *curaca* and wiped the blood from the tip of his lance on the man's multicolored cloak while young women and children stared at him from inside stone dwellings. He ran a hand through his beard.

"We'll be back next year for double the tribute," Gonzalo said. After wondering if the *curaca* understood, he repeated the message using the few Quechua words he knew.

Looking to the sky, he said, "I've done all I can, Lord."

He withdrew his dagger from its sheath and turned back to the sole man left alive in the settlement. "Now, to make sure you don't forget."

The five Spaniards and seven horses rested there that night, taking whatever food and women they desired. A messenger found them preparing for their departure in the morning.

"I've come from Cuzco," the Spaniard said.

"Another *encomendero* killing?" Juan said, licking his lips in anticipation for further revenge.

"No. Your brother's back."

"Francisco came back to Cuzco?" Gonzalo said, worried the oldest Pizarro had heard about the unrest in the countryside.

"Not Don Francisco. Hernando."

The Spaniards set out right then and there, not even waiting for the water on the fire to boil. Before leaving the murdered *encomendero*'s lands, Gonzalo dropped the *curaca*'s ears onto the hard-packed earth.

11

ANYTHING FOR GOLD

GONZALO AND JUAN went straight to church when they got back to Cuzco, dragging the other three Spaniards from their expedition with them. They crossed themselves upon entering.

At the disturbance, Friar Valverde stood from where he knelt in front of the altar and turned around. "Brothers," the priest said, approaching them with open arms.

"Father," Gonzalo said with a nod. "We can skip the pleasantries; none of us smell better than the horses we rode in on."

Friar Valverde continued as if he hadn't heard until he got within two steps of the party. Then, he came up against an invisible wall of odor and dropped his arms to his front, folding them on his small belly. Rings of gold adorned his fingers, jewelry Gonzalo hadn't noticed before.

"You've made it home safe," the priest said, smiling.

"By the grace of God above," Juan said.

Friar Valverde bowed his head and stepped to the side, beckoning the men forward with a single arm. "Juan, were you hurt?"

Juan followed the priest's eyes and looked down at the

bloodstains on his boots. He chuckled. "No, sir, this blood isn't mine."

"A native uprising?" the friar asked, a malicious glint in his eye. Gonzalo appreciated the priest's feigned ignorance. Everyone in Cuzco knew about the *encomendero* killings; half the reason they'd gone was because of the public outcry for retribution.

"They won't be a problem anymore," the thin, eagle-eyed man said, stepping forward.

"We hope," Gonzalo added as he passed the friar.

The men all kneeled in front of the altar and bowed their heads with the crucifix looming above them. Gonzalo thanked God for bringing him back safe, Jesus for the health of his horse, Castaño, and the holy spirit for the opportunity to teach the natives about Christianity. He assumed the other men's prayers gave thanks for similar blessings, though he wondered if there was much going through the brawler's mind at all.

Friar Valverde led a short mass for the men in which he read from the Bible and discussed the importance of evangelism. After a quick bite of body and a small sip of blood, the priest blessed them and beseeched they give thanks to God aloud.

"Thanks be to God," the men said, somewhat at the same time, but not in unison, before standing up.

"Have you seen Hernando?" Gonzalo asked.

"I have. Like you, he came here as soon as he got into the city, giving thanks for his safe journey."

"Where is he?" Gonzalo said.

"Last I heard, he's staying at your palace on the plaza," Friar Valverde told Gonzalo.

A wave of worry seized Gonzalo. Hernando was older than him, noble-born and educated. What if he wanted Gonzalo's palace for himself? Francisco wasn't there to enforce the initial distribution—it could be months before it got sorted out.

Juan and Gonzalo said goodbye to the other three members of their party and headed to the plaza. There, the Pizarro brothers split up, Juan going back to his own home for a wash and change of clothes.

Gonzalo passed over the threshold to his palace with a mixture of excitement at seeing Hernando and trepidation about what his brother would say regarding the Incan queen living there. Did his brother share Juan's attitudes towards native women, using them without regard, or did he find them beneath him as a noble? He couldn't recall any instances of Hernando taking liberties with the natives during their time in Cajamarca, but he also hadn't been paying attention.

"Hernando?" Gonzalo called out.

"In here," his brother replied from deeper in the palace, near the courtyard. His deep voice resonated through the halls.

Gonzalo had planned on changing after a quick greeting. He forgot everything when he saw the native man sitting with his brother at the table.

The last time he had seen that particular native, the man had been imprisoned at the monastery, the former Temple of the Sun. Now, Manco sat with his brother, enjoying a meal in a fresh set of clothes and all his emperor's jewelry.

Manco didn't act surprised upon seeing Gonzalo. In fact, he didn't act at all, just kept his eyes staring forward at the table, looking just past the dish in front of him.

"Gonzalo, it's good to see you again," Hernando said, his tone formal. He pushed the chair on his left, across from Manco, from under the table with his leg, gesturing towards it with his arm. "Manco was nice enough to join me for a meal."

Gonzalo looked at his brother, asking, "What are you thinking?" with his eyes. Hernando ignored the inquisitive look, instead turning back to the Incan Emperor. "And so your great-grandfather Pachacuti began teaching the other peoples around Cuzco about the powerful sun god?"

His brother spoke to Manco as if the native man was at the Spanish court with him—he sat bolt upright, kept his hands crossed on the table, and maintained a look of feigned interest that Gonzalo couldn't stand. He sat down at the table as Manco took a small sip of wine.

"Yes, Pachacuti started the expansion. His son Topa pushed our realms to the north and east, capturing Quito and building Saqsaywaman."

"Saqsa-*que*?" Hernando said.

"The stone fortress outside the city," Gonzalo interjected.

"And your father . . ."

"Huayna Capac. He spread our realms to the south and built all the connections. It's because of him our runners can travel throughout the lands on roads, with places to stay along the way."

Hernando made a show of exhaling in awe. He lifted the gold carafe on the table, topped off his cup and Manco's—the emperor didn't need more than a few drops—then filled up Gonzalo's. "Fascinating," he said as he poured.

An uncomfortable lull wiggled its way into the conversation. Gonzalo got a whiff of his own stench.

"Imagine my surprise when I arrived in Cuzco and found Manco in a room at the monastery," Hernando said, taking a passion fruit from a pile in the middle. He cut it in half, grabbed a spoon, and scooped out the flesh.

"He was leading a rebellion," Gonzalo said, staring at the Incan Emperor.

Manco still didn't look at him.

"A rebellion against who? The king appreciates the friendship between our two domains, always so important for continued trade."

Up until that point, Gonzalo had assumed that Hernando would agree with his and Juan's actions once he knew the truth about the duplicitous emperor. He wasn't so sure after hearing Hernando invoke the King of Spain.

"A stable government here is best for all parties involved," Hernando continued. "And it's my understanding that our young friend Manco here was an indispensable part in helping us gain a foothold in this country. Is that not true?"

Gonzalo took a swig of wine, a large gulp he wouldn't dare among the nobles in Spain. He couldn't deny Manco's usefulness during the early days of their arrival in Cuzco. "It's true," he said.

"Excellent. Let's have a toast," Hernando said, raising his glass. Gonzalo followed. When Manco didn't move, Hernando gestured that the emperor should do the same with a smile.

"To our renewed partnership. As the king himself said, 'Let's give thanks for the native emperor.'" All three men drank, Hernando and Gonzalo draining their cups.

How many times had Hernando mentioned the king so far? Gonzalo couldn't stand how his brother flaunted his nobility. He had dealt with it throughout their childhood and somehow he was still dealing with it as a wealthy man in the New World.

"Cura, more wine!" Hernando called out.

Gonzalo's stomach sank all the way to his stinking boots.

The Incan queen appeared right away, convincing Gonzalo that she had been watching the three men's discussion. Like Manco, she didn't look anyone in the eye while she walked around and filled each man's cup from a fresh carafe.

Gonzalo reached out a hand and grabbed the queen's backside as she left his side. Sneering, he looked at Manco.

The emperor had his eyes closed.

Hernando laughed after catching the exchange. "What, he

doesn't like the way we treat the servants? All those wives and he gets mad at us for keeping a few women for ourselves?"

Because of the way Hernando spoke, Gonzalo realized that his brother didn't know that Cura Ocllo had been Manco's primary wife.

"Maybe he doesn't think we're good enough for native women," Gonzalo said before sharing a laugh with Hernando.

"Ah, he'll get over it." Hernando turned his attention back to Manco. "So you mentioned this palace had changed since you had seen it last. Who lived here before?" he asked.

Manco unclenched his jaw before he spoke. "Topa," he said.

"Topa . . . the one who took Quito!" Hernando said, proud of his recollection.

Manco made no response.

"It's beautiful. The black marble, exquisite. There's so much history here," Hernando mused.

The way his brother said "exquisite" made Gonzalo wonder who in Spain he'd gotten the phrase from while he was there. Could the word have been a favorite of the king himself?

"He used to love sitting in this very courtyard. His servants would bring his body out here on special occasions so that he could see the sky," Manco said, looking up.

"Friar Valverde might have something to say about the way you worship corpses," Gonzalo said.

Manco lowered his gaze and his eyes settled on Gonzalo. His face stayed relaxed while his eyes adjusted to the changing light, an unsettling display of both control and a deep wellspring of patience in the moment.

"All this talk about ancestors reminds me of a statue of my father, Huayna, in a mountain cave two days north from here," Manco said, dropping his gaze back to its previous position.

Gonzalo felt a wave of relief wash over him, followed by

confusion because he hadn't been aware of any distress in his body.

"It's life-sized and might be of interest to you. Me and Villac Umu can bring it back," the emperor said, looking at Hernando's plate.

"So we can see what he looked like?" Hernando asked, leaning forward and resting his elbows on the table.

A rush of excitement overtook Gonzalo. A cave containing the statue of a former emperor might also have a cache of treasure. Though already rich, he could never have enough.

"It's very realistic, yes, but it's also made of solid gold."

Hernando choked on his spit. Coughing, with a hand held up to his mouth, he told Manco that they could depart together the following morning.

"I'm sorry, but it's a sacred site," Manco said.

Gonzalo got the sense that he no longer existed as a person when Manco turned his shoulders towards Hernando, that he was just a shadow watching events unfold.

"Only the priest can go."

"Well, how will you get a statue that big back here without help?" Hernando asked.

"There are men who tend the cave from the nearby village."

"And they'll help?" Gonzalo said.

Manco's cold eyes turned on Gonzalo once more. "I'm the sun's descendant on Earth. If they don't do what I say, I'll send them to the permanent night."

Neither man blinked until Hernando slammed both hands onto the table, then they both looked at the boisterous Spaniard. "Then it's settled! Manco, you and—Villac, was it?—go to the cave and bring back the statue. We'll be here waiting."

"But—" Gonzalo began.

Hernando cut him off by holding up a hand. Years of

tempering in Spain had taught Gonzalo that he couldn't push back . . .

Until Manco had gone. "What are you thinking? He's going to escape!" Gonzalo erupted as soon as they were alone.

"The king made it very clear that he's supposed to be treated like an emperor in his own right—it's all about the transfer of wealth out of this country and into Spain, you see. The emperor taxes the masses, the king taxes the emperor . . . And if the emperor wants to go out in the country for a few days, well, then that's what he'll do."

"Hernando, I'm telling you that he'll return with an army. They want us gone."

"Gone? Why? We're teaching them about God and Jesus Christ, showing them modern weapons and horses. No, a prosperous relationship begins with trust."

Before Gonzalo could utter another word, a commotion from the front of the house drew both of their attention.

"He said you let him free!" Juan roared after Gonzalo and Hernando succeeded in releasing Manco from his clutches.

"I did," Hernando replied.

"What are you thinking? They're going to kill us all!"

"I tried to tell him," Gonzalo muttered.

The pair brought their brother back to the courtyard.

Hernando rested his elbows on the table and steepled his fingers. "Look, it's no surprise that the two of you feel lost in these matters. Politics aren't simple! But the king and I feel that we need to establish a good working relationship with Manco—" Hernando's face relaxed but his eyebrows pinched in a mask of fury. "And that doesn't include keeping him prisoner. It smelled like piss in there—how long was he living in his own filth?"

Juan and Gonzalo looked at each other. Hernando didn't know that they had urinated on the emperor, and they would make sure he never found out.

"No, I don't want to know. I've apologized so much to him that I'm worried I won't have any more apologies left for weeks. We're lucky he seems forgiving."

"It's just an act! He's plotting revenge," said Juan.

Cura appeared and poured wine in a clean cup for the last arriving Pizarro brother.

Juan caught Gonzalo's eye, then asked outright. "Did Manco see her?"

Gonzalo closed his eyes and nodded once.

"Oh, then he's definitely coming back with an army!" Juan said.

Hernando alternated looking at his two half brothers. "What?"

"That's Manco's wife," Gonzalo said with a sigh.

"So?" Hernando said. "He has lots of wives. Losing one won't kill him."

"No, that's his *principal* wife. The Incan queen. He didn't give her up easily," Juan said.

Hernando closed his eyes and turned towards the heavens. "What *the hell* were the two of you thinking?" he whispered.

Gonzalo would have preferred he yelled like their father. He could take a beating but never knew what punishment would arrive from someone both calm and mad.

"Ok, when Manco gets back, we act like nothing happened. Cura stays here, since the damage is already done—we'll make sure she doesn't escape from the palace and join him on the road —and we move forward *remembering that he's our partner*. You two got it?"

Gonzalo and Juan nodded their understanding.

That night, a contingent of the Incan nobles opposed to Manco's rule requested an urgent meeting with the three Pizarro brothers. Hernando accepted and arranged an assembly on the construction site of the new cathedral.

"You made a mistake," their leader said without hesitation at the gathering. He was an older man with wooden plugs in his ears since his golden ones had been confiscated by the ravenous Spaniards.

"A mistake?" Hernando replied, amused, while crossing his arms.

"Yes. You have to go capture him again, he can't have gone far. If you leave now . . ."

"I still don't know what mistake I've made . . ."

"He's coming back with an army! The entire country has been mobilizing while he's been at the Temple of the Sun—"

"You mean the monastery," Hernando interjected.

"Yes, that building. The armies have been waiting for him ever since the night of his first escape. If you don't recapture him now, you're putting us all at risk!"

Hernando thought for a moment. "This is just a part of politics," he said. "We just have to show that we're willing to trust him, then he can trust us in return." He reached out and put a hand on the leader's shoulder before looking each of the nobles in the eye. "It's ok that you don't understand," he added.

An *encomendero* came into Cuzco two days later, reporting that he'd seen the emperor and the priest on the road between Cuzco and Lima.

"To the west, not to the north like he said," Gonzalo said to Hernando, pleading.

Hernando waved a hand, silencing his brother. "Did you talk to them?" he asked the *encomendero*.

"Of course. I asked where they were going," the *encomendero* responded. "I had a group of hired men with me for protection; we would have grabbed him if we knew," he added, speaking to Gonzalo.

"And what did he say?" Hernando jutted his face forward, eyes wide.

"That he was collecting gold to bring back here."

Hernando turned his smug face towards Gonzalo. "Looking for gold! *Just like what he said he'd do.*" He laughed and shook his head. "Thanks for letting us know," he said to the *encomendero*, dismissing him.

"Of course," the man said before leaving.

Seven days after Manco walked out from Gonzalo's palace to the minute, Hernando sighed with regret and looked at Gonzalo as the two of them inspected the ongoing construction of the expanded stables.

"Manco and the priest aren't coming back."

12

THE SIEGE OF CUZCO

"We told you! We told you, we told you, we told you," Juan said, pacing. The three brothers were in Manco's abandoned palace. The servants and retinue had disappeared overnight and the Pizarros had received word about a native army just fifteen miles to the north. Juan ran his hands through his hair then stroked his beard. "Didn't we tell him?" he said to Gonzalo.

"We told him," Gonzalo said, closing his eyes.

"And did you listen?" Juan said, turning his wrath back to Hernando. "No. You acted like we had no idea what we were talking about, like we haven't been dealing with Manco since day one!"

"Guy meets a king and all of a sudden knows better than anyone," Gonzalo added. An insult to Hernando had never escaped his lips before, since Hernando was a legitimized noble and Gonzalo was a bastard, but his newfound wealth and fear for his life injected courage into his veins. Plus, having a furious Juan nearby lessened the chance of reprisal.

Hernando slapped the wall. "The king said to reward him for helping us bring this country to heel," he said. He clenched his fist; Gonzalo couldn't decide if it was from rage or the stinging pain. "I came here and found him locked up. Why would I go against the king's wishes?"

"Because now we have to worry about the city getting overrun!" Gonzalo said, raising his voice for the first time.

"He wouldn't be so hell-bent on revenge if you never took his wife!" Hernando shot back.

"So it's all my fault?"

An exasperated Hernando rolled his eyes and exhaled. "He gave us all the gold and silver we asked for, right? Land, food, and supplies too?"

Both Juan and Gonzalo nodded.

"And the one thing he didn't want to part with was the queen?"

"He escaped the next day," Gonzalo replied, his voice little more than a whisper.

"And then you put him in a cell, degrading the one man in the empire *who can amass armies against us.*"

Gonzalo lowered his head.

"So I'll say it again: this wouldn't be happening if you didn't take his wife!"

Gonzalo swallowed his rage. Despite his considerable wealth, he was still looked down upon by the Spanish nobility for his plebeian tendencies. He swore revenge on Manco, and by extension the natives, for making him look foolish.

Juan came to Gonzalo's rescue. "There's no way he could have known Manco would rebel because of that. What kind of man gives up the entire wealth of his country but balks at losing a woman?"

Hernando shook his head. "Greece went to war for Helen . . ." He shook his head in disappointment at his brothers' blank stares. "It doesn't matter. Now we just have to fix this."

"It was fixed," Gonzalo muttered.

"What was that?" Hernando said, turning on his brother.

"I said it was fixed! And you let him go free to his waiting armies. This rebellion is as much on you as it is me."

The two brothers stared at each other, Hernando's nobility the sole reason Gonzalo didn't strike.

"We need to call a meeting," Juan said. "Let's get every Spaniard in Cuzco here and tell them what's happened. We can come up with a plan together."

Hernando led the late-morning meeting in the church. Without mincing words or laying blame on anyone, he laid out the situation they faced in plain words. He told the men how Manco had deceived him, that there was a rebellion brewing, and informed everyone present about the reported army to the north.

"How many men do we have in total?" Hernando said when he was finished describing their plight.

The Spaniards conferred and determined there were less than two hundred men, just over eighty horses, a dozen African slaves, and a thousand natives who either opposed Manco's rule or existed outside of Incan society proper and therefore sided with the Spanish.

"I think the best thing we can do is recapture the emperor. He can end the native rebellion if we can convince him that his continued peaceful reign is in everyone's best interest," Hernando said. He looked at the faces of the gathered men for any dissension. "It's what the king wants."

The king, the king . . . Gonzalo was so tired of hearing his brother drone on about his meeting with the king that he would have abandoned Cuzco and gone into the countryside if there wasn't a native rebellion underway.

"We already captured him once, we can do it again!" Juan said, lifting his hand in the air. The other Spaniards stared at the fiery Pizarro, uncertain.

"That's the spirit!" Hernando said. "God will lead us

through this if we work together. Let's send a force up to where the native troops are gathered and disperse them before they bring the fight to us! Any volunteers?"

Juan, his hand still in the air, looked at the assembled men. Soon, sixty cavalry had joined the enterprise, their infectious energy spreading like ripples in a lake to the rest of the group. Everyone left the meeting confident that they would teach the native dogs and their treacherous leader a lesson in short order.

The cavalry wasted no time, riding out that very afternoon. The Spaniards remaining in Cuzco were left with just twenty-six horses for their defense. Hernando and Gonzalo worked together in organizing strongholds, amassing weapons, and investigating their supplies of food and water. They posted sentries in high positions along the broadest paths into the city, assigning two men at a time to each so that they could keep each other awake overnight.

A night of collective bad sleep in the Incan capital of Cuzco ended with a strange calm descended on the valley. To the skittish Spaniards, it seemed that the animals didn't emerge from their burrows, the flowering plants never unfurled to the morning light, and the stream running through the city had stopped flowing. The sole indications that time marched on outside of the city's walls were the consistent breeze blowing through raised Spanish flags and the sun's path through the sky.

Every Spaniard visited Friar Valverde in church at least twice that day; Hernando and Gonzalo returned countless times in between their administrative duties. To a man, they all prayed for Juan's victory over the upstart natives, not quite realizing the true scope of the force Manco had brought to bear.

The truth dawned on them that night. Rather, it twinkled in the moonlight.

A messenger from the sentries, one of the African slaves brought to Cajamarca by Almagro, visited Gonzalo well after the sun had gone down. "I already told the other Señor Pizarro, he's waiting for us," he began.

"Out with it," Gonzalo replied, his frayed nerves sapping what little patience he had.

"You better come look for yourself, señor."

Gonzalo swore under his breath, claiming that he'd punish the slave himself for wasting his time. They gathered Hernando, and together the brothers followed the man through the city streets to the northern sentry post. They climbed a rough wooden ladder onto the slanted roof.

Thousands of small fires dotted the adjacent mountains. They were spread as far as Gonzalo could see to the left and right, as if the mountains had been waiting for nightfall before coming alive.

His dry tongue felt too big for his mouth. "Those are all native forces?" he choked out.

"Who else would they be?" replied the sentry, a grizzled *encomendero* who'd stopped going out into the country at the first word of native unrest. "That's not all." He turned to his slave. "Show them."

The African man scrambled to the top of the roof and held out a hand for Hernando. Gonzalo felt a glimmer of amusement, knowing his brother wouldn't accept the slave's help because that would mean touching the dark-skinned man. He himself didn't have such reservations, but the slave never offered him a hand.

Both Pizarro brothers climbed the roof and sat on the crest. There were more fires on the other side of the valley, thousands total. They surrounded the city, giving voice to native power without uttering a single word.

"It's worse than we thought," Hernando mused. "We need Juan and those horses, now."

"I was thinking the same thing," the old *encomendero* said from lower on the roof.

Hernando sent one of the natives who opposed Manco's rule with a message for Juan—reasoning that the man would have a better chance of avoiding detection than a Spaniard—telling his brother that Cuzco was under siege. The runner left the city before the sun rose on the field of Incan warriors and banners waving in the mountain breeze.

An exhausted Juan and his remaining cavalrymen arrived back in Cuzco before nightfall. Hernando and Gonzalo had spent the day watching the hordes grow and multiply outside of the city, feeling like a ship sailing straight into a gathering storm with no available alternative.

"How'd you make it through?" Hernando said as his returning brother dismounted from his horse. Gonzalo noticed that the native runner wasn't among their company.

"We crested the mountain," Juan said through heavy breaths while pointing to the mountain behind him. "And realized just how many native dogs there are. They must have been gathering for weeks!"

"We know," Gonzalo replied.

"Since his first escape, I'd guess," a sullen Hernando added.

Gonzalo thought for a moment that his brother might bring up his and Juan's hand in bringing about the calamity again, but Hernando never mentioned it.

"Well, we thought we'd have to hack and claw our way back to you guys. We said our prayers and charged. The natives kept pretending they'd make a stand but fell back whenever we got close. Flung plenty of stones at us though."

Hernando stroked his beard.

"Did you find the rumored army to the north?" Gonzalo asked.

"Oh, we found them all right," Juan said, fumbling with his armor.

Gonzalo lent his brother a hand.

"Caught them on the far side of a shallow river. Guess they didn't think we'd charge, but we did. They thought their copper axes and maces would save them, but they were no match for our horses," Juan said, tapping his steed on the side.

Gonzalo inspected the other horses. Blood and dirt covered the horses' legs up to their bellies—though the lower portions of their legs were washed clean by the river—and many of them sported deep gashes from the encounter.

"Never seen 'em fight so hard though, or so disciplined. It's like they knew Manco was watching."

"So you saw him?" Hernando said, breaking his reverie.

"No, but we did find his female servants and some gold serving ware when we pushed them back into the mountains. One of the men has it with him somewhere . . ." Juan looked around. "Hell, let him keep it for all I care. Lost a handful of men and horses—"

All three brothers crossed themselves.

"—keeping them from coming back down, but we couldn't press the attack; the horses are useless on the slopes, and they kept rolling huge rocks down whenever we got close. We were deep in the stalemate when I got the message about what's happening here."

"I wonder why they just let you through," Gonzalo thought out loud. "You were cut off, with most of the horses. Why let you pass unmolested?"

Juan chuckled. "What do natives know about warfare? They were probably scared of us."

Hernando looked at the two of them, his eyes heavy with resignation. "They're laying siege to the city. Sixty more men and horses to feed means a sooner end to our supplies."

Juan sobered, and Gonzalo sighed.

Hernando ordered every Spaniard into the town's plaza, where they camped alongside the stables under a sea of awnings. He deemed Manco's abandoned palace, where Huascar and Huayna had lived before him, as their command headquarters, formalizing his own power, making Juan second-in-command, and giving Gonzalo control of one of three groups of cavalry. Before retiring for the night, the Pizarros all climbed to the top of the building and looked at the nighttime panorama. Somehow, there were more fires than the night before.

"Looks like the stars in the night sky come all the way to our doorstep," Juan observed.

Gonzalo wondered why Juan waited until death had moved in next door before giving voice to the poet hidden inside him.

The following day found an industrious Hernando awake before sunrise. By the time Gonzalo joined him, letting Juan sleep after his exertions in the countryside, his brother was wearing his battle armor and was giving orders to a dozen men.

"There were more fires last night and more banners this morning," Hernando said, pacing with his hands behind his back in front of his mounted men. "And just yesterday, Juan got back without any real engagement. It's time to test whether or not these natives have any sort of backbone, or if they think we'll sit in the city scared of their numbers." He paused for a moment. "Are you scared?" he said.

The men shook their heads no.

"I said, 'Are you scared?'" Hernando roared.

The cavalry all raised a fist in the air and screamed "no" in unison.

"Then let's get to it!" Hernando said, walking over to his horse and climbing onto its back.

Gonzalo made a beeline for the stables and Castaño.

"Where do you think you're going?" Hernando asked.

"I'm coming with you."

Hernando made a show of deciding, then nodded his approval. Gonzalo donned his armor, grabbed his lance, and climbed onto Castaño's back.

"He's almost too fine a fighter for simply testing native strength; should save him for when we need him," Hernando said as the brothers rode side by side through the empty Cuzco streets.

"He gets jealous of the others if we leave him behind," Gonzalo replied, unsure if they were still talking about the horse.

They first prodded the strength of the native warriors to the east of the city, reasoning that if they discovered a soft path, they could send word to Francisco in Lima about their predicament.

Their appearance began a trumpeting and hollering that lasted all day. The numerous natives hurled a wall of stones that startled the horses and prevented the Spaniards from marching forward. Many of the projectiles clamored off of the nearby buildings with no effect, but the ones that struck Spanish armor produced a metallic ringing that rattled the bones of both horse and rider.

The second effort at probing outside the city produced the same results, but on the third it seemed the horses realized that the stones were no more than flies buzzing around their heads. The Spanish force kept charging forward, through the rock flurry, and found themselves surrounded on all sides.

"Miguel, get back here!" Hernando roared above the din. The Spaniard had pressed forward too far and was all alone. The natives surged forward, ignoring his probing lance, then his swinging sword, until they reached his mount, grabbed him by the legs, and pulled him down. While Hernando, Gonzalo, and the rest of the group watched, they beheaded both the Spaniard and the horse.

"Back to the city!" Hernando called out. "Gonzo, lead the way!"

Francisco was the only one of the brothers to call him the nickname given to him by their father. With a surge of pride and grim determination, he urged Castaño forth, trampling any natives in his path. His lance gushed forward, its eager edge searching for a path back to the city that the horse could follow. With Gonzalo at the point, the rest of the men fell into a formation like flying geese behind him, parting the native horde on their journey back through the dense jungle of bodies—it closed back up behind them, sending still more projectiles in their wake.

"I didn't expect so many rocks," Hernando said when they got back to the town square and dismounted. "It's like they're breaking up the mountain into small pieces."

"Maybe they want to bury the city," Juan said with a laugh. He was at the stables when the embattled group returned.

A single stone fell to the earth and tumbled to their feet. Then, low thumps rang out from the awnings when more followed.

"They're sending them in from the edge of the city!" Hernando cried out. They had never left the native war cries behind, but to Gonzalo it seemed as if they were now getting closer, squeezing the city and the Spaniards within.

Hernando began barking orders. He told some men to secure the horses in the stable, others to gather the supplies from out in the open and bring them into the large hall in Manco's palace that they used as headquarters, and the rest were responsible for making sure they had access to food and water as the majority of the Spanish forces took shelter in the palace. Native allies were stationed at other buildings surrounding the square with reminders that "if the city becomes overrun, you'll be killed just like the rest of us."

The fires started before the sun went down. Thick black smoke billowed up from the edges of the city; burning arrows arced through the sky into the buildings in the center, igniting the thatched roofs. Buildings would erupt as if by magic when struck by a stone, until one of them fell at Gonzalo's feet on his way back from Castaño in the stables and he realized they were red-hot, pulled from a fire and sent into the city's heart.

He had just got back into the palace, squeezing his way past his Spanish brethren in search of Hernando to tell him about the fire-starting stones, when thin white smoke started seeping down from overhead.

13

SPANISH WAR HORSES

HERNANDO, Gonzalo, and Juan, along with the wealthiest *encomenderos*, retreated into the adjacent rooms of the Incan palace as the African slaves, native allies, and poor Spaniards scampered to the sides of the large room, away from beneath the thatched roof. Tendrils of smoke poured down into the palace's large hall while the Pizarro brothers watched from an adjacent hall . . .

Then it stopped.

"Did it . . . did it go out?" Hernando said, walking forward into the abandoned open space.

"It looks like it," Gonzalo ventured.

"A miracle from the Blessed Virgin," Juan whispered. The handful of Spaniards still in the palace put their hands together and looked to the heavens, each man sending up his own private thanks.

One of their number stormed back into the palace. He looked up at the ceiling and, seeing that it wasn't aflame, hurried across the room to where the Pizarros stood. "They're everywhere," he said. "Every road out of the plaza is choked off by native forces."

The rest of the scared, haggard men from the stables appeared soon after, leaving the native forces in charge of its defense. Hernando prepared for their last stand inside the sturdy stone walls.

Smoke curled down from the roof again while the men prepared their defenses, again going out on its own. The third time it happened, a portion of the roof blackened before the spot stopped growing.

The room full of Spanish men, the trapped men of Cuzco, all fell to their knees and gave thanks to God.

Night fell, and the native army's attack ground to a halt. Gonzalo chanced leaving the palace under darkness, his path lit by the still-burning buildings, to check on Castaño. The jittery horse calmed when his owner appeared and strained on the rope keeping him in the stable when Gonzalo left him, headed back to the palace. On his way back, Gonzalo chanced a look out into the streets attached to the plaza.

Barricades built by the industrious attacking natives blocked off any potential escape route. In the distance, beyond the barriers, native warriors walked on the exposed walls now without roofs. Looking at the palace headquarters, he saw a handful of natives and the African slaves ready with buckets on the four corners of the roof, the rest lying on adjacent roofs.

A burning building collapsed in the distance, bringing Gonzalo back to the present. He hurried back into the palace and discovered Friar Valverde leading the terrified men in prayer. Swallowing the knowledge that the slaves had put out the flames instead of divine intervention, he fell to his knees and joined them.

Hernando stood up, placed a hand on the friar's shoulder, and nodded to the side, telling the priest without sound that he'd like to say a few words. The friar bowed his head and retreated.

"Men," Hernando began.

The men with their eyes closed opened them and saw the eldest Pizarro in Cuzco standing in front of them.

"I'll keep this short. Though we haven't been here long, this is now our home. We've already fought enormous odds in its capture; this is just another test. I'm asking you now, as Don Francisco's brother, to stand up and fight back against the native dogs instead of waiting for slaughter like some penned-up farm animal."

Juan also stood up and approached his brother. "Should we take the fight to them now, while they rest?"

Hernando shook his head. "We wait until tomorrow. We'll force the natives back with our superior willpower and with God on our side. Tonight, we rest and recover for the fight for our very survival. Not just for ourselves, but for Spain's presence in this land." The men nodded their agreement with a proud stoicism.

He ceded the floor once more to the friar, who announced he would be praying with the men and taking their confessions throughout the night.

The war cries began at first light the following morning as the native troops marched back into the city from their camps. The cacophony echoed off the buildings around the town square, stirring the Spaniards' hearts and dashing any trace of sleep from their eyes.

"Let's see how they handle this," Hernando said with an iron resolve from atop his horse. He stationed the bulk of the Spanish foot soldiers and all of the harquebuses at the southern entrance to the square, defending against native penetration into the heart of the city. The rest were split among the other three entrances. Their job, alongside their native allies, was the dismantling of the barricades so that the horses could press the attack.

"We're taking the fight to them," Hernando had said the night before.

As Gonzalo watched from his perch on Castaño, the native allies and Spanish foot soldiers rushed forward and started pulling apart the barriers in the street ahead of him. Hidden native archers punished anyone who exposed their flesh for too long with long, straight arrows that whistled through the air. As soon as a wide-enough crack appeared, Gonzalo put spurs to his horse and bounded into the waiting native forces in the broad avenue beyond.

Castaño, bred for battle, stomped and kicked, bit and twisted, while his rider maintained distance between them and the native forces with his lance. Arrows bounced off their armor and fell to the ground, broken on the Earth by the hooves of fifteen attacking horses. After decimating the native warriors in their vicinity and making it all the way to the edge of the city, where their horses had a definite advantage on the open ground, one of the cavalrymen told Gonzalo that "they could handle themselves, go check the other groups."

Gonzalo looked around at the carnage before pulling on the reins of his war beast. He went back to the plaza and reported to his brother. "That street's cleared for now," he said.

"Good. Juan just went to reinforce that one," Hernando replied, pointing to the street to the north. "Go check on the one to the east; I'll make sure the foot soldiers maintain their position."

Gonzalo galloped across the plaza in the direction of the still-rising sun, using a hand as a shield against the morning's bright rays. He leapt his horse over the dismantled barricade and, in the distance on his right, saw a wall topple over onto two horses and their riders. Urging Castaño to a gallop, he charged forward as the native warriors who pushed over the wall crawled over the stones with their axes and maces held high.

At the same time, another group of natives emerged from the adjacent building. Despite the difference in their dress from the warriors, Gonzalo feared the Spaniards would be lost before he arrived. However, some of the new arrivals started pulling the fallen Spaniards from the rubble while the others held the attacking warriors at bay. The horses writhed on the ground after taking the brunt of the fallen wall's weight, unable to get up. The thrown riders, clutching swords in shaky hands while half standing, half wobbling with the support of the native allies, swung their blades in wide arcs, forcing the attacking natives back. Their allies separated from them, scared of getting caught in the wild attack.

"Santiago!" Gonzalo roared at the top of his lungs.

The native warriors turned and saw the finest Spanish horse in the New World barreling down the road toward them, atop which sat a furious Gonzalo with his sword in one hand and a lance in the other.

Neither of the stunned Spaniards on the ground realized anything had changed, and they continued the wild swings of their swords, catching one of the surprised warriors on the shoulder. Before the blade dislodged from flesh, Gonzalo's lance had skewered the man, the force of the blow knocking the man to the ground. The sword followed, leaving the horseless Spaniard swordless as well.

The men on the ground didn't need their weapons. Gonzalo and Castaño made quick work of the tricksters, cursing them for resorting to duplicity instead of fighting.

Gonzalo made his horse prance in circles over the fallen warriors' bodies. Then, dismounting, he sliced the throat of both wheezing horses after confirming that they were beyond recovery.

"Sorry, brothers. You're both out of a horse," he said, wiping his blade on a fallen warrior's cotton armor.

"We owe you our lives," one of the men said, holding a hand to his chest with a small bow.

The other man bent down on one knee.

Gonzalo gestured to the native allies peering at him through the nearby doors. "Come here and help them back to the square," he said. Then, addressing the healthier of the two men, he said, "And you don't owe your lives to me. You owe it to them."

Getting back on his horse, he returned to the main eastern avenue and helped the cavalry repel a native attack. No matter how many the Spanish forces killed, there were more native warriors available to take their place. Native axes and maces couldn't kill through Spanish armor, but they did cause a good deal of pain and made a lot of noise. The armor was more or less the same among the native warriors, the difference being color, but the shields were of two distinct varieties: round and square. Each shield type had an associated fighting style. Those with square shields preferred an overhead strike, aiming for a knockout blow, while those with round shields used a quick blow before striking with the shield itself, either the edge on an exposed foot or chin or the brunt of the shield pushed into the opponent while making space.

A third type of shield appeared as the day wore on, a long rectangular shield worn on the backs of men with their arms and faces painted deep black. Gonzalo saw a group of men with this type of shield running along the burned walls towards his position, but to his surprise they never came down to Earth. Instead, they took up kneeling positions and withdrew longbows, notching arrows before a direct attack on the horses.

Gonzalo ordered a retreat after Castaño suffered a minor wound from the second arrow. Back in the plaza, he took off his helmet and swore. "Who were those painted men?" he asked a native ally standing nearby.

"They're from the Antisuyu—the jungle realm. They're the cloud warriors."

"I'm telling you, they were hitting at the small spaces between his armor," Gonzalo said to Hernando, handing over the reins of Castaño to the stable hand. He held up two fingers. "In a space this small."

The men took turns resting in the plaza for a quick meal while native allies replaced them at the front lines. Hernando was content with maintaining their hard-won positions—including the open field beyond the western edge of the city—until the men were fed and watered. Later, he called for a final push before nightfall so that any barricades erected by the Incan builders weren't so close to the plaza. But the Incan generals had a surprise in store for the Spaniards.

Horses had been the best Spanish weapon against the native troops since they captured Atahualpa in Cajamarca. No native warrior got close without risking an attack from sharp hooves and biting teeth, and the men on top were out of range for close-quarters combat while their armor protected them from arrows and stones. What they needed was a weapon that could take down a horse, and the late afternoon battles were the testing ground for a known method of taking down deer used by lowborn hunters from the realm in the south called Qullasuyu, the men who didn't have access to metal or arrows.

Since he preferred riding at the head of his men, Gonzalo was one of the first Spaniards these hunters attacked. His horse walked at a slow trot past the dismantled barricade along the eastern avenue. Native allies walked along his flanks, with the rest of his cavalrymen riding behind.

A solitary native man appeared up ahead. He wore a simple leather tunic with a red-and-white cape tied around his neck. In his hand was a series of long cords that almost touched the ground, each one weighted at the end.

Gonzalo charged, and the man crouched without fear. Then, the hunter started spinning the cords in his hand around his head.

Confused, Gonzalo withdrew his sword. He realized the weapon's unique power at the last moment and pulled on the reins with all his strength.

Castaño reared up on his hind legs as the man unleashed his weapon. The cords splayed out wide with the centripetal force of the attached weights; the center crashed into the horse's hind legs and the momentum of the weights spun them around twice, freezing the distance between two of Castaño's four limbs. Stunned, the horse brought his front two legs crashing down and stumbled forward, his hind legs useless.

The hunter smiled and disappeared behind the nearest building.

"Cut this damned thing off me!" Gonzalo roared at the natives he had left behind in his impatient attack. He scanned the tops of the nearby buildings for more of the cloud warriors, knowing he was exposed.

Without regard for potential attack, two of the native allies rushed forth and cut the leather cords, freeing the horse's legs. Stones inside leather pouches fell to the street.

"Two natives with every horse in case they do it again!" Gonzalo commanded.

The hunters struck again throughout the rest of the early evening's light skirmishes, even causing a few stumbles and fallen riders, but the natives cut the horses free each time before any real damage occurred. After clearing the eastern route all the way to the open fields beyond the edge of the city, Gonzalo trotted back to the central plaza in a good mood as the sun dipped behind the mountains ahead of him.

The pleasure of his achievement evaporated when he saw Juan's face.

According to Juan, the hunters had launched their bolas at his group too. Although Juan's horse emerged untouched from its first encounter with the new weapon, one of his men fell to the ground along with his horse when all four of the animal's legs became trapped.

The fallen man hadn't moved.

Juan relayed how he had dismounted, rushed forward, and started dragging his comrade to safety.

"Then, out of nowhere, a stone struck me right in the jaw," Juan said. His hand gestures made up for his slurred, heavy speech. He turned to the left side and showed his brothers the space below where his helmet protected—there was an indentation on his right jaw where there should have been solid bone.

"Well, I made sure Pedro was safe before I went and killed every one of them," Juan said, drool dribbling from the right side of his face. "They just kept coming though."

"It's that damned fortress," Hernando said, looking north at Saqsaywaman. "They just keep pouring out from there, right into the city streets."

"Not many open spaces for the horses in that direction either," Juan added.

Gonzalo felt a twinge of self-consciousness. Had they first given him the western route because they knew it was the least susceptible to attack, then the eastern route because he wasn't as good as Juan? "What if we take it?" he said.

Juan lifted his eyebrows and looked at Hernando.

The eldest Pizarro brother in Cuzco looked at the stone fortress rising above the city once more. "Honestly, I think it's our only shot of surviving this."

That night, while making battle plans, Juan convinced Hernando that, despite his injury, he should be in charge. "Let me get my revenge," he said.

Hernando nodded, his eyes filled with sadness.

Fifty horsemen rode out early the next morning. They didn't head to the north, towards the fortress; instead, they rode to the northwest, fighting their way out of the city through the native forces that had encroached on their hard-won territory overnight. Once out of the city, they turned to the right, approaching Saqsaywaman from the north—approaching from any other direction was even more of a suicide mission. As opposed to the southern side of the fortress, where the walls almost touched the city, the northern side had a wide plain where the Spanish cavalry could approach.

Knowing the fortress's weakness, the Incan generals had constructed barriers all along the plain. The Spaniards atop their horses fought through the masses without losing a single man. Their prize? A series of three terraced walls, on top of which stood the three recognizable connected towers—one conical, the other two rectangular. Upon each terrace stood hordes of native warriors staring down at the attackers.

Gonzalo and Juan led a series of charges against the lowest of the stone walls. The closer they got, the darker the day became from the increased volume of projectiles flying through the air. Three times that morning the Spaniards pressed then retreated, each time frustrated at their lack of progress.

Out of range of the native attacks, Juan discarded his helmet in anger. "This thing's killing me!" he said, prying open his tender jaw. Upon seeing Gonzalo's concern, he added, "I'll hold a shield over my head," picking up a discarded one from the battlefield.

Juan began pacing. "I have an idea, but you aren't going to like it," he said to Gonzalo. "Talking about holding my shield overhead gave me an idea . . ."

He was right. Gonzalo didn't like it one bit, but he didn't have a choice but to follow orders from his older brother.

The Spanish cavalry galloped towards the door at the center

of the lowest wall. It was sunken into the terrace, the passage to the door cut into the Earth so that native forces could look down on anyone approaching. When the attackers got close, they leapt from their horses and used native shields as protection against the incoming missiles.

"Santiago!" the men cried as stones and arrows fell on their head. They amassed at the door and, with a mighty push that required every ounce of their combined strength, forced their way through . . .

Where they found more natives on the stone steps that ended at the first terrace. The defenders on the walls at their sides poured bucket after bucket of rocks on the Spaniards, burying them in rubble.

Spanish knees at the front of the attack buckled, and they took a step back.

Juan, who rejected anything except forward progress, lunged forward with his sword and hacked at the closest native on the stairs. In doing so, he forgot about shielding his head.

As Gonzalo watched, the largest native man he had ever seen, with gold plugs in his ears and a jagged scar running the length of his face, lumbered into view with a large stone held overhead. Before he could warn his brother, the native threw the boulder—it struck Juan's head, leaving the leader of the assault in a heap.

14

THE FORTRESS ABOVE CUZCO

Somehow, Gonzalo rallied the men, commanding they cover Juan's body with their shields during their retreat. The natives, having already lost the passageway to the stairs up to the first terrace, let the men go so that they could take back the staircase and rebuild the door.

In a single stroke, the Spanish advance floundered and the Incan army gained a victory.

Back in the field and no longer in range of native projectiles, Gonzalo looked back at the fortress and saw the enormous warrior standing in front of a fire while holding a massive battle-axe overhead with one hand. Looking down at the lifeless Juan, a deep gash on the side of his sunken skull, he swore revenge. A single angry tear fell from his eye.

Gonzalo left thirty horsemen in the field outside Saqsay-waman and took Juan's body back to their headquarters in Cuzco with the other nineteen under the cover of night.

"Let me take the fortress—I'll have my revenge," Gonzalo said to Hernando after telling his brother about the imposing native warrior. "I can't get his face out of my head," he added.

Hernando stood up from his seat and put a hand on the

grieving Gonzalo's shoulder. "You're in charge now," he said. "Go back to your men and don't come back until you've taken the fortress!"

An inspired Gonzalo stood, kissed Juan's cold hand, then left, rejoining the men in the field for a few hours of rest before fighting resumed the next morning.

"Wake up, señor," Gonzalo heard in the distance. He was swimming across a river towards the woman who had rejected him in Spain. The flowing water pulled at the skirt of her dress while she called out to him, standing in the river up to her knees. Her father, friends with Gonzalo's father, waved Gonzalo forward with his hands as if beckoning a son who had just learned to walk. No matter how fast Gonzalo swam, or what angle he took against the rapid flow, the woman he loved kept getting farther away . . .

"Wake up!"

Gonzalo sat bolt upright. The morning mountain air hit his lungs, and goose bumps erupted along his arms.

"There's something you should see," the Spanish soldier said.

Realizing where he was, Gonzalo looked towards the Incan fortress. There, on the terraces, stood more native warriors than had been there the day before. They stood shoulder to shoulder, staring out into the field. Despite their numbers, he had no problem finding the largest among their group—the man stood a full head above the rest and was as wide as two of them put together.

"Manco sent reinforcements," Gonzalo said through gritted teeth.

"Sure looks that way," another one of the men said. He handed Gonzalo a hot corn mush ladled from a pot stirred by a native ally.

Gonzalo stood, holding the warm bowl with both hands

while he walked to Castaño. Between sips, he laid heated hands on his horse, hoping his animal absorbed some of the warmth in preparation for the day's exertion.

"It'll be a fight just to maintain this position," Gonzalo whispered to Castaño. The horse pressed his nose against Gonzalo's head and huffed. "You're right; nothing we can't handle."

Gonzalo and the other forty-eight cavalry were making the final preparations for resuming the fight when a native ally arrived and reported the heavy fighting in Cuzco.

"They attacked as soon as the sun came up. The streets are littered with bodies of the enemy, but the men are holding strong. Señor Hernando wanted me to tell you to make quick work of capturing Saqsaywaman to distract the natives in the city—" The messenger looked at the fortress. "But it looks like you might have a longer day of fighting than they do."

"Tell him we'll do what we can."

The native messenger scampered off, back through the safe passage between Cuzco and the field outside of Saqsaywaman still controlled by the Spaniards.

There wasn't a formal start to the day's engagement. The Spaniards sat atop their horses as soon as Gonzalo climbed onto Castaño, and they pushed forth in unison when Gonzalo's horse took its first step. Throughout the day, they would push forward into the range of the native projectiles, then wait while wave after wave launched from the fortress. There would be a point when the enemy decided they had sent enough arrows and stones at the Spaniards and the horses would gallop towards the lowest terrace, crashing into the natives stationed out front. After a period of slaughter, reinforcements would drive the Spaniards back through sheer volume, pushing the fight away from the fortress where the cavalry would mow down the natives in the open field. After every native push, the Spanish force would water their horses, catch their breath, then repeat the entire endeavor.

It was exhausting. The cavalrymen and their horses lasted less time on each successive push, but the natives, replenished from their vast store of men, continued driving the Spaniards back with a ferocity the Spaniards hadn't seen before. By the end of the day, the cavalry were waiting for a pause in the projectiles, galloping forward, then turning right around, hoping eager warriors followed them in pursuit of glory. Of course, the natives stood no chance against the horses—they fell soon after leaving the fortress' shadow.

Gonzalo kept an eye out for a massive warrior running across the field, hoping for revenge, but the warrior stayed perched on the first wall while commanding his forces.

Incan fires twinkled from the terraces as the sun went down. Gonzalo's men, sporting deep gashes and dark bruises but all still breathing, stayed at their temporary field camp, watching the bustling fortress.

"I don't think they'll attack again until tomorrow," Gonzalo said to his ragged men.

"There are so many of them," one man said.

"Don't know if the horses can make it all day tomorrow," said another.

Everyone present knew that he wasn't just talking about the horses. Two days of hard fighting had left many of them with dark circles around tired eyes; some of the men had started lying down between skirmishes that afternoon.

"Once we're sure they're done for the night, I'll go talk to Hernando and see what he thinks," Gonzalo said.

Back in the palace headquarters, Hernando told Gonzalo that he had been worried about the fighting men outside the fortress. "It's been tough down here too, but the native allies are a big help."

"Plus, maintaining a position isn't the same as taking one. Here, they come to you and you can cut them down as they approach," a weary Gonzalo said. On his way back into the city, he had seen piles of dead native warriors on every street corner, gathered and stacked by their allies.

"I know, I know," Hernando said. He smiled, his excitement evident. "I've got a plan."

An exhausted Gonzalo followed his brother through the plaza towards the cathedral's construction site. The main building's skeleton cast long shadows under the light of the full moon.

"One of our native friends was telling me about tonight's celebration," Hernando explained. "He said that Villac Umu himself is in the fortress tonight so that he can welcome the new moon from the highest accessible point."

"The mountains are higher though," Gonzalo replied, confused. He wondered if the physical exertion of the prior two days plus his lack of sleep, food, and water was clouding his thinking.

"You're right, but I think they prefer man-made structures. Something about their own efforts bringing them closer to the sky." Hernando waved a hand. "But that's beside the point. What's important: there's a ceremony tonight."

Gonzalo shrugged.

"And that's when we'll attack," Hernando said, slapping his fist into an open hand.

"They don't like fighting at night anyway . . ." Gonzalo added. "But they have entire camps on each terrace, with lookouts watching all night."

The brothers turned the corner around the building. In the open space beyond were a dozen wooden ladders. "I had the slaves work on these all day," he said. "The natives helped with the wood collection."

Gonzalo's eyes grew wide.

"I'm taking thirty-six men and twelve natives. We'll go up first, clear the area, then the natives will bring the ladders up behind us."

"And what do you want us to do?" Gonzalo asked, thinking of the men back in the open field.

"Watch and wait—you'll know when to attack."

Gonzalo ate a quick meal with his brother, received a blessing from Friar Valverde, then went back to his men. The ones who were sleeping cursed when they were awoken, but their eyes soon glittered in the firelight. "We have to be ready—we're taking the fortress tonight."

The men stayed by their fires—so any enemy spies wouldn't grow suspicious—and they kept their horses close. An hour passed, then two. The moon hung overhead, illuminating the field full of dead bodies with a spectral glow.

Native shouts on the night breeze drew their attention. "This might be it," Gonzalo announced. He waited until he saw movement in front of a fire, then stood up. "Let me go make sure," he said while climbing onto Castaño. From atop his horse, he saw a torch waving on the first terrace.

"Let's go, men!" he cried.

The Spaniards all hopped onto their horses, the exhaustion from the day before evaporating from their bones. They charged with every drop of speed their spent horses still possessed, arriving at the first terrace's door; it was wide open. The sound of fierce fighting emanated from above: steel on wood and stone, dying yelps from surprised men. Ditching their horses, they surged up the stairs and found bodies strewn throughout. Upon arriving on the second terrace, they found a host of warriors with their backs turned to them—since the Spaniards arriving on ladders were coming from the other direction—and made quick work of the unsuspecting men.

"It worked!" an exultant Hernando said when he saw

Gonzalo. They touched swords and turned towards the third terrace. Six of the surviving ladders rested on the wall where Spanish forces were navigating buckets of rubble, flying arrows, and thrown stones.

There, on the terrace wall, was the massive warrior staring down at the two Pizarros.

"That's the man who killed Juan. I'll kill him myself."

"No!" Hernando said, turning on his brother in surprise. "I told the men to capture him alive if possible. He's been on every terrace wall, pushing back our men and destroying the ladders. I even saw him kill one of his own men who tried to flee!"

"He killed our brother, and you want him alive?" Gonzalo asked, incredulous.

"The most courageous native we've encountered in the New World thus far—he deserves the respect we give enemy officers."

Gonzalo opened his mouth for a further argument, but Hernando held up a hand. "I've already given the order," the older brother said. The imposing native disappeared behind the edge of the wall . . . then reappeared a moment later holding a Spaniard who had just climbed onto the third terrace in a bear hug. He tossed the man down from the top of the wall as if tossing a sack of grain.

"Impressive, but pointless," Hernando said. Then, turning to Gonzalo's men, he commanded they push the door carved into the third terrace's wall. "We're taking this fortress before the sun rises!" he yelled.

Gonzalo's men attacked the enemy at the door, fueled by cries of "Santiago."

Hernando lost two more men taking the third terrace. The native warrior, the one the Spaniards had begun calling "el diablo," retreated into the center tower while Spanish fighters stormed the other two, climbing up on ropes and ladders.

Soon, the Spaniards had killed all of the remaining natives except for the one man Hernando had commanded they take alive, the warrior who had killed Juan. They pinched in from both sides of the parapet while he swung his gargantuan battle-axe at the approaching men, skittering from left to right while preserving his distance. Gonzalo and Hernando stood beneath the towers, waiting; Hernando couldn't wait to meet the warrior, Gonzalo scheming ways he would kill him.

El Diablo looked down at the waiting Pizarro brothers, then looked at the Spaniards encroaching on his position. Realizing his hopeless situation and future, he dropped his axe with a mighty thud. He wrapped his cloak around him, looked at the moon, and jumped headfirst from the tower, landing at the feet of the Pizarros.

"Truly a great warrior," Hernando said in awe.

Gonzalo spit on the man's twitching corpse.

The Spaniards spent the rest of the night clearing the dead and fortifying their position.

"Didn't you say Villac Umu was here?" Gonzalo asked, kicking another body over the edge and onto the second terrace.

"We saw a group of men escape when we first climbed up," Hernando replied. "Must have been him." He looked around and put his hands on his hips. "Oh well, we got what we came for."

In taking Saqsaywaman, the Spaniards had killed more than three thousand native fighters; they had lost five of their own, including Juan Pizarro. From then on, the fortress above Cuzco hosted at least two dozen Spanish men, flanked by hungry black Andean condors who feasted on the dead natives and always stuck around hoping for more. The sole problem with the fortress was the lack of access to water, but the streams running through Cuzco made transporting fresh water to the stronghold simple.

Food became more of an issue as the siege wore on. The fires set by the natives had destroyed several grain depots, necessitating incursions into Incan-held lands for food and supplies. The cavalry helped escort native allies whenever possible, but they still lost men and horses whenever Manco's forces overwhelmed them while the scavengers were away from the city. Fewer men meant fewer mouths needing food, but also fewer defenders.

One question hung on the mind of every Spaniard under siege: Were reinforcements on the way? They wondered if Francisco knew about their plight, or if the men left behind as a garrison in Jauja had heard about the trapped Spaniards and were planning a rescue mission. There were so many natives in the land under Manco's control that there was a good chance that Francisco himself was dealing with a similar situation in Lima, staring out at hordes surrounding the city on the coast while his brothers were trapped in the mountains. If so, their slow deaths were inevitable.

As the weeks wore on and Spanish willpower waned, Manco himself provided the spark that would keep their fire burning bright through the dark days.

Hernando, unsure if Francisco was even still alive, had arranged for fifteen of the remaining cavalry to set out for the coast, reasoning that it was better than death. While preparations were underway, Manco's troops left a grisly package outside of the city: a handful of severed Spanish heads and a pile of letters.

The Spaniards under siege learned that Francisco had sent out four separate groups of reinforcements, that he had repelled Manco's initial attempts at taking Lima because of the flat ground surrounding the city, and that their brother had requested help from the other Spanish colonies in the New World. They also found out about the arrival of Francisco de

Carvajal, who Francisco swore was one of the finest officers in the world, having been in the Italian wars and participating in the Sack of Rome in 1527.

The Pizarro brothers also learned about their father's death back in Spain, and that Gonzalo's mother had passed away.

"I'm truly alone in this world," Gonzalo said after receiving the news, his full brother Juan no longer by his side.

"No, we're not!" Hernando said, holding the letter from Francisco aloft. "Our brother's still out there, and men are coming to help us. They're attacking him too—Manco's finding out that a taste of Pizarro isn't quite to his liking!"

"But why did they even give these to us?" Gonzalo mused, holding a handful of the bloodstained letters.

"Who knows? Maybe he thought the severed heads would scare us?" Hernando said, laughing.

Gonzalo couldn't accept the explanation. Later that night, he asked the native allies if any of them had spies within Manco's camp. "Look, I know you have family. Hell, some of you are even related to Manco! I just want to know how he got those letters and why he gave them to us."

One man, who had been with the Spaniards during the storming of Saqsaywaman, said he could ask his cousin—their mothers were sisters and she lived in a nearby village.

"See what you can find out," Gonzalo said.

He didn't have to wait long. The following day, the native man asked for a moment alone with Gonzalo.

"Manco has a general, Quizo, who's killed many Spaniards: all of the men that were on their way here," the native ally said.

Gonzalo thought for a moment. "That must have been nearly . . . two hundred men!" he said, recalling the information contained in the letters and guessing the numbers by the language his brother had used.

"In the mountains—" the native began.

"Where the horses are useless," Gonzalo said, finishing the man's sentence. "Manco wants us to know that we're not invincible," Gonzalo thought out loud. He thanked the informant without ever letting him finish and promised a reward that never materialized as he left in a hurry to find Hernando.

Hernando's eyes grew wide when he realized that the promised reinforcements weren't delayed—they no longer existed. "So we really are on our own," he said, his voice heavy with sadness but a stern resolve emanating from his gaze.

15

MANCO'S TRAP

THE WEEKS under siege turned into months. Hernando's can-do attitude returned. He made finding enough food and rationing it out for the Spaniards his personal mission while leaving their native allies fending for themselves, reasoning that, "They're used to living off the mountain land." Despite his best efforts, the Cuzco inhabitants became thin and gaunt, the constant deprivation of food combined with the stress of attacks adding years to their faces.

"We can't go on much longer like this," Gonzalo told his brother.

"I agree, but what else can we do?" Hernando replied.

The pair walked into the temporary hospital and were met with the particular stench of unwashed men confined to their beds. Men wounded in skirmishes outside the city limits lay on makeshift beds while Friar Valverde nursed them back to health. Twice in the past week alone, the priest had been woken up in the dead of night because men needed their last rites after a festering wound took over their bodies.

"They're not healing anymore without food," the priest said, inspecting an open gash on an *encomendero*'s leg. The man had been a blacksmith in Spain—his thick forearms a testament to his craft—and had brought his talents to the Andes mountains.

Gonzalo and Hernando looked around. The other seven men in the large room looked back at them through tired, crusted eyes.

No one knew if Francisco was still alive—were the letters Manco gave them with the severed heads sent before the Incan forces overran Lima? And where were the reinforcements from Spain's other colonies in the New World? It had been long enough that they could be marching to Cuzco at any moment, if they were coming at all.

The uninjured men outside of the temporary hospital had no more hope than Friar Valverde. At times it seemed to the two Pizarro brothers that they were upholding belief in success for every Spaniard still in Cuzco.

Everything changed in August.

Hernando had sent out a small group of foragers, his most successful. One of them had become close friends with a cunning native man, and their group often brought back meat and vegetables from local towns and solider outposts with minimal fighting. Although their covert trips of a few days didn't put a dent in the native forces, they also didn't put Spanish lives at risk—and there were many more lives at Manco's command than there were Spaniards.

The Spaniards in Cuzco waited for the resupply while limiting their activity and therefore limiting their caloric needs, resting between the native attacks. But while the foraging men were gone, the native attacks slowed to a crawl then stopped altogether. The resting men woke up from an afternoon siesta to the sound of thousands of hooves stomping on the city's stone streets.

Gonzalo looked out from his palace and saw a sea of llamas, with still more streaming in from the east. His mouth watered at the thought of meat. Riding a fresh wave of energy, he found the Spanish forager and native friend and gave them both a hug.

The Spaniard laughed; the native man blushed.

"Where did you get these?" Gonzalo said, looking at the herd.

"About half a day's ride from here," the Spaniard said. "I think it was for Manco's men, but they've all disappeared."

Gonzalo blinked twice. "Disappeared?"

"For the most part," the Spaniard replied with a smile. He pointed to his native friend. "He talked to a villager, an old man with a belly, who said that a lot of the fighting men went home to plant their fields. The ones who stayed behind headed towards Ollantaytambo, a fort a day or two's ride away to the northwest."

Gonzalo's jaw hung open at their sudden reverse in fortune. A hand struck him on the back and he stumbled forward.

"This is why they're the best!" Hernando said from behind his brother, his eyes wide at the influx of livestock.

Gonzalo didn't even grow mad at the surprise strike. He told Hernando about the withdrawal of Manco's forces and watched as a pensive look passed over his brother's face.

"At another fort just a day away . . ." Hernando said, his voice trailing off. He walked away in the direction of the palace headquarters.

Gonzalo oversaw the building of nine massive cooking fires in the town square. Without the risk of native attack, finding wood took little time, and soon the men were bringing in cartloads of felled and cut-up trees. Butchered llamas spun on spits while hungry Spaniards watched, two of the animals eaten as soon as they were done. Despite his brother's belief that their native allies could feed themselves, Gonzalo made sure they got some of the first taste of meat as well, knowing that they'd played an instrumental role in keeping the Spanish forces alive over the previous months under siege.

He reserved two of the roasted animals for the men in the hospital under Friar Valverde's care. The other hungry Spaniards complained that eight men and a priest couldn't eat so much meat at once, but Gonzalo didn't care—he knew Francisco would do the same.

"Where did you get all of it?" Friar Valverde asked when Gonzalo brought the first tray laden with meat to the wounded men.

"There's a lot more on its way," Gonzalo replied with a smile.

Native helpers brought more trays inside, filling the room with the smell of roasted meat.

"Manco disbanded a lot of his men so that they could go plant their fields for next year. We don't have to worry about them anymore," Gonzalo said.

"Until they come back," Friar Valverde said, his eyes darkening.

"We'll worry about that when the time comes. Now, just eat and regain your strength." Gonzalo looked around the room. "All of you."

Weak smiles and nods were all the response the weak men could muster.

For the rest of their lives, everyone at the banquet that night talked about how it was the best meal they had ever had. There wasn't much besides llama meat and boiled potatoes, the vegetable eaten by the Inca for thousands of years, but after scant meals for so long the combination's taste matched even the best cuisine in Spain. Hernando joined in the meal but not in the celebration, eating while distracted as rowdy conversation raged on around him.

Gonzalo leaned back in his chair, filled to the point of a

stomachache. "What are you planning?" Gonzalo asked his brother.

Hernando shook his head and looked at Gonzalo with cleared eyes. "Just grateful we have the chance to regain our strength," he said, looking around. "Though we probably should have stopped everyone from eating so much—if Manco attacked right now he'd make quick work of us."

Gonzalo's heart skipped a beat. "You think this was his plan?" he asked.

"If they hadn't stopped attacking during the day, I was going to say something. But I think we're all right."

Hernando looked into the crowd of men. Gonzalo, following his gaze, saw that he was looking at the Spaniard and his native friend as they shared a laugh.

"I trust him," Gonzalo remarked.

"I do too. But you can't deny how useless the men are right now."

Gonzalo looked around and grew disgusted. Some of the men were asleep with bones still in their hands, while others took large breaths in between bites while they forced more food down their throats.

"I shouldn't have let them butcher so many," Gonzalo said, his gaze falling. He caught sight of grease stains on his own shirt and swollen stomach and grew ashamed.

"Sometimes, morale is more important than vigilance. It's no secret that we all needed a boost," Hernando said. He took a long drink, set down his cup, and excused himself from the table.

"Wait—what's the plan?" Gonzalo asked, repeating his earlier question.

Hernando paused, looked at his brother, and chuckled. "I'll tell you tomorrow. Tonight, just enjoy yourself."

The lingering effects of gorging on llama meat lasted for

days. In the meantime, Hernando stayed holed up in his palace, having small meals brought to him instead of joining the men. Every time Gonzalo asked about the secrecy, Hernando just replied that he should make sure the men regained their strength and keep them in high spirits.

On the third day, when Gonzalo's digestive system regulated to the consistent intake of protein and fat, Hernando unveiled the next step in the Spanish conquest of the Incan Empire.

"We're going to capture Manco again," he said.

Gonzalo felt his insides churn. If he hadn't just come from relieving himself, he would have run to the nearest hole in the ground.

"At his fortress?"

"Some of the natives told me what they know about it. Similar to Saqsaywaman, there's a side on a mountain and a side that faces an open plain. We'll ride our horses right up to the gate."

Gonzalo hesitated then spoke his contrary thought. "But that didn't work here—what makes you think it will work there?"

"We'll have the element of surprise," Hernando said, his eyes twinkling.

"What about staying here and replenishing our stores? We have to get ready for when they come back," Gonzalo said. After a moment's pause, he added, "Which they *will* do."

"I know; and it's why I took so long in deciding. Look, we don't know where the reinforcements are, but we have to assume Francisco is still alive—if not, all hope is lost. Therefore, to help Francisco, we can attack Manco and put an end to his little rebellion."

Despite the macabre logic, Gonzalo realized the mad genius of his brother's plan.

The Pizarro brothers, eighty other cavalrymen, and a large contingent of native allies set out before the end of the week, after everyone had gained a bit of flesh on their bones and their digestive systems had acclimated to the increase in calories. Hernando had their native guide take them a roundabout way through obscure mountain passes—he swore it was to maintain the element of surprise. Gonzalo knew his brother was also avoiding the Incan General Quizo or anyone who had learned the man's strategy of attacking Spaniards in the mountains, where their horses were useless. But they had no choice but to travel through the treacherous terrain on the way to Ollantay-tambo from Cuzco; nobody could lay a trap if they took an unexpected route.

The trip to the Incan fortress took three days on horseback. Scouts sent to the top of the mountain reported that they'd looked down on the fortress from above, that it was built into the side of the steep mountain itself, protected by rocky outcroppings and stone walls.

"Can we get the horses down from above?" Hernando asked.

"We'd be lucky to descend from above ourselves without any of us falling to our deaths," one of the scouts reported.

"The horses are our best weapon," Gonzalo reminded his brother.

"I know, I know," Hernando said, running a dirty hand through his long, greasy hair.

"But on the other side is a broad, open valley. We could take the horses that way, no problem at all. There are terraces built into the mountain leading up to the fortress, but you've dealt with those before," the scout said.

Hernando nodded, agreeing with the man. Gonzalo swallowed his momentary revulsion at the spineless attempt at flattery.

"Rest up!" Hernando said to the men at the night council. "We're heading out before first light. With any luck, we'll have Manco in our clutches before tomorrow's sun sets." Striding off, he repeated the short speech to each gathered group of men instead of shouting it so all could hear.

The native scout woke Gonzalo up in the middle of the night. "Your brother asked me to wake him up when the moon was at its highest, but he rolled over in his blanket when I tried."

Gonzalo shook his head. He emerged from beneath his blanket, and the cold night air bit his skin through his frayed clothing. Hernando received a toe poke in the back; then, when that didn't work, a kick in the backside.

"Get up," Gonzalo said when his brother turned on him in somnolent anger.

Realizing the situation, Hernando shook his head while leaving his cheeks loose so they clapped against his teeth then sprang up. "Today's the day," he said with false cheer.

"Today's the day," his brother repeated.

The Spaniards broke camp and set out within minutes. They trekked around the mountains to the far side of the stream that trickled through the valley. A sea of barricades sprawled into the distance, culminating at a stone rampart at the base of the mountain. On the far side of the plain, the stone fortress keeping watch over the valley was visible in the moonlight.

"Crossing shouldn't be a problem—not a lot of water," Hernando remarked.

"Maybe there's another stream where they get their water, one closer to the actual fortress?" one of the Spaniards remarked.

Their native guide stared at the eastern mountain, where the first rays of the sun made the clouds above a bright mix of pink and orange.

"Maybe. Unless they didn't consider a source of water at

this fortress either. The natives don't have the same planning skills we take for granted," Hernando mused. After a moment's pause, as if divine inspiration had struck, he commanded they begin their approach. "Before they wake up," he said.

The cautious Spaniards passed by abandoned barricades while making as little sound as possible. Gonzalo heard a few of the snickering men whispering to each other in surprise, delighted at the success of their clandestine attack plan.

"Those native dogs built all these and don't even keep men in them."

"What kind of defenses let the attackers walk right up to the front door?"

"We'll just keep these here for when we have to defend this place for ourselves!"

Hernando slowed down his horse and rode alongside Gonzalo. "Let's just hope we're not too late to save Francisco from being overrun," he said.

Thinking about helping his brother sobered Gonzalo's racing heart. They were close to the stone wall at the base of the mountain; he could see a lance propped against the parapet's edge.

All of a sudden, the weapon disappeared.

"Wait," Gonzalo hissed to his brother.

Hernando continued on, undeterred.

"Wait," Gonzalo said, louder.

As Gonzalo watched, dozens of men stood on the top of the wall, their arms and faces painted black. Square shields on their backs framed their shoulders, and what Gonzalo thought was a lance was in fact one of their longbows.

"The cloud warriors!" Gonzalo shouted. He realized that their mission wasn't a surprise at all; in fact, it was a trap. "Get back!" he shouted.

It was too late. The spray of arrows clouded the sky,

throwing shadows over the Spaniards. Despite the protective metal armor covering the men and horses, the sheer number of arrows meant that some found the cracks of exposed flesh.

The Spaniards scrambled out of range of the arrows and regrouped, taking stock of the damage done by Manco's surprise attack.

"It's a bunch of flesh wounds," Hernando remarked. "Nothing we can't handle!" he shouted, attempting a fresh injection of courage into his men.

Gonzalo could see the effect of the surprise attack on the spirit of his forces: downcast eyes, slumped shoulders. Moments before, they had believed they were headed for a swift victory against an unsuspecting enemy. Now, they realized they were facing a prepared force of elite archers. Who knew what else lay behind those walls?

"We might need a new strategy," Gonzalo said to Hernando in front of all of the men.

"A new strategy? We're here to take Manco back into our custody—that's the strategy!" He laughed, a condescending bark Gonzalo had hated since the two of them were children.

Juan had hated their brother's laugh too; remembering the detail filled Gonzalo with sadness.

Hernando looked at the oldest of their group, an *encomendero* with a gray beard and deep lines around his eyes. "Well, the young ones seem to think we're crazy."

"That's what they told me back in Spain too," the graybeard replied.

"Why don't we show them how crazy we really are?" Hernando said with a mischievous grin.

The *encomendero* shrugged. "What else do I have to do today?"

Together, Hernando and the eldest of their group galloped all the way to the walls, taking sharp, ever-changing angles during their approach so the arrows wouldn't find their mark. They touched the wall, drove their lances through a native defender each, then streaked back to the waiting Spaniards while arrows darkened the sky behind them.

"That was fun!" Hernando said after taking off his helmet.

"I've had worse mornings," the old man replied, laughing.

Gonzalo shook his head. He knew what their challenge meant despite it remaining unspoken. He turned to the other seventy-seven men. "First one through the door?" he said, pointing to the lone door in the rampart.

They all raced at the native defenders with cries of "Santiago!" while ignoring the stone and arrows pouring down on them. Outside of the door, they dealt with native foot soldiers wielding maces and bolas, the painted cloud warriors, and heaps of rubble poured over the edge onto their heads.

Gonzalo felt himself transported back to Juan's death. The bodies and sounds blended together until his heartbeat drowned them all out. Light from the sun, manageable in the morning, grew to a blazing source of pain in his eyes and head . . .

Until he heard a loud snap. One of the horses had stepped into a hole and broken its leg. The rider, on the ground after the stumble, hopped onto a friend's horse.

"Retreat!" Gonzalo said, turning Castaño around and racing away from the fortress. The arrows didn't follow. Confused, he turned and saw the native warriors streaming out of the single door at the base of the mountain.

"They're chasing us," he said to Hernando when he got back to the two waiting men. Hernando's horse lifted its feet, squelching mud with each step.

"Where did the water come from?" Gonzalo said.

"Who cares? Let's teach these dogs a lesson!" Hernando roared.

The cavalry held back the onslaught of the native forces as

the ground grew wetter around them, then as the water started flowing around their horses' feet. It wasn't until the water was almost at the horses' bellies that their movements became restricted—but still, the inexhaustible supply of native warriors trudged towards them.

"Manco diverted the river!" the graybeard said. "Must be why the stream was so low!"

The Pizarro brothers looked at each other. They knew it was the truth right away.

The Spanish forces retreated to Cuzco, traveling nonstop on the most direct path while being chased by native forces the entire way. Manco, as it turned out, had learned from General Quizo that stopping the Spanish horses offered the best chance for an Incan victory.

16

ALMAGRO'S RETURN FROM CHILE

MANCO'S FORCES harassed the Spaniards along all of the major routes in and out of Cuzco throughout the rest of 1536. The stranded men continued scraping by with the help of resupplies from their native allies; the hierarchy, with the Spaniards at the top, persevered in complete disregard of the native assistance received.

Escape to Lima had been floated among the Spaniards on multiple occasions, but after a few probes by the cavalry into the countryside, it became clear that Manco's primary concern was keeping the Spaniards entrenched in Cuzco.

The trapped Pizarro brothers learned about the fate of their older brother during the months after the failed attack on Ollantaytambo. Francisco, facing the famed General Quizo, had withstood numerous attacks before managing a death blow on Manco's prized military leader. The loss of this single man's life had resulted in a complete retreat of the Incan army at Lima's door and, the besieged Pizarro brothers hoped, the imminent arrival of reinforcements from the coast.

A Spanish army arrived in early 1537, but it wasn't the one they expected.

"Two hundred men from Almagro's army are at Urcos but he's not . . ." Hernando said when Gonzalo arrived at Manco's abandoned palace. The large hall, used by the Incan Emperor for public spectacles, had two large doors facing the plaza that had survived the fires at the start of the siege with little more than black stains on the highest portions.

"Urcos?" Gonzalo said.

"Town on the Urubamba River half a day's ride from here," Hernando said. "The news came from a native farmer after the men took his land."

"Then we're saved! We can take the fight to Manco and we won't fail this time—" A look from Hernando interrupted Gonzalo's excitement.

Hernando shook his head. "No wonder you and Juan made a mess of things in Cuzco when the two of you were left alone. Juan never had a head for politics, but I had hoped you could see the scheming behind the scenes."

A bright red flush crept up Gonzalo's neck while he held back a sudden murderous urge.

Hernando launched into an explanation. "Almagro left for the south with five hundred Spaniards—less than half are now in Urcos. Now, if you were a one-eyed bastard coming back from the south with Manco's brother Paullu—who you'll remember went with Almagro—and you heard about your countrymen under siege, where would you go?"

"To Cuzco, to help them out."

"And if he's not here, where else could he be?"

Gonzalo's eyes opened wide when he realized the truth Hernando had laid out for him. "He went to see Manco!"

"Behind our backs," Hernando said with an emphatic nod.

One effect of the additional Spanish forces in the region became clear right away—the Spanish cavalry could traverse the countryside unmolested. Manco, because of either discussions with Almagro or fear for the loss of his own warriors, had withdrawn his troops from the areas surrounding Cuzco. But escaping to Lima was no longer an option—Almagro and his army would take Cuzco the second the Pizarro brothers and their men left, opening the question of the city's ownership all over again. This meant that the *encomenderos* still in Cuzco faced a problem that had first appeared years before, one that they had thought well behind them: they could lose their land to Diego de Almagro's followers if the one-eyed man took over Cuzco.

Gonzalo and a sizable contingent of Spanish landowners impressed upon Hernando the need for discussions with the army from the south once they realized the necessity for the continued occupation of Cuzco.

"What if Diego de Almagro died on the way back?"

"Could the native have been mistaken about Almagro not being there?"

"Perhaps they don't want to get caught in the siege themselves?"

"Maybe they found gold at Urcos!"

Convinced of the need for a meeting, the Pizarro brothers and a group of fifteen additional men rode out to Urcos as a light drizzle fell. They scanned the horizon for signs of troop movement and sent scouts out ahead searching for traps as they passed between grass-covered mountains and through native villages, annoyed at the distances without appreciating the vistas. Hoping they could return to Cuzco before sundown, they rode their horses hard.

The Spanish army from the south had made camp on the shores of a blue lagoon. The two forces spotted each other over the water, and the group from Cuzco watched a small force leaving the main camp headed in their direction while they continued their approach.

One of the men from Almagro's army rode forward alone when the two groups were within shouting distance of each other. In response, the two Pizarro brothers rode forward by themselves.

Gonzalo soon recognized the man approaching him and his brother. It was Rodrigo Orgóñez, Almagro's second-in-command. His face and horse were gaunt, and his clothes hung together by a thread.

"You made it back alive," Hernando said when the three men met. The sun peeked down on them through the light-gray clouds, warming the ground. The resulting steam clung to their clothes and condensed on their skin in beads of salty moisture, further matting their greasy hair.

"We did," Orgóñez said.

"And Almagro?" Gonzalo asked.

"He made it back alive too," Orgóñez said.

"He's not here," Hernando observed.

"No, he's not."

"He went to see Manco, didn't he?" Hernando said, his voice quavering with rage.

"With Paullu, yes. The native was very excited at the prospect of seeing his brother once again after our trip south."

Hernando stared, enraged.

"Did you find anything on your expedition?" Gonzalo asked. Based on Orgóñez's appearance, the men had found nothing but hardships.

"Mountains covered in snow, a desert no man should cross."

"And the natives?"

"More stubborn than those here, if you can believe it. They somehow captured three of our scouts one time, early in the trip," Orgóñez said with a faraway look in his eyes. "In response, we sent the natives a message that blazed ahead of us no matter how far south we went."

"What was the message?" Gonzalo asked, still aware of his seething brother beside him.

"We gathered thirty of their local chiefs and burned them alive. Took a few days but saved us a lot of future problems."

Gonzalo raised his eyebrows and crinkled his chin, impressed at the forward thinking.

"Cuzco will never be yours," Hernando said, breaking his silence.

Orgóñez turned cold eyes on the older Pizarro. "You don't really have a choice in the matter. From what I understand, you hardly have enough men to occupy the place."

The two men stared at each other, Orgóñez with a smile on his lips and Hernando flexing his jaw.

All of a sudden, Hernando withdrew his sword. He pointed it at Orgóñez. "What if we save ourselves a lot of future problems and cut you down right here?" He looked around at the blue waters, the mountain peaks rising in the distance, and the lush greenery dripping with moisture. "There are worse places to die."

The men behind Orgóñez started forward but were stopped by a raised hand from their leader. "Killing Spaniards now? Why, worried you won't have enough food for the extra mouths?"

Gonzalo took out his own weapon; Orgóñez didn't flinch.

It was no secret that Gonzalo was one of the best fighters wherever he went, and with Hernando by his side, the insolent Spaniard didn't stand a chance.

Instead, Hernando laid his sword over Gonzalo's and forced his brother's sword down.

Orgóñez laughed. "It seems you remembered how to count!" he said.

Nobody talked on the way back to Cuzco. Hernando asked

for a native messenger the second they walked into the palace that served as headquarters.

"Remind Manco that Almagro has no claim on this land, that Francisco is the king's man in this empire, and that Almagro claiming otherwise shows his treacherous soul," Hernando said. He handed over an accompanying letter so that Diego de Almagro could receive Hernando's words himself and confirm to Manco that the messenger spoke the truth.

The native messenger returned a week later without a hand.

"Who did this?" Hernando demanded while the native man held his wrist, bandaged where his hand used to be. "Manco?"

The man shook his head no. "A bearded man with one eye."

"Almagro," Gonzalo said.

Hernando cursed and dismissed the unfortunate man.

Gonzalo sighed. He didn't need his brother's political acumen or translation; it was clear that Manco had taken a side in the Spanish feud and left the Pizarros out in the cold.

The brothers spent the rest of the day debating possible courses of action. While they were in possession of the city everyone coveted, they also had the fewest available men and resources.

"The first thing we need is a truce; keep Almagro at bay until we figure out what to do," Hernando said. Another messenger set out for Urcos at first light the next day, Hernando reasoning that Almagro wouldn't dare attack Cuzco without his full army behind him.

Word trickled in from Ollantaytambo about a battle between the Incan and Spanish forces. From what the Pizarro brothers could discern, Manco had launched an attack on Almagro's camp and had suffered enormous casualties as a result.

"So they can still fight," Hernando muttered in between bites while he ate lunch with Gonzalo. "I was beginning to wonder if their blades had dulled after so long away."

"They have horses, so they have the upper hand," Gonzalo remarked before taking a bite of stewed llama meat and potatoes.

"Speaking of horses: Have we had any luck with the foals?"

Gonzalo swallowed and nodded. "They're growing fast now that we have a steady supply of food for them. Castaño's sired three born in the last month, and two more mares are now pregnant."

"They should be larger than they are now," Hernando said, shaking his head in disappointment.

"We were fighting for our survival; any extra food went to us."

"*They* are going to be our survival," Hernando said under his breath.

A man named Rui Diaz rode into Cuzco on a worn-out horse with Almagro's response to the suggested truce. Before heading south with the one-eyed Spaniard, Diaz had been a friend of both the Pizarros and the Almagristas despite having arrived with Almagro's reinforcements when they showed up at Cajamarca. Diaz and Juan had been good friends, riding together the entire trip from Cajamarca to Cuzco.

The Pizarro brothers found the Almagrista at Juan's tomb in the monastery built atop Coricancha. After hearing about his arrival in the city, they had waited in Manco's abandoned palace, imagining that the rider would request an audience straightaway. Their spies brought the brothers to the monastery when he didn't show up, where more of their men stood watching Almagro's man from the back of the nave.

Gonzalo and Hernando approached Diaz from behind as he knelt in front of Juan's tomb. It was a simple stone rectangular cuboid on a raised stone platform. At chest height, on the stone lid, sat Juan's helmet and sword.

"Imagine arriving in a city, eager to see an old friend, then being directed here by giggling men when you asked for their whereabouts," Diaz said without turning around.

"He died fighting—" Gonzalo began.

Hernando laid a hand on his brother's arm, stanching the flow of information.

"What does Almagro say?"

"He says the truce is fine," Diaz said with a dismissive wave of his hand. He stood up with great effort, bringing one knee up then pushing against it for support. "We're not getting any younger," he said with a smile.

"Don't we know it," Hernando said, his face a cold mask. "Come to the palace—we have a lot to discuss."

During the walk, Diaz revealed that Almagro never stopped believing that Cuzco fell within the land granted him by the king.

"That's ridiculous. The king extended Francisco's land even farther south; I procured the extension myself," Hernando said.

"And still Cuzco doesn't lie clearly in either sphere," Diaz replied.

Hernando grabbed Diaz's shoulder and spun the man so that they were facing each other. "Are you calling me a liar?" he demanded.

"No, señor, I wouldn't dare. I'm merely offering Almagro's point of view," Diaz said with a shrug.

Almagro's man told them all about the situation between Almagro and Manco. The Pizarro brothers' meeting with Orgóñez had far-reaching consequences—Manco, discovering that the two armies had met near the lagoon, assumed that they were working together. That's what had precipitated the attack on Almagro, forcing the one-eyed man back to Urcos without hope for an alliance with Manco.

"So he was going behind our backs! Did he think Francisco would allow it?" Gonzalo said.

Hernando pried open his clenched jaw enough for a sip of wine.

"With all due respect, Almagro and Manco united wouldn't have much trouble dealing with him."

Gonzalo realized the truth of Diaz's words and crossed himself, thankful for God's grand plan keeping them safe from the snakes lying unseen behind obstacles in their path.

"How do you know that's why Manco attacked?" Hernando said, his eyes narrowed in suspicion.

"I was with him before I came here," Diaz said without apprehension. "I knew Manco well before I left, and I thought maybe I could facilitate an agreement between our parties. Almagro had no idea about my plan; he thought I was headed straight here. Unfortunately, I might have made things worse," he said with a sigh.

"Even after you told him that our groups weren't working together?" Hernando pressed.

"He seemed to think for a moment after that information came to light. Then, he asked me another question—he kicked me out after I answered."

The Pizarro brothers sat in silence, waiting.

"He asked if all the mountains were made of gold and silver, and if he, Manco, gave all this treasure to the King of Spain, would he withdraw the Christians from the Four Realms?"

Gonzalo groaned. Hernando closed his eyes and laid his head back.

"I told him no, then he dismissed me."

Hernando rested his elbow on the chair's arm, then rested his chin on his hand. "And now you're dismissed for a second time. Go, tell Almagro that we'll refrain from hostilities until we measure the true dividing line between our lands."

Rui Diaz hadn't even left the city before Hernando began

its fortification, going against the terms laid out in the initial truce sent to Almagro's camp.

Almagro might have attacked Cuzco if he had heard about the Pizarros strengthening themselves in the city, but a new piece of information swung the balance of power well into the Pizarro camp and forced his hand.

Alonso de Alvarado, one of Francisco's men in command of more than five hundred Spaniards and hundreds of horses, was on his way to Cuzco. He had been far to the north, near Quito, when word from Lima brought his forces back south. The army was in Jauja, close enough for a meaningful impact on any future hostilities.

The Pizarro brothers heard about Manco's response to the newest arrival first. Now facing the potential for hostilities against three Spanish armies, he left Ollantaytambo for Vitcos, doubling the distance between his headquarters and Cuzco.

They didn't have to guess *what* Almagro's response would be; the sole question was *when*—it had to be before Alvarado arrived in Cuzco.

On a stormy night in the middle of April, the entirety of Almagro's forces descended on Cuzco. The cavalry took up positions on all major roads in and out of the city while Orgóñez went in search of the Pizarro brothers.

Gonzalo woke up inside Manco's abandoned palace to a banging on the massive wooden doors. Along with Hernando and twenty of their finest fighters, they had slept in the head-quarters since the news of Alvarado's arrival, knowing the swing in fortune would inspire Almagro to action. Every man got out of bed, grabbed their weapons, and waited as the rain pelted down and thunder crashed overhead.

"Open the doors!" a deep, resonant voice yelled from the other side. Gonzalo recognized the voice—they had last met on the shores of the lagoon at Urcos.

"I wouldn't dare surrender to a lowborn soldier like you!" Hernando shouted. The men inside gripped their lances and swords tighter.

The noises outside of Manco's palace ceased after some more ineffective banging and shouting. Gonzalo looked around at the men standing with him, pride swelling in his chest. They smelled, their hair was long, and their beards were matted, the results of almost a year spent under siege. The Spaniards outside their door were just the latest obstacle that God would see them through . . .

A mighty crash, louder than any thunder, rang out from the double wooden doors. They bowed and splintered. The second crash dislodged a few pieces of wood, and on the third crash the doors came flying open.

Standing in the Cuzco plaza, soaked by pouring rain and framed by lightning, stood Orgóñez and thirty shouting men. The forces protecting the Pizarro brothers, standing their ground instead of pressing the attack, took out a handful of the invaders before Orgóñez shouted for a regroup.

Through the broken double doors, Gonzalo saw Orgóñez pointing to the thatched roof over their heads. Within minutes, flames emerged from the corners closest to the plaza; the roof's consumption approached their position in the middle.

"What should we do?" one of the fighting men asked.

Hernando and Gonzalo watched as the roof burned, both hoping the downpour would extinguish the flames like when Manco attacked almost a year prior. Luck wasn't on their side, and the rafters started falling on the outer edges of the large room.

Gonzalo looked at the men he had come to love as brothers. "We have to surrender," he said, taking responsibility for their protection.

Hernando stared at the roof, then looked out the double

doors at the grinning Orgóñez. He walked forward and tossed his sword to the ground at his enemy's feet.

Gonzalo followed, discarding his weapon at sword point. The rest of the men did the same, the last man leaving the palace as the roof collapsed behind them.

Through the driving rain, Gonzalo saw Cura Ocllo running away from his palace.

17

BROTHERS IN PRISON

DIEGO DE ALMAGRO kept the Pizarro brothers under lock and key within the same building of Manco's imprisonment: the monastery built atop Coricancha, the former Incan Temple of the Sun. The holy men living within ensured that the two prisoners from the aristocracy never lacked comfort or sustenance under the watchful eye of Almagro's most faithful men.

Almagro's takeover of Cuzco resulted in few changes for most of Cuzco's residents. In fact, realizing that he knew little about operating the former capital of the Incan Empire, he had placed one of the Pizarros' officers in charge of maintaining the city's operations. The average resident continued through their days the same way they had before, despite the officer answering to Almagro, other than dealing with the influx of Spanish troops that accompanied the usurper.

Francisco's one-eyed business partner often joined the imprisoned Pizarro brothers for their midday meal while they ate in shackles, discussing the political situation with the brothers under the pretense that they were fellow diplomats reviewing events within the city.

"Alvarado imprisoned our messengers," Almagro said

through a mouth full of food. "They should have been back from Jauja days ago."

"What did you expect? Honestly?" Hernando said after chewing and swallowing his food. The ranking Pizarro hadn't spoken much during their first weeks of meals together—leaving the pleasantries to Gonzalo—but the brutish conquistador wore down his resistance with good-natured camaraderie. It was the same disposition that inspired such fierce loyalty from his men.

"I expected him to honor my position in charge of the city," Almagro replied. He wiped his mouth with the back of his hand, then the back of his hand on his pant leg.

"You don't have to explain yourself to them," Rodrigo Orgóñez snarled. Neither the Pizarro brothers nor Orgóñez cared if he was at the meal, but Almagro insisted on bringing his second-in-command at least once each week. The Pizarro brothers and Orgóñez made no efforts at cordiality, instead speaking their minds without apprehension.

"It's what happens when your primary counsel is a soldier from a poor family," Hernando remarked as he took another bite.

Orgóñez slammed his hand on the table. "Noble blood runs through my veins, the same as yours!" he declared.

One of the worst kept secrets among the Spaniards in Cuzco was Orgóñez's real last name: Mendez. In fact, his brother Diego Mendez, also a member of Almagro's army, went along with Rodrigo's denial of their kinship in public but talked about it without reservation in private. In essence, Rodrigo claimed he was the bastard son of a nobleman in Spain in hopes of improving his station back home.

Gonzalo understood the motivations for the scheme; his goal in the New World revolved around proving his perceived worth in the eyes of the Spanish elite as well.

"Of course it does—no lowborn could capture men like us

from our home the way you did," Gonzalo said with a sly grin. He knew Hernando would call him submissive when they got back in their cell, but he found amusement in the feigned deference.

"That's right," Orgóñez said, sitting back down, ignoring or missing the sarcastic jab.

"We're marching on him tomorrow," Almagro continued, returning the subject back to Alvarado. "Our spies tell us that he's on the far side of the Abancay River. Half of his men are guarding the bridge and another group are in charge of protecting the lone ford downriver."

Orgóñez smiled. "And he has no idea about Lerma."

"Lerma?" Gonzalo said, a faint recollection of the last name floating like wisps of smoke in the back of his mind.

Almagro told the Pizarro brothers about the communication he had received from Pedro de Lerma, the officer in charge of protecting the ford. The man was tired of dealing with Alvarado, ashamed at their sham "protection of Jauja."

"He said Alvarado's staying put because he's scared of going against the Pizarros," Orgóñez interjected, smiling with meat tendons dangling from his teeth. "There's nothing worse than a breathing Pizarro. I tell Diego every day: cut their heads off! Dead men don't bite," he said before taking another ravenous bite of roasted llama.

"Well, the decision isn't up to you," Almagro said to his second-in-command.

"I guess we should be grateful," Gonzalo observed.

Almagro retook control of the conversation. "He said he'd allow us safe passage across the ford, where we can take Alvarado's back and force his surrender. We just have to hope this isn't some dishonorable ploy of Alvarado's . . ."

When Almagro and his men returned in July 1537, the Pizarro brothers learned that Almagro's foretelling of the battle rang true. The main force encountered Alvarado's men at the bridge crossing the Abancay River, each group maintaining their position until night fell. Then, under the cover of darkness, Orgóñez took half of the army down to the ford, where Lerma let them cross unmolested. In the morning, after seeing the reduction in Almagro's forces, Alvarado raced to the ford as the men with Almagro rushed over the bridge. Faced with attackers from both sides, Alvarado surrendered, his men following Lerma's example and joining the ranks of Almagristas.

They learned all of this from Alonso de Alvarado himself, now Almagro's third prisoner.

"Orgóñez was begging Almagro to let him attack your brother in Lima next," Alvarado said. The three men had nothing to do all day but talk, and it was the third time in as many days that Alvarado had told them about Almagro's upstart officer. "He kept talking about how he took my entire army from right under my nose, that he'd do the same thing to Francisco's city on the coast."

"And let me guess—Almagro got quiet and started thinking about the benefits of controlling a port city," Hernando said, his head leaning against the wall as he stared up at the ceiling.

"That's right. But Orgóñez keeps forgetting—"

"That Francisco is much better liked than you," Gonzalo interjected.

"I was going to say that he has fortifications built for defense," Alvarado began, his pride wounded. "But yes, that too, I suppose."

Meals with Almagro never included Alvarado. The Pizarro brothers kept waiting for word about a march on Lima, wondering if the one-eyed man's brashness extended far enough for a confession about upcoming action against their brother. Instead, they learned about Orgóñez's journey to Vitcos in pursuit of Manco.

"And there's going to be a celebration!" Almagro exclaimed, full of bluster and cheer. Beads of sweat had left streaks through the dust on his unwashed face. "We're crowning Paullu emperor!"

Manco's brother, another one of Huayna Capac's sons, had spent the previous two years with the Spaniards. As Almagro told it, Manco sent a message each day requesting that Paullu join him in Vitcos.

"Manco keeps saying that Paullu's duty is done—he thinks that his brother's still here because of his orders!" Almagro said, slamming the butt of his fork on the table. "He told me himself that he's not foolish enough to take up arms against us. He's seen what we can do!" Spit dribbled onto Almagro's beard while he laughed.

"Why attack Manco though? He's holed up in Vitcos," Hernando said.

"And now you have your own emperor. I'd let him rot there if I were you," added Gonzalo.

Almagro paused for a moment while he chewed. Uncharacteristic for someone who had no problems talking with his mouth full. "We don't want to leave ourselves open to attack."

"Of course," Hernando said. Both brothers knew that Manco could attack Cuzco if Almagro sent his men to Lima. But the one-eyed conquistador would have to deal with Francisco at some point; both of Francisco's living brothers were now prisoners. If Almagro didn't press Lima, Francisco would show up at his doorstep.

The Pizarro brothers finished the meal without saying anything more than vacuous pleasantries. They heard the celebration for Paullu's coronation from their cells, the partying city keeping them awake the entire night.

A triumphant Orgóñez returned without Manco but did bring back a valuable prize: Titu Cusi, Manco's son. They kept him imprisoned in the monastery but, since he was still young, they let him associate with the friars. They supplied him with a firm foundation in their religion, hoping he could one day replace Paullu and lead the natives of the country to Christianity. It was a newfound source of souls while Protestantism and Muslims pressed in on Christian Spain from all sides.

Almagro's second-in-command even showed up at the monastery soon after his return. Somehow, he had learned of Gonzalo's taking of the Incan queen, and he wasted no time in relaying news about her to her kidnapper.

"Guess who else just got away from us?" Orgóñez said after relaying the story of how Manco had escaped his grasp in Vitcos by fleeing into the jungle beyond the mountains.

Neither Pizarro brother responded.

"You're going to like this one," Almagro said, grinning.

"Cura Ocllo!" Orgóñez said, staring at Gonzalo. "Guess you weren't good enough to keep her from running back to Manco," he said with a wink to Almagro.

Shame coursed through Gonzalo's veins at her memory. The ungrateful woman, given a life of luxury alongside one of the preeminent men in Cuzco, had run away at the first chance she got. Now, Orgóñez had insinuated his manhood wasn't equal to that of a native. He stood up and lunged forward, forgetting the chains around his hands that connected to the shackles around his feet. The taut chain caught the edge of the table and Gonzalo's hands shot downwards; he stumbled, and the chains around his feet kept him from regaining his balance.

Orgóñez stood and looked down at the furious Gonzalo. A smile overtook his bearded face, and he exploded with laughter. Almagro joined. Even Hernando snorted and shook his head, suppressing a chuckle.

Gonzalo shuffled out in a rage, his short steps inspiring even more laughter from his captors. His bad mood lasted for days, persisting until a visitor from Francisco arrived in Cuzco.

Gaspar de Espinosa was one of the men who had helped finance Francisco and Almagro's initial conquest of the Incan Empire. Having heard from Francisco by letter about the siege of Cuzco, the aged lawyer answered the call for support, leaving his home in Panama and heading to the fledgling capital city of Lima. The events with Almagro had taken place by the time he had arrived, and Francisco took advantage of their business associate's relationship with Almagro by sending him as an emissary to Cuzco.

"Your brother will be happy to hear that you're both healthy and well-fed," Espinosa said to the imprisoned Pizarro brothers. He was well into his fifties, with soft hands and a pooch belly. Contrary to the rest of the Spaniards, he kept his face clean-shaven, revealing deep lines that extended from the sides of his nose to the corners of his mouth.

Almagro had introduced the lawyer, telling Hernando that he had already spoken to the man and was permitting them a private discussion; Gonzalo hadn't spoken to Almagro since the incident with Orgóñez. But their conversation wasn't conducted with any semblance of true privacy—everyone present knew that the nearby guards would relay all that was said to the one-eyed Spaniard.

"Just in chains," Hernando replied, opening his arms and gesturing to the room, his prison. The Pizarro brothers didn't wear shackles in their cells.

"Regrettable, this entire affair," Espinosa mused.

"How's Francisco?" Gonzalo said. Part of him felt neglected because Francisco hadn't come to their rescue in force.

"Furious but calm. His anger bubbles below the surface while he calculates his next move," Espinosa said, assuaging Gonzalo's sentiment. He filled the captives in about their brother's movements over the previous months—how he had set out in force with the reinforcements sent to him by none other than Hernán Cortés but turned around when he heard Almagro had taken the city and defeated Alvarado, worried Lima would be next. "He had already lost the other four groups of reinforcements, from what I understand, and felt he would become overextended if he continued his trip here."

"Almagro wanted Manco dealt with before attacking Lima," Hernando explained. "He was worried about an attack from the natives."

"And Francisco was worried about attacks from both," Espinosa said, nodding his head. The lawyer looked at the two men standing guard, reminding Gonzalo of a wizened owl. "My main purpose in coming here is to impart some counsel to the two of you." He looked at Hernando. "Especially you."

"Me?" Hernando said, wrinkling his forehead.

"You don't strike me as someone who forgets any slight, no matter how small."

Gonzalo closed his eyes and suppressed a smile at the accuracy of the lawyer's statement.

"If and when Almagro releases you, forget all thoughts of revenge," Espinosa began. "There's no option besides peace in this matter. Trust me, I've been involved with the New World since 1513. If there is any quarrel whatsoever, the king himself will seize the property and punish the transgressors. All of you could end up imprisoned for a long time—"

"How can the king find fault in anything we've done?" Gonzalo exclaimed.

"Look at it from his point of view. The king wants peace in his lands. Your two parties are responsible for the breakdown of that peace—even more so if you insist on taking revenge once you're released. Once the king's men set foot in a new territory, the original governors never rule again. Mark my words; I've seen it happen more than once." His narrowed eyes inspected the chastened Pizarro brothers. "I'm here to work out a settlement. But first, I need to know you won't start a war right after I secure your release."

Both brothers agreed that they wouldn't seek retribution, though Gonzalo doubted Hernando meant it.

Espinosa turned to the guards. "Now go tell Almagro that I've advised them not to strike back if they want to keep their lands," he said as he walked towards the door. Taking a last look at the Pizarro brothers, he added, "Time to go find a settlement we can all live with," before walking out the door.

The aged lawyer never found that mythical agreement; Almagro arrived in their cell two days later and reported that Espinosa had died of natural causes. He pointed at Hernando and told him that they were going on a trip. "Time to establish my own port city, and you're coming with me," he said with a twisted smile.

"What about us?" Gonzalo said, referring to himself and Alvarado, who was also present in the cell.

"You're staying here," Almagro said before slamming the door.

Gonzalo and Alvarado found the guards friendlier without Almagro and Orgóñez around. After a few days of relaxed cordialities, they all shared a spirit of mutual fellowship, laughing about how all of them had traveled to the New World to sit on holy Incan land.

The prisoners found out that Almagro had taken Orgóñez because the city was no longer under threat of native attack.

"Then why not march on Lima? The risk of attack by Manco was the sole reason they didn't press Francisco in the first place—" Gonzalo's voice trailed off as a wave of nausea took hold of his bowels. "Wait, are they headed to Lima?"

One of the guards, a round-faced man whose dry skin shone

red, shook his head. "No, not that we know of. His brother Diego had a hand in it," he said, gesturing with his chin to Alvarado.

Gonzalo knew Alvarado had a brother among the Almagristas, but he couldn't imagine how the man had convinced Almagro and Orgóñez against marching on Francisco.

The second guard, a short, disheveled man with filthy fingernails, chimed in. "It's no secret that Orgóñez wants you and your brother dead," he said to Gonzalo. "Well, Diego de *Alvarado* told Diego de *Almagro* that executing the two of you would outrage the other Almagristas—"

"Why would they care?" Alvarado interjected.

"Murdering fellow Spaniards because of a disagreement over land? What if the Pizarros adopted that policy? It's barbaric," the second guard said. "And, more importantly, the Spanish court wouldn't look kindly on Almagro murdering a fellow Spaniard."

"Well, Orgóñez wasn't happy about that. He swore up and down that the two of you would come for vengeance as long as blood still ran through your veins!" the first guard said with a chuckle.

"He's wanted our heads since our first days in chains," Gonzalo mused.

"And he still wants them! I heard him say so right before he left!" All four men laughed together, blurring the power balance in their relationship.

A bolt of genius struck Gonzalo while he slept, waking him up the night after the discussion. He waited until the four friends—two guards and two prisoners—found themselves in easy conversation before putting his plan into action.

"I wonder how the Spanish court would look upon the men who took action to end the hostilities between our two factions," Gonzalo mused.

"What do you mean?" the round-faced guard said.

"Well, our conversation got me thinking—if Almagro's worried about punishment for wrongdoing in the dispute over Cuzco, I wonder what his feelings are about the rewards for fixing the situation."

Alvarado sat up; he smelled blood. "We all know Francisco would appreciate it; there might even be a hefty reward! Not to mention all that the court would do to acknowledge the level heads that took control of the matter."

The two guards looked at each other. "How could you fix it?" the disheveled guard asked.

"We can't do anything—we're imprisoned! But the two of you . . ." Alvarado said.

"What can we do? We're just guards."

"You *could* forget to lock the door. I'm sure Francisco, Spain, and God would reward the men brave enough to do the right thing," said Gonzalo.

The round-faced man forced back a nervous laugh. The second guard stared at the two prisoners. "I think I remember seeing Manco's son playing near the door tonight—he must have unlocked it without anyone noticing."

18

THE BATTLE OF LAS SALINAS

"THAT SCOUNDREL!" Francisco said, slamming his helmet onto his wooden desk. The oldest Pizarro brother sat down across from Gonzalo. "I can't believe I ever went into business with a bastard like him in the first place."

It was the middle of November 1537. Gonzalo had been in Lima for a few days, having arrived on Castaño with Alvarado after their escape from Cuzco. After their trek to the coast and a quick trip to the cathedral to thank God for their successful journey, Alvarado had taken up residence at an inn frequented by sailors; Gonzalo went straight to the governor's mansion in search of his brother. Once there, Gonzalo had learned that Francisco and Almagro were meeting at a small coastal town called Mala, halfway between Lima and Chincha, Almagro's chosen spot for his own port city. A priest from Lima's cathedral oversaw the negotiations.

"Thank God for Friar Bovadilla's patience—Almagro's got his hands full keeping that dog Orgóñez under control," Francisco said, crossing himself. He looked at his brother. "I'm sorry. We don't see each other for two years and my first words to you are cursing Almagro's name! How are you? How did you get away?"

Gonzalo smiled. "I'm much better now! Staying at a palace such as this could return even the weakest traveler back to full strength," he said. He told Francisco about the guards who let him escape, reminding his brother that not every Almagrista had the burning hate of the Pizarros he had witnessed in Orgóñez.

"We'll have to take care of them once this is all over," Francisco mused.

"And how have you been? The City of Kings looks like it's been here for ages, not just a few years," Gonzalo said. Watching the bustling city's rhythms had taken up a full third of his time spent during recuperation, along with eating and sleeping.

"Founding a city on Three Kings Day turned out to be a blessing," Francisco said. "It's been a lot of work, but I'm proud of what we've accomplished so far."

The two brothers caught each other up on their lives during the intervening years over the course of the day. Silence from one inspired some new nugget of news from the other. Gonzalo told the story of Juan's death over dinner, then asked if Francisco had seen Hernando at the negotiation.

"They had left him in Chincha," Francisco reported. He then told Gonzalo all about the meeting at Mala, how he had argued with Almagro before the one-eyed man grew suspicious and left in a hurry.

"He didn't even hear Friar Bovadilla's verdict, even though he agreed to the arbitrator!"

"What was the decision?"

"We are to send a navigator to measure the exact position of the Rio Santiago, the northern border of our land. From there, we can measure and determine whether or not Cuzco falls within our borders based on the distance south granted us by the king. In the meantime, Almagro is to abandon Cuzco and release Hernando, who must leave for Spain in six weeks."

"He has to leave the country?" Gonzalo asked, appalled.

"That's the agreement. Oh, and Almagro has to go back to his own undisputed land, while we have to stay in ours." The brothers walked back to Francisco's study, each carrying a goblet of rich red wine.

"The priest sees through Almagro's thin reasoning," Gonzalo observed as he sat down.

"And I'm going to make Almagro a better offer so that we guarantee Hernando walks free; I'm worried that he'll take action against him in response to the friar's verdict." He called for a scribe, then started pacing with his hands behind his back while dictating his letter.

After a handful of empty pleasantries, Francisco got to the meat of the offer. "In exchange for the release of my brother, I'll permit you and your men to stay in Cuzco until we figure out the true boundary between our lands," he said.

He sent the letter with his fastest messenger and a handful of natives for protection the following morning. Their reply arrived four days later, in the evening.

"I agree to the terms. I'll send Hernando to Mala in two days' time." The messenger clarified Almagro's message, adjusting for time spent traveling. "In essence, Hernando's leaving Chincha tomorrow morning."

"Then we'll be waiting for him in Mala tomorrow afternoon!"

Diego de Almagro had sent his half-native son in his place. The two free Pizarro brothers sat on their horses on the northern side of the dirt road through town, and the seventeen-year-old Diego de Almagro II—nicknamed "El Mozo"—sat on his horse on the southern side. Francisco had stationed his men in the surrounding trees on the chance that Orgóñez had convinced the elder Almagro about the need for an offensive strike. The Pizarro brothers assumed that any of Almagro's support, if they weren't attacking, sat just beyond their view.

The hostilities never materialized. El Mozo helped Hernando from his horse and let him walk forward. The two Pizarro brothers urged their horses forward and met Hernando in the center of town, the three brothers together for the first time in years.

"Come here, young man!" Francisco shouted to El Mozo with a wave and a smile. Under his breath, he added, "And you two: don't say a word until he leaves."

Even if El Mozo didn't want to approach, both halves of his blood required he listen to the elder Spaniard.

"Well, aren't you turning out to be a fine young man!" Francisco said when Almagro's son halted a few steps away.

"Thank you, sir."

"Tell your father that I'm proud of the job he's done with you. And, once we get over—" Francisco waved his hand around. "—this *unpleasantness*, I look forward to getting to know you better."

El Mozo flashed a handsome smile, showing straight white teeth, and thanked Francisco again before turning around and returning south.

Gonzalo couldn't help but wonder what Diego de Almagro might look like without such a brutal upbringing. Almagro's uncle had locked him in a cage as a child back in Spain, the horrible treatment crafting the man's brutish features.

And now, because of a string of hideous decisions, Diego de Almagro had sealed his fate.

A flurry of curses erupted from Hernando's lips once El

Mozo disappeared around a bend. He called Almagro every name under the sun, mocking his appearance, his aptitude for leadership, and his manhood. The tirade persisted while they made camp, paused while Hernando slept, then began anew the following morning.

Francisco let Hernando talk all the way until they arrived in Lima; he held a hand up and asked, "Are you done?" when they arrived.

Hernando massaged his aching jaw. "I think so."

"Then good. There's something I want to show you," Francisco said with a twinkle in his eye. He looked at Gonzalo. "Not even you know about this."

Francisco dismissed their escort and led the three brothers down to the port and onto a large ship. "These came in from Santo Domingo before I left for Mala the first time—I was keeping them a surprise."

Gonzalo and Hernando went into the ship's hold and discovered rows upon rows of three-foot harquebuses. "They arrived with a hundred infantrymen well-trained in their use," Francisco explained. He looked at Hernando. "I suggest you set them up in the middle of your ranks."

Hernando looked at Gonzalo, confused. "I thought I was going back to Spain?"

"You're under command to lead the army against the traitors. Gonzo will be your second-in-command. The crown put their faith in me, and I'm putting my faith in you because I'm too old to go on another campaign."

"Duty to Spain supersedes some silly agreement over stolen land," Gonzalo said.

Hernando looked torn.

"You wanted revenge, didn't you? This is your chance to take it!" Gonzalo added.

"But I gave Almagro my word as a knight," Hernando said.

"And as a knight, it's your responsibility to do as command-ed," Francisco reminded his brother.

Staring at the rows of weapons, the finest collection of guns anywhere in the New World, Hernando nodded.

"Then it's settled!" Francisco said. He showed his brothers the three cannons that had also arrived on another ship, doubling their supply of the heavy firearms.

Back in the governor's mansion, Francisco dashed off a letter to Diego de Almagro, declaring an end to the treaty and commanding that he abandon Cuzco. He told the brothers that they would have eight hundred Spaniards—many of whom had been sent to fight Manco's native troops during the siege of Cuzco instead of their own treacherous countrymen—and two thousand native troops under their command. "I have one more surprise," Francisco said with a mischievous grin. "There's a man here by the name of Carvajal . . ."

Hernando and Gonzalo had first heard of Francisco de Carvajal in the letters delivered by Manco during the siege of Cuzco; Francisco had called him one of the finest officers in the world. The seventy-four-year-old man had the vigor of a man half his age and was twice their size. Francisco left Carvajal and his two brothers in charge of drawing up battle plans.

Carvajal convinced the brothers that they should wait until the rainy season ended in March for easier transport of the cannons. "Nothing worse than dragging one of them through the muck," the bald, heavyset man said. "It's possible, but we need every available horse for the cavalry." Hernando didn't like waiting months for revenge, but Gonzalo answered for both of them. "So we set off in March."

"That gives us three months," Carvajal said, setting his jaw. The old officer spent six days a week drilling the men, himself working just as hard or harder than any of the soldiers. Even on their Sundays off, Carvajal brought the officers—which included Alonso de Alvarado, who had escaped with Gonzalo—together and talked strategy after mass. Their ranks swelled every few days from soldiers arriving back in Cuzco, most of whom had been a part of Alvarado's force that lost to Orgóñez and Almagro.

Gonzalo and Hernando were so busy preparing for the fight against Almagro that they couldn't even enjoy the city their brother had built and didn't realize how much the city grew during their stay. They set off for Cuzco at the end of March with their well-trained army with both Carvajal's and Francisco's blessings ringing in their ears, arriving in the final days of April 1538.

They first spotted the encamped Almagrista forces in the afternoon at a field just south of Cuzco called Las Salinas. The center of the field was covered in pits where Incan natives leached salt from the groundwater, from which the field derived its name. A small stream bisected the plain; the soaked ground on the Almagristas' side created a soft-ground marsh until the final quarter nearest Cuzco.

"Why would he choose this spot?" Gonzalo asked Hernando as they looked at the opposing force across the field. They both knew that Almagro had a superior number of cavalry —though fewer overall troops—and the battleground was a poor choice for horse movement.

"Maybe he believes it most defensible?" Hernando ventured. "Not what I'd choose, but it's as good a place as any to die."

Hernando led his forces all the way to the banks of the stream before ordering they set up camp. While the men prepared for the final night before the clash, the Pizarro brothers inspected the mountains and hills around them. They were covered with natives, news about the impending conflict having spread by word of mouth to all the surrounding villages.

After losing thousands of warriors to the Spanish because of the superiority of their war beasts and weapons, a fight between Spaniards offered a tantalizing display of strength and strategy. Plus, Manco had called for rebellion and the elimination of the bearded men from Incan lands; seeing the Spanish forces fighting each other meant fewer available for fighting the natives.

Dawn arrived cool and bright. Hernando gathered all of his troops together as the natives watched from the surrounding vantage points. He stood on a log so that everyone could see him.

"First, let us pray," he began. Everyone bowed their heads as Hernando asked God for strength in the coming trials. He decried the men across the field as honorless barbarians not living Christian ideals, describing how the Incan land had transformed their foes into avaricious savages. "God, give us the power to preserve the virtue described by your holy words in the Bible, to make sure that none who disobey your commands goes unpunished," he said, his head bowed. "Amen."

"Amen," the men responded.

The Pizarro forces arranged themselves in the formation drilled into their heads by the old officer Carvajal. The infantry —which included the harquebusiers and native auxiliaries—was in the middle, led by Gonzalo, and cavalry was on each flank, one led by Hernando and the other by Alvarado.

The Almagristas on the far side of the field arranged themselves in the exact same manner.

Hernando paced his horse in front of the assembled men and spoke once more. "It's no secret that Almagro struck the first blow against the Pizarros," Hernando said, his voice more forceful than during the prayer. "He took Cuzco from us for no reason other than greed, attacked his own men at Abancay—"

He looked at Alvarado, who had been the losing commander in the rout.

Alvarado and the men who had been at the river nodded in agreement.

Hernando paused for a moment, letting the men's murmuring rise to a boil. "And now it's up to us to take back what Almagro stole—for Francisco, the governor in this land, the King of Spain, and God. Behind them lies our prize. Let us release the sparkling jewel from Almagro's covetous grasp!"

The men all responded with shouts of excitement while raising their weapons high overhead.

Movement on a nearby hill caught Gonzalo's eye. To his surprise, Spanish inhabitants from Cuzco were setting up for a view of the spectacle, among them a litter carrying what looked a lot like a particular Spaniard with one eye...

Rustling in the trees between the hill and the field drew Gonzalo's attention before he gave the spectators another thought. After another flash of movement, he realized that natives were running through the trees; he turned to his own native troops and told them to keep an eye out for a flanking attack. Hernando and Alvarado, the men in charge of the cavalry on their flanks, could make quick work of them, but Gonzalo worried about what would happen if the cavalry were otherwise engaged.

"Gonzalo!" Hernando screamed.

Pulled from his thoughts, Gonzalo looked at his brother.

"It's time. Press the attack."

Gonzalo nodded. The infantry marched forward in crisp lines that would have made Carvajal proud. They crossed the shallow stream with little effort and laughed as Almagro's cavalry stayed back because they couldn't approach through the sodden ground.

Their laughter ended as the first volley of cannon fire tore through five of the leading men. Despite Carvajal's best efforts at discipline, the men's hesitance appeared as clear as the blue sky above them. Gonzalo, sensing the reluctance, rushed forward and stood ahead of his men. He pulled some, pushed others, shouting the entire time while cannonballs whistled past; his men made it to the firm ground beyond the marsh because of his immense willpower alone.

For some reason, the Almagrista infantry didn't press the attack. It was as if they didn't believe the Pizarro forces were real, that somehow this was a dream that they would wake up from if they pinched themselves hard enough.

Gonzalo didn't care why they stood still. As soon as the mire ended, the harquebusiers took a knee, raised their guns to their shoulders, and let off a devastating volley. The front row of infantrymen in the middle of the opposing forces collapsed as the shots pierced their armor. Carvajal had taught the shooters on the edges about aiming at the cavalry since they shouldn't "waste two bullets on an infantryman when one will do." Because of his foresight, dozens of cavalrymen and horses also fell.

Gonzalo saw a familiar man gallop over to one group of cavalry, shout an exchange, then streak at the Pizarro infantry . .
.

Because of how long loading another shot took, Orgóñez killed two harquebusiers and injured a spearman before returning to his troops without a scratch.

Inspired by shame, every cavalryman rallied around Orgóñez. Then, they charged.

Gonzalo heard his brother yelling behind him. He turned around just in time to see Hernando and every cavalryman streaking towards the enemy after navigating the stream and marsh. Thanks to Carvajal's training, there were clear lanes between the infantry for the horses so none of the allies got trampled.

The two groups of cavalry slammed into each other. Between the yelling, the horses, and the clang of weapons on weapons and weapons on armor, Gonzalo couldn't hear a thing, not even his own thoughts.

But he did know that he wanted Orgóñez dead.

He found the rival officer in the thick of the maelstrom and pointed him out to his shooter with the best accuracy. The man lined up his shot, fired, and Orgóñez's head jerked back.

As Gonzalo watched, Orgóñez shook his head as if clearing himself from a daze. Then, his horse fell from under him, dead.

Gonzalo started running as Orgóñez pulled himself from beneath his horse, revenge burning him from the inside and inhibiting all reason. As he watched, Almagro's second-in-command sat on his knees, inspecting the unfolding scene.

Orgóñez's men were falling all around him while he sat in a moment of calm.

Two of Pizarro's men found the confidential circle and dismounted. Orgóñez placed his hands together and looked up at the men. One of them withdrew his dagger and stabbed him in the heart, pushing him to the ground as he withdrew the blade. The other swung his sword and beheaded the unfortunate officer, holding the head up by the hair with a shout.

The Almagristas retreated once they realized Orgóñez had fallen. The infantrymen sprinted away behind the men on horseback, all of them pursued by a rabid Hernando . . .

All of a sudden, native troops emerged from the trees and began attacking the fleeing Almagristas. Gonzalo turned around. All of the Pizarros' native auxiliaries were behind him.

Turning back to the slaughter, Gonzalo realized the men were taking orders from Paullu, Manco's brother. The puppet emperor had turned on Almagro at the last minute, turning the hour-long battle into a complete and utter defeat.

"Where's Almagro?" Hernando yelled after stomping through the field of bodies.

Gonzalo looked at the hill where he had seen the Cuzco residents watching the battle and caught sight of a litter hurrying away on native shoulders.

19

GUERRILLA WARRIORS

The Spaniards in the Incan Empire lost one hundred and fifty of their number in the Battle of Las Salinas. Among them were Pedro de Lerma, the man who had betrayed Alonso de Alvarado—he had been skewered by Hernando's lance—and Rui Diaz, the Almagrista who had attempted a personal negotiation with Manco on behalf of the one-eyed conquistador. The rest of Almagro's men made it back to Cuzco, where they watched as the Pizarro brothers entered the Incan capital city once again.

Looting began as soon as the victorious soldiers stepped foot in the city; the sole caches worth plundering belonged to Almagro's officers. Once the treasure was all taken, the native women who called Cuzco home became the next available prize. Pizarro's men pillaged without reservation.

Paullu brought back Rodrigo Orgóñez's head and presented it to Hernando on bent knee. The Pizarro brothers exchanged a quick glance and both understood that Manco's brother, the other Incan Emperor in the land, had earned their mercy after his change in loyalty. Hernando inspected the morbid visage before ordering it displayed in the town square; the rope wrapped around the gaping mouth and hung from ropes attached behind each ear.

While the three hundred and fifty surviving Almagristas kept their distance from the Pizarro forces—Hernando had lost a mere dozen men during the battle—the victorious brothers searched high and low for the missing leader of the rebellious forces.

"He has to be here somewhere!" Hernando said, seething. Having spent longer in captivity, his burning desire for revenge shone brighter than Gonzalo's.

Paullu proved his worth once more, eliminating all traces of doubt about his allegiance. "The litter-carriers took him to Saqsaywaman."

Gonzalo looked at the three towers of the stone fortress that stood guard over the city. He turned Castaño towards the site of his brother's demise and trotted away. Hernando followed, interrupting his men from their looting and conscripting their service.

Almagro was in the center tower, the same location where the impressive Incan warrior had made his last stand before jumping to his death. His discarded litter sat in a heap on the spot where the warrior met his demise. Standing in front of the tower, Gonzalo wondered if the one-eyed fugitive had the same strength of character.

"It's over, Diego!" Gonzalo yelled from the base of the tower. Hernando and two dozen cavalry took their place by his side, all of them looking up at the stone structure looming above them.

They didn't wait long. Within minutes, the conquistador appeared at the tower's base looking older than ever, shuffling because of an attack of gout.

"I can't even hold a sword, my hands are so swollen," he said with a meek smile.

"Let's go," Hernando said. They made him walk all the way back to Cuzco and to the monastery, keeping him captive in the same room he had kept the Pizarro brothers.

"Orgóñez swore up and down you wouldn't attack in the field," a breathless Almagro said when he had sat down.

"He thought we brought an army from Lima just to see the countryside?" Gonzalo asked, laughing.

"No, he assumed you'd feint then make a run for Cuzco. That's why I chose that field for the battle, so that his men wouldn't push too far forward before giving chase." Almagro chuckled. "He based it on his knowledge of the *Italian campaigns*—he never shut up about that experience."

"Well, no other words are coming from his lips again," Hernando said with a malicious smirk.

"He's dead? He didn't surrender?"

"Nope, he died fighting. Like a real man," Hernando said, his words dripping with scorn.

The brothers started walking out the door.

"Francisco's coming, right? It's about time we settle our differences face-to-face so that we can put this unpleasantness behind us," Almagro said.

"He's looking forward to seeing you again," Hernando replied. "And if he doesn't come, I'll take care of you myself."

It was clear that Almagro assumed Hernando referred to his release, a reciprocation of Almagro's final treatment of Hernando. He rested his head against the wall, folded his hands over his belly, and murmured, "Good, good," with his eyes closed.

Gonzalo's brother then slammed the door and gave strict orders to the chosen pair of guards that nobody could enter but him.

The setting sun had touched the western mountains by the time the Pizarro brothers emerged from the monastery. Both men were exhausted, but they still had one more concern before they could return to their palaces: El Mozo stood outside the monastery, wringing his hands.

"What?" Hernando said when he saw the young man.

"Can I see my father?"

"Absolutely not," Hernando replied. He thought for a moment. "In fact, go home and gather your belongings—you're going to Lima."

"Lima?" the stunned youth repeated.

"You'll stay with Francisco," Hernando said.

Noticing the young man's trepidation, Gonzalo added, "Trust me, he's much nicer than we are. You'll love it on the coast."

Hernando sent the young man on his way and the two brothers returned to their palaces, finding everything in similar conditions because of the natives employed at each residence.

The following morning, right after El Mozo started for the coast, Hernando declared a start to the proceedings in the trial against Diego de Almagro. He encouraged the participation of anyone with cause for complaint against the one-eyed conquistador. In a strange twist, many of Almagro's own men testified against their former leader in their attempts at currying favor with the Pizarros. During the prolonged evidence collection, Hernando kept Almagro sated with delectable food from his own table and promises of Francisco's impending arrival.

The process ended in July 1538, and a sentence of public execution was handed down. Hernando gave the list of charges against Almagro to Friar Valverde, with orders that the priest tell the prisoner. The claims against Francisco's former partner included the death of the Crown's subjects by making war against fellow Spaniards, working with a known enemy by colluding with Manco, and theft against the governor of Cuzco.

Almagro demanded a meeting with Hernando when he

learned about the accusations. Gonzalo didn't accompany his brother to the conversation, but he heard afterward about how Almagro had "begged for his life like a scared woman" and "claimed I owed him because he had released me, that he alone saved my life when everyone wanted my head."

"And then he said that the Crown would repay my treachery in kind. *My* treachery! The nerve of the man," Hernando said to Gonzalo as they walked around the town square after a heavy meal and too much wine.

Hernando didn't pay attention, but Gonzalo couldn't help but notice the stares from their fellow Spaniards; they ranged from incredulity to outright anger. Diego de Alvarado, Alvarado's brother who had spoken to Almagro about the folly in executing the Pizarros, approached the brothers with concern.

"The punishment is too steep," he said after exchanging idle pleasantries.

"It's not yours to mete out; I'll sleep just fine tonight," Hernando replied.

"You're not worried about what they'll say back in Spain? How one man decided the fate of someone in Almagro's station?"

Hernando glared at Diego de Alvarado. Gonzalo put a hand on his brother's shoulder, convinced he would strike.

"I'm going to pretend this conversation never happened, and I suggest you do the same," Hernando said.

Rumors swirled throughout Cuzco in the following days, all of them echoing Diego de Alvarado's sentiment: How could one man, after being in power for such a short amount of time, decide the fate of one-half of the enterprise that began the conquest of the Incan Empire? Even Francisco would require external arbitration, and the king had granted him the other half of the captured land!

Hernando's sole capitulation was a change to the manner of

execution: instead of in public, it would take place in Almagro's cell. On the appointed day, the Pizarros employed the hundred harquebusiers given to them by Francisco and spread them outside the homes of Almagro's principal followers, a preemptive step against potential conspiracy.

Friar Valverde heard Diego de Almagro's final confession and supervised the notary recording his will—everything went to El Mozo. The executioner, his garrote in hand, entered soon after the notary left.

Almagro's screams rang out along Cuzco's stone streets, reverberating off of the stone buildings and walls. Then, silence descended on the city.

Friar Valverde and the executioner accompanied the two natives carrying Almagro's corpse into the town square. Under the watchful gaze of the Pizarros, the executioner removed Almagro's head from his body and the notary read the charges against the deceased, as well as his last will and testament.

The flies buzzing around Orgóñez's head dispersed when Almagro's joined the exhibit, then descended on the still-warm flesh as the wind caught in the head's open mouth and started it ticking like a metronome. His body ended up at the small church attached to the convent called the Church of our Lady of Mercy, where his remains sat on display for a number of days before their final interment beneath the holy establishment.

Guerrilla attacks began in the weeks after Almagro's death, as if Manco had been waiting to see if the Spaniards would eliminate themselves before devoting more of his own troops to the cause. *Encomenderos*, traders, supply convoys, and everyone else traveling to and from Cuzco feared surprise attacks from native warriors, and rumors swirled that Manco himself was in the Andes directing the assault. In addition, the native forces destroyed Spanish farms, scattered livestock, and razed settlements.

The Pizarro brothers, communicating via letters, lamented the loss of horses more than the loss of men. "Send escorts with everyone traveling between the cities," Francisco declared in a letter. "We need to keep Manco from obtaining his own cavalry."

"And from breeding his own," Gonzalo said as Hernando read their brother's letter to him.

News of Manco's terror campaign reached Cuzco as the year 1538 drew to a close, carried back by distraught Spanish women. The first time it happened, the Pizarro brothers in Cuzco thought one of Manco's officers had gone rogue. After the fifth, they knew the orders for the frightful treatment had come from above.

Each devastated woman reported the same incident. They had been captured on the road to Cuzco while traveling with their husbands, the native warriors having taken their procession by surprise. Within minutes, a large man with a thick spear arrived. As the women were forced to watch, the stake entered into each of the men of their party in the lower part of their body, continuing until it emerged from their mouths. Then, the women were taken to within walking distance of the city.

The Pizarro brothers in Cuzco received another letter from Francisco not long after the latest survivor arrived. In it, he outlined how he had sent two hundred cavalry into the mountains in search of Manco and "a large native whose brutality I won't repeat; no Christian should have the knowledge of what the savages are doing to our countrymen."

"I'm guessing some of the surviving women have made it to Cuzco," Hernando said when he had finished reading the letter.

"Or they have come up with some other form of torture we haven't yet heard about," Gonzalo added.

Cuzco received word about what had happened to Francisco's cavalry from an escorted messenger sent by their leader.

"We had Manco cornered," the man began while sharing a meal with Hernando and Gonzalo. "His back was against the river. Suarez sent a young captain by the name of Villadiego and twenty-nine men around his back to the lone bridge in the vicinity, Manco's only escape back to the jungle."

The messenger took a bite and shook his head. "You see, we knew Manco was in the area, from natives we had interrogated, but we didn't know exactly *where*. So the plan was, once he was trapped on our side of the river, we'd find him and attack while Villadiego waited at the bridge . . ."

"It would have been so easy!" the messenger added, slamming his hand onto the table.

"What happened?" Gonzalo asked, enthralled.

"Well, the cockroach heard about where Manco was before we did and decided to attack on his own! We found their naked bodies on a steep hill, where their horses were useless."

Hernando leaned his elbows on the table and steepled his fingers. "And what about the horses they had with them?" he said.

"Gone! Along with the natives, back into the jungle. The rest of the men went back to Lima."

The Pizarro brothers shook their head; the meal continued in silence.

Word of Manco's successful skirmish against Villadiego spread, and soon reports of native attacks led by Villac Umu trickled in from the area around Lake Titicaca, to the southwest of Cuzco. Then, news emerged about two murdered *encomenderos* in the northwest.

Hernando didn't wait for a letter from Francisco before taking action. He sent one of his lower officers—Captain Chávez, a man known for his brutality—to the northwest, telling him to "make the native lives miserable. Destroy everything—

make them beg for peace." Unspoken, but understood: make no exception for women and children.

In the coming years, Chávez often bragged about killing hundreds of natives below the age of three, before they had a chance to cause trouble for the Spanish.

Hernando and Gonzalo headed south with a sizable cavalry force, accompanied by Paullu and his native auxiliaries. Along their march, they murdered any chiefs who didn't provide their men with food and women.

The situation near Lake Titicaca was worse than reported. Every group of natives stood armed and ready to defend their homeland against the Spaniards during an infuriating barrage of guerrilla attacks. Whenever the Pizarros defeated a local tribe, it seemed like two more took their place. When they fought against a large group comprised of three separate factions, Paullu reported that he had never heard of those men working together before.

"It seems they want you gone," he said, shaking his head. Paullu would lose an empire if the Spaniards ever left, however tenuous his power in the current situation.

On the shores of Lake Titicaca, Paullu pointed across the water at the land on the other side. "If we cross here, we can come up behind the Lupacas." They had heard that Villac Umu whispered into the Lupaca chief's ear, leading them to victory and causing the most destruction to the Spanish settlers.

"Cross? With what rafts?"

Paullu looked at the Pizarro brothers and smiled. "Give me one week."

The natives worked on the rafts both night and day. Gonzalo, when marveling at their industriousness, often heard from Paullu that "they do as their emperor commands." He wondered how often Manco took pride in the potency of his orders and if he could ever command men with the same authority.

With the vessels completed, the Spaniards hurried across the lake in the early morning hours—it took two trips before everyone was on the far shore. Then, they turned north, finding the first fringe members of the Lupaca tribe late that afternoon, which they murdered without a second thought. The Spaniards spread out among the local farms, eating crops and taking women.

A scout or a surviving native farmer reported the presence of the Spanish force behind the Lupacas, alerting the chief. Without means for escape and with the Spaniards already in their land, a head-to-head fight was the sole remaining option.

The Lupaca tribe never stood a chance. Gonzalo himself ran down the fleeing Lupaca chief and put a spear through his thigh, keeping him alive on purpose while the rest of the cavalry chopped down the native warriors. Some of the warriors succeeded in stopping Spanish horses by using the bolas their people were known for, but it earned the men hacking deaths instead of a quick slice through the throat or heart.

Gonzalo let the Lupaca women live long enough to watch what he did to their chief with a wooden stake. Then, one at a time, he made each woman stand against a tree while two of his men used the stake with the skewered chief as a battering ram, piercing their bellies.

Hernando laughed when they performed the execution on a pregnant woman; Paullu threw up.

They discovered Villac Umu while setting fire to the village. He scurried out of one of the buildings, unrecognizable without his priest's vestments.

"Get him! First man wins!" Hernando shouted. There had never been a prize other than being the murderer.

Gonzalo squinted into the morning sun. "Wait," he muttered. "I think that's—wait!" he shouted. "Keep him alive!"

Hernando looked at his brother, then echoed the order.

"How did you recognize him?" Hernando said when they had the native priest tied and slung across a horse.

"I remember him from when he first emerged from the woods with Manco. He didn't have his robes on then either," Gonzalo said.

The Pizarro force started back towards Cuzco having killed thousands of natives, continuing their terror campaign all the way until they reached the walls of the former Incan capital. They threw Villac Umu into the cell Almagro had died in, grinding his face into the bloodstained floor before slamming the door behind them.

They were met with a surprise outside of the monastery. Chávez stood outside holding up a mutilated, well-built native man.

"Who's that?" Hernando said.

"Is he even alive?" said Gonzalo. Upon closer inspection, he saw the man's chest rising and falling, blood spurting from a hole near his right lung.

"It's General Tiso!" Chávez said with pride. "All the native tribes surrendered to save their children. He was left without a single soldier under his command!"

20

THE SEARCH FOR VILCABAMBA

"Leave the horses! We'll continue on foot," Gonzalo said to the three hundred Spaniards in search of Manco. They were in the jungle on the other side of the Andes Mountains, having passed Vitcos, Manco's old stronghold that Orgóñez had attacked, in search of his new base of operations called Vilcabamba. The horses had made it over the mountains despite the steep slopes and loose footing that gave native warriors the edge in skirmishes with the Spanish on that terrain, but the vegetation in the jungle infringed upon the path too much for their continued involvement.

Gonzalo stared off into the trees, wondering how many hidden cloud warriors were watching him and how many Manco had under his command now. Since Manco's elite bow and arrow fighters were Gonzalo's largest concern with the mission, he relied on a sizable contingent of the Santo Domingo harquebusiers scattered in clusters throughout the procession for protection from incoming projectiles.

Finding the Incan Emperor became the Pizarro brothers' priority after seeing the reduction in hostilities following the capture of Villac Umu and General Tiso. Once again, they reasoned that the continued Spanish prosperity in the lands granted to them by the Spanish king relied on the capture or elimination of Manco, which would bring an end to the persistent threat of guerrilla warfare. The Spanish landowners agreed; many of them accompanied Gonzalo on the operation.

Their group included three litters carrying Paullu and two recent native additions to the Spanish cause: Cura Ocllo's two brothers. As Paullu had explained to the Pizarro brothers, accepting the Incan queen's remaining family into their party would help legitimize his claim to the title of emperor in the eyes of the populace. With them was a sizable group of native troops and the ghosts of rumors about those who called the jungle home.

According to accounts given by the highland natives, the people who lived in the eastern part of the empire on the other side of the mountains, the jungle realm called Antisuyu, enjoyed feasting on human flesh. The stories that circulated during their march from Cuzco included descriptions of butchered troops sold in the market and a gruesome ritual reserved for those of higher rank: the nobles would tie the captured officer to a stake, cut tender slices of flesh from his body, and consume them raw while the unfortunate captive watched.

Every Spaniard wondered if the Antisuyu warriors would consider their rank fit enough for quick slaughter or if they were marching into potential torture.

Without the horses clogging the trail through the rainforest, the entire company walked two abreast, stretching in both directions as far as the eye could see and then some. The mosquitoes feasted on both Spaniard and native alike, but the Spaniards also contended with a persistent heavy sweating underneath their armor.

"If they don't see us or hear us coming, they'll certainly

smell us," Paullu said to Gonzalo as they sat together during a break in their march.

Gonzalo responded with a grunt.

An ear-piercing scream from deep within the trees commanded everyone's attention. Gonzalo stood up. "Is everyone accounted for?"

A serene native guide beckoned for Gonzalo to sit back down.

Furious, Gonzalo asked an interpreter for an explanation.

"It's just a monkey," the native said.

A series of barks rang out in response to the scream. "See? There's another one."

Gonzalo cursed his luck and then Hernando for letting Manco escape in the first place.

A short while after resuming their journey, the Spaniards in front discovered a brand-new bridge spanning a shallow river. They called Gonzalo to the front.

"We're on the right track!" Gonzalo said, looking ahead as the path receded into the undergrowth. "Everyone, get ready! No telling how close we are now."

The men who heard Gonzalo's directive couldn't suppress a chuckle. They had been ready since leaving their horses behind, clutching their weapons as they stumbled through dense foliage and entertained thoughts of the gruesome torture they could expect if captured alive.

They stumbled upon another bridge a short distance from the first, spanning another shallow river that one could ford without too much difficulty. While Gonzalo crossed the bridge with his sword in hand, he watched as the twenty-man vanguard started walking up a slight incline flanked by two bluffs emerging from the trees . . .

They disappeared behind a boulder that fell between them from above.

"It's a trap!" he yelled, turning around as more boulders came crashing down. He pushed the men blocking his path as the sound of snapping wood filled the air, worried about the large rock rolling down the incline towards the bridge and the cloud warriors shooting arrows with pinpoint accuracy.

The harquebusiers had set up on the bank and were aiming into the jungle by the time Gonzalo got back to safety. He stood behind them and watched the scene unfold.

Three men who had been right in front of Gonzalo had survived the initial boulder drop. Because it had landed on open ground, it had sunk into the dirt instead of rolling back down the incline. But during their retreat back to the bridge, they had been overtaken by additional rolling boulders and smashed before parts of them ended up in the river. The rest of the men in front had fled into the thin line of trees on each side of the path upon finding their way back blocked by the massive stones.

Gonzalo could still hear a combination of native shouts and Spanish cries but knew he couldn't risk sending more of his men into the trap—it was through God's good graces and a heaping dose of native impatience that he hadn't lost his life or more men. As he watched, the surviving Spaniards emerged from the trees on the far bank and flew into the river, many bleeding and some with arrows sticking out at awkward angles from their bodies. Protected by cover fire from the harquebuses, Paullu's natives helped the wounded Spaniards from the water.

A second wave of attacks began soon after; Gonzalo later found out that the first bridge they had encountered wasn't destroyed by a hidden native force because the sheer number of men under his command meant that some still hadn't crossed, providing a defense force for their sole means of escape. While the combined Spanish and native force attempted a retreat after the ambush, the cloud warriors emerged on both sides and began firing arrows into their flanks. The archers didn't display a unified front that Gonzalo could attack and overwhelm with bodies; instead, they darted in and out of the trees, firing a shot then disappearing before emerging for another shot somewhere else.

Even after the engagement, Gonzalo couldn't say for certain how many cloud warriors his men had faced. All he knew as he approached the snorting and stomping horses they had left behind was that he had lost more than thirty men in the day's attacks. Worse, he couldn't find a single member of his own party that could say for certain that they had killed a native warrior.

"We have to send word back to Cuzco," an exhausted Gonzalo said to Paullu. The native allies had secured the perimeter and started a fire in the damp jungle under the impressed gaze of miserable and hungry Spanish onlookers. "And we need to stall them long enough for help to get here."

Gonzalo and Paullu decided that negotiations with Manco would keep the renegade emperor from sending another force against them right away. Sending Paullu was out of the question —if Manco killed Paullu, the Spaniards would lose their puppet emperor. Instead, they decided that Cura Ocllo's brothers would go despite Manco's tendency of killing any natives that helped the Spanish.

"Orgóñez told me that she escaped from Vitcos with him— she has to be at Vilcabamba!" Gonzalo said, masking his wounded pride with apparent enthusiasm.

"He wouldn't murder her flesh, she'd never forgive him," Paullu said.

Gonzalo turned a curious eye towards Paullu. "How do you know that?"

"We all grew up together, I've known her since we were children," Paullu said.

For some reason, Gonzalo hadn't realized how familiar the

Incan aristocracy had been with each other before the Spanish arrival. He looked at Paullu with fresh eyes, at his Spanish armor and clothing and the wooden cross hanging around his neck.

Paullu flashed a lopsided smile, showing a slight gap between his two front teeth.

"Why can't your brother be more like you," Gonzalo said with a sigh.

"He still thinks he stands a chance against Spanish influence," Paullu said. Anger flashed in his eyes. "But he doesn't realize that we were once a conquering force in the land too— it's the only reason he has any power to begin with. So everyone in the Four Realms is supposed to bow down to him because his ancestors conquered them, but now he won't bow down to another after he's been conquered?"

Gonzalo covered Paullu's hand with his own, aware of the taboos regarding physical contact with the son of the sun. "God smiles down on those who can recognize truth," he said, dismissing the part of himself that told him he hadn't sounded quite as profound as he would have liked.

Paullu nodded. "Amen."

They waited for a reply from Manco that never came. Paullu's scouts, while out searching for Manco's hidden capital, stumbled upon and captured one of the enemy's warriors. After a torturous interrogation, Gonzalo and Paullu found out that Manco had killed Cura's two brothers and had begun reinforcing a stone barricade in "the sole canyon that stands between our camps."

The warrior died before they could get any more information from him, but it didn't take Paullu's men long before they found the location the warrior had described.

"We'll have to take the barricade if we want to get to Vilcabamba—there's really no other way past it," Paullu said, relaying information given to him by his lead scout. "Maybe a few could go around, but the numbers we need couldn't make it without risk of falling or being attacked."

There were still a few days before reinforcements from Cuzco could arrive, if they had left as soon as they had received the letter or were coming at all. "Let's take it then," Gonzalo said. "That way, we can strike Manco's base of operations as soon as the men from Cuzco get here."

The next day, Gonzalo and most of the Spaniards followed Paullu's scouts to the barricade. He snuck forward with Paullu, a handful of officers, and Paullu's lead scout, staying hidden in the trees while assessing the situation. Ahead of them was a natural formation of stone sandwiched between two cliffs that were covered with dense vegetation—Gonzalo doubted even the best Spanish climbers could scale either. Atop the stone in their path was a man-made stone wall made of smaller rocks protecting a sizable group of native warriors.

"There were ladders here before; my men found a broken segment of one in the trees," Paullu whispered.

Gonzalo nodded and beckoned for them to head back to his men waiting a short distance away. If he were Manco, he would have chosen a new command post on the far side of this obstacle as well.

"All right, everyone, listen up!" Gonzalo said to his eager men. "We take this and we should have a clear shot at Manco's new capital—all reports suggest it's vital to his protection." He continued with a rousing speech, reminding them that they had God on their side and that he would see them through the crisis. "Now, get your weapons out. We'll approach through the trees, before emerging onto the main path and climbing up to meet the natives head-on."

Gonzalo turned to the puppet Incan emperor. "One native guide for each side of the path."

Paullu nodded.

"Let's teach these dogs a lesson!" Gonzalo said, remembering Hernando's battle cry as the water rose at their feet in the field outside of Ollantaytambo. He raised his sword and beat a rhythm against his chest—the men did the same, matching his beat.

As Gonzalo watched well out of range of arrows from the cloud warriors, his men scrambled up the rock face. Because it had a slight slope, the men could find purchase in the cracks and seams littering the natural barrier. Gonzalo saw native warriors shuffling behind Manco's constructed rock wall through cracks in the structure. Then, it seemed as if a native face filled each space before disappearing.

Loud cracks erupted from atop the barricade, like the sound of breaking tree trunks, followed by wisps of smoke issuing from the cracks in the wall.

"Did they—did they have harquebuses?" Gonzalo said, looking at Paullu.

"It seems like it . . ." the Incan replied.

The Spaniards, caught off guard, leapt from the wall and ran back to Gonzalo's position. They hadn't lost any men.

"I looked up and saw a handful of barrels pointing at us through the rock!" one of the Spaniards said.

"Where did they get firearms?" another exclaimed.

"Probably from some unlucky Spaniards," Gonzalo said.

"Well, I don't think they know how to use them. I saw a lead ball falling down the rock, like they dropped it from above," the Spaniard who had spotted the barrels said.

It took another cautious day before the Spaniards realized that Manco's warriors had no clue how the harquebuses operated; the natives managed just one more ignition. By then, the cloud warriors had appeared on the rock, firing down on Spaniards as they searched for an opening in the native defense.

Over the following days, Gonzalo tried spreading out his men over the entire stone barricade at once, condensing them at a single point on the rock, and using the cover of night for a stealth breach—none of the tactics worked.

Until fresh troops arrived from Cuzco and Paullu offered up a plan.

Native scouts had discovered a potential way up the back side of one of the cliffs flanking the stone barricade. Manco's defenders didn't know that their force had doubled—why not send the fresh men around so that they could shoot at the warriors from above while the defenders were busy with attackers on the rock?

Gonzalo fell in love with the idea. Instead of sending the fresh troops up the cliff, he decided on sending his best marksmen, putting the additional men from Cuzco in their place on the frontal assault.

"Keep them occupied," he said to the men attacking the barricade's front after the marksmen had left.

The plan bore fruit as the sun peaked in the sky. All of a sudden, the characteristic cracks of gunfire erupted from above the stone wall and Gonzalo watched native bodies fall. The men in front of the barricade, smelling blood, surged forward.

"Most of them dispersed into the trees," one of Gonzalo's men reported after Gonzalo joined them on top of the captured barricade. Three ladders leaned against the wall. "We saw a handful of natives carrying the emperor that way," he said, pointing.

"Well, what are we waiting for?" Gonzalo said, withdrawing his sword.

"It could be another trap," Paullu observed. "We should wait for the rest of the men."

Gonzalo, used to absolute authority, stood stunned at the emperor's interjection. After a moment, he decided that the advice was sound and sheathed his weapon. "Have one of your men follow him," he said in a way that left no room for questioning or disagreement.

"Already did," Paullu said with a smile.

One of the native scouts sent by Paullu had returned by the time Gonzalo and Paullu's full force had made it up the ladders. According to them, Manco made it across a nearby river and had turned in their direction and shouted, swearing that he'd "kill every invader in his land."

Gonzalo chuckled. "We'll see about that."

The combined Spanish and native force continued along the well-worn path for a full day before reaching Manco's abandoned settlement. As Gonzalo predicted, they faced no more obstacles, not even from cloud warriors hiding among the trees.

Cooking fires still smoldered from the hasty retreat of the city's inhabitants while Spanish soldiers searched for gold and silver. Paullu, sitting on his litter, commanded his native troops help gather all the precious metal, forever playing the Spanish game of conquest. Gonzalo and a group of handpicked men went searching throughout the upstart city for Manco in hopes of surprising him after his flight across the river. They walked into the largest house, which they assumed had belonged to the former Incan Emperor, and found golden plates, goblets, and jewelry.

They also found Cura Ocllo lying on the ground between the headless bodies of her two brothers. Flies buzzed around the severed heads, which lay a few steps from the bloody necks, as if they had been kicked.

If the sight hadn't turned their stomachs, the smell did. It was obvious that the bodies had laid decomposing for days, and the filth around the Incan queen made it clear that she hadn't moved in just as long, not even for her own biological needs. She had given up and was waiting for death's embrace between the bodies of her brothers.

Furious at her for humiliating him by going back to Manco, Gonzalo put his nose inside his shirt, receiving a waft of his own reeking sweat, and pressed into the miasma. He reached down, grabbed Cura's forearm, and lifted her off of the floor . . .

Her screams startled everyone in Vilcabamba; the birds took flight and the monkeys screamed in response. She twisted out of his grasp and lay back down.

"Get up!" an angered Gonzalo said, trying again.

After twisting away once more, she rubbed her arms in the excrement and caked blood on the floor before covering her body with the paste. Then, she lay back down between her brothers, laying an arm over one as if they were sleeping.

Gonzalo kicked her as hard as he could on the thigh, then continued battering her legs because the bodies of her brothers protected her torso. His breathing grew heavy and he released his face from his shirt for a deep breath; he threw up as soon as the stench hit his nostrils.

"Any of you ever want to feel what a queen's like on the inside? Now's your chance!" he said to his waiting men, wiping his mouth as he walked out.

21

THE SILENT QUEEN

THE EXPEDITION STAYED in Vilcabamba for weeks while they searched the surrounding jungle for Manco. Under Gonzalo's orders, mixed groups of Spaniards and natives fanned out north, south, east, and west in ever-expanding arcs, always keeping a force behind in case Manco came back for his queen. Despite coming from the highlands, the natives under Paullu's command were far better at navigating the wilderness than the armored Spaniards, but the Spaniards held every advantage during the numerous skirmishes with the hidden cloud warriors.

Paullu, when he wasn't otherwise occupied with lounging in camp, met with hostile local chiefs, offering them titles and gifts in exchange for information about his missing brother. More than once, he heard how the chiefs in the Antisuyu had no way of knowing who the true ruler was, that the "mountain squabbles" didn't concern them.

Gonzalo wanted the obstinate chiefs punished, but Paullu convinced him that there was no quicker way of forcing them into Manco's waiting arms.

"Who knows how many flesh-eaters are out there just waiting for permission to storm our camp?" Paullu said.

Gonzalo shuddered at the thought.

Paullu spent part of each day with Cura Ocllo. Each morning, his oldest soldier—who often joked about how the expedition into the Antisuyu was his last—washed the Incan queen after she had covered herself in filth as a repellant against brutal nighttime visits from Spanish soldiers. She didn't utter a word during the scrubbing, then ate as much as she could in preparation for another night's defenses.

While she was clean, Paullu tried apologizing for bringing her brothers into the power struggle, reiterating that she should instead be mad at Manco for murdering them in the first place. It was his own guilty conscience interpreting her silence as anger towards him—she never said a word against either emperor, or spoke any words at all.

"It's as if her tongue's been cut out," Paullu reported to Gonzalo. The two men met after each meeting, Gonzalo eager for any information his puppet emperor might have acquired from the queen. He couldn't visit her himself—she was still a reminder of Manco's insolence, how he had failed in bringing his flock to heel like Friar Valverde had done.

A lingering surge of Gonzalo's former adoration erupted beneath his breastbone. "Has it been? Have you checked?"

Paullu chuckled. "It's still there. She has chosen silence."

Her vow continued through the trek back to Cuzco. Some of the Spaniards, when they had heard of the mute queen, knew about Gonzalo's standing offer and snickered while they plotted ways of making her scream when they made camp at night.

None could make it past her defenses.

Francisco was in Cuzco when the failed expedition arrived. After a quick trip to the church, where he gave thanks for surviving another mission, Gonzalo hurried to Manco's former palace, now Hernando's, without washing.

He found his brothers seated at a large table with a handful of soldiers standing at the walls. Three rotting heads, two natives and one African, sat on the table, their eyes gone.

"Why are those here?" Gonzalo said, covering his nose and sitting down.

Francisco reached out and pulled Gonzalo's hand down. "They don't smell any worse than you," he said.

Gonzalo flushed red but didn't dare a reply.

"There's a dead horse's head outside too," Hernando said.

"Why?"

Hernando sighed. "Francisco was on his way here—"

Francisco interrupted his brother. "After I made sure Lima was secure, I came here to help you take care of the rebellions; you were gone by the time I arrived. We received a letter from Manco—"

It was Francisco's turn to be interrupted by Hernando. "Well, we thought it was from Manco . . ."

Francisco turned an icy glare on his half brother. "Saying he wanted to negotiate the terms of his surrender. I assumed he had heard of your forays into his territory and wanted assurances of safety. So, I sent these three." Francisco pointed to the heads on the table. "With gifts for the emperor. This is what he sent back."

Gonzalo shook his head. "From what I've seen, I don't think he'll ever surrender. He left his queen behind and didn't make a single attempt at rescuing her."

"And where is she now?" Francisco asked, his curiosity piqued.

"I told the men to throw her in the prison at the monastery."

Francisco folded his hands and bowed. "Dear lord, thank you for providing a way of teaching a lesson to those who oppose your holy commands."

Gonzalo and Hernando met eyes and joined their brother in prayer.

"Give your humble servants the strength to do what must be done so your blessed word can flow throughout this land. Amen."

"Amen," Gonzalo and Hernando said in unison.

Francisco looked at his brothers with a spark of rage burning in his eyes. "Have some men erect a stake in the plaza. There's going to be an execution."

The following day, Friar Valverde led a despondent Cura Ocllo from the monastery to the town square. Word had gotten out about the day's events and a sizable crowd of both Spaniards and natives stood waiting.

In addition to the three Pizarro brothers, a group of native archers under Paullu's command waited for the prisoner in the center, separate from the crowd but within earshot of Paullu's litter.

As Gonzalo watched, the crowd parted for Friar Valverde and the Incan queen. His heart raced with shame at the intense feelings he once felt for the native woman, then in anger for her rejection of his advances. He cursed Manco for rebelling because he took her, blaming the Incan Emperor for the entirety of the fledgling colony's problems without accepting any of the responsibility for himself.

"The queen, as you commanded," Friar Valverde said with his head bowed.

"Did she convert?" Francisco asked.

"I tried, but she hasn't uttered a word," the priest reported.

"So nothing's changed," Gonzalo joked with a nervous laugh. His smile evaporated at a look from Francisco.

"Then she's condemned herself," Francisco said. He strode forward, grabbed the woman by the wrist, and brought her to the waiting stake. Pointing to two nearby foot soldiers responsible for keeping the crowds in order, he told them to come tie her hands behind the stake so the wood was at her back. Once secure, he ripped her rough clothes from her body and exposed her for everyone in the crowd.

Cura didn't even flinch.

"Manco thinks that he can reject our advances of friendship, after we're the ones who put him on the throne in the first place!" Francisco roared.

The Spaniards in attendance nodded in agreement.

"Well, now we're going to take something from him—the same way he's trying to take this country from us!"

Francisco turned a rabid eye on the natives in the crowd. "And let this be a lesson to you: God doesn't place any stock on the rulers decided by mere mortals. His holy commands are all that matter, handed down by his chosen emissary on Earth: the pope. The pope gave this land to the King of Spain, and the king gave *me* the right to rule."

Francisco paused, as if waiting for a challenge. Gonzalo searched for any Almagristas, wondering if they would bring up how the right Francisco referenced had been split between him and Diego de Almagro.

"Remember, and tell your children so that they can tell their children: this is what happens when you go against God."

Francisco pointed to the native archers, and they backed away from the queen at the stake. He pointed to the crowd on the opposite side of Paullu's men, waving them apart. The members of the crowd jostled each other as they cleared the space behind the queen.

Satisfied all was ready, Francisco commanded Friar Valverde try for one final conversion to Christianity.

"Do you accept the Christian God, or would you rather spend the rest of eternity in hell?" the priest asked.

A native man yelled something in their tongue, pleading with the queen. He received a swift punch in the gut from a nearby Spaniard.

Cura made no sign she understood, or even heard, the priest.

Friar Valverde turned to Francisco and shrugged.

Francisco turned to the archers and pointed at Cura. They notched arrows into bowstrings and drew. The crowd grew silent.

"Fire!" Francisco said, dropping his hand.

The arrows flew, whistling in the wind. They lodged in the queen's legs, sticking out from her thighs and shins; flowing blood pooled on the ground. She didn't make a sound.

At a wave of Francisco's hand, the archers all strode forward, retrieved their arrows, and walked back to the firing line.

"It wasn't her fault?" Hernando roared. He ran forward and seized a Spanish man in the crowd by the jaw. "Did I hear you correctly?" Hernando said.

The man's eyes grew wide, and he looked past the angry Pizarro in front of him to the two other Pizarros in the center of the square.

"You did," the Spaniard stammered, deciding against lying. "It's Manco's rebellion, not hers."

"And this is his punishment!" Hernando said, pushing the man away and spitting on him.

Gonzalo put a hand on his sword and swore to himself that he would cut down anyone, Spanish or native, who brought up how she was the reason Manco had rebelled in the first place.

Nobody had a death wish.

Francisco held up his hand again then dropped it once the archers were ready. Another volley of arrows flew, this one burrowing into Cura's torso.

She lifted her head before the archers reached her, smiled, and said in her native tongue, "Not much longer and I won't be able to fight back while you satisfy all of your desires." Her eyes met Gonzalo's before she let her chin rest against her chest; both of them struggled for each breath.

"Wait!" Francisco told the archers. They froze, some men mid-stride.

Francisco, Hernando, and Gonzalo gathered around the native interpreter while he relayed what she had said. Francisco and Hernando grew angry, Gonzalo heartbroken—it was that same innate pride that had attracted him during Manco's coronation a lifetime ago. She was a woman worth an empire, and now she was paying the price.

Under Francisco's instruction, the archers withdrew their arrows from Curo Ocllo and more blood poured from her wounds. None of them flinched, their dedication to Paullu and by extension Francisco absolute.

Hernando walked in front of the archers with his hands up when they were back in position. "Let her suffer for her disrespect!" Hernando urged his older brother, implying they let her bleed out.

"Tell them to aim for her heart," Gonzalo muttered under his breath.

Paullu sat up and turned his head as if he had heard the words but didn't register their meaning and needed a second exposure.

"Speak up; if you're going to say something then say it like you mean it!" Francisco told Gonzalo. There had been few times that the eldest brother spoke with impatience towards his brothers, but his bloodlust blurred the edges of his values.

Gonzalo glared at Hernando for his cruelty, then turned to Paullu and repeated himself so everyone present could hear. "Tell them to aim for her heart!" he said, pointing to the upper left side of his chest. Then, he watched Cura's labored breathing while she bled.

Paullu brought his lips together and nodded then looked at

Francisco for confirmation. Francisco tilted his head in acquiescence before beckoning Hernando to his side while Paullu relayed the instructions to the waiting archers.

Francisco dropped his arm one last time, the archers fired, and every arrow burrowed deep into Cura's chest.

Nobody said a word. When the masses realized the spectacle had ended, they filtered out from the town square, back to their normal lives in the various quarters of Cuzco.

"Should we hang her head like we did to Orgóñez and Almagro?" Hernando suggested.

Francisco shook his head no. "There's no point in striking at Manco without him knowing about it." He turned to the archers. "Take her body and float it down the river in a boat towards the emperor. Let's make sure he knows about the consequences for his actions."

After clarification from Paullu, the archers untied Cura's body from the stake and carried her away.

The Pizarro brothers spent the rest of the day planning for their future. One of Francisco's primary concerns was having Hernando return to Spain before the king found out about Almagro's execution in an unfavorable light from Diego de Alvarado, who had gone to Spain on El Mozo's behalf after Almagro had left everything to his son.

"You have to go back and explain what happened from our point of view. Otherwise, you simply murdered one of the king's subjects," Francisco explained. "It could turn the Crown against us all."

"Do you think the king would seize our land?" Gonzalo asked.

"Of course not!" Hernando exclaimed. "That traitor Almagro held us prisoner first; how can we be at fault?"

Francisco leaned back in his chair, folding his hands and placing them in his lap. "Because he didn't kill you," Francisco said. He turned to Gonzalo. "And yes, he could, if he becomes convinced of Hernando's guilt."

Hernando looked at the ceiling and sighed. "So what do you want me to do?" he said.

Together, the three brothers came up with a written account of what had transpired at the end of the siege of Cuzco. They included the events preceding Almagro's arrival, how Hernando had kept Cuzco out of the Incan Emperor's hands before the one-eyed Spaniard came back and tried working alongside the enemy.

"But didn't the king want 'a good working relationship with Manco' for the transfer of wealth out of this country and into Spain?" Gonzalo asked. He didn't forget how Hernando had claimed that he and Juan were lost when it came to political matters when his brother had first returned from Spain, back when Juan was still alive.

"That was before Manco gathered his army at our door!" Hernando shot back.

"We told you he was leading a rebellion; you didn't listen."

Hernando opened his mouth but didn't get a word out before Francisco, slamming his fist on the table, demanded both of their attention.

"Let's focus on fixing the problem, not laying blame at each other's feet," the oldest Pizarro said, his voice quavering with rage.

"All I'm saying is that the king might interpret Almagro's actions as following his instructions more closely than we did," Gonzalo said, braving his brother's wrath.

"And that's why we'll send a sizable shipment of gold, as proof that we're still in a position to extract wealth from this country," Francisco replied.

Hernando's anger bubbled below the surface, but Gonzalo

didn't care—his brother would be on his way to Spain soon enough.

"And while you're there, you can try and have the king declare Almagro's lands as our own so we can settle the Cuzco issue once and for all," Francisco said.

"That should be easy," Hernando said. "Almagro left everything to El Mozo, and there's no way the king wants a half-native like him in charge of half the country. By the way, where is the runt anyway?"

"Still in Lima; I told my men not to let him leave."

"Smart. You have to be careful with everyone who was with Almagro; they're looked down upon by every Spaniard in this land as traitors. Since they struggle finding jobs, I suggest you feed them and make friends with them." Hernando looked at both of his brothers. "Don't let them gather or else you're asking for trouble."

Francisco gave his brother a dismissive wave. "They're nothing to worry about—Manco's a far greater threat."

"I'm telling you: keep an eye on them."

The coming days saw the final preparations for Hernando's departure. They received word that Manco had discovered Cura's body and taken her back to Vilcabamba, giving orders for a period of mourning for his rogue state.

"Well, at least we know that Manco's men won't attack you on your way to the coast!" Francisco said at the edge of Cuzco. The Pizarro brothers had stopped there for their final goodbyes before Hernando went back to Spain.

Hernando laughed. "Anything else you want me to tell the king?" he said, smiling.

"I think the king's heard enough from us," Francisco said.

Gonzalo stared at the mountains in the distance on his right. "I can't help but think . . ." he began before pausing.

"What?" Hernando said, the corners of his lips returning to neutral.

Gonzalo turned to his departing brother. "You're heading into the lion's den without any of us there by your side. I can't help but think it would be better that you stay here, safe from accusations, while we defend the country against Manco." When neither of his brothers responded, he added, "You could keep an eye on the Almagristas!"

"What do you know?" Hernando said, a cold glare aimed at Gonzalo. "You don't know the king or how the court works. These are the types of things only educated people understand."

Francisco, himself uneducated as well, thought for a moment before saying, "Daniel made it out, and *he* didn't have his brothers with him."

"Exactly! I'm leaving, and I'll be hoping every day that I return to a land without Manco." With that, Hernando urged his horse on, taking the main road between Cuzco and Lima while Gonzalo and Francisco stayed behind.

"I'll be heading back to Lima soon—I have an assignment for you, now that you're second-in-command," Francisco said with a proud grin. He told Gonzalo about rumors regarding cinnamon in the wilderness east of Quito—a commodity approaching gold and silver in value—saying that he wanted his brother at the head of an expedition in search of the spice.

"Of course," Gonzalo said, excitement boiling in his gut. Another adventure, another chance for wealth. "But if neither of us are in Cuzco, who will be in charge?"

"Friar Valverde can take care of it. He's taken enough of the land for himself in the name of the church, let him take responsibility for his overreaching."

Gonzalo thought Francisco would have looked down on the priest for taking advantage of the power granted him by God;

instead, his brother had accepted it and turned it into leverage. "And what about the prisoners? We still have Villac Umu and General Tiso in the monastery—Manco could attack if he finds out they're still alive."

Francisco shrugged. "Burn them and scatter the ashes. We can't leave their bodies intact just because of some native superstition."

22

THE LAND OF CINNAMON

Gonzalo brought one man from Cuzco with him to Quito at the end of 1539: Francisco de Orellana. The heavyset Spaniard came from the same hometown as the Pizarro brothers and had made a reputation for himself in the defense of Lima when it was attacked by General Quizo while Manco's forces laid siege to Cuzco. He had stayed in Lima until accompanying Francisco to Cuzco, and jumped at the chance for further conquest.

In Quito, which had been founded by Sebastián de Belalcázar in 1534, they found another three hundred and fifty men who shared their lust for exploration. After the addition of four thousand native porters, the expedition set out for beyond the eastern fringe of the empire in early 1540.

The men were in high spirits when they left the city, their party stretching far into the distance behind them. The Spaniards joked and laughed as they meandered up the mountain past the snow line, their last major obstacle before they descended into the jungle on the other side. Despite being wrapped in layers of Incan wool, the cold bit into their extremities as night fell.

Gonzalo decided that they would set up camp when he first

saw his breath. In a jovial mood, he told the men, "Hurry, before our fingers get too stiff to even start a fire!" They melted snow for drinking water and dug into the provisions that would spoil first.

He saw the curious looks from the natives in his company but ignored them.

The Spaniards and their horses—Gonzalo had left Castaño back in Cuzco, opting for a sturdier option—spent a cold night around dozens of fires, wrapped in blankets and shawls stolen from native storehouses. Dawn was a blessing, and Gonzalo awoke to a thin blanket of fresh snow. Together with Orellana, he roused the camp, shouting "Wake up!" as he made his way to the sleeping natives.

"Wake up!" he said again, standing over one of the native men he had put in charge. The man hadn't erected any type of shelter and the snow covered his blanket. Under orders from Gonzalo, he had slept apart from the men he oversaw, a lone mass of human flesh.

The man didn't move.

"Wake up!" Gonzalo repeated. Annoyed, he kicked the man's leg.

Still no response.

Gonzalo leaned over and pulled at the man's blanket. To his surprise, it was a single thin piece of wool. The snow fell from the fabric onto the native's face. Upon closer inspection, Gonzalo realized that the man's skin had lost most of its color; he had died overnight.

Gonzalo checked more nearby natives, the ones sleeping alone because of their rank. None of them woke up. He grew angry at the weak native constitution for succumbing to the cold, then grateful that he was responsible for fewer mouths.

"Icy wind came down from the top of the mountain last

night," Orellana said behind him, pointing to the mountain's peak.

Gonzalo nodded without turning around.

"We didn't lose any of our countrymen, thank God," Orellana added.

Both men crossed themselves.

The native porters who had huddled together for warmth while they slept reported that the previous night's cold had been an anomaly. They said it was a bad omen; a sizable number of Spaniards agreed.

"I always expected we'd lose some natives along the way—why do you think we brought so many?" Gonzalo said with forced humor, grasping for some of the previous day's good mood. He rubbed his hands together then blew into them for warmth.

"But fifty? And all of the men we put in charge?" Orellana said when the two of them were alone. "Some of the men say we should go back, that this doesn't bode well for the mission's success."

"Go back? We just started!" Gonzalo snarled. "Who said it?"

Orellana shook his head. "Nobody's deserting, just rumors."

"They'll be begging for the cold once we get into the jungle," Gonzalo muttered, remembering his days searching for Manco in the wilderness around Vilcabamba. "Leave the bodies but take the blankets," he ordered.

Orellana nodded once. "No Christian burials?"

Gonzalo looked at his comrade, checking if he was joking, then burst out into laughter. "Even if they *claim* they've converted, we still don't have time to take care of every single body. They're just natives, after all." Gonzalo walked away, shaking his head while suppressing a chuckle.

The expedition began their descent within hours of striking

camp. They stayed in the mountains for another four days, leading their horses on foot because of the unstable footing, but none of the nights grew as cold as the one on the peak that had claimed the native lives.

A vast expanse of green appeared in front of the men at the end of the first week. The Spaniards erupted in cheers while the natives looked on in mute stoicism, understanding that they had emerged from one challenging terrain right into another.

Gonzalo looked down the slope at a small village erected just above the tree line. It was situated between two ridges, hemmed in by the mountain on one side and the jungle on the other. He wondered whether the villagers were highlanders who didn't want a life in the dense foliage or lowlanders who dreamed of cooler days.

A deep rumble brought everyone in their company to their knees. The horses reared up, the swine screamed, and the natives placed their palms on the ground. Gonzalo turned towards his caravan, looking at the rising mountain behind them while searching for falling debris. A loud crack followed by a groaning creak turned his attention back to the village in their path.

As Gonzalo watched, the tips of the two ridges approached each other; the village sank beneath them in a burst of gas. He thought he saw people collapsing outside of the houses but with his shaking vision he couldn't be sure.

"It's a message from the underworld!" he heard a Spaniard say behind him.

The natives were screaming in their own tongue, but Gonzalo's limited understanding of their language kept him from understanding what they were saying—he guessed it was a similar sentiment.

The rumbling stopped, and the expedition recovered from the earthquake.

"We have to hurry before this mountain throws up," a native interpreter told Gonzalo.

"Throws up?" Gonzalo asked.

"The mountains don't always swallow," the native said, pointing to the village. "It could come from any of these," he added, looking at the peaks surrounding them.

"We shouldn't continue," Gonzalo heard, in Spanish. "There are signs everywhere."

Gonzalo withdrew his sword and walked towards the group where he had heard the complaint. Everyone stepped away from a stout man with red cheeks who had joined the expedition in Quito. Streaks of gray dotted the man's dark beard and long hair.

"Do you think you're more situated for command than me?" Gonzalo asked, holding the point of his sword just below the man's Adam's apple.

The man gulped, and the sword nicked his throat. "That's a message from the underworld, clear as day," the man said.

Gonzalo admired the man's bravery. He lifted his sword and put it back in its scabbard. "And how do you know the devil's not worried about what we'll find if we continue? Wouldn't it be our job to thwart the devil's plans despite his attempts at dissuading us?"

The objector tilted his head, thinking.

Gonzalo pressed. "According to your logic, you're listening to a message from the underworld and following the devil's commands."

"No, no, I just—" the man stammered.

Gonzalo looked at the Spaniards, winked at Orellana, then turned to his men. "And who here feels like they could use a dose of God's good favor . . . maybe by eliminating the devil's messenger in our midst?" The expedition was his first role as second-in-command in the country—it couldn't suffer anything less than complete obedience.

A limping Spaniard with a lopsided face and heavy eyebrows stepped forward, a dagger in hand.

Gonzalo crossed his arms and looked down his nose at the stout Spaniard who'd suggested the group turn around. "Get on your knees."

"Señor, I—" he stammered. He ran both hands through his greasy hair. "I would never question you."

"What did you think you were doing with your *interpretation* of an earthquake? As if you're some priest." Gonzalo scoffed. "On your knees!"

Tears welled in the stout man's eyes as he knelt before Gonzalo. Gonzalo looked at the volunteer and nodded.

One quick slash and the man's head lolled back, his neck opening into a wide, bloody grin.

"Now, what do you all say we get going?" Gonzalo said with a cheerful smile.

Everyone nodded. They continued down the mountain in their long procession, going around the smoldering chasm where a village had stood moments before, the Spaniards and natives stepping over the first Spanish casualty on their journey.

"That should keep them in line," Orellana said. Having both grown up in Trujillo, Spain, they shared a similar brutality. "Think we have to worry about any friends who might want revenge?"

Gonzalo led his horse around a large boulder in their path.

"Did you see how fast everyone stepped away from him when I approached? No, I doubt we have to worry about anyone."

The fierce cold of the mountains transformed into insufferable heat as soon as the caravan descended into the jungle. The vegetation closed in on them, and all manner of creatures watched them from the surrounding trees, some curious and others hungry.

Continuous rain began on their third day in the jungle. Thunder woke them each morning, drizzle and sunlight followed them through the afternoon, and dark clouds choked out the sun before night fell each evening.

"We don't listen to the devil!" Gonzalo said as encouragement for his men whenever he sensed any failing morale. He made sure the volunteer executioner stayed by his side in case anyone else interpreted the signs as a message from the underworld that they should turn around.

He found out that the limping man's name was Fernando de Guzman. He had come to the New World after hearing about Hernando's exploits during the Pizarro brother's first trip back to Spain.

"I didn't do much before I found myself in Quito," Guzman said. "And when I heard a Pizarro needed men, I knew where I was headed."

The company continued on for weeks on end, exhausting themselves and their supplies as they hacked through the jungle. When they ran out of swine, they relied on fallen horses for meat. When they ran out of horsemeat, they resorted to dried provisions carried by the natives. Their clothes tore and rotted from the moisture and the constant snagging on branches, and many men developed problems with the skin on their feet because of walking in damp boots.

Their native porters succumbed to disease or exhaustion or escaped into the jungle. Any native jungle dwellers they encountered—called *antis* because they lived in the Antisuyu—were captured and enslaved. Despite the introduction of fresh bodies, ones made for life in the jungle, they lost more than they ever replaced.

They made a breakthrough discovery at the end of the sixth

month, a few days after their last horse fell. It came during a lull in the rain, when the steaming jungle sent wisps of vapor into the sky. Guzman smelled it first. He grabbed Gonzalo's shoulder and told him to stop.

"Why?" Gonzalo said, ripping his arm away. Everyone's interactions had devolved from civilized into something far more feral.

Guzman made a show of taking a deep sniff. "Do you smell it?"

Gonzalo smelled the air; his eyes grew wide. "Cinnamon!"

Excitement tore through the Spaniards. They had made it after their excruciating journey! Gonzalo demanded one of the captured natives brought to him.

"Do you smell that?" he said after sniffing the air.

The confused native didn't reply.

Gonzalo repeated his question, and a look of understanding passed over the slave's features. He led Gonzalo and pointed to a nearby tree with mottled bark, small leaves, and green fruit hanging beneath a brown cap. It wasn't the cinnamon they were used to in the old world, but it was a spice nonetheless.

Once they knew what to look for, the Spaniards found hundreds of similar trees. They cut them down, stripped their bark, then removed strips of the wood and dried it out over small fires—because of the humidity, the strips didn't dry on their own. Guzman disappeared during their harvest, annoying Gonzalo, but he returned with a captured native sporting two bloody stumps where his hands had been.

Guzman kicked the native behind the knees, forcing him to the ground. "You'll want to hear what he says," he said.

Gonzalo called for the native interpreter.

"Oh, you don't need that," Guzman said. He withdrew a gold cross hanging from a chain around his neck and showed it to the kneeling man. "Where?" he said.

The man pointed farther into the jungle with the stump of his arm.

"There's gold," Guzman said, his greedy eyes crinkled at the corners.

The single utterance of the precious metal brought the entire cinnamon harvest to a halt. Within moments, every Spaniard in the Antisuyu realized the potential for greater riches waiting in the darkness of the dense rain forest beyond their current position.

With the help of a native interpreter, the expedition found out that the gold was located ten days of walking along a river farther into the jungle. It had taken a bit of encouragement, including the loss of feet and ears, and afterwards Gonzalo had Guzman put the native out of his misery.

For the first time, Gonzalo put the decision to a vote. They gathered around a clearing where dense growth had stood before their arrival, and Gonzalo asked for a simple show of hands.

"Take the cinnamon back or continue in search of gold?" he said.

Every single Spaniard voted for gold. None of the natives were given a vote.

They set off the following day, leaving the bundles of dried bark behind while convincing themselves that they'd be back for the bounty. Gonzalo had Guzman and Orellana take a clipping and seeds of the tree for planting back in Quito, hoping the plant could somehow survive the different climate.

Hungry and sustained only by thoughts of the gold awaiting them, they stumbled upon a gorge with a river running far below.

"Is this the river the prisoner was talking about?" Gonzalo asked the interpreter.

The interpreter thought for a moment before restating the

conversation he had had with the captured native. "He said we had to walk along the river's edge until we found the tribe with the gold," he said. "I don't know how we could walk along this river . . . but we could try if you want."

Gonzalo peered over the edge. "Let's cross over and hope we encounter another," he said.

It took a day and a number of fallen trees, but soon the Spaniards and their natives were on the far side of the gorge, marching forward in search of a larger river—all except one, who had slipped and fallen after looking down. Hunger groans accompanied the group; whenever they captured an Antisuyu resident, the first thing they asked for was where they could find food instead of where they could find gold.

Gonzalo deemed finding the river a miracle when they stumbled upon it days later. The men found frogs and snakes on the riverbanks and ate them raw accompanied by leaves, anything for their aching stomachs. After hearing from a captured native about a fruitful country a few days downriver, the Spaniards grew hopeful that their luck had turned. They set off through the dense vegetation, but it soon became apparent that a sizable number of the Spaniards could no longer press forward at any appreciable rate.

"We're making a boat," an exhausted Gonzalo proclaimed.

Building it took two months, during which the men sustained themselves with fish and whatever jungle animals they could catch. Since their own clothes were disintegrating and they still had months of travel ahead, they started saving animal skins and wearing them, joking that they were becoming more like the Antisuyu natives with each passing day. His men dropped in clusters; there were stretches of days where none turned up dead, until a single day when the morning was devoted to digging graves for fallen Spaniards or tossing dead natives into the river.

The raft, made from rubber and nails crafted from saved horseshoes, set sail with three dozen of the most feeble men on board, with Orellana as a steersman; the healthy members of the company rotated through time on the boat so they could rest. Letting natives on board was never an option. Gonzalo thought it best he lead the men from the shore with Guzman's help so that nobody could accuse him of taking the easy route, imagining his older brother Francisco would do the same.

Progress down the river continued in lockstep, the boat matching the speed of those on land. Gonzalo worried about the men on the boat—he could see that they were exhausted, sick, or both, none of them moving much more than a slight rise and fall of their chests. His men onshore chewed on leather belts and straps between their meager meals, joking how it was better than the meat their mothers-in-law cooked back in Spain, even if they were unmarried.

The hungry men onshore started rising later and ending earlier each day, worrying Gonzalo; it continued until they came to a waterfall. Guzman found a reasonable path down to the land below, but the men were too weak for a trip while carrying their boat, even if dismantled.

"Let me ride it down the waterfall," Guzman suggested. "I'll bring it to shore downriver and everyone can get back on board."

"How do we know you won't take it and leave us behind?" Orellana said. Persistent hunger frayed everyone's nerves.

"By myself? What good would that do? Where would I go?" Guzman retorted.

"Let him take it, unless you want to do it," Gonzalo said.

Orellana watched the foaming water rushing over the precipice. "No, no; I'll walk."

"Then it's settled," Gonzalo said.

The men crowded at the top of the waterfall as Guzman pushed away from the shore. He avoided a protruding rock using his long pole, and his shoulders rose and fell as his heavy breathing became more pronounced.

He went over the edge calling out, "Santiago!"

Gonzalo watched the entire scene occur in slow motion. Their raft tilted over the edge surrounded by white foam, Guzman suspended above it after jumping. It struck the water below sideways, then sprang back out of the white water as if the pool had spit it out.

Guzman met the leading edge of the raft while still horizontal, the edge striking his back and sending him tumbling into the depths.

23

ORELLANA FLOATS AWAY

Gonzalo chased after the raft in a daze. Alone and without a second thought, he raced down the steep incline as the voices of his men receded in the distance. His feet slipped on slick rocks twice; both times he sat down and slid while braking with his hands, receiving deep gashes on his palms. At the bottom of the waterfall, he spent a moment looking for Guzman before pushing forward along the river after finding no sign of his body. Branches and vines reached out for his limbs.

When crossing a small stream that fed into the flowing river, Gonzalo stepped onto what he thought was a large rock—it sunk, and he stumbled into water up past his knees. The rock reemerged and continued until it reached the main body of water, sunlight glittering off the patterned carapace.

He cursed the jungle with each sloshing step.

The intact raft was on a beach at a bend in the river, surrounded by dozens of caimans lying in the sun. Gonzalo, furious at the continued run of wretched circumstances, grabbed a stick and approached the mass of reptilian bodies with long, powerful strides. The first one he approached hissed, opened its mouth . . .

And received a swift blow on the snout.

Gonzalo made sure he stayed well out of range of the powerful jaws while he attacked each animal until they retreated back into the water. A few charged him instead of retreating right away—those received a swift poke in the eye from the expert lancer, leaving bright red streaks on the dirty sand when they gave up and ran away. By the time Gonzalo was alone on the beach with the last caiman, he was drenched with sweat and weak in the knees. Despite his exhaustion, he realized the bounty of meat in front of him and withdrew his sword, holding his stick in one hand and the sword in the other.

The caiman gave a perfunctory open-mouthed hiss and Gonzalo inched forward so he could plunge his stick deep into the caiman's throat. When the reptile instead turned and started towards the water, Gonzalo chopped off the creature's tail with his sword. It turned around and snapped at its attacker, tasting flesh in the air where Gonzalo's hand had been a moment before.

Gonzalo danced around the angry reptile, slashing and slicing, his body forgetting about the intense weariness in his bones. Panting, he stood over the animal while it tried wiggling backwards into the water without any of its four legs. A chuckle escaped his lips while he watched, then a full-bellied laugh.

"Did you really think I'd let you get away from me?" Gonzalo said between fits of laughter. "I'm going to call you Manco—the two of you really believe anything is possible!"

With that, Gonzalo brought his sword down between the reptile's eyes, forcing his blade through its skull. It twitched then lay still.

Orellana and the rest of the expedition emerged from the jungle onto the beach and found Gonzalo sleeping naked on the raft, his drying clothes spread out around him.

"Gonzalo!" he cried out.

Their leader blinked in the afternoon sun and rolled over while getting up, ending in a seated kneeling position.

"What took you guys so long?" Gonzalo said. He pointed to the raft. "I caught up to it," he added with a smile.

"I see that," Orellana said. He gestured to the bloody sand. "How many natives did you kill?"

Gonzalo shrugged and didn't bother correcting his second-in-command's flawed assumption. "Everything in my way," he replied. "This too," he said, pointing to the butchered caiman meat sitting in piles on leaves on the beach.

Orellana pointed to one of the underlings. "Get a fire going," he said.

Gonzalo noticed an Antisuyu man with his hands tied. "Who's he?" he said while putting on his dried pants.

"That's what took us so long," Orellana replied. "Hunter from a local tribe, we ran into him while we were following you."

"So one more mouth to feed? Great," Gonzalo said with a heavy exhale.

"Yes, but wait until you hear this," said Orellana. He told Gonzalo again about a nearby native village, on the water, where they could get food. "He said they never go hungry," Orellana said, wrapping up.

Gonzalo leaned his head back and looked at the sky. A few stars had appeared in the fading daylight. "How many times are we going to hear about these villages just a few days away?" he mused.

"We don't really have much of a choice," Orellana whispered. "The men are already getting excited, thinking we're close to the one with gold we were looking for in the first place."

"Always just days away . . ." Gonzalo said. He looked at his pitiful men, some of them lying dirty in the sand and looking like they would never get up. "Take the raft, a few men, and the native. Let's use him as a guide instead of just following his instructions," he said to Orellana.

"That was my thought too; that's why I kept him alive and unmolested. And Guzman isn't here to cut off hands anymore." Orellana looked at Gonzalo with a question in his eyes.

"No sign of him," Gonzalo replied with a forlorn shake of his head.

Orellana set out the following day with promises of forth-coming supplies to the most exhausted men. "We'll be back soon, don't you worry," he said while kissing the foreheads of his weary comrades.

Gonzalo and Orellana stood in front of the raft, each man with a hand on the other's shoulder. "If I don't find it in one week, I'll turn around and come back."

"No longer than two weeks gone," Gonzalo said with a nod.

Orellana, fifty Spaniards, and the captured native set off downstream one year after their expedition had set out from Quito, every available space on the raft not occupied by a body used for their meager supplies. Gonzalo and one hundred men, plus the remaining three thousand natives, started setting up their temporary camp, clearing a patch beyond the sand for their living space.

The first few days at the beach brought a handful of culinary surprises. With plenty of fresh water, their main concern was finding food. Caimans appeared on their beach each day, and Gonzalo soon had a foolproof method for killing the reptiles, making a game to see how fast he could cut off all four legs. Native scouts spread out into the surrounding jungle—each accompanied by a Spaniard so that they didn't desert—and gathered an assortment of fruits, roots, and greens.

Even a local mammal contributed to the food collection.

While relieving himself on the shore a short distance from camp, Gonzalo saw a motionless monkey leaning over the water while holding onto a branch with its long arm, staring into the depths. After a moment, it reached down into the water and withdrew a brown shell before disappearing into the trees.

Curious, Gonzalo went to where he saw the monkey hunt. Just below the surface, clinging to the floating tendrils of a submerged water plant, he discovered a field of brown snails. He grabbed the same branch the monkey had used, leaned over, and paused, wondering which one he should grab.

"No wonder that monkey didn't move—it's hard to decide which one looks best!" Gonzalo said to himself with a chuckle. Instead of choosing just one, he took off his shirt and harvested as many as he could carry with it.

Back in camp, one of the captured Antisuyu natives told Gonzalo that he should let the snails sit in water overnight, then boil them before eating. It took a day before he tried the meal he'd gathered himself; he realized that he preferred caiman meat, but the act of scooping the snails from the shells made the meal last longer, giving him something to do besides wait for Orellana's return.

By the end of the first week, Gonzalo's weakest men started showing signs of rapid improvement. The number of men available for food collection grew, starting a virtuous cycle of plenty that everyone, including the natives, benefitted from while they waited.

The grumbling started the day after the two weeks had passed; the men had split themselves into two basic camps. The first thought that they should erect more permanent structures and continue gathering supplies in case their comrades weren't coming back for them. The second thought they should push forward along the river now that they had recovered their strength, reducing the distance between their beach and Orellana.

"Do you realize how slow we walk compared to floating downriver in the boat?" Gonzalo replied whenever the argument between the factions grew large enough for his involvement. "We'd be putting ourselves in another delicate situation for what could save but a few hours on the boat."

"Then why don't we build another?" the de facto leader of the group in favor of traveling suggested. He was a stubborn man with the bushiest beard in camp.

"The first one took two months! And the only thing we can do with a boat is follow them into the unknown—if we stay here and gather our strength, we can head back to Quito if they don't come back."

Gonzalo, torn between both ideologies, didn't choose either. The camp stayed in their temporary structures, as if Orellana could come back any day, while collecting as much food as they could.

One day's hunt brought a gruesome discovery and pried the Spaniards away from their beach, but not towards Orellana.

It started with shouts coming from the jungle, in Spanish, requesting help from the men in camp. Three Spaniards closest to the tree line plunged into the undergrowth; Gonzalo sat up from where he was lying down, looked at another pair, and gestured they follow. After hearing calls in their native language, a dozen porters also ran into the jungle.

Snapping twigs and strings of curses grew louder as the group approached the camp. The first two men broke through the trees carrying what, at first, looked like part of a tree. As they continued, Gonzalo saw the sag and realized the men weren't carrying wood, they were pulling a snake.

The rest of the men pulling the anaconda were scattered at

various points along the enormous creature, wrapping their arms around it and heaving with all their might until the headless animal emerged from the jungle. Sweat poured from their matted hair and soaked their rotting clothes. The men at the front of the procession, pulling on the snake's tail, ended up turning away from the water after passing through the clearing and the beach because of the anaconda's length.

"We'll have enough meat for days!" the Spaniard who had gone with the native said with pride. One of the two Bernardos in the camp, he had a penchant for hunting elusive prey.

"How are we going to cook all of this?" Gonzalo said. He sighed with a smile and a shake of his head.

When he heard another Spaniard mutter something about the snake in the garden as told in Genesis, he proclaimed that, "This land is no Eden, and we're no Adam," without turning around.

Upon butchering the carcass, they discovered the body of a young naked native girl in its stomach. Every Spaniard crossed themselves.

"This body is fresh," Gonzalo said. He looked into the jungle. "How far away was the snake?" he asked the Spaniard who killed it.

"The better question: Was she given to the snake, or did the snake take her?" a man named Lope said. He was notorious for quoting scripture and predicting the end of days, and was in all likelihood the one who'd referenced Genesis.

"Not very," Bernardo replied, ignoring the question of sacrifice. "It took us forever just to pull the damned thing back."

Looking at the nearest captured native, one of the many they had added to their group, Gonzalo asked how far a snake that large could travel with such a large meal in its belly.

"No more than half a day's walk," the native ventured.

At Gonzalo's instruction and without the need to hunt for more meat, native and Spaniard pairs fanned out from where Bernardo had found the snake in search of the native settlement. They found it two days later.

"And you're sure they didn't see you?" Gonzalo asked after hearing the report.

"Positive," came the reply.

"Then we're striking out at first light tomorrow. Let's see what we can gather from the village." Everyone in camp hoped for more gold.

When Gonzalo and two dozen Spaniards, led by a handful of their most trusted natives, got to the village's clearing, they didn't stop or wait at the fringes. They walked in like they were conquering lords, their swords drawn, and killed every native man that stood up to them while the women and children fled into the trees. A few received arrows for their efforts, and two men fell convulsing on the ground a short while after being shot by poisoned tips.

"Stay vigilant for archers in the trees!" Gonzalo roared while his men searched the small huts for gold.

"Come take a look at this," a Spanish soldier told Gonzalo, beckoning him to a building in the center of the village.

Gonzalo walked into a smoke-filled room and wondered how the entire structure didn't burst into flames. Seated in the center was a naked and wrinkled woman sitting cross-legged on the dirt floor with scattered snail shells in front of her. When she saw Gonzalo, her eyes rolled to the back of her head, exposing her sclerae, and she started speaking in a native tongue, repeating the same message over and over again.

Just one of the natives with them knew the language. He listened to the woman's ranting, letting her talk for tense moments before turning to Gonzalo.

"She says they aren't coming back," the native man reported.

Gonzalo's eyes opened wide and the blood drained from his face. He walked forward and chopped off her head in one swift swing.

None of the men said a word on their way back to the beach after finding nothing of value in the village. All they brought back with them was the cursed prophecy, and every Spaniard in camp knew about it by the day's end.

Gonzalo, sitting alone on the beach, watching the river flow by as night fell, heard shouting in the clearing behind him. He turned and saw the majority of his men congregated near the tree line.

"What is it now?" he said with a groan as he stood up and approached the mass of bodies. When he arrived, he saw two of his men holding back Lope from walking into the trees.

"Let me go!" Lope roared, twisting against the grip of his captors.

"Why are you holding him like that?" Gonzalo said, striding forward and swatting the men away from Lope.

Once freed, Lope bent over and picked his tattered Bible up from the ground, kissing it and apologizing in whispers. He started walking into the trees until Gonzalo stopped him by grabbing his arm.

"Where are you going?" Gonzalo asked.

"We're cursed! Even the natives know it: 'They aren't coming back.' They laugh at us for believing Jesus will come back for our souls!"

"Jesus?" Gonzalo said. "She was talking about Orellana!" He looked around at the rest of his men, questioning whether they had the same interpretation of the prediction.

Almost two hundred Spanish eyes nodded in agreement.

Lope twisted away from Gonzalo's stunned grasp. "Just like

Adam and Eve, I'm going into the wilderness. Either God will protect me or he won't; it's all in his hands now."

With that, the religious man crossed into the jungle.

"This land isn't Eden!" Gonzalo shouted after Lope had disappeared from view.

"And you're no Adam," came the reply.

After a few stunned moments of silence, Gonzalo told one of his men to keep a large fire lit overnight where Lope had walked into the jungle. When he didn't show up by the next morning, nobody talked about the religious man again.

Gonzalo still had to deal with the growing belief that Orellana wasn't coming back. The men who had thought they should push towards Orellana in the first place brought up a point Gonzalo hadn't considered: What if Orellana couldn't navigate against the current?

"He could be waiting for us with food and supplies but we've been staying put!" a vocal Spaniard who thought they should push forward said.

Bernardo, who had been an advocate for staying put because of the fertile hunting ground, said he agreed with pushing on towards Orellana. "They might even need our help!"

With no other options, Gonzalo decided that they would continue downriver on the one month anniversary of when Orellana and company had left. They pressed forward for an entire second month, living off the land without losing a single Spaniard, until they reached a river so large that it dwarfed the one they had followed.

"If they got pulled into this beast, there's no way they could have made it out alive," Gonzalo mused while watching the heavy flow.

"You'd have better luck crawling out from an anaconda," Bernardo observed.

Gonzalo had his men set up camp so that they could spend a few days looking for signs of Orellana's group. On the very first night, a blazing fire attracted a mammal they hadn't expected.

"Hello?" a hoarse voice called out from the darkness. Cries of joy soon followed as a man named Sanchez de Vargas stumbled into the firelight.

"It's you! It's you! You're finally here!" he said, clinging to Gonzalo.

Gonzalo tolerated the outburst of emotion for a time before pushing the man away to arm's length. During the trials they'd experienced on their trek, Gonzalo had grown used to seeing emaciated men. But the pitiful man in front of him put all of them to shame. Ribs and sharp hip bones poked out from his skin, and his sunken cheeks gave the impression of a corpse.

"Why don't we get you fed and we'll hear all about your ordeal in the morning," Gonzalo said. It was a generous plan, but Sanchez had other ideas.

"I've been alone for so long I can't wait until tomorrow," he said between ravenous bites of roasted fish. "We got here in three days," he began.

Gonzalo almost choked on the white fish flesh he had in his mouth. "Wait, three days? It took us a month of walking!"

"Oh yeah, once we got in the middle of the river, there wasn't anything in our path." He took another large bite. "Well, we got here and realized there wasn't any way back to where you were—you saw those whitewater portions, no?"

Gonzalo nodded. There been a heated discussion during their trek about whether navigating against the rapids was even possible.

"But we were here and still didn't have any supplies. Orellana said that we should go to the mouth of the river, navigate its length in the name of Spain. He wanted the glory, and so did the men."

"And what happened? Did you crash nearby and you're the only one who survived?" Bernardo asked.

"Oh no, they took off into the larger river and left me behind —I was the only one who said that we shouldn't abandon you," Sanchez said, washing down the fish with a gulp of water.

24

"WE'RE STILL ALIVE"

HOPE DISSIPATED from Gonzalo's expedition as fast as the morning mist faded in the sunlight. On the first day after hearing Sanchez's tale about Orellana's trip down the mighty river in front of them, the men decided that they should press forward as well so that the traitor didn't garner all of the glory from the Spanish Crown for himself.

"It isn't fair!" the men grumbled.

"He'll become governor of a new land after leaving his countrymen to die!"

"How can the men with him trust him not to leave them behind too?"

Just under one hundred Spaniards and over two thousand native porters walked along the Amazon River in single file. A stunned Gonzalo got swept up in his men's spiteful march, putting one foot in front of the other with little thought given to what he in fact wanted. Where had it all gone wrong? He had come for cinnamon, heard about gold, and now had nothing but a trail of bodies in his wake.

Malice sustained the troop for just a few days. On the fourth morning, nobody roused the camp for another day of marching—it was as if every Spaniard dreamt the same dream overnight and had come to the consensus that they were done moving forward. Their surrender wasn't localized to their continued advancement; nine of them had died overnight. The remaining men didn't eat, didn't drink, and didn't work on fortifying their camp.

Gonzalo spent a hopeless morning wondering what the eldest Pizarro would do in his situation. Would his brother Francisco make another raft and pursue Orellana? It was what the treacherous Spaniard deserved. No, Gonzalo decided, Francisco wouldn't let something like revenge put his men in danger. In fact, his men would take priority. What would keep them safe and alive so that they could live to fight another day?

"We're going back to Quito," Gonzalo whispered. As soon as the words left his lips, he felt a large weight lift from his chest; air filled his lungs.

"We're going back to Quito," he said again, a bit louder. Then, a third time, louder still.

"What?" a Spaniard replied, his voice sodden with lethargy.

"We're going back to Quito," Gonzalo said. Speaking the words out loud, to a listening member of his crew, cemented his conviction. His conviction, in turn, solidified his words.

"We're going back to Quito!" he shouted, sitting up. "We're going back to Quito!" he roared.

"We're going back to Quito?" the sluggish voice said.

Gonzalo stood up and walked to his supine comrade, grabbed him by the wrists, and pulled him to standing. He put both hands on the man's shoulders, looked him in the eye, and repeated his talismanic phrase.

The man nodded in time with the saying. His eyes grew wide as he became invigorated with the fighting spirit, the exchange reminding Gonzalo of times he had seen holy men work wonders on the sick and despondent.

Gonzalo and the first man each inspired another man, then the four of them each inspired yet another. Before long, the entire camp had come together and repeated the magical phrase in unison: "We're going back to Quito!"

Thousands of natives watched in amazement. They had no choice in the matter but could sense the electricity of change in the air. The Spaniards, insisting on leading the procession, walked past the small native camps until they were on the other side of them, then started for civilization.

Inspiration runs out given enough time, and soon Gonzalo was faced with the distressing reality about their situation. They had nothing to show for their exhausting journey, had been living off of the land for months, and had lost most of their men, yet somehow had to make it back the entire length of their trek without any of their initial provisions.

Their walk slowed to a crawl despite Gonzalo's continual repetition of the magical phrase for the sake of his men. While on the banks of the first river they had followed, he started wondering how his brothers might inspire the men. Hernando would appeal to their love of country, reminding them that they were Spaniards, a race who didn't quit. Juan, if he were still alive, would harp on the fact that they had no other option, that they needed to face their fate like men.

For the entirety of a day's slow march, Gonzalo tried to decide what Francisco would tell the men. He put one foot in front of the other, remembering that each step took him closer to home, finding solace in the simple act of continual effort. He realized that Francisco never worried about what was approaching in the distance—he took each challenge in stride, trusting that God and his own good judgement would lead him through whatever happened.

Another thought struck him, and he stopped walking when the revelation sunk in: Was it Francisco who acted like that, or was it him? He turned his head sideways, staring at red flowers along a single vine hanging down from the trees above. The vine continued up until it met branches high overhead, merging with a tangle of other vines in the trees.

Did it matter? He realized, in that moment, that he was a conglomeration of all three of his brothers, a single vine hanging down and reaching forward from Mother Spain. All of his life had led to this single point in time; the heartache of rejection by his beloved in his homeland, the lessons he had learned from his absent father, and his attempts at teaching the natives Christian values were parts of him that he couldn't ignore. There was no point in separating who or what had contributed a particular aspect, just like there was no point in dwelling on anything other than getting home—including their miserable situation.

The world transformed in front of Gonzalo's eyes. Instead of seeing damp misery, he started seeing the vibrant colors of the foliage all around him. Insects underfoot were no longer a nuisance; they were evidence of a thriving jungle community.

Those traveling in his immediate vicinity detected the subtle change in their leader and stood taller while they walked towards home. What was persistent stifling humidity to well-bred men like them? They laughed at their aching stomachs, knowing they had enough strength for the upcoming steps and daring nature to try knocking them off course.

But the invigorating sentiments couldn't persist very far without proximity to Gonzalo sustaining them. The morale was as low as ever just a dozen men back, and Gonzalo knew it. He tried walking with different groups of his men, rotating among the Spaniards so that he could get a sense for how his men felt on any given day. Upon discovering that five of the men were so weak from issues with their bowels that they couldn't continue, he had native porters carry them, the entire procession slowing so that they wouldn't leave their countrymen behind. Severe dehydration set in three miserable days later, and all five men grew so weak that they couldn't lift their heads. Gonzalo, realizing that they were on death's door, had the natives clear a large swath of the jungle and told everyone they were making camp until their comrades recovered.

They didn't wake up the next morning.

Gonzalo wondered if Francisco would give a speech before deciding that it didn't matter—he'd give one because that's what he would do.

From the top of a fallen tree, Gonzalo began by speaking about the dead.

"As I'm sure you're all aware, we lost some of our brothers overnight," he said, crossing himself.

The gathered men all responded in kind.

"The natives are digging graves right now, and we'll gather around their bodies and say kind words later. The reason I'm talking to you now is because I'm obsessed with living."

He paused and looked out at a sea of confused stares. Some of the natives stood listening behind the Spaniards, and he wondered how much they understood.

"Back in Quito, I took responsibility for your well-being upon myself. I gathered natives for help, brought food and weapons, and promised future riches for everyone. In my mind, providing for all of you meant giving you supplies so you could stay alive. I even brought a man I thought was my friend, that bastard Orellana, who turned out to be no more than a cheap traitor!"

Murmured curses erupted from the crowd.

"But I realized that being in charge means more than just providing *stuff*. It involves showing you what you're capable of, making you understand the great power that rests inside your bones. First, let me start by saying that none of you have anything to prove. *Anything*. Just by making it this far, you've defied the odds, stood up against natives and creatures and everything this cursed land has thrown at you. Think about it: *we're still alive*. We're still alive! After all that we've gone through, we're still alive!"

The men nodded in agreement.

"But the fact remains that we're Spaniards. We have Christian blood running through our veins and a string of faith in us that leads all the way back to God."

One perplexed man furrowed his eyebrows; flecks of mud covered his face and beard.

"Who had faith in you for this expedition? Me. And who had faith in me? Francisco, the governor of this land. Who had faith in Francisco?"

Gonzalo delighted in seeing the recognition dawn on the face of his confused comrade.

"The king! And who trusted the king with this land? The pope!"

Gonzalo looked out at the proud faces, delight rising in his gut.

"And I have just one question for you: Who trusted, who had faith in the pope?"

"God!" his men responded in unison.

Gonzalo stood tall on the tree trunk. "That's right. God himself has faith in us, and I have faith in his judgement. Now, we've lost five men today, and there's—" He took a moment to count the remaining Spaniards in his company. "Eighty-five left. I'll say this once and one time only: all eighty-five of us are making it back to Quito!"

The men raised their hands and shouted in response.

"This is the only option we have left, and we'll meet it like men—Spanish men! Every step takes us closer to home, closer to our loved ones, closer to a future where we look back on this expedition and laugh at the devil's attempts at making us doubt ourselves. Imagine, anywhere you go in this country, you'll know you walked into the jungle and made it back to tell the tale—even the natives will be impressed with your vigor!

"Now, who's ready to show this jungle, the natives, and our countrymen all over the world just why we all deserve to be called a Spaniard?"

The rabid men cheered. Some patted each other on the back, others closed their eyes as if they were scared the spirit of brotherhood would escape if they left them open.

Gonzalo made many more long speeches during their trek back to Quito, each time succeeding in stirring his men's emotions and inspiring their continued progress. His body withered away from the meager sustenance they could gather in the unforgiving rainforest while his belief in his own abilities at leading men grew in proportion to his diminishment. Thoughts about impressing his brother with his newfound oratory skills filled his mind as he walked over the fallen trees spanning the canyon, and he wondered what might be the best use of his particular set of skills in the colonies.

And, most important of all, he looked forward to the time when he could impress the Spanish nobility who had humiliated him when he had asked for Don Antonio's daughter's hand in marriage. Oh, the looks on their faces when he returned after leading men in the New World!

The trip back to Quito from the excursion's farthest point took more than a year. They walked past the bundles of cinnamon, now rotted and worthless, and realized they still had half a year of walking ahead of them. The fact motivated some of the men and left others dejected, but they continued on nonetheless.

As Gonzalo and his men approached the city in June 1542, he let the two thousand natives in his company—half of what he had set out with—go back to their home *encomiendas* instead of making them march all the way into the northernmost Incan city.

But Gonzalo kept his word: all eighty-five Spaniards limped into Quito, though some of them required support because of the state of their feet after spending more than two years in the jungle without new shoes. They had no horses, their swords and weapons were rusted through, and they stank—a combination of their own rancid odors mixed with the rotting animal hides they wore.

The locals in Quito stared as the ragged men went straight to the church. Gonzalo ignored the whispers about the men's matted hair, their emaciated figures, and the sores and scars on their skin, delighting in the comfort of civilization.

"Water," Gonzalo croaked to the priest at the front door. "And food." He turned to his company. "Stay here and he'll make sure we're taken care of," Gonzalo said, gesturing to the priest.

The men didn't need a second urging. They collapsed in the square outside the front door of the church as the priest sent some underlings away.

"How long has it been, señor?" the priest asked.

"We departed over two years ago, by my calculations. It's June, correct?"

"The twenty-sixth," the priest said with a nod. He kept his head at an angle so the men's stench wouldn't strike his nostrils head-on.

"We left in February 1540," Gonzalo said with a sigh. He looked at the cross high above the front door. "And we have nothing to show for it."

He had no way of knowing then, and he found out much later, but the expedition was a success in one particular aspect: Francisco de Orellana was the first European to traverse the length of the Amazon River.

The priest beckoned Gonzalo to have a seat on the stairs in front of the church while he waited for the sent-for food and water, but Gonzalo insisted the sole sustenance he needed was the Holy Spirit and started walking inside. The priest, his feelings about the traveler's odor evident, stepped back and waved him forward while maintaining a healthy distance.

Kneeling in front of the altar, Gonzalo gave thanks to the Almighty for letting his men return alive and said prayers for Francisco and Hernando. He didn't get up when he heard the commotion brought about by the arrival of the rations for his men, instead asking the Lord for the continued prosperity of the colony and Mother Spain.

Sebastián de Belalcázar, the Spaniard in charge of Quito, was waiting behind Gonzalo when he stood up from his prayers. "We assumed you had died in the jungle," he said with a smile. The conquistador was taller than almost every Spaniard in the New World and sported a mustache with raised tips.

"Hell couldn't hold us," Gonzalo said with a smile. He approached the governor but stopped short when the man held out his hands.

"Let's save the greetings for later; I could smell you as soon as I walked in."

Gonzalo laughed for what felt like the first time in a long time as the pair walked outside.

On the paved square outside the church, his men were digging into a small feast. There was water and wine, roasted meats, stewed potatoes, and bread.

Gonzalo grabbed a jug of water and drank, spilling no small portion of its contents onto his chest. Belalcázar braved the stench of him and his men and sat with him the entire time, keeping the conversation light despite Gonzalo's continued requests for news about what had occurred while he was gone.

"There's time for that," Belalcázar replied each time before changing the subject.

The priest and some local women made sure the men didn't eat too much during their first real meal back among civilization despite their protests. With their meal finished, local Spanish men took groups back to their houses so that they could bathe.

Gonzalo accompanied Belalcázar back to the governor's mansion.

"We'll talk once I've washed," Gonzalo said. He had grown tired of seeing the looks of repugnance on the faces of his fellow Spaniards.

"I'll be waiting," Belalcázar replied.

That evening, over a light dinner so that Gonzalo wouldn't gorge and make himself sick, the men discussed what had happened while Gonzalo was in the jungle.

"Well, one of the first things you should know about is the new special investigator sent by Spain."

Gonzalo slammed his hands on the table and stared at Belalcázar with wide eyes. "Why did they send him?"

"Initially, to sort out the land situation between Francisco and the younger Almagro. The elder Almagro left everything to the younger, including the southern portion of the colony. Oh, and it's now called Peru."

Gonzalo mouthed the word, measuring the feel of it on his tongue. Then, he asked what Belalcázar had meant by "initially."

"Well, now he's hunting down the younger Almagro for assassinating Francisco."

The news of his brother's death broke the small scraps of hope that had sustained Gonzalo during his long years of traveling. He didn't collapse, didn't cry, just sat there with his mouth hanging open as he listened to Belalcázar tell him what had happened.

"You chose a fascinating day for your return; it happened a year ago today. June 26, 1541. The remaining Almagristas, under the younger Almagro's command, stormed Francisco's Lima home and murdered him in cold blood. He then claimed control of the entire country with the support of Manco and Paullu."

Gonzalo couldn't believe what he was hearing. Out of all of the possibilities for the future of the conquered Incan Empire, he'd never expected anything approaching what he had returned to after his miserable trek into the jungle.

Belalcázar kept talking about how the special investigator was working with Gonzalo's old friend Alonso de Alvarado, which nobles threw their lot in with the younger Almagro, why Cuzco hadn't fallen into Almagro's hands, and how the infighting among Almagro's officers had led to the loss of his top three generals.

Gonzalo didn't hear any of it. All he could wonder was why God had sent him into that hell of a jungle and returned him to another.

25

STOLEN REVENGE

It took a month after hearing about his brother's assassination before Gonzalo left Quito for Lima. The delay wasn't for lack of effort—Gonzalo had tried leaving Quito the day after he arrived as little more than a skeleton and was held back by Sebastián de Belalcázar because he was "in no shape to travel." Furious at the setback, he had slept and ate as much as he could, recovering his strength so that Belalcázar couldn't stop him even if he tried.

He learned more about Francisco's murder while he recuperated, using the knowledge as further fuel for his broken body. The men who had carried out the deed were the one-eyed Almagro's former followers, adrift men who had turned to Almagro the younger as a leader. They had spent two years searching for gold in Chile with nothing to show for it, captured Cuzco, then lost the Battle of Las Salinas before the Pizarros imprisoned their beloved leader and killed him. The events had left them at the bottom rung of society—they couldn't hold office, weren't trusted for work, and scraped together a living by relying on each other.

Hernando had warned Francisco about letting the Almagristas gather before leaving for Spain, but the eldest brother hadn't listened. El Mozo, Diego de Almagro's son, had a house in Lima that became a rallying point for the alienated men. But without access to the wealth that the elder Almagro had left behind, the men were reduced to sharing a single cloak among twelve men, taking turns using it so that nobody learned about their dire financial situation.

Other than refusing the right to the elder Almagro's wealth, Francisco Pizarro ignored the faction and didn't make friends with them, again against Hernando's sage suggestion. The situation was ripe for bursting, and events split at the seams when the promised special investigator Vaca de Castro—who was sent to settle the question of the inheritance—was rumored lost at sea after he hadn't appeared months past when he was expected.

The Almagristas knew that Francisco was a pious man, attending mass every Sunday, and that he went to and from the cathedral unarmed. One of the assassins, either because he got cold feet or because he wanted absolution from God for his participation in the upcoming enterprise, confessed to the priest the planned date for Francisco's demise.

Word got back to Francisco and he stayed home that Sunday; the priest came to the governor's mansion for a private mass instead. The desperate Almagristas showed up during Francisco's usual sizable Sunday meal.

Captain Chávez, the man who had bragged about killing hundreds of natives under the age of three, tried negotiating with the attackers instead of locking the door to Francisco's dining room and keeping the mob at bay. With the door open, the assassins continued forth and attacked five of the twenty diners—Francisco and four other men—after killing the captain.

Francisco's last stand resulted in three dead Almagristas and the murder of all five defenders. Hidden Almagristas emerged from the city's every corner; by the end of the night, the younger

Almagro had more than three hundred men swearing their allegiance to the King of Spain and Governor Almagro.

But where were the men who had claimed loyalty to the Pizarros? Why hadn't they fought back after his murder? A furious Gonzalo mulled over the events surrounding Francisco's assassination each day and dreamed about them every night. He knew, without ever being told, that his brother had fought until his last breath, that the pitiful Almagristas needed more than a dozen men for the oldest Pizarro brother.

But there was still one left in the New World, and he was coming for revenge.

Eighty of the men who'd made it back to Quito followed Gonzalo to Lima when Belalcázar could no longer say that Gonzalo wasn't strong enough for the road. They left at the end of June, arriving in Lima at the end of August; the trip was relaxed and enjoyable compared to walking back to Quito through the jungle.

Gonzalo didn't know what to expect upon his arrival in Lima; did the city still have some respect for the Pizarros, or were they all set on Almagro as their leader, despite his mixed blood? Would any Pizarro allies even dare show their face after accepting the assassins as their leader so soon after Francisco's death? He and his men were ready for a fight, eager for revenge. It turned out that the majority of the city's residents weren't in either camp—all anyone cared about was proclaiming their devotion to the King of Spain, regardless of who led them in the Americas. Plus, the Almagristas were all away, having gone on the warpath against a Spanish force under Pedro Álvarez Holguin leaving Cuzco on their way to reinforce Alonso de Alvarado, who was aligned with the special investigator Vaca de Castro. Ceding control of the colony to the king's representative wasn't a part of their plans, so if they could strike blows against the Spanish armies under his command, they could force Castro's acceptance of their rule.

The first thing Gonzalo did upon arrival, instead of visiting the church and giving thanks for his safe passage, was search for Francisco's remains so that he could pay his last respects. His brother's final resting place was the one thing the many stories about the assassination had left out. He ignored the men who came from every corner of the city when they heard about his arrival, believing them sycophants who couldn't fight back against the exchange of power when it mattered.

It didn't take long before Gonzalo learned that his brother's bones were in the cathedral, and so he ended up there as priests-in-training lit the night's first candles.

"I'm here to pay my respects to Francisco," Gonzalo said to the attending priest, Friar Bovadilla, the man who had overseen negotiations between Francisco and the elder Almagro during the final days of the siege of Cuzco.

The friar, his leather face sporting a sparse beard, nodded and led Gonzalo to a nondescript corner of the cathedral. A small cross drawn in charcoal was on the bricks above an exposed space on the floor.

"He's underneath these stones," Bovadilla said with a solemn nod.

Gonzalo collapsed onto his knees and laid his forehead on the cool floor. He let his tears flow—for Francisco, for Juan, for himself and the men he lost in the jungle. All of the time between when he had last seen his brother in Cuzco and this moment in the cathedral rolled through his head in a flash. Instead of wondering which of his actions God deemed deserving of his recent struggles, he blamed curses from his enemies as the driving force behind the string of bad luck. He lifted his head and looked at the puddle beneath his face. The liquid disappeared beneath cracks between the stones, dripping down to his brother's decaying corpse. "Why is his grave marked by a single drawn cross?" he croaked.

Friar Bovadilla laid a hand on Gonzalo's back. "We're lucky we got this much," he said. He explained how one of Francisco's attendants, a native man and his wife, brought the body wrapped in a cloth. "They said Almagro let them take the body instead of listening to his men and displaying Francisco's head in the plaza like the elder Almagro's."

"Why would he let them do that?" Gonzalo said, choking back another sob.

"Francisco's friends promised a peaceful transition of power. That's why nobody raised arms against the upstarts."

In that moment, the hatred Gonzalo felt for the Pizarro allies in Lima evaporated, replaced by gratitude that his eldest brother's corpse hadn't been subjected to public display.

"Two dozen men attended the midnight service, lit by a handful of candles. Those who know pass by this spot before and after every mass but don't dare offer more public respects because of the Almagristas' control of the city."

"They don't have control of the city anymore. A Pizarro is back in charge," Gonzalo said through gritted teeth as he stood up.

"*The* Pizarro," the friar corrected. "You're the last one left."

Despite the desire for revenge coursing through his veins, two reasons kept Gonzalo in Lima for weeks: one, he didn't know where the younger Almagro and his forces were and therefore couldn't pursue them; two, Lima's residents needed him.

His first order of business, before taking care of any Spaniards, was finding the native attendant who had taken Francisco's body from the mansion and rewarding him for his loyalty. Since Manco and Paullu had thrown their lot in with

Almagro, Gonzalo wanted an example made of this instance of native devotion in hopes more would follow.

Gonzalo didn't bother hiding his admiration when the native refused all manner of compensation because "Francisco was a Christian and he deserved a Christian burial." With a smile and a pat on the man's shoulder, Gonzalo promised that he would ensure every Spaniard in Lima knew about his actions that fateful night. "We'll make sure your family gets taken care of," Gonzalo said.

He felt a sharp pain in his stomach when he remembered how Francisco had ordered native bodies burned after their death despite knowing their beliefs, but he attributed the ache to spoiled meat.

Gonzalo learned that the Almagristas had drained the city's coffers, both taking the money set aside for the Crown and further taxing the Lima residents. In addition, they had taken all the horses and arms they could find before leaving on the march against the two Spanish armies under Holguin and Alvarado. Gonzalo promised the repayment from his own personal wealth, ingratiating himself with the Spaniards in Lima and bringing the city back into the Pizarro sphere of control.

The majority of Gonzalo's time in Lima involved personal meetings with every prominent Spaniard in the city—with witnesses present—so that they could attest to what had been taken by the Almagristas while suffering his watchful gaze. He believed that, if left alone, they would try claiming more than their fair share, and many Spanish claims lessened under his imposing presence and persistent inquiring.

A letter for Gonzalo from Vaca de Castro arrived halfway through September, requesting Gonzalo's presence in Cuzco for a meeting with the investigator. Hoping for word about the younger Almagro's location from the man hunting him, Gonzalo set out the next day, his forces now including the men from Quito and an equal retinue from Lima.

Halfway through their journey, at a town called Huamanga, Gonzalo learned about a recent decisive battle between Castro's forces and the younger Almagro's assembled army from Spaniards Castro had stationed there.

"The forces met on the fields of Chupas, a short distance from here . . ." the Spaniard in charge began.

Gonzalo didn't care about specifics. He knew Castro had won, and all he cared about was revenge. "What happened to Almagro? Was he killed?" Gonzalo asked, interrupting the man's tale.

"No, he fled to Cuzco. Castro made us stay here and round up the rest of the Almagristas." A sinister smile played on his lips. "Some of them thought they would get sanctuary in the church—they're sitting in prison right now. Do you want to see them?"

Gonzalo shook his head. "No, all I care about is cutting off that traitor Almagro's head."

With that, Gonzalo led his company to Cuzco, pushing his men and their horses to their physical limits.

They found a desolate Cuzco on their arrival. After passing vacant stalls and walking through empty streets, Gonzalo's force reached the town square and discovered a mass of people watching a public execution. Nobody paid any attention to the one hundred seventy new arrivals on horseback.

In the distance, Gonzalo could make out a young man on an elevated platform. A large man stood on one side with a heavy axe that gleamed in the noon sunlight, and another man on the other side rolled up a scroll before walking away. The young man stood tall, his face uncovered, then knelt down, turned his head sideways, and rested his ear on a large block of wood.

The executioner didn't waste a moment. He leaned back,

wound up, and sent the axe in a wide swinging arc, bringing it down with a resounding thud on the wooden block.

The younger Almagro's head rolled off the block and onto the platform. El Mozo was dead.

A collective gasp from the crowd and subsequent murmuring drowned out Gonzalo's curses.

"His death was for me," Gonzalo muttered to himself. He told his men they could go wherever they wished in the city. "Almagro's dead now—I'll tell you where we're going next after I talk to Castro."

After greeting his horse Castaño, which he had left behind in Cuzco when he departed for Quito, Gonzalo met Castro in Francisco's former palace. By then, part of the crowd had dispersed—the rest had stayed while El Mozo's head went up on display.

Castro stood up from the dining table as Gonzalo strode in. He took one look at Gonzalo's snarling face before launching into an explanation. "This isn't permanent," he said, gesturing at the palace with his hand.

"It belongs to the Pizarros," Gonzalo said through gritted teeth.

"And it remains in the Pizarro family, I'm just using it," Castro said, tapping the table with the knuckles of a closed fist.

Gonzalo noticed how the man didn't offer to leave. "Taking the palace just like you took over as governor. It seems Francisco's death worked out well for you," he said, sitting down. A native girl set down a cup of water and poured another of wine.

"If you think I orchestrated this in any way . . ." Castro said, his voice trailing off.

"Sit down. I don't think there's anyone to blame but Almagro." He waited until Castro sat. "But you can tell me why the country didn't pass into my hands."

Castro folded his hands on the table and looked at Gonzalo in the eye. "It would've, if the king hadn't already sent me."

The men stared at each other. Gonzalo cracked first. "What happened?" he said.

"You'll have to be more specific," Castro said, leaning back with his cup in hand. He took a sip.

"With Almagro. Tell me about what happened at Huamanga."

Castro started his tale the same way the man in Huamanga had begun his. "We met at a lowlands called Chupas," the man began. "It was late in the afternoon; too late, I thought, but Alonso de Alvarado told me otherwise."

Gonzalo learned that Alvarado had lined the men up similar to how Gonzalo had at the Battle of Las Salinas, when he had defeated the elder Almagro: infantry, artillery, and harquebusiers in the middle, cavalry on the flanks.

"Carvajal's old strategy," Gonzalo observed.

"Your old friends Alvarado and Carvajal played important roles in the victory," Castro replied. "Almagro arranged his forces in much the same way. Carvajal had our footmen advance on a longer, safer route that wouldn't expose them to the guns, but encountered Paullu's forces—"

"That traitor!" Gonzalo exclaimed. He grabbed his water and drank, some of the liquid splashing onto his shirt.

"The native leader turned on Almagro's men later on and redeemed himself," Castro explained.

Gonzalo realized that history had repeated itself—Paullu had pulled the same trick against the elder Almagro. He wondered if El Mozo had known about the Inca's treachery before trusting him with repelling a flanking attack.

"Almagro's men fired on Carvajal as soon as they appeared over a ridge, but their guns were angled too high. A divine act of providence," Castro said, crossing himself.

Gonzalo doubted a higher power had anything to do with the mistake. Spaniards fighting Spaniards in the New World left plenty of potential for sabotage.

"The second volley took down a number of men. Since we couldn't wait for reinforcement from the heavier guns, the cavalry charged."

"Into the line of fire? Were they decimated?"

"They would have been, if Almagro had sat waiting. Instead, he gave the order to charge. Our forces met in the center of the field . . ." The memories affected Castro; he took a deep breath and continued. "It was terrible. Brother against brother.

"Almagro's cannons tore through our infantry—our own heavy guns were still far behind. Our men took just a single step back before Carvajal noticed and yelled at them." Castro chuckled. "That old fat man is crazy! He grabbed a banner and admonished the men, saying he was twice their age and double their size, then took off his helmet and charged forward on his horse. Can you believe that not a single shot hit him?"

Gonzalo shook his head and smiled, glad Carvajal was on their side.

"He ended up taking all of their guns for our side by himself, grinning like a fool until his men caught up." Castro took a sip of wine. "As night fell, Holguin died in combat and the left flank lost ground. Alvarado, on the right, pushed forward. That's when I came in with my reserve troops, diving right into the center of the maelstrom," Castro said with a faraway look in his eye. "And that was it. By midnight, the natives who witnessed the battle descended on the plain, looting what they could. No doubt some of them ran straight to Manco with news of the battle."

"If Paullu is with us now, where does Manco's allegiance lie?"

"Against us, as always. Paullu is at least willing to work together; Manco never will."

"Paullu also works with whoever can keep him alive and in power."

Castro looked at Gonzalo with a clever look in his eyes. "Isn't that the best any of us can do?"

Gonzalo didn't bother putting up a resistance. He sighed, leaned back, and asked, "And what do you have in mind for me, now that you've stolen my revenge?"

Castro stood up, put his hands behind his back, and started pacing. "Rest, relaxation, and the accumulation of wealth. You've heard of the Incan legend about the mountain of silver, La Plata?"

Gonzalo said that he had.

"I think we've found it, and I'm giving it to you. It's right outside a town called Potosí."

26

THE NEW LAWS

GONZALO SPENT the next year and a half overseeing the silver mines, more than doubling his wealth in the process. The hungry mountain required thousands of native lives as tribute each year in exchange for its guts, and he made their efficient collection his personal mission. His agents spread out over a vast area of land—up to four days by horseback in every direction—conscripting desperate native men. Those who complied uprooted their families and brought them to the Spanish settlement; those who didn't scattered beyond Gonzalo's sphere of influence for fear of violence. Because of the shift in population density away from the fields and the production of agriculture, many of the natives near the silver mines then perished from famine and malnutrition. They couldn't turn to llamas—the extensive Spanish hunts had dwindled their numbers to small flocks taking shelter in the highlands closer to Cuzco.

Despite the vast numbers of native lives lost to starvation, many more native laborers died in the mines. Workers were sent deep beneath the Earth with scant rations and remained belowground for at least a week at a time. The overseers expected falling rocks and poor ventilation to reduce the workers by half; the survivors found that the meager amount of food sent down with them was just enough for their reduced numbers. Those who survived the week in hell were tasked with carrying loads of silver back to the surface from deep beneath the Earth, often falling from ladders and plunging to their deaths or left crippled. Anyone who left the warmth of the mine and arrived on the cold surface risked serious illness, death's final opportunity for collection of their soul.

Gonzalo crunched the numbers and determined that replacing native workers was cheaper than nursing debilitated ones back to health. Those who were sick or injured were removed from contention for rations and left to their families, who had no resources for their recuperation because of the upstart economy.

"It's cheaper to work them to death than to replace them," Gonzalo often said, referencing the costs of paying Spaniards for native collection and relocation. From his vantage point, veiled by a false belief in the unending supply of native labor surrounding his silver mine, the numbers made sense.

While watching his stores of silver accumulate around him, Gonzalo heard about Vaca de Castro's opposite approach to the treatment of the native population. The special investigator from Spain, in charge after eliminating El Mozo and sending Gonzalo away, opened schools for the indigenous population and encouraged their resettlement to Spanish communities.

Everything changed when the Spaniards in the New World heard about the passing of the New Laws in early 1544. King Charles the fifth made all indigenous peoples vassals of the Crown. In essence, this meant that natives should be taxed at a moderate rate, eliminated compelled native labor, and entitled them to fair compensation for their work. Anyone that owned a native could keep them until the owner's death, at which point the natives would fall under the Crown's protection.

The king's edict included stipulations that certain people and institutions could no longer call natives their property, regardless of whether they were alive or dead: slave owners who neglected or abused their charges, public functionaries, and religious bodies. Friar Valverde had a sizable retinue of native servants under his command in Cuzco, though he claimed they belonged to the church—that distinction cost him his workforce.

A collective roar emerged from conquistadors from New Spain to Peru, but the shouts were loudest in the former Incan Empire: included in the New Laws was a clause that stated that anyone who participated in the feud between Pizarro and Almagro must forfeit their native slaves.

What's more, there was a man coming from Spain named Blasco Núñez Vela who would enforce the New Laws with the help of four judges.

Gonzalo heard about various gatherings of Spaniards throughout the colony through letters from his friends. They were livid at the turn of events—every Spaniard in the former Incan Empire had participated in the feud between Almagro and Pizarro! Each letter ended with a plea for his interjection with the government on their behalf; they couldn't entrust Castro, the Crown's agent in Peru, with the task. Gonzalo couldn't help but smile whenever he read these requests for help; they were proof of his status, that which he had sought when first leaving Spain a pitiful, lovesick pauper. That knowledge alone held greater value than every drop of silver in the mountain.

A letter from Castro in Cuzco arrived for Gonzalo in response to the murmurs among the Spanish elite, begging that he remember his allegiance to the Crown and not make any rash decisions. He threw it into the fire, just like every other letter he had received about the situation, focusing instead on the efficient extraction of silver from the mountain.

"He better get out of Cuzco before the *encomenderos* turn on him," Gonzalo muttered to himself, though part of him wouldn't mind Castro's demise. Then, remembering that the New Laws abolished the *encomienda* system, he added, "If there's even time for that."

Another letter, this time from his old friend Alonso de Alvarado, changed Gonzalo's attitude toward the unfolding situation. While en route to his new post, Blasco Nuñez Vela had stopped in Panama, where he had encountered a ship containing silver from another mine in Peru. His first act as viceroy, according to Alvarado, was the seizure of the treasure on behalf of the government, since the goods were the result of slave labor. Then, while crossing the isthmus, he freed hundreds of Peruvian slaves and sent them back to their country.

"He's as obstinate about the law as they come; I don't see how your own operation won't be affected upon his arrival," Alvarado wrote. "Plus, nobody else played a larger part in the feud with Almagro than you."

This time, instead of throwing the letter into the fire, he laid it flat on his desk and stared at the words on the page. Confused and wanting a distraction, he called for his favorite native woman and spent the evening draining himself of the confusion plaguing his bones.

The viceroy arrived in Lima in May 1544. According to Alvarado, Vaca de Castro was there to meet him, having left from Cuzco at some point in the preceding months.

"He's freed slaves all the way from Tumbez to Lima, if you can believe it. There are rumors that the judges don't even agree with his heavy-handed approach," Alvarado wrote. "But there's nothing they can do to stop him. And, what's more, he's already made statements that you would be dealt with according to the law."

Gonzalo stared at the correspondence, letting his anger wash over him. Who was this foreigner, who played no part in the conquest of the Incan Empire, and why should Gonzalo suffer for expanding Spanish lands? He realized he was no longer satisfied with just the knowledge that his power in Peru existed—it was time he take it, act on it, and stand up for the Pizarro name on behalf of his fellow Spaniards. Even though his father and older brother were dead, and even if it meant that Mother Spain rejected him, he would stand up for what belonged to his family.

The Pizarros had built Peru, and he wasn't losing his hard-won wealth without a fight.

"I'll be damned if they're taking my workers, my mine, or my silver," Gonzalo proclaimed at an informal town meeting. Everyone present had a stake in the mines around Potosí.

"Amen!"

"You've earned this!"

"Nobody's done more for this country than you!"

"And I'm not going to stand by while this *viceroy* comes in and undoes all the hard work we've put into this land! He already stole an entire shipload of our silver—I see no reason why the actual mines aren't next!" Gonzalo paused and took a breath while wiping an errant hair off his face. "Now, the men in Cuzco have requested my presence, and I need twenty men—"

Dozens of volunteering hands shot up.

"Wait, wait," Gonzalo said, holding up his hands. "Before you agree, I just want you to realize that I'm going up against the Crown's man in Peru. There's a chance he won't listen when I ask that he revoke the New Laws on behalf of every Spanish landowner in the country. He could decide we're traitors instead, despite the love in our breasts for the king."

The hands stayed raised, determined eyes staring back at him.

"Very well," Gonzalo said. He chose twenty men he knew that he could trust, men that he also believed had well-functioning households that could continue without their direct supervision.

Allied messengers from Cuzco met Gonzalo's entourage on the way into the former Incan capital city, informing him of his new title: Procurator of Peru. The position had originated in the Roman Empire—it meant an agent who represented others in a court of law. Gonzalo had always imagined his homecoming would take place in Spain, after disembarking from a ship and traveling to Trujillo, so he was quite surprised when he felt immense pride swelling in his chest while he rode into the city on Castaño. Cuzco was now his home, Peru his country, and its citizens needed his help.

The messengers also told Gonzalo about Friar Valverde's flight from Peru. He had left while Castro was still in charge, displeased with the forced ceding of control of Cuzco to the investigator. Natives outside of Tumbez, where Francisco had burned local chiefs and scattered the associated families during his initial arrival into the empire, captured the priest and killed him.

Gonzalo crossed himself when he heard about the man's fate.

"The first thing I need, before I go plead my case to the viceroy," Gonzalo said to an assemblage of Cuzco landowners in his palace on the town square. "Is an army."

The assembled noblemen squirmed while meeting each other's quick glances. Gonzalo's entourage, standing behind the seated guests, smiled, displaying rows of brown and decaying teeth.

"We don't want to go to war with him—we just want him to listen," the Cuzco landowner left in charge of the city said, a mountain of a man who had been a tax collector before coming to the New World. His comrades nodded their acquiescence when he looked at each of them.

"I don't want to go to war with him either," Gonzalo said. "It's for our protection, in case the viceroy takes our request as a declaration of revolt."

"Why would he do that?" the leading nobleman asked.

"Why would he take silver, and free slaves? Our countrymen are already being robbed—the army is just so Núñez will think twice before he continues taking what's ours."

"Manco's still lurking in the distance, ready to descend on what we've built at the first chance. An army could be useful in a hunt to rid ourselves of him once and for all after you meet with the viceroy," another landowner said, a stocky man with a bushy gray beard.

He hadn't expected another hunt for Manco, but he was glad for another shot at the elusive prey. "Exactly! Can't kill Manco without sufficient manpower." Sensing the hesitance in the room, Gonzalo poked fun at his own past failures. "And even with enough men, he can always just hide in the jungle."

Nobody dared smile. Hernando would have shied away from bringing up the various failed attempts at assassinating the former emperor because of a shared belief of discretion among the Spanish elite. Gonzalo didn't have such pretensions; now that he was the last Pizarro left in the New World and at the cusp of being in charge of the Spanish populace in Peru, he could set his own standards for elite behavior.

"Can you give us some time to confer among ourselves?" the

former tax collector asked. "We can give you an answer this afternoon."

After the nobles left his palace, Gonzalo spent the afternoon trotting around the city on Castaño, marveling at the ways in which it had changed since he'd left for the silver mine. Somehow, there were even more churches, more natives, and more Spanish children running along the avenues. Seeing the growth made him consider starting a family of his own, and he wondered if the people's Procurator should find a young Spanish woman or content himself with a native, despite his previous experience with Cura Ocllo.

"We can't provide you with an army—it's beyond the scope of our authority," the leader of Cuzco said on behalf of the landowners when the assembly reconvened.

Gonzalo closed his eyes and nodded. "Well, I guess I'll just go back to the silver mines then," he said with a sigh. "At least I got to see the city I love once more, and Castaño got some exercise. It's important for him, in his old age, to remember that he isn't sitting at home just waiting to die."

The stocky man with a bushy beard stood first. "Your help is contingent on us providing an army?"

"You would rather I march to my potential arrest without support?" Gonzalo replied.

The stocky man turned to his brethren, who looked at him with apprehension. "I'll send whatever men I can. Including my son," he said, hanging his head.

"It's much appreciated, but it might be too little too late. The rest don't agree."

"Let me ask for volunteers," another landowner said.

"There are a few dozen men in my employ."

"I don't have many men, but they're yours, along with me."

The former tax collector spoke last. With a heavy sigh and

sagging shoulders, he pledged what he could. "And we'll gather what forces we can from the rest of the city," he said.

Gonzalo smiled. "Excellent. I was hoping I hadn't come all the way up here for nothing."

"But," Cuzco's leader said. "Make sure you tell the viceroy about our plan to get rid of Manco once you leave the meeting. I don't want him thinking we're revolting against the Crown."

"Of course," Gonzalo said with an emphatic bow of his head.

An unexpected piece of news arrived in the early days of assembling the men. Castro, who had done an admirable job at keeping the peace in Peru until the announcement of the New Laws, had requested Núñez suspend the implementation of the edict because of the unrest in the country.

"He pushed for an appeal and a suspension until the Crown can be informed about the potential consequences of enforcement," the massive leader of Cuzco told Gonzalo. "Núñez agreed to start the appeal process but refused to stop carrying out his orders."

Gonzalo shook his head. "Núñez is a fool and drunk on power. Doesn't he realize he's an entire ocean away from Spain?"

Reports of seized natives, lands, and treasures poured in over the following weeks as the New Laws went into effect. News also flowed in the other direction, and word soon got out about Gonzalo's arrival in Cuzco and the subsequent gathering of men. Spaniards were meeting all over the country, deciding on whether they should submit to the king's authority and lose their property or stand up for themselves and join Gonzalo.

A letter from Núñez himself arrived as Gonzalo made his final preparations for leaving Cuzco with four hundred men, the first correspondence addressed to him from the viceroy himself. In a flurry of pretentious language regarding his authority, the king's representative in Cuzco demanded that Gonzalo disband his forces. The letter ended with a simple thank-you, without a single threat or promise, as if the request alone would convince the man.

Núñez had never met a Pizarro. Gonzalo laughed and tossed the letter into the fire.

There was one final surprise in store for Gonzalo and his men while they were still in Cuzco. He was poring over maps in his study, staring at cities and towns while deciding how many additional men he could wrangle from each. The four hundred men he had with him weren't imposing enough, in his estimation, to intimidate the king's agent in Lima. Plus, Manco had slipped through his fingers when he had six hundred men during his last attempt at eliminating the Incan Emperor. But with eight hundred under his command attacking at once, Gonzalo believed he could strike the heart of Manco's dwindling empire and wipe the rebels from the face of the Earth.

"But how am I going to feed all of them?" Gonzalo muttered to himself, leaning back in his chair.

"Make them live off the land," a familiar growl said behind him.

The startled Gonzalo almost fell from his chair. He turned around and saw an old bald man, now eighty, standing in his doorway, his imposing gray facial hair split by a smirk.

It was Francisco de Carvajal. He had always been big, fond of saying he was twice the man as any of his troops, and he had maintained his corpulent size since Gonzalo had last seen him before the Battle of Las Salinas.

Gonzalo smiled. "I couldn't decide if I should send word about a feast or a fight to get you here . . ." he said.

"Why not both?" Carvajal said with a roar of laughter. The two comrades embraced each other before sitting down with the maps between them.

"I had planned on leaving when I heard about the New Laws—sold everything and headed to the coast," Carvajal said. His fist tightened as he spoke. "But I never got the chance. Once the viceroy showed up in Lima, there was no way I was getting out of the country with anything but my name. You heard about the shipment of silver he stole in Panama, right?"

Gonzalo nodded. "Of course, that's why I'm here," he said. "I'm not about to let Núñez take everything we've worked so hard for. And it appears God's sent me some help," he said as the men turned their attention to the route between Cuzco and Lima.

27

ASSEMBLING AN ARMY

GONZALO SET out from Cuzco confident that he was approaching the viceroy from a position of strength. According to reports and common sense, Spaniards throughout the country were hell-bent on keeping their stolen wealth, which meant that the entire country rooted for the Pizarro brother's success in the upcoming discussion with Blasco Núñez Vela. After all, no Spaniard in the conquered Incan Empire could claim they hadn't been involved in the dispute between Pizarro and Almagro, and everyone who played a part in that conflict would lose their native workforce, according to the New Laws. In short, suspending the implementation of the ordinance was the sole path to continued peace among the Spaniards in Peru—but would Núñez listen?

The presence of Carvajal guaranteed the finest military mind in the New World was on Gonzalo's side and in charge of his troops. The old man's tactics had won the Pizarro faction the battle against the elder Almagro, and his valor had turned the tide against the younger one. Gonzalo was certain that after proving the popular support for his cause and convincing the viceroy of the potential harm in carrying out the New Laws, the old man could help him get rid of the initial thorn pestering the Spanish existence in Peru: Manco and the last remnants of the Incan Empire.

Their procession of horses hadn't been out of the former Incan capital city for long before news arrived that threatened the entire operation. It involved the last remaining Almagristas, seven men who had played a part in Francisco's assassination.

The renegade Spaniards had somehow evaded capture after the Battle of Chupas in 1542, where the younger Almagro had met his demise. Among them was Rodrigo Orgóñez's brother Diego Mendez. After having cast their lot with the losing forces, there was just one place where they could escape the Spanish sphere of influence: the remnants of the Incan Empire, led by Manco.

A wary Manco kept them at Vitcos while he stayed at Vilcabamba, making use of the two capital cities he had fled to after abandoning the siege of Cuzco. The Spaniards became Manco's instructors in all things related to the invaders, teaching him about European warfare, how to use seized firearms, and how to care for stolen Spanish horses.

In truth, the exiled Spaniards were biding their time. They saw an opportunity for a reemergence into Spanish society when the new viceroy arrived. Hoping for pardons for the part they had played in Francisco's death and the younger Almagro's revolt in exchange for ending the Incan Empire once and for all, they waited until Manco visited Vitcos from Vilcabamba and stabbed him in the back while his fourteen-year-old son Titu Cusi watched. They fled towards Cuzco but were caught and killed by native forces.

Another one of Manco's sons, Sayri Tupac, became emperor.

After hearing about Manco's death, many of the Spaniards with Gonzalo could no longer understand why he needed an army. Without a native empire looming large and threatening the Spanish colonizers, there was just one potential enemy left: the viceroy and the Crown's agents in Peru. Gonzalo and Carvajal started receiving reports of grumbling throughout the ranks by men who couldn't stomach outright rebellion.

The first deserters abandoned Gonzalo's march in the days following the news of Manco's death. They left when Gonzalo was meeting with a ten-man delegation of a small town's fighting-age Spanish men.

"What do you mean you're not interested in resisting?" Gonzalo said to the gathered landowners. They were in a large room attached to the modest church, Gonzalo standing in front of them while they sat on wooden chairs. "You could lose everything!"

"And there's a greater chance of losing it all if we march on the king's man in Peru," the aged spokesman for the group said, the words seeping out of him as if he suffered from intense exhaustion. His big red nose dominated his face.

"We're not *marching* on him. We're going for a negotiation on behalf of every landowner in Peru!" Gonzalo said.

"Then what's the army for?" The red-nosed man crossed his arms and looked at Gonzalo with smugness.

Gonzalo shifted the subject of the conversation, since he could no longer claim that they were going after the emperor. "Núñez isn't just taking native laborers—he's taking everything earned through native work as well. Have you heard about the shipment of silver he took because it was mined using slave labor?"

"Of course, but we don't have any goods like that for him to take. We have workable land, and we've already taken steps towards paying our workers and taxing them as Spaniards," the spokesman said.

Gonzalo stared at the men, appalled. "You earned your *encomiendas* through your own sweat and blood . . ."

"And the king decreed that system abolished. We're Spaniards, at the end of the day. What can he do, take our land and give it to the natives? Who will collect the taxes?"

"So you're relying on becoming the king's tax collectors in Peru?" Gonzalo said, his poisonous words dripping from his tongue. "What happened to the men who conquered a barbarian race?"

"Think of it however you like. We're not joining your cause —we all have families and farms to take care of." With that, the landowners left Gonzalo alone.

Carvajal poked his head in as soon as the last man left. He walked in when he saw that Gonzalo was alone. "How'd it go?" he asked.

"Not well. They're convinced we're marching on the viceroy and don't want any part of it."

"None of them joined?"

"Not a single one."

Carvajal sat down, his immense thighs spilling over the sides of the chair. "Then we're down thirty men."

Gonzalo blinked twice, stunned.

"I heard through one of my informants that some discontents were heading out—they don't have the stomach for rebellion—"

"We're not rebelling!" Gonzalo insisted, though he didn't quite know the truth himself.

Carvajal ignored his outburst. "Of course, the rascals didn't bother telling me to my face, and I'm assuming by your reaction that they hadn't told you either."

Gonzalo shook his head.

"When I heard that they were leaving, I raced to the western road out of town—"

"But Cuzco is to the east . . ."

"And sat on my horse in the middle of the road. Twenty-two of the men headed in that direction—the other eight went back to Cuzco."

"They're . . . they're headed to *Lima?*" Gonzalo stammered.

"That's what they said. On their way to pledge their allegiance to the viceroy." Carvajal spat on the floor. "The dogs . . ."

Gonzalo collapsed into one of the wooden chairs, leaving a space between himself and the old veteran.

"At first they stopped, said something about how I couldn't stop all of them." Carvajal shook his head. "I'd cut through them like pork fat, make no mistake."

"I believe it," Gonzalo replied, his voice not much more than a whisper.

"But I told them that I wouldn't stop them, that God was watching how their allegiance shifted quicker than a teenage girl's crush; they didn't like that," he reminisced with a chuckle. "But none of them said another word as they steered their horses around me. I almost wish one of them had swung . . ."

Silence hung from their shoulders like a heavy, wet blanket.

"And the other eight went back to Cuzco? How do you know?" Gonzalo said. His tongue felt strange in his mouth, and his stomach churned.

"I sent my informant to watch the eastern road. Wasn't hard for him to count."

"And how did you know to watch the road to Lima?" Gonzalo asked.

"They don't want the viceroy thinking they're a part of your cause—what better way to prove it than pledging their allegiance to the king's man?"

"Even if it costs them in the long run," Gonzalo whispered, shaking his head once more. "Núñez will take everything."

"Seems they haven't quite absorbed that lesson yet,"

Carvajal said. He folded his hands over his prodigious belly and waited.

"Think more men will follow their example?" Gonzalo asked after a spell. "We could always go back to Potosí and form a new government there; I know of fifty stout men who won't bow down to the pressure from Spain . . ."

Carvajal turned his bald head and looked at Gonzalo. "Do you think Núñez will just let you walk away and leave you alone? Your path's been set ever since you took the first step out of Cuzco."

Gonzalo let his head roll back and stared at the ceiling.

"There's only one course of action available: we see this thing through to the very end. Who knows what will happen to the country if you back down now? Everything you've worked for, everything *Francisco* worked for, could be gone, up in smoke. The viceroy can't ignore our demands—we're proving that not only are there hundreds of men opposed to the New Laws, we're also willing to be seen as rebels *because that's how much we believe in our cause.*"

Gonzalo sat up straight and nodded at the mention of Francisco. Would his brother want him second-guessing himself? "The men's resolve might falter if they think I'm unsure of myself," he said, thinking out loud. "So what if some men leave? They could be the ones stirring up the others in the first place!"

"Exactly!" Carvajal said, urging Gonzalo on.

"Pruning our ranks might be just what we need. Let them give up their hard-won wealth if they want, and leave the resolute men behind. We're better off without them!"

Carvajal reached over and patted Gonzalo on the back.

"We can do this. The men in Cuzco have trusted me with presenting their case, and that's what I'll do."

"Not just the men of Cuzco; the men of *Peru*."

Gonzalo stood up. "Should I make a speech to the army?"

"No, no, no. That won't be necessary. I'll have my informants spread the word that you're happy the men deserted, that you've had your eye on the malcontents for a while. They'll make sure everyone knows that only the most determined are still here," Carvajal said.

Gonzalo marveled at Carvajal's management of men and counted himself lucky that the veteran was on his side. When had he set up the informants? How many were there? He decided that he didn't care. "And if they think that the men they're marching with are also bought in . . ."

"They'll have less reason to question anything," Carvajal said with a smile.

Gonzalo had better luck recruiting in the next town. The residents cheered the name Pizarro upon his entrance into the settlement, and he almost made up for the deserters after a single request for assistance.

All he said was, "We're on our way to suspend the implementation of the New Laws!" and the men signed up on the spot.

This success prompted a string of fruitful recruitment, his ranks swelling at each stop. There was a handful of further desertions, but the new additions more than made up for the men of weak constitution, growing their number by hundreds.

And then, with one stroke, Gonzalo had more than twice as many men as he had set out with from Cuzco.

It happened when they were outside of Huamanga, at the plains of Chupas. Carvajal was regaling Gonzalo and the other officers with the tale about the battle against El Mozo's forces, telling them about the time he'd taken over the enemy's artillery all by himself. The rest of their army rode and walked a good distance behind them.

"So there I am, smiling like a fool while my men slink forward on their horses, looking like sheep. Guess they didn't know they were fighting alongside a wolf!" he said with a roar of laughter.

His infectious joy spread to the other men, and they all shared a laugh.

"Sir?" an uncertain voice said behind them.

Gonzalo turned around. He saw the man in front of him first, then movement in the distance caught his eye. Approaching them were hundreds of men on horseback, led by a man carrying the Spanish coat of arms. The standard wasn't strange, since every man in Peru, even Gonzalo, swore fealty to the king, but there was just one place of origin for such a large force of cavalry: Lima.

"Fall in!" Gonzalo shouted, putting spurs to his horse and racing to the front of his men. His officers followed, while Carvajal organized their forces into formation.

Gonzalo and Carvajal had thought about the possibility of Núñez sending forces against them before they presented their case, but they hadn't expected any resistance until they were closer to Lima. Encountering the men at Chupas, near the halfway point between Cuzco and Lima, took them by surprise.

And they were surprised once more when the man at the front of the troops called his men to a halt then continued forth with just the standard-bearer.

He waved once within range of Gonzalo's bowmen, then continued until he was within talking distance. Despite showing up with a significant force at his back, nothing else suggested he had come for a fight.

"My name is Puelles," the man said. He pointed behind him with his thumb. "And those are my men."

Gonzalo waited, staring. Carvajal sat on his horse beside him.

The man named Puelles smiled. "We've come to join your ranks."

Over the course of the afternoon, Puelles told Gonzalo about how Núñez had sent him on Vaca de Castro's suggestion. "Castro sent sixteen cannons to Huamanga before he left for Lima because he didn't trust the men in Cuzco with the artillery. They sent me here to make sure you didn't take it."

"And they didn't suspect your true intentions?"

"I doubt it. These are the finest men and horses in Lima, all landowners who don't want their livelihoods taken because of the conflict caused by that traitor Almagro."

After hearing Puelles curse Almagro's name, Pizarro didn't need any further proof of the man's fidelity. He welcomed him and his men into their ranks with open arms.

Dozens more Spaniards signed up in town. Before leaving on the road to Lima with his swelling force of Spaniards, Gonzalo conscripted six thousand natives for transporting the cannons and the rest of their supplies. "Núñez would have a fit," a smiling Gonzalo told Carvajal, Puelles, and his other officers as they headed for the western coast. "He thinks I should pay all of them, just to tax them later!"

Everyone laughed.

"Even though some of them won't even survive! Just a waste of money, time, and a bad idea overall. They're not Spaniards, and the king needs to stop acting like they are." Gonzalo laughed again but the rest of the men didn't offer more than a chuckle.

News from Lima arrived that convinced Gonzalo of the righteousness of his actions. Blasco Núñez Vela had had Vaca de Castro arrested for conspiring with the men of Cuzco, the ones who had named Gonzalo Procurator of Peru and supplied him with his initial forces. The special investigator Castro had been the one man keeping the peace in Peru, having encouraged Gonzalo's isolation and enrichment in Potosí before requesting the viceroy suspend the implementation of the New Laws until after the appeal process. He was thrown on a ship in port along with other men from Lima charged with conspiring with Gonzalo.

"Núñez is hell-bent on standing alone against the entire country!" Gonzalo told Carvajal after hearing the news. "Imprisoning his main ally . . ."

"See enemies everywhere, eventually they appear," Carvajal said, shaking his head. "Someone had to stand up to the tyrant—they're lucky it's you."

Gonzalo swelled with pride, not realizing that the line between standing up to the king's man in Peru and standing up to the king didn't exist.

On their final approach to Lima, when they were just days away, they encountered another force sent by Núñez led by a man called Diaz, this time sent in direct opposition to Gonzalo's march. After a quick discussion with Puelles, the entire unit joined the cause, swelling Gonzalo's ranks to more than a thousand Spanish men.

"The viceroy won't like this one bit!" Gonzalo said with a laugh. "Who can he trust? They all come over to our side!"

From the new addition to their ranks, Gonzalo learned about the preparations Núñez had made for war. "He's barricaded all of the streets and armed every outpost," Diaz reported, acting as if a Pizarro was back in charge of the country.

"Then let us take some time to rest and come up with a plan," Gonzalo said. "I'll talk to Carvajal."

A group from Lima arrived within days of their march's temporary pause. Friar Bovadilla, now Bishop of Lima, sat down with Gonzalo and Carvajal with hardened men standing behind both parties.

"So he's interested in negotiating?" Gonzalo said when the friar told him the purpose for his trip.

"An army led by a Pizarro stops outside his door—what do

you think?"

"Look, if he agrees to stop enforcing the New Laws, I'll turn around right now," Gonzalo said, leaning back in his chair.

Friar Bovadilla sighed. "You know he won't do that."

"Just until after the appeal process."

"Castro was imprisoned for the same sentiment."

"Then I really don't know what to tell you," Gonzalo said with a shrug. "Does he think the men who brought an empire to its knees for the king will just hand over all of their hard-won wealth?"

"Under orders of the king? Yes."

"The viceroy is a greater fool than I thought," Carvajal chimed in.

"We already knew that," Gonzalo added.

The priest looked down at his hands. "He has more than sixteen hundred men under his command," the priest said, bringing his eyes back up and looking at Gonzalo. "And he considers you a traitor. How do you think this is going to end?"

Carvajal laughed. "Can he even trust these men? Two of his officers met us on the road and both joined our march instead of submitting to his inflexible rule."

Friar Bovadilla closed his eyes and nodded his head as if voicing the truth was causing him pain. "He hasn't told me his personal feelings about his forces, but nobody in the city trusts their neighbor—they all wonder who will come to your side next. Many of them ask me for guidance in the decision, saying they don't agree with the king but don't want to go against his decree."

Gonzalo shrugged. "Well, he shouldn't have tried stealing from every Spaniard in Peru." He stood up and held an open hand up to the door. "You can tell him my conditions for leaving: no enforcement of the New Laws. If he doesn't agree, I'll take the country for myself and throw him in a cell."

28

WHO CONTROLS PERU?

As it turned out, Gonzalo Pizarro didn't have to imprison Blasco Núñez Vela—the judges the viceroy had brought with him from Spain did it for him. Gonzalo learned of the circumstances while he waited outside of Lima for a reply to his message.

The four judges, called the *audencia,* were sent with Blasco as a way of giving the king's man more authority in Peru. As Alvarado had told Gonzalo in his letter, they didn't agree with Blasco's heavy-handed approach to the seizure of the ship laden with silver in Panama or the releasing of slaves, but their hands had been tied. From Diaz, the officer who had changed sides, Gonzalo learned that the judges had also disagreed with the continued enforcement of the New Laws before the appeal and the defenses erected around the city.

"They say that he should trust the negotiations, that his preparations signal the lack of faith between honorable Spaniards," Diaz reported.

Gonzalo agreed and added it to the list of grievances he had with the viceroy.

The first crack in the viceroy's control appeared soon after

Friar Bovadilla left Gonzalo and went back to Lima. Blasco, out of fear, imprisoned a number of Lima's landowning Spaniards, worried that they would defect to Gonzalo's side while his enemy waited in close proximity.

Gonzalo and Carvajal held up cups of wine and toasted to the viceroy's folly. "He might as well have armed and sent them to come join us in the field," they said with a laugh.

The judges, understanding the sparks falling onto an explosive situation, visited the prison and freed the men at once, creating a rift between the viceroy and the *audencia*. The Spanish citizens in Lima celebrated the cool logic of the judges and the public sentiment shifted in their favor, maintaining a tentative peace in Lima by ostracizing the viceroy—to Gonzalo's disappointment.

But nobody dared make a move against the king's sent man. Not even Gonzalo, not yet, who waited outside of Lima for word about how the situation played itself out.

Blasco's next mistake was the one that cost him his freedom. A man named Suarez, who had been a popular member of Lima's government and responsible for convincing many Spaniards to follow the viceroy upon his arrival, turned up dead, his body found in a shallow grave. His last known location was a meeting at the viceroy's office late the previous night, where, according to witnesses, Suarez had been accused of treason.

"Everyone's calling it the 'ungrateful murder,'" a new defector from Lima told Gonzalo. "I'm not sticking around in the city until he decides I'm next."

Gonzalo opened his arms wide. "Welcome," he said with a roguish smile.

The viceroy, scrambling, made plans to leave Lima behind and march north, laying waste to the country as he went. The *audencia* objected, saying their authority depended on their presence in the capital. When Blasco tried using force against the judges so that they would follow his command, the citizens of Lima protected the men. A call from the judges for his arrest went out within the hour.

A mob appeared outside of the viceroy's residence. Blasco, who had summoned his forces, was inside with two hundred men. Overnight, his officers and most of the men joined Lima's citizens. By dawn, the viceroy was in custody without a single life lost.

Gonzalo received a response to his offer, but it wasn't from the viceroy. "They want me to lay down my arms and go home," he told Carvajal. "They've suspended the New Laws until they hear from the court in Spain."

"We've already received an influx of men who would rather join us than listen to the judges," Carvajal said, his eyes closed and hands folded over his belly. "They know we can take the city whenever we want."

"The entire purpose of our march has been addressed," Gonzalo said in a faraway voice.

Carvajal, resting just a moment before, sprang up and looked at Gonzalo with wide eyes. "You are so near your goal! Just reach your hand forward and take what belongs to you— everything else will follow."

Gonzalo looked down at the letter, reading it once more. "This man Cepeda, one of the judges. Something about the way he wrote this letter makes me believe he wants power for himself . . ."

Carvajal sat back down. "Trust your instincts, they've gotten you this far. Are you going to let him take what belongs to your family?"

Gonzalo clenched his jaw and composed his simple response. "The people called me to be the government of Peru, and if you don't hand Lima over, I'll have no choice but to take it by force."

He gave the *audencia* a few days, during which time he heard that they tried talking to Vaca de Castro while the special investigator was still imprisoned on the boat outside of the city. When Gonzalo believed too much time had passed, he talked to Carvajal about storming the capital.

"It won't be easy after they set up the barricades, but it's still possible," Carvajal said. A malicious glint appeared in his eye. "But I have an idea about how we can convince the good judges without losing any of our own men."

Carvajal launched into a presentation of the devious scheme, claiming he had been thinking about it for some time.

Gonzalo chuckled. "I'm glad you're on my side."

Carvajal entered the city under the cover of night, kidnapped three men from Cuzco who had deserted and come to Lima, and brought them to halfway between Gonzalo's camp and the city's limits, where Gonzalo was waiting with his highest-ranking officers.

In a clearing, the captured men were permitted a quick confession with a local priest.

"All right, that's enough," an impatient Carvajal said. The men knelt on the ground in a row, their heads hanging in shame.

Carvajal put his hands behind his back and paced in front of them. "Now, because of your rank, I'll give you an honor most men don't receive," he said. He paused, a grin displaying his rotten teeth. "You can select the branch where you'll hang until your final breath!"

The men broke down in quivering sobs, angering the ancient commander.

"What did you think the consequences were for betraying your countrymen?" he roared.

"Just choose," Gonzalo said despite his churning stomach.

All twitching stopped within ten minutes of the six feet leaving the ground. They left the three bodies hanging from the tree and sent word back to the *audencia* that no traitor was safe.

The judges responded right away, inviting Gonzalo into the city and proclaiming the government placed in his hands for the security of the country. "We look forward to your arrival," Cepeda added in an additional personal note.

Gonzalo walked into Lima in the middle of October 1544 alongside more than twelve hundred Spaniards. Several thousand natives entered first, dragging the cannons and supplies, followed by the infantry, composed of spearmen and harquebusiers. Gonzalo, riding on his prized horse Castaño, led the cavalry alongside Carvajal, the men flanked by the Spanish flag and the Pizarro coat of arms.

The judges wasted no time in proclaiming Gonzalo Governor of Peru, with the stipulation that they still needed approval from the King of Spain. Gonzalo, certain the king would appreciate a united country, had no doubts that his position would become permanent in short order. He took up residence in Francisco's old mansion, the same one his brother had been murdered in over three years before.

Carvajal, when offered a residence of his own, declared that he would also stay in the governor's mansion. "The *audencia* might try something if we split up," Carvajal whispered to the new governor.

Gonzalo nodded, grateful for the old man's wisdom. Then, he declared a weeklong celebration for the entire city.

Cepeda, the judge Gonzalo believed wanted more power, requested a personal meeting with the new governor on the first day of the festivities that Gonzalo ignored. Then the second, then the third, before Gonzalo told the judge's messenger that he wouldn't talk with the man until the city calmed back down.

"Whatever he wants can wait," Gonzalo said, drunk on power and wine.

At the agreed-upon time, Cepeda strode into Francisco's former dining room, now Gonzalo's office, stepping over the bloodstains still present on the floor. "They can't clean those? Or replace the wood?" Cepeda said in disgust.

Gonzalo looked at the judge from behind his desk. He had seen the man many times during his week in Lima but had never been alone with him. The judge had a growing bald spot on his head, a wide face, and a broad neck. His large arms and barrel chest were genetic, not earned, and were soft.

"I keep them as a reminder," Gonzalo said. It had been Carvajal's suggestion, as had using the former dining room as his office. He gestured for Cepeda to sit down.

With the judge across from him, Gonzalo folded his hands and rested them on the desk. "Now, what did you want to see me about?"

"Well, it was two things. Now, just one. What do you want to do with the former viceroy?"

"I'll have Carvajal deal with him," Gonzalo said.

"You can't leave him to that demon," Cepeda said. "He'll kill him."

"So? What else are we supposed to do with him?"

Cepeda shook his head. "Didn't you learn anything from Hernando?"

Gonzalo stiffened at the mention of his brother. "I haven't heard from Hernando for a long time. Do you have news about him?"

"News? The same old news. He's still at the Castle of La Mota."

"Yes, he said he's been living there while waiting for the sluggish legal process."

Cepeda tilted his head and blinked. "Living there? He's imprisoned there, for killing Diego de Almagro."

Gonzalo's gaze fell and his breath quickened.

"And Almagro was an upstart who happened to find gold for the crown," Cepeda continued. "I can't imagine what the king will do if he finds out that you oversaw the murder of his handpicked man in Peru, a nobleman no less."

Gonzalo leaned back in his chair. "I'll figure it out later. What else did you want to discuss?"

"What else?" Cepeda repeated.

"You said there were two things," Gonzalo snapped. "What was the second?"

"Oh, it was about Vaca de Castro. But he's already gone."

Gonzalo's features contorted into disbelief. "Gone? Where did he go?"

"Back to Spain. The captain had to leave three days ago—I tried speaking with you beforehand to see if you wanted to send a message back to Spain along with him."

"It's too late now," Gonzalo mused. "But I expect I've gone too far to expect favor from the Crown."

Cepeda nodded in agreement.

"I would've liked to talk to him before he left, hear from him about this obdurate viceroy we have on our hands. He seemed like an honest, pragmatic man."

"Which he was. If only the country was left in his hands instead of Blasco's . . ."

"If only," Gonzalo said. Then, after a moment, he added, "I think it's time I meet the man who threw the country into disarray."

Cepeda said he'd arrange a visit for that very afternoon. Gonzalo entered into the storage building where the man was held prisoner and introduced himself.

"You," Blasco Núñez Vela said, the words poison on his lips.

316

"What do you want? Have you come to rub your victory in my face?"

Gonzalo sat down at the simple wooden table in the center of the room and gestured to the second chair across from him. "I just came to talk. The Bible tells us to love our enemies."

Blasco scoffed as he took a seat. "You're taller than I expected."

"And I didn't expect anything from you," Gonzalo responded with a shrug. The man seated across from him still had the pallor of a man accustomed to the indoors. His beard ended in a severe point below his chin and his mustache flared out. Gonzalo wondered how the man maintained the shape of his facial hair until he watched the viceroy slick back the hair on his head with a hand and twist one end of his mustache.

In essence, the man reeked of nobility. The same kind of man that looked down on the bastard Pizarro men in Spain—but they weren't in Spain anymore. This was Gonzalo's Peru. Finally.

"You don't quite realize what you've done here, do you?" Blasco said. He sat tall with his head tilted back so that he looked down his nose when he spoke.

"What do you mean?" Gonzalo replied. A smile played on his lips at the powerless man's condescending body language.

"Not you personally," Blasco said, adopting a nonchalant air while he played with the point of his beard. "I mean all of you, from the first Pizarro down to the last *encomendero*."

Gonzalo leaned back and crossed his arms. "Why don't you enlighten me?"

"You're a Christian man, correct?"

Gonzalo nodded.

"As am I. Friar Bartolomé de Las Casas, a priest from the Dominican Order, convinced King Charles the fifth about the need for preventing the exploitation of the natives by the *encomenderos*."

"Yes, I know the argument. It's not right."

Blasco slapped the table. Gonzalo stared at the hot-tempered man.

"It *is* right! They're subjects of the Crown as well."

"And they are taken care of by the Spaniards in charge of the land. Taught Christianity, offered schooling."

Blasco scoffed. "Maybe some of them. How many have died in your silver mines? Were they educated, or were they just fodder for your own personal enrichment?"

Gonzalo stared at the impudent man.

"Let me tell you how I see it; I can assure you the king shares my sentiments:

"Your older brother stumbled upon a vast empire already in place, filled with more treasure than any civilized nation had ever seen. These people, on their own, had a functioning society where the wealth funneled up. The lowest native knew he owed the emperor taxes each and every year and they worked—"

"I already know all of this, I've lived here longer than you. What's your point?"

"My point, my simple friend, is that the *encomendero* system upended an entire functioning taxation network. Instead of sliding our own men into various points along the chain, you ruffians eliminated the structure's backbone. Now, instead of taxing an entire empire's worth of workers, the king can only tax a few landowning elite."

Gonzalo relished how he now belonged to the so-called "elite"; the rest of Blasco's word washed over him. "Taxing the natives simply flows through us now," he said with a shrug.

Blasco rolled his eyes and huffed. "But they aren't surviving! There won't be a workforce if protections aren't enacted right away!"

"What kind of protections?"

"The New Laws!" Blasco exclaimed, shaking his head. "How on Earth did someone as dense as you end up leading this entire country?"

Gonzalo stood up, knocking his chair over, and withdrew his sword. He pointed the tip at Blasco's throat.

Blasco didn't flinch. The two men stared at each other for a long moment before Blasco lifted his shackled hands. "You'd strike a chained man?"

Gonzalo stayed still.

"All right, I apologize," Blasco said through gritted teeth.

Gonzalo sheathed his sword and sat back down. "And what do you propose we should have done?"

"You should've kept the empire functioning."

"For how long?"

"Forever! Who cares, as long as they pay the king? Everyone stays happy—the Dominicans, because the natives are taken care of, the king, the colonists join a thriving economy instead of squabbling over land after being left destitute . . ."

Gonzalo was surprised at how well-informed Blasco was about the younger Almagro's rebellion. "And what about all the gold we sent over? I suppose we should have let them keep that too?"

"Why would you do that? The empire still existed after you took their stores of gold, correct? That was just a standard part of the conquest."

Gonzalo thought back to how helpful Manco had been during the gold collection and removal to Spain. Back when the young native still ruled from Cuzco.

"What I want to know, what the king wants to know, is why the emperor rebelled after we had taken almost everything from him? I've been asking around and heard a few rumors, but I wanted to hear it from you."

Gonzalo bit the inside of his cheek and looked at a corner of the room.

"So it's true?" Blasco waited a moment before he continued. "The emperor rebelled because you took his wife?"

Gonzalo looked at the viceroy and shrugged. "They weren't married in the eyes of God . . ." He didn't mention her rejection of him, his deepest shame.

"The king lost a functioning empire because you wanted to take a queen to bed? Incredible." Blasco raised his shackled hands to the heavens. "We could have had decades of consistent revenue, centuries even . . ."

"This all would have happened anyway; our men deserved land for their conquest of the empire!"

"And you can't possibly envision a future where you lived on a plot of land supported by the emperor? He could have guaranteed workers, supplies. And think how many natives we could have brought to the church! I'll tell you one thing, the clergymen back in Spain aren't happy with the death toll from the *encomiendas* either—every dead native is one less chance for conversion."

Gonzalo didn't say a word.

"But I'm sure you all thought about this, you and Francisco and Hernando and Diego de Almagro when you walked into the country and set about enslaving the natives. Even the *leader of an entire empire* couldn't escape becoming your property. Then, once the king realized the folly in the system and sent me to fix it, you show up outside my door and take over the country for yourself."

Gonzalo pushed himself away from the table, stood up, and walked out of the door.

"How do you think this is going to end?" Blasco said as Gonzalo left the prisoner alone.

Gonzalo marched straight to the judge's house after leaving the prisoner. "I want him killed," he said to Cepeda.

"And face imprisonment like Hernando? Trust me when I tell you: the king will send over an entire fleet if he finds out a Pizarro has killed his viceroy. Why don't we send him back to Spain and we can wait until we find out about the appeal? There's no way the king wants a revolt on his hands."

"Fine, send him on the next ship," Gonzalo said, storming out of the room.

One of the four judges left with Blasco within days. Soon after setting out from port, the judge had a change of heart and declared Blasco Núñez Vela a free man, handing over control of the ship.

29

THE BATTLE OF AÑAQUITO

"WE'RE MARCHING out to end this," Gonzalo said from the raised platform overlooking his troops. "This has gone on long enough."

Their target was San Miguel. Blasco Núñez Vela, after gaining control of the ship, had landed in Tumbez in October of 1544. After he put out the call to arms, Spaniards from the area flocked to the king's standard, seizing the opportunity for favor with the Crown. He had marched to Quito for a spell and obtained assurances of support from farther north courtesy of Sebastián de Belalcázar, the Spanish governor in the new colony above Peru, before returning to the coast and setting himself up at the city between Tumbez and Quito.

Gonzalo heard about the alliance with Belalcázar and couldn't fault his fellow governor for aligning himself with the Spanish king's man, despite their time spent together in Quito when Gonzalo emerged from the doomed expedition into the jungle. He still held out hope that the man would prove a poor ally for the viceroy, switching allegiances when presented the chance just like Blasco's former officers Puelles and Diaz.

In response to Blasco's entrenchment, Gonzalo ordered that

his officers in the area engage the new five-hundred-strong army. Quito and San Miguel were still under his command, after all. Somehow, Blasco won three straight skirmishes, sending shock waves down the coast that kept Gonzalo awake at night.

Gonzalo marched out from Lima with the judge Diego Vázquez de Cepeda in March of 1545, eager and excited for the end of his rival. He had long since cursed Cepeda for staying his hand, then twice cursed the judge who had given control of the boat back to the viceroy. He led his forces straight up the coast and arrived in San Miguel yearning for a fight.

"They just left," one of Gonzalo's men reported with a shrug when the Pizarro force arrived in San Miguel. He wrung his hands and continued despite obvious nervousness. "We were waiting for you before we attacked again."

Gonzalo looked out at the man's forces. They were an odd assortment of simple landowners and weapon-wielding natives, little more than one hundred strong. Small wonder they couldn't stand up to the viceroy without him.

"It's fine," Gonzalo said, making no effort at hiding his frustration at their amateur stench. "How long ago did they leave?"

"Hours ago. The men clamored for a retreat when they heard that a Pizarro was bearing down on their position. One of the soldiers said that they all wanted to go back to Quito and wait for reinforcements from Belalcázar, despite Blasco wanting to fight."

Gonzalo smiled, happy that his family name struck fear into the hearts of those who stood against him. "This soldier you talked to . . . is he still here?"

"He rode out to his farm in the east," Gonzalo's nervous officer reported.

Gonzalo sighed. "From now on, give anyone who fought for him the chance to fight for us. If they refuse? Kill them for treason."

The officer's eyes got wide, and he nodded multiple times in rapid succession. "Of course, of course, my mistake."

Gonzalo tapped the man's cheek with an open hand. "It's okay, how could you have known?"

Carvajal, who had stood behind Gonzalo during the meeting, spoke up as soon as the officer left. "Blasco's men have more sense than he does. Still a bunch of cowards though."

"It doesn't make sense. Why would he brave coming back into Peru but won't stand up to fight?"

Carvajal laughed. "You think it was his decision? Like the man said, the *soldiers* wanted to go back to Quito. What was he supposed to do, fight us all by himself?"

The two men laughed at Blasco's ineffective leadership.

"What should we do? They've already escaped into the mountains," Gonzalo asked his longtime officer.

"Give me a few dozen cavalry and I'll have them for you by morning."

Gonzalo inspected Carvajal's face, searching for the punch line that never came. "You're serious?"

"What? They're fleeing. Just got to make sure my men stay alive while we pick off the ones in the back." Carvajal smiled. "Haven't you ever been hunting before?"

As the sun went down overhead, Gonzalo and the rest of his forces set up camp outside of the city while Carvajal streaked away towards the mountains.

The ancient commander returned in the morning, harried and disheveled.

"It's my fault," Carvajal said while handing over his sword. He got down on one knee and lifted his chin. "Make it quick, if you can—I've got a thick neck. No more than two strokes."

Gonzalo, mortified, dropped the sword and pulled Carvajal to standing. "What? Why on Earth would I do that?" he said.

"Because I've let the enemy slip through my fingers."

Carvajal went on to explain how they had caught up with the viceroy's slumbering army just after midnight. "We could've slaughtered them, made a game of it," he said in a faraway voice. "But for some reason, one of my men blew his trumpet before I ordered the attack—we were still getting into position." Carvajal shook his head. "Everything went sideways after that."

"Did you kill any of them?" Gonzalo asked. His first thought wasn't the safety of his own men.

"Kill them? We could hardly save ourselves! They sprang awake—half mounted their horses and the other half poured harquebus shots into the trees where we hid. We're lucky we even escaped."

Gonzalo stroked his beard. "How many men did you lose?"

"Seven, by the last count. A few injured might soon expire, we'll have to see in a moment here. Blasco's men chased us almost all the way here; they left us at dawn."

"Maybe they feared an ambush?"

"Whatever the reason, we barely got back here alive." Carvajal picked up the sword from the ground and handed it to Gonzalo once again. "Make it quick."

"Why would I execute you?" Gonzalo said, his confusion real. Nothing from Carvajal's tale required such drastic consequences.

Carvajal stood tall, his chin held high and arms stiff at his side in a military posture. "What good is a commander that can't maintain discipline among his men?" he said.

Gonzalo tapped the old soldier's belly twice. "Hey, at least your men don't convince you to retreat just because someone's coming for a fight."

Carvajal looked at Gonzalo and smiled. "That poor fool has no idea what he's doing," Carvajal said.

The comrades laughed at Blasco's unfortunate situation.

"And I need my poor fool to help me keep a country,"

Gonzalo said, laying a hand on Carvajal's shoulder and looking him in the eye.

Carvajal nodded and took the sword back from the last Pizarro brother in Peru. "I have one request."

"Name it," Gonzalo said.

"Let me make their lives miserable until you catch up."

Gonzalo smiled. "Take whatever you need."

The comrades met again in Quito; Blasco had already passed through. Carvajal strode up to Gonzalo all by himself while the Pizarro brother prayed inside the cathedral—the same one he had entered after emerging from the jungle. The ancient soldier stood behind the governor of Peru with his arms behind his back, falling in behind Gonzalo when he finished his prayers and walked out.

"Where are the rest of your men?" Gonzalo asked once the pair were outside.

"They're still resting. They're not as . . . hearty as I am, sir."

"Nor as boastful," Gonzalo said with a smile. "Tell me about your trip."

Carvajal launched into an explanation about the harassment of Blasco's march. "I was closer to them than flies on an ass," he said. "At first, they left behind all sorts of supplies in their camp—discipline must be lacking. Ammunition, clothes, even a mule once." He looked at Gonzalo and tapped his temple. "I made sure they knew I was so close behind that they couldn't sleep. It made them sloppy."

"And how did your men hold up?"

"They didn't have a choice! What man is going to complain when the eighty-year-old man leading them weighs twice as much as them and doesn't ever quit?"

The men turned the corner and ran into one of Carvajal's cavaliers retrieving water. He looked exhausted; his hair stuck out at odd angles and his eyes were still puffy from lack of sleep, but he still managed a military bearing when he noticed Carvajal. "Is it time to leave again?" he said, feigning alertness.

"Not yet," Carvajal replied.

The soldier exhaled with relief. "Just let me know," he said with pretend enthusiasm.

Gonzalo chuckled while watching the man walk away. "He's dog tired! Why aren't *you* still resting?"

Carvajal shrugged. "Don't need as much sleep now that I'm an old man," he said with a smile. He tapped his diminished belly. "And I always carry enough food with me for the road."

The pair passed the time in idle conversation until they got to Gonzalo's temporary headquarters. "Anything else about your mission worth noting?" Gonzalo said as the pair sat down.

"Those bastards ran their horses into the ground, leaving them behind when they couldn't continue at the same pace. You know what they did?" said Carvajal.

"What?"

"Cut their hamstrings so we couldn't nurse them back to health. Nothing I wouldn't have done, but I didn't think they had it in them."

"I also didn't think Blasco would land back in a country that had risen up against him, but here we are. His pride will be his downfall."

Carvajal inspected his leader, seeing if he was joking because of the parallels with Gonzalo's situation and temperament. Gonzalo picked at a fingernail, oblivious.

"We stumbled upon many bodies too, deserters and the like. Caught a couple of stragglers who used to belong to your forces —let's just say that I doubt they lasted long in the wild without their eyes or tongue."

Gonzalo once again felt grateful that Carvajal was on his side.

"Our efforts are working, I suspect," Carvajal continued.

"Three of the bodies were dressed as officers and seemed well-fed; their throats were cut. My guess? Blasco is seeing enemies all around him and is fighting for some semblance of order within his ranks."

Gonzalo folded his hands and rested his chin in the crook between his thumbs and forefingers. "What happened when he got here, to Quito?"

Carvajal released a deep belly laugh, as if he had been waiting for this joke during their entire conversation. "Everyone ignored him! Nobody offered shelter or support for him or his men. The church did what they could before the cowards ran when they heard I was almost here," Carvajal said with a heaping dose of arrogance.

"Yet Belalcázar said he'd come to his aid from up north . . ."

"All he knows is that it's the king's man, not the actual state of his army. I doubt anyone would throw their lot in with him if they knew that he can't even trust his own men. He's heading there now, to Bogotá, no doubt hoping for protection from you."

Gonzalo winked at Carvajal. "And from you."

Carvajal shrugged. "Want me to head out this evening and continue the pursuit?"

"No, we're getting closer to Belalcázar's land. It's best that we stick together. We can all leave in the morning."

Carvajal leaned back, gathering momentum, before placing his hands on his knees and standing up. "I'll go tell the men to sleep tonight so they can be ready for the march in the morning —no telling what they might do in the city if left to their own devices."

"We'll chase him clear to the sea if we have to," Gonzalo muttered while making a fist, more to himself than to his officer.

Carvajal nodded and stepped out into the late afternoon sun.

The Pizarro vanguard caught up to the viceroy's men

outside of a town called Pasto, within Belalcázar's land holdings. They had been a fair bit ahead of the main body.

"And the men were exhausted from the march—we had heard about Carvajal's mission and wanted to prove that we could move as fast as the old man could," Diaz reported. Together with Carvajal, they were in Gonzalo's tent on the banks of a shallow river.

"We went to take a drink, not realizing that the viceroy's forces were hidden in the trees across from us."

"Did they attack?" Gonzalo asked.

Diaz laughed. "That's the thing. We realized that we had stumbled upon the enemy because we heard Blasco calling for the charge—but the men wouldn't have it. We were close enough to see their terrified eyes as they shook their heads no." Diaz sobered. "They could've crossed the river and slaughtered us before you had even arrived . . ."

"The mere sight of Pizarro's men struck fear into their hearts!" Carvajal roared, slapping his knee. "Let me guess: they retreated again."

"Couldn't get away fast enough," Diaz said with a haughty smile.

"That's the only reason you're alive," Gonzalo said, deflating Diaz's growing pride.

Carvajal stood and put a hand on the younger officer's shoulder. "Let that be a lesson to you: either you go slow enough that the men stay alert, or you *make them* stay alert."

"How would I have done that? How do you do it?" Diaz said, thirsty for the old man's wisdom.

"Make them fear you more than they fear the enemy."

Later that night, Gonzalo and Carvajal stood on the banks of the river and looked towards Bogotá. "Should we keep going?" Gonzalo asked.

"The farther we go, the greater the chance we encounter

Belalcázar. Might be worth going back to Quito—Blasco wants what we have; he's bound to come back."

Weeks in Quito turned into months. Gonzalo thought about returning south a single time, but then word arrived that one of his officers had declared his allegiance to the viceroy.

"That dog Centeno—I trusted him with the mines at Potosí and he turns against me!" Gonzalo said to Carvajal.

"Let me go take care of him, you stay here and wait for the viceroy. The fate of the entire country rests on you eliminating him."

Gonzalo turned to his adviser with hatred burning in his eyes. "Make him regret stepping foot on the boat that brought him to the New World," he said.

After Carvajal left, Gonzalo learned about the state of Blasco's forces from an opportunistic man from the north selling information. The viceroy had had five hundred men when he had first retreated from San Miguel, and Gonzalo found out that Belalcázar had provided an additional three hundred, including himself.

"They have four hundred men prepared for the march south."

Gonzalo thought about the numbers for a moment then laughed. "Just one-fifth of his men made it to safety before he received Belalcázar's reinforcements." Carvajal's methods had proven themselves effective once again.

"And those were near collapsing, to hear them talk of it."

Gonzalo dismissed the man after paying his price. Then, he came up with a plan for drawing the viceroy back to Quito.

First, he ordered that his men get ready for a march south, to "protect his silver mines and teach the traitor Centeno a lesson." Then, he made sure messengers left with word of his departure from Quito. Leaving a garrison under Puelles in the city, Gonzalo marched south, away from the city, and waited until he heard that Blasco had set out from Bogotá in January 1546. He waited a few more days before returning to Quito, assured that the viceroy couldn't turn around without embarrassment.

Gonzalo's manipulation of Blasco's honor worked. On January 17, the forces stood across from each other an hour's ride from the city, so close that they could hear the men in the opposing camp. They called each other traitors, both sides believing they fought for Crown and country. Gonzalo's army, seven hundred strong, slept ready for a battle in the morning.

But Blasco's forces were gone when they awoke. All that remained were the ashes from decoy fires.

It wasn't long before Gonzalo learned that Blasco's army was in Quito, behind them. "They must have spent all night marching!" he said in disbelief.

None of his officers, including the judge Cepeda, responded. Everyone realized the void left from Carvajal's absence, none more than Gonzalo. "Just get the men ready to march," he snapped at his officers. "We're not losing them again."

"They'll be tired," Gonzalo imagined Carvajal saying. "Not everyone has this old man's reserve!" If he closed his eyes, he could see Carvajal tapping his belly.

Within the hour, and before Gonzalo had set out, more news arrived that Blasco's army had set out from Quito in the Pizarro army's direction.

Gonzalo smiled when he heard the news. "Finally."

They met each other late in the afternoon. Both sides arranged themselves into Spanish Peru's standard battle formation: harquebusiers and infantry in the middle flanked by cavalry troops. Gonzalo sat atop Castaño as he watched the viceroy's standard playing in the wind.

Blasco pressed the attack first. Once they were within range, Gonzalo had his harquebusiers open fire. Smoke issued forth from dozens of barrels, obscuring the field of battle. The viceroy's infantry approached under the limited visibility and the fighting began.

Pizarro's cavalry made quick work of the exhausted opposing forces. The bodies of horses and riders dotted the field, their blood creating mud underfoot.

In a cruel twist of fate, the judge Cepeda and the judge who had handed over control of the ship to Blasco, two of the four original members of the *audencia*, met on the field. Cepeda, well-rested and with an unquenchable lust for power, tore through his counterpart, a far cry from their previous battles in court.

It wasn't long before the fighting turned into a rout—the viceroy's men, already at a numbers disadvantage, couldn't find the energy after their ill-advised march. A full third of the viceroy's men perished while Gonzalo lost just a handful of men.

Belalcázar was one of the men taken alive from the Battle of Añaquito. Gonzalo sat down with him after the fighting ended. "Why did he order the march to Quito before the fight?"

The governor from Bogotá cast his eyes down to the ground. "That was my idea. We had less men and you had a strong position, so I thought a surprise attack from the rear would work. The guides made me believe the path was easier than it was . . ."

Gonzalo banished the governor, making him swear on his honor that he wouldn't take up arms against Peru ever again.

The majority of the defeated foes were permitted into Gonzalo's ranks, save for those who had once been under the Pizarro banner and had defected. Those were put to death.

And what happened to the viceroy? Gonzalo found out from Puelles.

"I stumbled upon the former viceroy on the ground,

stunned and unarmed, being circled by none other than Suarez's brother on horseback," the officer reported.

"Suarez?" Gonzalo asked.

"The Lima man Blasco killed, the reason the judges took control of the city in the first place."

Gonzalo looked up to the sky, closed his eyes, and folded his hands. "Thank you for giving the man justice." He turned his attention back to Puelles when the officer coughed.

"He didn't swing the sword that decapitated the viceroy—I didn't want him facing that dishonor."

"There's no dishonor in executing a traitor."

"He was a Spanish nobleman, sent by the king . . ." Puelles didn't mention Hernando by name.

Gonzalo narrowed his eyes and waited.

"I commanded one of the black slaves to swing the sword. Then, Suarez's brother speared the head from atop his horse and rode around with it and celebrated his revenge."

30

THE DEMON OF THE ANDES

SPAIN'S RESPONSE to the transfer of power in Peru came quicker than expected. Gonzalo found out about it in a letter from Admiral Pedro de Hinojosa, his trusted man in charge of Panama. The admiral's dominion included the port of Nombre de Dios, the key entrance to the isthmus.

"He tricked our man in charge of the port into letting him in, but I place no fault in the officer. The new president is a man of the cloth, and came with a small force that included your old friend Alonso de Alvarado."

Gonzalo squeezed the edge of the letter in his fist, crinkling the paper. Alvarado had gone back to Spain soon after Blasco Núñez Vela had arrived in Lima, after sending Gonzalo news of the viceroy's movements. The last Gonzalo had heard, his old friend was married and growing old in Spain. What was he doing helping the king's man take what rested in the Pizarro name at long last?

"He has absolute authority of the land, or so he claims; he balked when I asked him if he could confirm you in your present post. His answer? 'I'll demonstrate my powers when the time comes.'

"But he does have two interesting proposals: one, he's revoking the New Laws. And two, he's offering pardons for everyone involved."

Gonzalo groaned at the news. Hinojosa went on about how the Spanish Crown had decided to treat the colonists with grace. Spanish troops, if war had been the decision, would have to cross an entire ocean, then the continent, arriving in a rebellious country filled with unknown terrain, marching against a populace united under a beloved commander.

"Some of the soldiers might have even joined our cause, for the right price. The king didn't have much of a choice," Hinojosa wrote. He then went into a description of the president, Pedro de la Gasca.

Gonzalo digested every detail about his newest enemy.

"He's a simple and humble man, as you'd expect from a priest. I've heard from Alvarado that he declined all manner of compensation for his role and rejected the pomp associated with the position. I can see why the king would grant him absolute authority as President of the Royal Audience, if he in fact did so.

"One interesting note: he mentioned that his powers included sending home the viceroy, if he saw fit, and that he had only learned of the man's death when he landed in the New World. According to him, the Crown started the preparations for his role way back when the viceroy first left Lima on a ship."

Gonzalo set the letter down on his desk. He folded his hands, rested his elbows on the table, and reread the words while his chin sat on his joined fists.

"Señor," the judge Cepeda said, poking his head into Gonzalo's study. "The guests are waiting."

Gonzalo folded up the letter and slid it into one of the many pockets on his new embroidered surcoat. Gold jewelry covered his neck and hands. Together with Cepeda, he walked between two rows of his bodyguards, the ten men a small portion of the eighty charged with his continual protection.

Every night's dinner had been an affair ever since he'd arrived in Lima, and tonight was no different. One hundred of Lima's finest residents sat awaiting his arrival, and they stood until he took his seat at the head of the table. Besides Gonzalo, three diners were there every single night: Cepeda, the judge, on his left; Paullu, the recognized emperor of the Incan Empire, on his right; and the officer Lorenzo de Aldana somewhere in the crowd.

The same conversation played on the lips of the diners as on previous nights: whether or not the country should throw off the yoke of Spain that still held them in place. Gonzalo listened, half paying attention, absorbing both sides of the argument that would have been cause for charges of treason even a few short months ago.

Yet again, the same as countless nights before, Gonzalo felt himself justified in taking action against the king's men but refused thoughts of rebelling against the king himself. Like a man who sins all of his life but makes a deathbed confession, Gonzalo believed that the king possessed a benevolence that would guarantee forgiveness in the end. God granted authority to the pope, who passed it along to the king, who gave it to those who conquered the Incan Empire. Breaking belief in any link on the chain meant he was no longer following God's will, but the devil's.

Gonzalo speared a morsel of meat with his fork and brought it to his lips. He paused before taking a bite.

What if the priest was in Peru for an exorcism? What would that make him?

"And what do you think, señor?" Cepeda said.

Lost in thought, Gonzalo didn't respond.

"Señor?" Cepeda repeated.

"What?" Gonzalo said. He finished taking a bite and looked at the judge.

"I was asking if you thought we could set up a horse race. Entertainment for the good citizens of Lima!"

Gonzalo recovered from his distraction and a sly smile grew on his face. "What's the point? Castaño will win, even in his old age!"

Everyone within earshot laughed at his brash confidence. Those who hadn't heard joined in the laughter when they realized the joke had emanated from the Pizarro.

Gonzalo laughed with them, once again confident that he deserved all he had earned during his time in the New World.

Over the following weeks, word began trickling in about letters sent from Gasca to cities all over Peru. Each one had the same message, that he was abolishing the New Laws and offering pardons to everyone who gave their obedience.

"How is he corresponding with every corner of Peru?" Gonzalo roared, slamming a copy of the letter down on the table. It had come from Jauja, along with another declaring the city still in Pizarro's control.

Cepeda and Aldana, his two most trusted advisers while Carvajal was still at Potosí securing their silver production, cowered at the outburst.

"I'm not sure, señor. We check every letter coming from Panama," Cepeda said while wringing his hands.

"Maybe it's the natives? Think they're working with him?" Aldana suggested.

"Paullu assures me that I still have his support."

"No, I meant those under Sayri Tupac, the one that replaced Manco. Maybe he's helping spread the news . . ."

Gonzalo looked at Aldana with disgust. "They're hiding in the jungle. How would Gasca have entered into negotiations with them?"

Aldana dropped his gaze.

Cepeda lifted a finger and waited.

"Well, say it!" Gonzalo yelled.

"You said that Gasca is a man of the cloth," Cepeda began.

"The *chaplain*," Gonzalo sneered. He turned his head to the side and thought for a moment. "That's a good name."

"It is," Cepeda agreed. "I was just thinking—maybe the priests are helping him?"

Gonzalo ran both hands through his greasy hair. "What can I do?" he said, shaking his head in dismay. "Kill priests who go against me?"

What would that make him?

"We would need proof, at the very least," Aldana suggested.

"Even with proof—" Gonzalo began.

"It might be too far for most," Cepeda said. "At this point, I suggest we trust the country. They followed you against the viceroy, why not follow you against the president?"

Gonzalo thought for a moment. "Plus, Hinojosa is still fighting for Gasca to make my position permanent . . ."

The advisers seized upon the glimpse of light in the darkness. "Exactly!" they exclaimed in unison.

"I did unite the country, after all."

"You did!"

Gonzalo looked at Cepeda. "Why don't we compose a letter to Gasca and present the case for keeping me in charge of the country. Maybe we can sway the chaplain with your gift for words and Hinojosa's stubbornness."

"I'll get started right away," Cepeda said. He pulled at Aldana's sleeve on his way out, bringing the man with him and leaving Gonzalo alone.

Before Cepeda finished the first draft, four letters arrived in August 1546 that changed everything.

The first, a short one from Hinojosa, detailed how the accompanying correspondences were the first he had permitted sent by the king's man since he had arrived in Peru. The admiral requested forgiveness, saying that he knew Gasca was sending messages despite Hinojosa's best attempts at limiting his influence.

"You could have thrown him in jail," Gonzalo mumbled.

The second letter was from the King of Spain himself. In it, he acknowledged that Gonzalo's actions were justified because of the viceroy's actions before the completion of the appeal process. He deferred leadership of the country to Gasca and requested Gonzalo work with the new arrival.

The letter from Gasca was the longest. It began with flattery, detailing the ways in which Gonzalo had united Peru under a common cause. "Only a true leader could pull together a country under such circumstances." But it stated in clear language that the reasons for the rebellion were gone, the points conceded—the New Laws were revoked and all parties involved pardoned. Including Gonzalo. "Now it's time you demonstrated your allegiance to the Crown. Continued revolt after removal of the viceroy shows that it wasn't the viceroy you had issue with, but the king."

Gasca ended with a charge for Gonzalo: prove to the world that your conduct was patriotic, not for selfish ambition, by ceding control of Peru.

The final letter was for Cepeda, the judge. In it, Gasca offered a seat on the Royal Audience of which he was president, saying he needed a man with experience in the country.

The effect of the four letters was immediate. Gonzalo summoned Carvajal to Lima and Cepeda stopped writing his letter to Gasca. Gonzalo also prepared for a trip to Spain.

"What are you thinking, going to Spain?" Carvajal roared during their first meeting in Cuzco. He had arrived a month after Gonzalo sent the letter, riding in ahead of a caravan laden with silver fresh from the Potosí mines.

"I want to explain myself to the king. He sent a letter to me personally," Gonzalo said, showing him the king's correspondence.

"This says that you're to listen to the president," Carvajal growled.

"Who won't confirm my position. Hinojosa already pressed the man."

Cepeda, sitting off to the side, listened but appeared deep in thought.

"He already said your conduct was justified—" Carvajal began.

"But he doesn't pardon me; that's also left in Gasca's hands."

"But Gasca gave you that!"

Cepeda made a show of his substantial sigh. "He just wants the king to confirm his position and thinks he has a better chance of getting it from him in person. Wants both remaining Pizarros imprisoned."

Gonzalo glowered at the judge. "What did I tell you about saying that?" he said.

Cepeda shook his head. "That you'd take a finger every time I brought it up." Cepeda held out his left hand. "Maybe just take the little guy on the end? I don't use that one so much."

Gonzalo huffed and turned back to Carvajal.

The old man rubbed a hand over his bald head. "You took up arms against, then killed, the viceroy. What more can you expect from the Crown? You've gone too far already. But if you want control of the country, you have to push further: proclaim yourself king."

Gonzalo recoiled in horror.

Carvajal continued. "Marry the young Incan lord's wife and unite our people. We can work together for a better Peru

—the king would have no choice but to accept the arrangement."

Cepeda chimed in before Gonzalo's thoughts settled. "Why doesn't he have any choice?"

Carvajal looked at the judge like he was a schoolteacher explaining a lesson to a pupil. "The king's man was killed after an armed revolt. Don't you think he would send an army against us if he could? No, his sole option is leniency."

"Hinojosa said the same," Gonzalo muttered.

"See? Reach out and grab what you want; it's there for the taking."

Gonzalo thought about Manco's son now in charge of the rebellious Incan state, Sayri Tupac, and his wife, Cusi Huarcay. Would the son have the same reaction as the father to giving up his queen? He blushed, then grew angry, when he thought about the irony of the situation. Taking Manco's queen had initiated the rebellion—which he still believed to be an overreaction because, in his mind, she was just another native woman for his bed and they were unmarried in the eyes of God. Carvajal's suggestion would initiate another rebellion, this time against the Spanish king. What was it about the native women that put them on the same level as Helen, capable of bringing men to war?

"The people will support you," added Carvajal in what was, for him, a deferential tone.

Gonzalo shook his head, clearing thoughts of native queens from his head. "No. That would make me no better than Manco, fighting against the natural hierarchy because of foolish pride."

Carvajal shook his head. "Well, you can't go to Spain."

Cepeda agreed. "Leaving will be your surrender. Of the country and your freedom."

Gonzalo looked at his two counselors and shrugged. "If the

341

two of you agree, then I won't. But what should we do about this?" he said, putting a finger down on Gasca's letter, the one that offered pardons.

Carvajal leaned back in his chair and folded his thick fingers together, resting his hands on his generous stomach, right below his ribs. "That right there is more dangerous to your position than any army the king could have sent."

"Well, should we accept?"

Carvajal laughed, a hearty one from his belly that shook his shoulders. "Should we accept? *Should* we? Of course! I'd pave the street in the silver I just brought from the mines for whoever guarantees it!"

Gonzalo furrowed his eyebrows. To him, the answer wasn't so clear.

"It will cost you the country," Cepeda whispered.

"So? He can retire a rich man—we all can!"

Gonzalo looked at Cepeda, waiting.

"I'm disgraced," the judge began. "I came here to support the viceroy, then turned on him. What grace is there for me? No Spanish court will have me—"

"Didn't Gasca offer you a position on his Royal Audience?" Carvajal interjected.

"He can't possibly mean it! I'll be a ruined man if Spain ever regains control, no better than the Almagristas left destitute once the one-eyed conquerer died."

"So you think I should reject the offer?" Gonzalo pressed.

A solemn Cepeda nodded. "The chaplain isn't as simple as you think. It's all political—he knows what promises to make. Everything will change once he's in charge."

"You don't trust him," Gonzalo said.

Cepeda shook his head no.

Carvajal threw his hands up in the air. "What other option do we have?"

"All you're thinking about is your own futures," Cepeda shot back at the ancient cavalier. "You can go back to your silver mines; both of you can. I can't." Before either man could respond, he added, "And I won't impress upon you for charity, so don't even try."

Carvajal found Gonzalo's gaze. "*You* know how much weight I give my life. He doesn't know what he's talking about."

Gonzalo's two closest advisers glared at each other.

"But I'll go along with whatever the two of you decide," Carvajal added.

"You will?" Gonzalo said.

Carvajal nodded. "I don't care for further rebellion, but look at me: my hands are spotted and my cheeks hang down to my neck. I can't expect to live much longer, so it doesn't really matter to me."

Gonzalo grew quiet. He looked down, then at the two men, then up at the ceiling. After standing, he paced back and forth behind his desk, pausing for sips of water. "I'm with Cepeda— let's reject the terms offered by Gasca."

Part of the trio's plan included pleas to the king for confirmation of Gonzalo's position in the form of a letter, instead of the last free Pizarro going himself. "The king already wrote to you once; he wouldn't have begun the conversation if he didn't want a reply."

They chose Aldana as their envoy. "I trust him with my life," Gonzalo said in defense of the officer.

"As evidenced by your choosing him," Carvajal replied.

Cepeda got to work drafting two letters, one for Gasca and one for the king. In the message to the president, they agreed that congratulations for his safe arrival were in order. "But inform him that he's arrived too late—the country is already taken care of, the situation settled when I overthrew the viceroy," Gonzalo said.

Cepeda took notes as his leader spoke.

"And tell him that Aldana is on his way to Spain to request confirmation of my post. *Don't say we're asking for a pardon;* that implies wrongdoing."

"And there wasn't a crime," Cepeda said, pointing the quill at Gonzalo.

"Exactly."

"Remind him that the country doesn't need further distractions and make sure he understands the dangers of landing on our shores." Gonzalo thought for a moment. "Be political, of course."

"Of course, of course," Cepeda replied, nodding.

"And in the letter to the king, justify our actions and request official confirmation of our authority."

Cepeda scurried away to his study.

In the weeks Cepeda spent writing the letters on which the future of Peru rested, Gonzalo heard all about Carvajal's exploits in the south over a number of shared meals.

Carvajal, after gathering more troops at Cuzco, rode straight to Potosí, where Centeno had begun his rebellion. Like Blasco Núñez Vela, Centeno had retreated, eliciting another of Carvajal's now-famous pursuits through mountains, swamps, forests, and ravines.

"My men had trouble keeping up," Carvajal said with a laugh. "They don't like sleeping in the saddle."

Gonzalo found himself wondering what creature best described his savage commander as the man described killing every traitor he got his hands on.

Carvajal took a swig of wine. "We chased him clear down to the ocean but never found him; the natives must've helped him hide." Carvajal wiped his greasy mouth with the back of his hand. "Then, I went back to the silver mines before coming here!"

Every telling of the story brought new details and vivid descriptions of torture and execution.

"Nothing to a demon like you," Gonzalo said during one of their meals. It was an offhand remark, but something clicked the moment he said it.

"A demon?" Carvajal thought for a moment. "I like that. *The demon of the Andes.*"

Cepeda finished the letters in October, many weeks after they had first received the letter from Gasca. The trio sent Aldana away with a large quantity of gold, "in case Gasca needs further persuasion."

"Time to exorcise the chaplain," Cepeda muttered as Aldana rode north.

"He's probably saying the same thing about us," Carvajal said with a laugh.

What else would a priest do to demons?

31

THE FLIGHT SOUTH

A LETTER from the envoy Lorenzo de Aldana dated the November 19, 1546, sent Gonzalo into a depressive spiral. His handpicked man, upon arriving in Panama, had met with Pedro de la Gasca, heard about the man's authority and offer, and accepted the chaplain's terms instead of going back to Spain.

After seeing Gonzalo's trusted man turn against the Pizarro name, Pedro de Hinojosa, the admiral in charge of Panama, did as well. Sebastián de Belalcázar followed soon after, still smarting from the loss against Gonzalo after helping the viceroy Blasco Núñez Vela in his march on Quito.

"That's our entire fleet, gone," Gonzalo said, his voice trembling with rage after cursing Aldana's name and family for the defection. "Securing it cost me a fortune . . . the ungrateful dog," Gonzalo said, slamming the letter onto his desk. "There wouldn't even be a fleet if it wasn't for me!"

Francisco de Carvajal sighed. "At least we still have command of the ships here, I suppose," he said.

Diego Vázquez de Cepeda, the judge and third member of their command, shrunk into himself.

Carvajal took notice of the change in the sheepish man.

"What?" he snapped.

"We had the ships destroyed so that nobody from Lima could join the president," the judge said. He hurried to add, "But this was before you got here."

Carvajal stared at Cepeda, then Gonzalo.

"It was his idea," Gonzalo said, shaking his head.

"You trusted Hinojosa *that much*? You destroyed Lima's guardian angels; now we can't do anything when the fleet shows up on our doorstep," Carvajal said. He thought for a moment. "Guess it's a land battle, then. Good. That's what we prefer."

Cepeda dropped his gaze to the floor.

"I trusted him," Gonzalo muttered while rubbing his temples.

"And look where that's gotten you," Carvajal said.

More news arrived in the following days that further soured Gonzalo's mood. The first, from the north: Puelles, Gonzalo's man in charge of Quito, had been assassinated.

"Hey, at least he stayed loyal," Carvajal quipped when they heard the news. He wasn't so nonchalant when he learned about the developments in the southeast. Diego Centeno, the man Carvajal had chased clear to the coast, had reemerged and taken Potosí. Again. From there, he had marched to Cuzco, where he aligned himself with the city's leaders in support of the president.

Gonzalo didn't leave the governor's mansion in Lima. He took to staring at the bloodstains left on the floor after his brother's assassination, part of him wishing he hadn't found out about the traitors in the country until they showed up for the final fight to the death. The native servants grew accustomed to his near-constant brooding—punctured whenever he yelled at some perceived slight—and remained vigilant for signs of drunkenness so they could steer clear of his blows. Insomnia-filled nights gave way to days where he wouldn't eat, and the effects of the stress showed up in deep creases on his face that highlighted his persistent frown.

Preventing further defections became his primary objective. At a meeting with Lima's preeminent citizens, the hypervigilant Spaniard told the assembled men that the president's powers had been granted before the king found out about the Battle of Añaquito, where Blasco had lost his head. "The Crown could never pardon those who rose up against the viceroy!" he proclaimed, as much a warning for them as a justification for his own actions.

Taking Cepeda's advice, he struck coinage with his own profile, creating the new money from the royal fifth that, under normal circumstances, was earmarked for Spain. Lima's gentry didn't push back against the measure, both from fear for their own safety and an indifference to the design, so long as the gold and silver weighed the correct amount.

Combining the royal fifth with his own vast holdings, Gonzalo paid for an army. One thousand men started drills with Carvajal, spending days in the field in preparation for the upcoming fight for the country. Acquiring horses proved more difficult, and Gonzalo had to take mandatory loans from Lima's richest citizens in exchange for exemptions from service. His mounting anger was on full display during the negotiations with the city's landowners; ignoring all measures of civility, he yelled and assaulted whoever offered the slightest resistance to his requests.

"You didn't have a problem when I put my name on the line against the viceroy!" he roared after slapping one man across the face. The rich Spaniard stared at Gonzalo with murderous rage playing in his eyes before nodding his assent, sending the enraged Pizarro away with a dozen horses from his personal stable.

Gonzalo saw threats everywhere. The constant drinking of

wine didn't help. His once-proud face, with fresh lines from worry, adopted a rosy hue, with puffy cheeks. Thick hair fell out in clumps, and his eyes stayed bloodshot for days.

Thoughts of the viceroy's reaction to the persistent defections played through Gonzalo's mind; Blasco was the sole man he knew of who had dealt with a similar situation. He found himself talking to the man's imagined ghost, seeking guidance and asking what steps might have produced different results. Whenever a native servant walked in on him during these conversations, he explained that he was praying and seeking counsel from his dear older brother Francisco—they never thought speaking to the ancestors strange, and in fact said that mummification of former emperors served a similar purpose for confused descendants.

But Blasco had deserved his men's treachery for attempting the theft of hard-fought Spanish land. Gonzalo didn't because he had fought for the people. The same people who were turning their backs on him.

Cepeda sought a justification for Gonzalo's actions so that the men of Lima wouldn't revolt. Calling upon his old method for waging war, he charged Gasca, Aldana, and Hinojosa with treason. After a sham trial—none of the men were present—they were convicted and sentenced to death.

"What's the point?" Carvajal sneered when the judge reported the results in their council meeting.

"The point? So that they can be executed right away."

Carvajal laughed. Gonzalo sulked.

"Here I was thinking that sentencing them to death might strike them down in Panama!" Carvajal said with a laugh. "Let one of them fall into my hands and I'll kill him without waiting for the courts," he added, full of bravado.

"Well now you don't have to wait for the courts," a defensive Cepeda shot back, fuming.

Aldana appeared on a ship off the coast of Lima in March 1547. As Carvajal had predicted, they were powerless against him anchoring in port.

Cepeda developed a strategy in advance of whatever actions Aldana planned. He brought together every male citizen in a large gathering and expounded on Gonzalo's history of service and all the Pizarro name had done for them since the founding of Peru. After that, he told everyone in attendance that they could remain under Gonzalo's protection or transfer their allegiance to the enemy. Then, he made whoever continued under Pizarro swear their loyalty under penalty of death.

"Not a single man chose the president," Cepeda reported to Gonzalo and Carvajal with pride. The two men hadn't been allowed at the ceremony because, as the judge said, "The people would be scared of revealing their true feelings with the two of you there."

Carvajal roared with laughter until tears streamed down his face. "How long do you think their oaths will last? Once we leave, they will scatter like dust!"

Gonzalo, noticing Cepeda's crestfallen shoulders, told the judge that it had been a good idea. "Better than doing nothing," he said with sadness.

"Waste of time," Carvajal said with a condescending chuckle.

The chaplain sent a letter to Carvajal, his first message to the aged cavalier, outlining the president's powers and extending the offer of a pardon once again. Gasca's previous letters had been sent to Gonzalo and Cepeda, so extending the same generous hand to Gonzalo's third adviser ensured a thorough exploration of diplomacy.

Gonzalo marveled at his well-informed opponent, wondering how many and which of Lima's citizens continued correspondence with the enemy.

The next move in the paper offensive targeted both Lima's citizens and Gonzalo's soldiers. Aldana sent word about the president repealing the New Laws and pardoning every man in Peru for actions taken against the viceroy.

Gonzalo pulled at his hair when Cepeda told him about the resulting escape of Lima's elite at the concrete offering of pardons. Men escaped in the middle of the night, running into the mountains.

"What are the people saying?" Gonzalo asked the judge. It was just the two of them during a late-night meeting; Carvajal went to bed when the sun went down and woke up when it rose.

"That they didn't realize the extent of his powers, or his generosity. There's general confusion because of the revocation of the New Laws, whispers that there's nothing left to fight for."

Gonzalo stared at Cepeda. "Nothing left to fight for? Nothing left to fight for! I'm fighting for the entire country! The country that already belongs to me!" He gathered himself while taking a series of deep breaths. "To us."

Cepeda held his hands up. "I'm on your side. Gasca is trying to take what you worked hard for, and the people are ungrateful, giving up at the first sign of trouble when you risked your neck for them!"

Gonzalo stared off into space. "I won't give up on them so easily," he said, more to himself than the judge.

"They don't deserve your benevolence," Cepeda whispered.

One man's defection hurt Gonzalo more than any other and swayed public opinion in favor of the president once and for all. Suarez, the brother of the man Blasco executed who had then displayed the viceroy's head on a pike, snuck out in the dead of night. Fearful of Gonzalo, he left without a word, reserving his reasons for a letter distributed early the next morning.

"If the president can pardon even someone like me, after my

quarrel with the viceroy, every man in Lima is eligible for the king's grace," Gonzalo read to Cepeda and Carvajal, his voice quavering. Carvajal had brought a copy of the letter sent to him —Cepeda didn't receive one.

He continued reading despite his mounting rage. "Don't let the grasping Pizarro convince you otherwise: Gasca knows full well what happened with the viceroy and extends his mercy regardless. Don't be scared! You don't have to take part in Gonzalo's revolt against Crown and country."

The memory of being trapped in the burning palace in Cuzco by Rodrigo Orgóñez crept into Gonzalo's mind. He recalled the smell of smoke, the flames crawling along the ceiling, the anger knowing his enemy stood right outside the front door . . .

"Do you think we'll see any of our army leave?" he asked Carvajal once he suppressed his thumping heart.

"I'm sure of it. Suarez was much loved among the men," Carvajal replied. After a moment, he assured the other two men that he would execute any traitors he got his hands on. "We'll chase them down and drag them back so we make an example of them."

Two hundred members of Gonzalo's army left within days. Carvajal sent out three hundred in pursuit and just one of them returned a week later, saying the rest of the men changed allegiances.

"I almost struck him down, I was so angry," Carvajal said. "But instead I rewarded his loyalty."

Gonzalo, lost in thought, didn't respond.

"We're down to five hundred men. We can't afford the loss of any more."

Silence descended on the room until Gonzalo broke the spell. "How well do you think we could defend ourselves from Chile?"

Cepeda blinked in surprise. Carvajal stroked his beard with thick fingers.

"We'll lose Lima the second we walk away," Carvajal said, shaking his head.

Cepeda turned towards Carvajal, his eyebrows weighed down by confusion. "The men swore—"

"Those oaths meant nothing! Mark my words."

"How well?" Gonzalo urged.

"Much better than here. The men won't be tempted day and night by the president."

"The people will get tired of their new ruler and call upon me again, just like they did against the viceroy. We just have to survive . . ." Gonzalo said, his voice trailing off.

In June, they received word that Gasca had landed in Tumbez, to the north, with Hinojosa and Belalcázar at his side. South of Lima, Centeno stood between Pizarro's forces and Chile in the area surrounding Lake Titicaca.

When Gonzalo told Carvajal that the time had come for their trip south, Carvajal rubbed his hands together and said that he'd been waiting for another encounter with the officer he had chased to the ocean. "His death won't be swift."

Gonzalo smiled. His old war dog had caught his quarry's scent once again.

Early on their march south, the Pizarro camp received word that Lima had opened its doors to Aldana, welcoming the president's envoy with open arms. Gonzalo heard the news while atop Castaño. He looked out among his army, five hundred men strong, and smiled.

"Bad luck teaches us who our friends are," he said, meeting the gaze of Carvajal, then Cepeda. Leaving Lima injected new life into his veins, the open country reminding him of the years of hard work required for conquering the indigenous empire. The reflections gave him a renewed belief in his abilities.

He turned around and looked at the bulk of the army trailing behind them. "As long as anyone still believes in the Pizarro name, I will again take control of Peru!"

The men around him responded with hearty huzzahs that spread the length of the column.

After a meandering march that lasted months, the Pizarro army encountered the Centeno forces on the shores of Lake Titicaca. Gonzalo, knowing Centeno had once been a close enough ally that he had entrusted his silver mines to his care, sent his opponent a letter in the spirit of negotiation.

In truth, he didn't want a single man of his meager army lost.

Gonzalo's sole request was safe, unmolested passage into Chile. Once he left Peru, he wrote, Gasca and the rest of the country would find peace.

Centeno didn't succumb to Gonzalo's counterfeit kindness. In his reply, he requested Gonzalo have faith in him and Gasca, that they could secure favorable surrender terms from the president.

Gonzalo tossed the letter onto the ground and stomped it into the mud. "There's nothing left but to fight," he said with disgust.

Carvajal grinned like a fool, saliva gathering at the corners of his mouth.

The two armies met on the plain outside of Huarina in October 1547. Centeno had one thousand men, two hundred and fifty of them on horseback, and one hundred fifty harquebusiers. Across from him, Carvajal commanded half the total number of men, five hundred, one hundred of them cavaliers, and three hundred fifty harquebusiers, each with multiple weapons. The rest of each army consisted of simple infantry equipped with spears.

Centeno lined up in the familiar Spanish battle patterns of

Peru: infantry and harquebusiers in the middle flanked by cavalry. Gonzalo, not having enough horses, put all of his cavalry on the right side of his infantry, where he would lead them himself while seated on Castaño. The spearmen protected the exposed left side of the infantry.

Gonzalo sported a gaudy crimson surcoat over his armor that matched Castaño's thick, protective caparison. His garb drew the attention of every opposing soldier.

Carvajal, by contrast, was indistinguishable from the rest of his men. His simple battle armor matched that worn by those of the lowest rank, with the exception that it covered more of his body and was therefore more effective.

Both Gonzalo and Carvajal looked for Centeno, the leader of the opposing army, but couldn't find him on the field.

After a series of false starts and small skirmishes, Carvajal succeeded in provoking Centeno's army into the first attack. They surged forth while Carvajal's harquebusiers stood still as the stones at their feet.

"Remember what I told you!" Carvajal reminded them. That morning, he had instructed his infantry to aim at the opposing chests instead of heads, reasoning that a misplaced shot could still do damage instead of flying into the sky beyond their foe.

"Fire!" he roared.

The first wave of shots erupted in a cloud of smoke. More than one hundred men and horses fell, with many more wounded. Before Centeno's harquebusiers could line up their own retaliatory shots, Carvajal's shooters had their second guns in hand and fired another devastating volley.

Centeno's forces scattered, the infantry in full retreat. Just in time for the most difficult fight of Gonzalo's life.

The Pizarro cavalry faced the opposing force's superior numbers. Centeno's left-side cavalry, knowing their advantage, surged forward and overran their opponents in the field, driving them back but still well ahead of Carvajal's flank.

Dead bodies, horses and human, littered the ground that Gonzalo tried taking back. Cepeda, fighting alongside Gonzalo, received a slash across the face that forced him from combat. Then, Gonzalo found himself surrounded by four opposing cavaliers, bloodlust in their eyes.

They soon found out why Gonzalo Pizarro was counted among the best soldiers in Peru; they never imagined Castaño played a large role in his success. The horse and rider dodged and weaved as one, Gonzalo manipulating his body weight while his sure-footed horse kept him from danger. His sword found human legs and arms, and horse flanks; his attacks focused on one attacking cavalier while Castaño danced out of reach of the other three.

The horse's luck soon ran out and the beast received a gaping slash across his back. Gonzalo disengaged and urged one last burst of speed from the wounded animal while blood soaked Castaño's coat on both sides of his body. One of the assailants grabbed hold of one of Gonzalo's reins, holding Castaño back from achieving his full speed. Gonzalo grabbed the man's axe, raised it high in the air, and swung, cracking the opposing horse's skull.

The rider, in a desperate attempt at bringing Gonzalo with him, reached out. His hand plunged into the horse and seized a portion of the wound as his own horse fell. It ripped a large swath of flesh from Castaño's back, exposing glistening muscle beneath.

A handful of Carvajal's harquebusiers saw Gonzalo's flight and shot the pursuing three cavaliers. Castaño waited until Gonzalo had dismounted before collapsing.

32

THE BATTLE OF JAQUIJAHUANA

GONZALO FELL to the ground without a sound, grief leaving him stunned. Castaño had come with him from Spain, had carried him to victories in Cajamarca and Cuzco. They belonged to each other, their bond beginning back when Castaño was just a foal. Horse blood seeped from the exposed flesh and trickled to the earth, joining the rest of the sanguine fluid from both horses and men turning the ground into mud.

There were garbled words from somewhere close; Gonzalo couldn't make them out.

Unseen hands grabbed Gonzalo beneath the armpits and lifted him to standing. Victorious trumpets rang out in the distance, from Centeno's side of the battle.

Gonzalo twisted away. What use was there in fighting? The cavalry was gone, demolished, their best horse and rider falling after almost making it to safety. Centeno's camp had already proclaimed victory.

Turning, the distraught Pizarro caught sight of Carvajal's strict discipline in action. At a command from the grizzled veteran, the entirety of his infantry turned to the left, where Centeno's right-side cavalry charged after recomposing themselves following the two volleys from the harquebusiers that had left them scattered. The spearmen lowered their weapons as a single unit moments before the wave of horses crashed into them . . .

The wall of infantry held firm as dozens of horses met their demise. The gore provided a natural barrier while Carvajal's fearless men finished off the fallen riders. As they completed their lethal work, the harquebusiers unleashed a third volley, decimating the remaining cavalry.

Centeno's left-side cavalry, after defeating Gonzalo's forces, had made a sweeping arc—out of range of Gonzalo's harquebusiers—and now approached Carvajal's infantry from the rear, along with the rest of the cavalry that had survived the spearmen. Carvajal turned his entire infantry *again*, so that their rear became their front, and somehow had another wall of spears ready for another charge.

The renewed attack yielded the same result: Carvajal's well-trained men stood firm, a porcupine with barbs ready for an attack from any direction. The time between attacks had been plenty for reloading the harquebuses, and the men wielding them fired as soon as they were ready.

It wasn't long before Centeno's cavaliers, their ranks decimated, realized the folly of their continued attacks and followed Centeno's infantry in retreat.

A trumpet from the middle of Carvajal's forces rang out, declaring victory.

Gonzalo, surprised out of the distress of losing Castaño, pursued the withdrawing forces as far as their camp, laughing alongside his comrades as they discovered lunch prepared for a victory celebration.

"There's a victory all right," Gonzalo yelled out while standing over the laden tables. "Ours!"

The hair on the sides of Carvajal's bald head stuck to his

scalp. He took a few bites of food, replenished the water he'd lost from sweat in one long drink, then asked Gonzalo if he could continue the pursuit of Centeno's cavalry and, in particular, their leader.

Gonzalo shook his head. "Don't you ever get tired?"

Carvajal put his helmet back on his head. "Not when there's fighting. Who's with me?" he shouted.

Two dozen men, inspired and bloodthirsty, raised their hands. They shoveled whatever food they could down their throats before setting off with a sizable portion of the Pizarro force's remaining horses.

Gonzalo surveyed the battleground the following morning. He had lost one hundred men, most of the losses concentrated on the portion of the battlefield where his cavalry had been overrun. Scattered alongside them were the bodies of more than one hundred horses. Centeno had lost three hundred and fifty men during the battle, and three hundred more infantrymen opted for joining Gonzalo instead of retreating through the countryside.

The day's victory struck all thoughts of fleeing to Chile from Gonzalo's mind. He declared that they were heading to Cuzco and sent out messengers to the surrounding cities asking for funds, supplies, and men.

If God oversaw his victory in a battle against twice as many foes, what chance did Pedro de la Gasca have? Peru belonged to Gonzalo, after all, and with a demon like Carvajal on his side he would remind the president of the fact.

Carvajal met Gonzalo in Cuzco in the final weeks of 1547. "Centeno escaped my grasp yet again," he said with a heavy sigh. He plopped down onto the chair at Gonzalo's table in the palace that had belonged to a former Incan Emperor—Gonzalo forgot which one—and set his filthy helmet next to his plate. "I would've stayed on the hunt, but the men were done."

"Did you catch any of the other retreating men?" Gonzalo asked.

"Executed a few dozen," Carvajal replied while biting a hanging thumbnail. "Everyone we captured." After a few wordless moments, Carvajal added, "So no Chile?"

"We beat them once, we'll do it again," Gonzalo replied, the same well-practiced phrase he used when speaking to his men.

The ancient commander stopped biting his nail. "What preparations have you made?"

Gonzalo, having made none, grew ashamed, as if Carvajal was a schoolmaster chastising him for not completing an assignment. His shame transmogrified into anger, and he looked at Carvajal from beneath a furrowed brow. "I've been letting the men rest."

Carvajal snorted. "I can tell. There aren't any barricades, no fortifications. Any stockpiles?"

"Of course!" Gonzalo replied. Collection had begun, but he knew the tally wasn't anywhere close to Carvajal's standards.

"Bet it isn't enough."

Gonzalo's hands balled into fists beneath the table. He kept them hidden.

"Huarina was the beginning, not the end," Carvajal said. He touched his temple twice and pointed to Gonzalo. "Discipline won us the day on the battlefield, and it's our only chance in another."

"You don't think I know that?" Gonzalo shot back.

Carvajal looked at Gonzalo with the full weight of his eighty-four years. "Doesn't seem like it. Can you honestly say you've done everything to prepare for Gasca's arrival? By all accounts, he'll have more men than Centeno did."

"Well, we'll have more too. Three hundred men from Centeno's army are now under our banner."

"They'll change direction faster than one of our flags when

the wind blows," Carvajal replied. "Do you think they'll hold a line against charging cavalry? If anything, they'll slaughter their neighbor and join the enemy."

A wave of irrational arrogance swept over Gonzalo, starting in his toes and ending when his ears turned red. "They understand who has power in Peru! We just proved it to them."

Carvajal laughed. "Get rid of them. They're just biding their time, grateful they're still alive."

Gonzalo took a breath and let it trickle out of his nose, getting snot on his mustache. "And what would you have me do instead? Face Gasca with three hundred fewer men?"

"Destroy Cuzco, leaving nothing they could use, and begin fighting from the mountains, like Manco. There won't be anything here for Gasca when he arrives! Think about how much more effective we'd be if—"

Gonzalo slapped the table between them. The serving ware rattled. "You'd have me adopt *native* tactics, like some animal?" he said, shaking his head.

"Manco didn't invent it—"

"I'm not doing it. I'm the leader of Peru! I saved the people from the viceroy! I'm not leaving the city until it's time to meet Gasca in the battlefield."

Carvajal shrugged. "So that's it then."

Gonzalo felt something he hadn't felt since falling from Castaño's back in Huarina: fear. Was the old commander leaving him?

"I guess we'll have to prepare as best we can," Carvajal said before leaving Gonzalo alone.

Gonzalo had one more discussion about adopting a plan other than meeting Gasca's forces in battle. The judge Cepeda suggested it after Carvajal began drilling his men in the morning and overseeing the manufacture of arms.

"Why don't we negotiate?" Cepeda said as the two men

rode horses together alone in the immediate countryside around Cuzco. The judge had spent the first few weeks in Cuzco recovering from his battle wound and now sported a jagged scar from his right temple to his left jaw. Somehow, he had avoided infection and losing his right eye but had lost a portion of his nose.

Gonzalo laughed. "So *now* you want to talk to Gasca. What changed from before, when Carvajal wanted to accept the pardon?"

Cepeda squeezed the fabric of his pants between his fingers. "Well, we're in a better position now. We've proven we can fight."

Gonzalo shook his head no. "If you were worried about not being pardoned before, we haven't done anything but stoke the president's anger. Why would he offer us the same treatment?"

"He may offer us better! Why go to war against you? No need to shed Spanish blood."

"It's already begun. This all started when he landed in Panama and wouldn't go back to Spain. The rest is out of my hands."

"Gasca is marching his entire army to Cuzco as we speak. It's the largest force ever assembled in Peru." The latest reports put Gasca's forces at two thousand.

"So there won't be anyone else when we beat them. I'll risk it all on a single throw of the dice," Gonzalo said with a smirk.

Cepeda crossed himself and looked up at the sky.

By the end of January, the Pizarro faction learned that Centeno was back with the president's army, to the annoyance of Carvajal. The soldiers suffered his worsened mood for days, drilling for hours at a time under his withering glare. It continued until he heard of the arrival of Pedro de Valdivia to Gasca's cause. Like Carvajal, the officer had served in the Italian Wars and had been there during the Sack of Rome.

"Finally, a worthy opponent!" Carvajal cried out when he learned of his counterpart.

From then on, his soldiers suffered extended drills because of his eagerness, not his irritation.

Gonzalo didn't do much during the winter in Cuzco. As the leader of a conquering force, he felt he had earned a respite from the rigors of war. Plus, if everything was dependent on a dice roll, he thought it made sense that he enjoy the palace, the lifestyle, and the city the Pizarro brothers won through their own blood and sweat. He did make one decision, however, during the winter that proved effective against the president's army: the destruction of the bridges crossing the Apurímac River. The body of water ran north to south to the west of Cuzco; Gasca couldn't touch him without crossing it.

"Give me a hundred handpicked men and I'll bring you the chaplain in chains," Carvajal said when news arrived that Gasca's men were rebuilding the closest bridge. "I know that spot well—the ground slopes upward on our side of the river. They wouldn't stand a chance!"

Gonzalo put a hand on the enlivened old man. He could tell that Carvajal had glory in his sights and blood in his nostrils. "I can't risk you being so far away from me. What would happen if you fell? You're needed for the final battle."

Carvajal swatted the air with a huff. "We won't need a final battle if I stop him now," he grumbled. "They'd need more men than there are in all of Peru to take that hill from me."

"I believe you, I do," Gonzalo soothed. "But what if we send someone else with *two* hundred men, since you're twice the man as most?"

Carvajal didn't let Gonzalo's flattery shake his sour mood. But he did help Juan de Acosta, Gonzalo's chosen cavalier, prepare for the excursion. The young man set out with two hundred cavalry, all of them equipped with the best firearms in Cuzco.

The next news the leaders in Cuzco heard came from a messenger, sent by Acosta. Because of the state of the roads, Acosta had arrived and found a large group of Gasca's men already encamped at the summit on the Cuzco side of the Apurímac.

Cepeda hung his head, Gonzalo looked at the sky, and Carvajal stood and started pacing with his hands behind his back.

"I told him to hurry!" Carvajal said. "I bet you made camp at night, didn't you?" he asked Acosta's man.

The messenger, still a teenager, affirmed Carvajal's suspicion.

Carvajal threw his hands up. "As if the entire cause didn't depend on his success!"

Gonzalo, still confident in their chances during a final battle, shrugged. "Is he on his way back? Does he need reinforcements?"

"He's requesting three hundred more men, sir," the youthful messenger reported.

Carvajal turned his now-red face to Acosta's man. "Did you even try an ambush?"

Somehow, the messenger's face turned even brighter red than Carvajal's. "We were preparing for one when a deserter told the enemy our plans." He avoided Gonzalo's gaze.

Gonzalo slammed a fist on the table and pressed it down as if he could break the wood with enough pressure. "Cepeda, take care of getting the needed men on the road within the hour."

Cepeda blanched. "Señor, that's not enough ti—" The look on Gonzalo's face took the words from the judge's mouth, and he agreed that he would make it happen.

The trio waited for news after the reinforcements left and

heard it from Acosta himself. "They were in full force by the time help arrived," the contrite officer reported, his eyes on the ground.

"The golden opportunity snatched away by incompetence," Carvajal growled.

"At least we didn't lose any men," Cepeda observed.

"And now we wait for their arrival on our doorstep," Gonzalo said in a faraway voice. He had the look of a man hungry for prestige and thirsting for revenge—a far cry from the lovesick boy who had arrived in the Incan Empire sixteen years before. That boy had craved his father's approval and relied on Francisco's benevolence; the man took what he deserved.

Gonzalo moved his force to the valley of Jaquijahuana on Carvajal's reluctant suggestion—the old man still thought they should abandon the city and fight from the mountains alongside the remnants of the Incan Empire. Nine hundred men made camp alongside six cannons. Natives poured in from the nearby locales and took up residence in the surrounding hills, their anticipation palpable; Spaniards killing Spaniards meant fewer oppressors in their homeland.

Carvajal's choice for the battle's location sparked even greater resolve in Gonzalo's chest. A vertical mountain cliff protected one flank, while a river protected the other. The river wasn't wide or strong but made the surrounding land soft and difficult for horses—dragging the cannons through the mire had been a nightmare. The two natural formations protecting his flanks made a narrow approach from the front where Gasca's superior numbers wouldn't present much of an advantage. Direct supply lines to Cuzco meant they could fight for days on end.

Gasca's forces appeared on the morning of April 8, 1548. The first fighting took place that afternoon, when a small group sent by Carvajal to a hill just within cannon range encountered

Hinojosa's men. Pizarro's defeated men had been back in camp for less than an hour when the first boom of a cannon rang out, the sound reverberating off of the surrounding geography.

The shot killed two men.

"Take down the tents!" Gonzalo commanded. "No need to give them an easy target!"

A shaken Cepeda approached Gonzalo. "They . . . they were . . . right next to me," he stammered.

Upon closer inspection, Gonzalo noticed the blood and bits of flesh caked on Cepeda's front. He clapped the judge on the back. "Lucky it wasn't you!" he said.

The judge nodded then wiped sweat from his brow, getting blood from his hand on his face.

Gonzalo didn't tell him.

Carvajal worried that deserters would leave the Pizarro camp under the cover of night. He spread word that there would be a night assault on Gasca's men, "so that anyone who thinks about leaving won't find a good time to do so. Plus, if Gasca hears about the rumor, his camp will be up all night instead of resting for today."

Cepeda, still wallowing in his misery, observed that their own men would also stay up all night because of the rumor.

Carvajal laughed. "Sleeping before you attack is different than sleeping while worried about demons arriving in the night," he said. "You'd know if you spent less time writing laws and more time fighting wars!"

There was an edge to Carvajal's quip that Gonzalo didn't address. Cepeda sulked away, lost in thought.

The next morning, the trio of leaders in the Pizarro camp looked out over the battlefield and inspected their enemy's formation: two groups of infantry flanked by cavalry.

"Double the conventional," Cepeda observed, his voice cracking.

"That devil Valdivia's just showing off—don't let him get to you!" Carvajal said. Somehow, everything was still a joke to him.

The Pizarro forces arranged themselves in the typical formation, infantry flanked by cavalry on each side. As in Huarina, their plan relied on their superior firepower instead of men; they also depended on the enemy's overzealous attack.

"Me and Carvajal will each take command of one side of the cavalry. Cepeda, you're in charge of the infantry. They're well-trained, just make sure the enemy's close enough for that first volley."

"You'll know when it's time," Carvajal said with a reassuring nod.

Cepeda looked at both men with his scarred face, lingering on Gonzalo's face for a moment longer, before putting spurs to his horse and advancing to the front of the infantry. All of a sudden, he took off at a full gallop, heading straight for the bulk of Gasca's forces.

"Hold!" Carvajal yelled at the infantry, a resonant command that froze every man to the spot but Cepeda. Two cavaliers looked back at the ancient officer like expectant dogs; at a nod from him, they raced after the judge.

All Gonzalo could mutter was, "Cepeda?"

The judge rode one of their older beasts wearing a heavy caparison for close-quarters fighting. Carvajal's cavaliers caught up to him and, once within striking range, threw a spear that felled the aged horse and escaping rider. Before they could dismount and grab the judge, a contingent from the president's camp stormed in and forced their retreat.

Cepeda's desertion was contagious, and the plague tore through Gonzalo's army before he could move. Every cavalier that raced to the opposing army was a stone removed from beneath his feet; each infantryman who tossed down his arms and started marching across the field knocked him further off-balance.

Gonzalo realized that he couldn't wait for Gasca's advance; he might not have an army if he did. "Attack!" he yelled in a rush of clarity. His reluctant forces set off towards the enemy.

Gasca's men advanced in lockstep. "Valdivia!" Carvajal cursed at the impressive show of discipline.

Centeno's men in the infantry chose that moment for their abandonment. A group of cavaliers followed.

The chaplain's men came to a halt when they realized the approaching men weren't fighting.

The natives watching from the hills saw the men from Pizarro's camp who couldn't stomach surrender take to the hills and flee back to Cuzco. The condors circling above began looking in adjacent valleys for carrion, understanding that there wouldn't be a feast.

Gonzalo, Carvajal, Acosta, and a few cavaliers were all that remained. "What should we do?" Gonzalo whispered.

"Attack," a young man's voice said. Acosta. "There's nothing else left!"

Gonzalo nodded and led the charge, knowing that he still had one trick up his sleeve. Peru's leading men had followed him before, against Manco, then Almagro, and finally Blasco. What if they were given one more chance?

An officer accepted Gonzalo's surrender. The remaining Pizarro forces, surprised at seeing their leader's capitulation, gave up their arms as well, knowing there was no hope for a pardon; their execution loomed on the horizon.

Gasca's man took Gonzalo straight to the president and forced him to his knees. The president's captains, upon seeing the enemy, began their withdrawal so they wouldn't witness Gonzalo's disgrace.

"Wait!" Gonzalo commanded.

They stood still. Gonzalo smiled, certain in his power over them. This masterful scheme, inspired by Gasca himself: *Take the men from under his nose.* Why hadn't he thought of it sooner?

"Why did you throw the country into such confusion? Countrymen should be united on foreign soil! Instead, you've pitted brother against brother and sent countless men to their death," Gasca said, his voice never rising. A true chaplain.

Gonzalo looked up at Gasca and smiled. He looked at each captain in the face, madness in his eyes. "Together, we will rule the whole of this continent," he said as if the words were a curse, his lips twisted into a snarl.

He didn't hear the sword withdrawn from its scabbard behind him, nor sense the man holding the weapon high above.

"Who else is with me?"

COULD YOU DO ME A FAVOR?

Please help other readers learn more about this book by leaving a rating and review!

Then head over to my website authormarcoshernandez.com and subscribe to my email list. You'll hear about upcoming releases and deals you don't want to miss!

ALSO BY MARCOS ANTONIO HERNANDEZ

Android City Chronicles

The Return of the Operator

Before Anyone Finds Out

Good Enough in a Pinch

The Edited Genome Trilogy

Awakening

Alternative

Absolution

Hispanic American Heritage Stories

The Education of a Wetback

Where They Burn Books

They Also Burn People

Demons in the Golden Empire

Indigenous Magic

Jesus Chan and the Return of Mayan Magic

ABOUT THE AUTHOR

Marcos Antonio Hernandez writes from the suburbs of Washington, D.C. An avid reader of both fiction and non-fiction, his favorite authors are Haruki Murakami and Philip K. Dick — in that order.

Marcos graduated from the University of Maryland, College Park with a degree in chemical engineering and a minor in physics. Since graduating, he has worked as a barista, a food scientist, and a CrossFit coach.

authormarcoshernandez.com

www.ingramcontent.com/pod-product-compliance
Lightning Source LLC
Chambersburg PA
CBHW070907260626
47162CB00007B/2585